Pierre Souvestre, Marcel Allain

A Nest of Spies: Fantômas Saga

OK Publishing 2021

Pierre Souvestre, Marcel Allain
A Nest of Spies: Fantômas Saga

Published by
MUSAICUM
Books

- Advanced Digital Solutions & High-Quality book Formatting -

musaicumbooks@okpublishing.info

2021 OK Publishing

ISBN 978-80-272-7887-9

Contents

I
SUDDEN DEATH

She sought in vain!

The young woman, who was finishing her toilette, lost patience. With a look of annoyance she half turned round, crying, "Well, Captain, it is easy to see that you are not accustomed to women's ways!"

This pretty girl's lover, a man about forty, with an energetic countenance, and a broad forehead adorned with sparse locks, was smoking a Turkish cigarette, taking his ease on a divan at the far end of the room.

He jumped up as if moved by a spring.

For some time the captain had followed with his eyes the gestures of his graceful mistress; like a good and attentive lover he guessed what she required. He rushed into the adjoining dressing-room and returned with a little onyx cup in which was a complete assortment of pins.

"There, my pretty Bobinette!" he cried, coming up to the young woman. "This will put me into your good graces again."

She thanked him with a smile; took the needed pins from the cup, and quietly finished dressing.

Bobinette was a red-haired beauty.

The thick braids of her abundant tresses, with their natural waves and curls, fell to where the lines of neck and shoulders meet, their tawny hues enhancing the milky whiteness of her plump flesh. This young creature was of the true Rubens type.

It was half past three in the afternoon of a dull November day. A kind of twilight was darkening the ground floor flat in the quiet rue de Lille, where the two lovers were together.

For some months now Captain Brocq had been on intimate terms with this intoxicating young person, who answered to the nickname "Bobinette." Her features, though irregular, were pleasing. Sprung from the people, Bobinette had tried to remedy this by becoming a past mistress of postures, of attitudes. Like others of her kind, from her very childhood she had learned to adapt herself to whatever company she was in, picking up almost intuitively those shades of taste, of tact, which can transform the most unconsidered daughter of the people into the most fastidious of Parisiennes.

It was the contrary as regards Captain Brocq, an artillery staff-officer and attached to the Ministry of War. Notwithstanding his intellectual capacities and his professional worth, so highly valued by his chiefs, he always remained the man of humble origin, somewhat gauche, timid, who was evidently better fitted to be at the head of a battery on the bastions of a fortress than frequenting the gossipy clubs of officials or society drawing-rooms. Brocq, who had passed out of the Military Academy exceedingly well, had been given an important post recently: a confidential appointment at the Ministry of War. During the first years of his military life Brocq had been entirely preoccupied by his profession. Of a truth, as pretty Bobinette had just told him, he was not at all "a man accustomed to women." This was why, when verging on forty, his heart, as young, as fresh as a student's, had suddenly caught fire when he happened to meet Bobinette.

Who was this woman?

Brocq could not place her with that mathematical exactitude dear to his scientific mind. She puzzled this honest man, who fell deeper and deeper in love with her. Whenever they met, and their first tender effusions were over, the lovers exchanged ideas, and always on the same subject.

Bobinette had completed her toilet. In leisurely fashion she came over to her lover and seated herself beside him. Brocq, who was thinking deeply, remained silent.

"What are you thinking about?" Bobinette suddenly asked, in a chaffing tone. "Have you solved a new problem, or are you thinking of a dark woman?"

Brocq smiled. Amorously he put his arm round the girl's supple figure; drawing her to him, and burying his lips in her abundant and perfumed hair, he murmured tenderly:

"I am thinking of the future, of our future."

"Good gracious me!" replied Bobinette, withdrawing herself from his arms. "You are not going to bore me again with your ideas of marriage?"

The captain made a movement of protestation; but Bobinette went on:

"No, no, old dear, no chains for me! No gag, no muzzle for me! We are both independent, let us remain so! Free! Long live liberty!"

Brocq now got in a word: "In the first place," he said, "you know quite well you would do a very stupid thing if you married me; I have not the usual dowry, far from it! Then I am not of your world. Can you see me in a drawing-room, playing my tricks with the colonel's wife, the general's wife, with the whole blessed lot of them? Zut! I am just what I am, just Bobinette.".…

Brocq now got in a word: "In the first place," he observed, "as regards the dowry, you know very well, my pretty Bobinette, that I have already taken steps about it, on your behalf — now don't protest! It gives me pleasure to make your future safe, as far as I can: a modest competence. On the other hand, I am not a society man, and if you wish it.".…

The captain drew nearer his mistress and brushed her lips with his moustache.

Bobinette drew back, got up from the divan, stood in front of her lover, erect, arms crossed, her look sullen: "No, I tell you, I wish to be free, my own mistress.".…

Brocq grew impatient: "But in spite of your ideas of independence, my poor darling, you are always in a state of servitude! Why, only to give one example, for the last two years you have been content to occupy an inferior position in the house of this Bavarian diplomat — or Austrian — I don't know what he is?"

"Naarboveck?" asked Bobinette, surprised. "But don't imagine that I am the Baron de Naarboveck's servant: still, if it were otherwise, I can't play proud. I can't bring out the title-deeds and pedigree of my ancestors for inspection!"

"It's not a question of that," observed Brocq.

Bobinette had launched forth. She continued:

"But that is the question. You are always imagining that I have things given me to do which lower me. I have told you a hundred times how it was I went to the Naarboveck's. One day the poor man came to the hospital: he was almost beside himself. His daughter Wilhelmine, who is barely nineteen, had just been taken ill — it was typhoid fever — he was obliged to go away and leave her — not a soul in whose care he could leave the child with confidence. I was recommended to Naarboveck. I came, I nursed Wilhelmine. This went on for a month, then for two, then three — now we are the best friends in the world. Wilhelmine is a girl whom I love with all my heart; the baron is an amiable man, all kindness and attention.…It is true that I am now a kind of companion, in an 'inferior' position, as you choose to put it in your absurdly vain and jealous way of looking at things; but, my dear man, there are ways and ways, and I assure you I am treated as one of the family. And, besides, you ought to consider that it was precisely at the Naarboveck receptions we met."

With the utterance of these last words Bobinette glanced at Captain Brocq as if she would annihilate him: the remembrance of their first meeting seemed more odious to her than pleasing.

Brocq, whose eyes were obstinately lowered, saw nothing of this. He suggested: "I am not the only one you have met at M. de Naarboveck's. There is that handsome cuirassier, Henri de Loubersac.".…

Bobinette crimsoned. She shrugged her shoulders. "How stupid you are! Lieutenant Henri does not give me a thought, if he comes to the house.".…

Brocq interrupted: "Yes, I know he comes on account of the fair Wilhelmine." His tone was conciliatory. Once more he drew Bobinette to him; but she seemed to object more and more strongly to the captain's caresses. Glancing at a clock on the mantelpiece she cried: "Why, it is four o'clock! High time I should leave."

Brocq, who had followed her glance, added, suddenly serious: "My faith! I must call at the Ministry!"

Both rose. Bobinette took up her hat and went to the looking-glass. Brocq exchanged his jacket for a black coat. He went into his study, separated from the other room by a heavy curtain.

"Bobinette!" he called.

That young person responded to his call, but with no show of haste. She found the captain seated before his bureau rummaging in an immense drawer crammed full of papers.

"You know, my little Bobinette, that I have made you my sole legatee," cried the captain, with an adoring look at the pretty girl who suddenly appeared in the doorway. He continued his search among his papers: they were in great disorder.

"I wished to show you — it's a question of spelling your name correctly. You are called Berthe, are you not?"

The girl had come forward. She quickly caught sight of a mauve sheet of paper on the blotting-pad. A few lines were traced on it.

"Ah! you wretch!" she cried, while she glanced through the words. She pretended to be angry. "I've caught you! You were writing to a woman! Ho, it starts well:

"*My own darling adored one, how long the hours seem when I await.*"...

Captain Brocq shouted with laughter.

"Ah, here's a joke! Why, it is you who are jealous now!"

Bobinette questioned him with a look. He explained:

"But, you great idiot, don't you understand that I was writing to you, and that only a couple of hours ago! You know I am always afraid you will not come to our meeting-place, and you are always late!"

Bobinette, reassured, now helped Brocq to go through his drawer methodically.

There could be no doubt of it — the captain was a most untidy man. Family letters, papers covered with figures, handwritten military documents, even some bank-notes, were jumbled together in great disorder.

Bobinette noticed her own handwriting on some sheets of paper. How well she knew them!

She feigned anger. "It is abominable to compromise me like this!" she cried. "See! My letters! Love letters! Intimate letters lying about like this! No, decidedly!"...

Brocq put her right. "No, no, my pet! Your precious letters are most carefully preserved by me — put together — see — there they are — there are not many of them — but not one is missing!"

"You are sure of that?"

"I swear it."

Bobinette reflected. The captain, however, returned to the adjoining room, hoping to come across the deed of gift he had set his mind on finding. "Come with me, Bobe!" he called. He opened a little writing desk. He thought his mistress had followed him, but she had remained in the study.

"Bobinette!" he called again, astonished to find himself alone.

She lingered.

Brocq went back.

He collided with the girl who, with a furtive gesture, slipped something into her muff.

"Well," said he.

"Well, what now?" she retorted.

They gazed at each other for a moment in silence.

"What were you doing?" questioned Brocq suspiciously.

"Nothing," answered Bobinette coldly.

But the captain caught hold of her hands. He was uneasy, almost angry: "Tell me!"

The red-haired beauty jumped back with a defiant air: "Very well, then! I have taken my letters, they belong to me! I wish to have them! It disgusts me to think that they are left lying about your rooms. Do you think it funny that your orderly should read them to his country-woman? That your concierge should know all about them? I declare men like you have not a scrap of tact, of nice feeling!"

"Bobinette!" the captain implored her.

"No, no; and again, no!" cried the girl more and more angrily. "I have them. I keep them!" The captain grew pale. She added, a little more gently:

"But, you great stupid, they are of no importance! I'll give them back to you later — when you are good. You are behaving like a schoolboy! Come, kiss me! Tell your little Bobe that you are not angry with her! If you don't I shall cry!"

Already she was beginning to sob, and great tears were dropping. Captain Brocq, struck dumb, gazed at her sorrowfully. And whilst he clasped her in his arms, anxiety strained at his heart, anguish convulsed his soul. Did she really love him, this woman with her whimsical ways, her independent attitude, this elusive woman who never gave herself entirely? Was he the dupe of a comedy? Did she consent to these meetings three times a week through pity, through sympathy only, or through habit, or, worse still, for some mercenary reason? And this when he himself would have given up everything so that he might not miss them! Ah, if that were the truth! The captain felt an immense void opening in the depths of his lonely soul. He apologised in a low voice, hurriedly, with bent head, humbly, and Bobinette listened with curled lip and haughty air: She bore no malice, she declared. Then, a few moments later, for she was really much upset and did not wish to show it, she hurried away, dropping a hasty kiss on her lover's forehead as a token of peace. How ardently he wished that this peace might last.

"I am very much behind time," she had murmured by way of farewell.

Directly his mistress had gone, Brocq went to the window, watched her turn the corner of the rue de Lille, enter the rue des Saints-Pères, and go towards the quays. While he watched her he was trembling. A roll of paper was sticking out of Bobinette's muff. Brocq knew this paper: its appearance and colour were familiar to him. Nevertheless, his mind was so full of his love affair that he immediately forgot this detail. But, in a minute, the turn of events forced him to recall it.

"In Heaven's Name!" shouted Captain Brocq, as a violent blow from his clenched fist made the scattered papers on his bureau tremble. "By Heaven! It is impossible!"

When he found himself alone, sadly alone in his little flat, Brocq saw it was five o'clock, and more than time to start for the Ministry of War. Hastily putting on overcoat and hat, he had hurried into his study to look for the big leather portfolio he always carried when taking his work from the office to his own home.

Owing to his special knowledge of fortress artillery Brocq had been requested to put the finishing touches to a confidential report on the defences of the eastern forts of Paris and the distribution of the effective forces of the companies of mechanics in time of mobilisation. He had searched feverishly in his drawers for this report, which was of no great bulk. For the last ten minutes he had anxiously searched, but in vain: he could not find a trace of it!

"It is impossible!" he cried. He swore aloud as if the better to convince himself. "The title is in big letters, 'Confidential,' in red, and twice underlined. Oh, it is quite impossible that it should pass under my eyes unperceived!"

Again the distracted man ransacked his papers and shook his portfolio. Almost beside himself with exasperation, he cried: "My excellent Bobinette, by her rummaging, has put the finishing touch to this confusion. Heaven knows, it was bad enough before!"

He paused. Anguish seized him. He fell into an arm-chair, while drops of sweat broke out on his forehead. Suddenly he had remembered the roll of papers sticking out of Bobinette's muff. He uttered a cry: "My God! But supposing!" ...He did not put the rest of his thought into words. For an instant he had the idea that through thoughtlessness, by mistake, an involuntary one assuredly, his mistress had taken this document to wrap up her letters ...without suspecting. That was it! No doubt she had carried off with her this secret plan of mobilisation — but if the plan got lost? If it were dropped in the street!

Brocq cursed his untidy ways once more. He would never forgive himself for having allowed that girl to ransack his drawers — but he must act, and at once! He must, without fail, find that mislaid document. Of one thing he was sure — the document was not on the premises. Brocq jumped up. "Good-day, Captain!"

"Good-day, Captain!"

The man in charge at the cabstand, on the quay des Saints-Pères, at the corner of the bridge, saluted Brocq cordially.

Brocq, ghastly pale, his face showing signs of intense anxiety, gasping for breath, asked: "Tell me! Just now, ten, five minutes ago — did you not see a lady — young — she had red hair — did she not pass this way? Come now!"

The cabstand than winked. "My faith, Captain, you are just in time. Only a moment ago a lady, such as you describe, but prettier than that, got into a taxi; she."...

"Ah!" interrupted the captain, "do you know what address she gave?"

"Why, yes I do. I was almost touching her when she spoke to the driver."...

"Well?"

"Faith, what she said was 'Take me to the Bois,' and the cab turned by the Saints-Pères bridge. Probably it went by the Tuileries quay after."

"The number? The number of this taxi?"

"Why, we will ask the policeman at the kiosque: he has certainly entered it, as usual."

Stamping with impatience inside a landaulet whose hood he had had lowered that he might more easily see around him, Brocq had rushed off in pursuit of Bobinette's taxi, 249 — B.Z.

Shaking from head to foot, Brocq held in a tight grip his leather portfolio, which contained all the documents he wished to lay before the Ministry of War, less, alas! the mislaid plan of the eastern forts. He scrutinised the Place de la Concorde, the Avenue des Champs-Elysées. He was asking himself why Bobinette, after telling him she must hurry away, had driven to the Bois as if she were one of the leisured crowd? This troubled the lover in him as well as the soldier. Why had he rushed after his mistress in this fashion? What definite reason had he? After all, it was exceedingly improbable, surely, that she had carried away this document without noticing it, for it was composed of three or four large sheets of paper!...In that case, she must have lost it before getting into the taxi. As to supposing for an instant that she had taken it away intentionally — Brocq would not suppose it. Why should he? There was nothing to lead him to think.

But, all the same!...

All the same, the captain had a presentiment, a conviction, an instinctive certainty that, at all costs he must overtake Bobinette — he absolutely must.

Why?

Brocq could not have said why. He did not reason about it. He felt: a feeling as indefinable as it was irresistible drove him to pursue, to continue the chase at top speed.

Again and again he had shouted to the astonished chauffeur, who was driving his taxi as fast as the crowded street permitted: "Get on! In the devil's name, go faster — faster!"

Night was falling. The close of this November day was particularly beautiful. Behind the Arc de Triomphe a broad band of red on the horizon reflected the setting sun in its winter glory. The breeze was wafting the last red-brown leaves from the trees, turning them over and over before they fell on the autumnal greensward and the black earth of the empty flower-beds.

Rows of carriages were moving towards the Étoile. As they had cleared the Rond-Point of the Champs-Elysées Brocq uttered a cry of joy. Some fifty yards away his keen eye had caught sight of Bobinette's taxi: he had identified the number.

"There it is!"

He urged the chauffeur to follow it up closely, regardless of consequences.

"A moment more and we shall have caught up the 249," said Brocq to himself. His landaulet was gaining ground.

The crowd of vehicles, the police holding them up where the roads intersected, impeded the advance. Brocq, wild with impatience, could not keep still. At last they reached the Place de l'Étoile. The carriages, conforming to rule, rounded the monument on the right, going more and more slowly owing to the increased crush. But the captain felt relieved; only one cab, drawn by a horse, now separated him from Bobinette's taxi, and assuredly her vehicle and his would be abreast, side by side at the entry to the avenue of the Bois de Boulogne.

Brocq loved Bobinette dearly, but frankly, if for a joke or inadvertently she had carried off the document, he would give her a piece of his mind. He would let her know that it would not do to play tricks with things of that sort. Nevertheless, his heart was wrung with anxiety.

Supposing Bobinette had noticed nothing — if the document had fallen in the street?

Suddenly the poor fellow saw Bobinette's taxi cut across the line of carriages to the right and turn into the Avenue de la Grand-Armée.

Brocq's chauffeur did not seem to have noticed this: he continued in the direction of the Bois de Boulogne.

"Oh, you idiot!" shouted the captain. And, in order to give his instructions as rapidly as possible, he leaned almost entirely out of the vehicle.

But a second or two had passed when the chauffeur stopped dead, that he might see what had happened to his fare. Something must have happened, for Brocq had abruptly stopped short in the midst of his directions. He had collapsed on the cushions of the taxi, and remained motionless.

Other vehicles surrounded the automobile. Some ladies passing in a victoria noticed the captain.

"Look, my dear," exclaimed one of them, "do you see how pale that man is? He seems to be ill!"...

At the same moment, the pedestrians were struck by the officer's strange attitude. Brocq had suddenly subsided in a heap on the cushion, his head had fallen to one side, his mouth was open, his eyes were closed: he seemed to have fainted.

A crowd gathered at once.

The chauffeur got down, shook his fare by the arm, and the arm was inert.

The crowd increased.

"A doctor!" cried a voice. "It is plain that this man is ill!"

A man stepped out from the crowd. His hair was white, he wore a decoration ribbon, and he had descended from a private brougham. With an air of authority he made his way through the curious onlookers, and when a constable came forward he said: "Kindly make these people stand away. I am Professor Barrell of the School of Medicine."

There was a murmur of respectful sympathy among the onlookers, for the professor was famous.

This master of medicine with a sure hand had undone the collar, the cravat of the mysterious sufferer, half opened his overcoat, put his ear to the patient's heart, then, straightening himself, considered the face attentively, not without a certain amount of stupefaction.

The constable made a suggestion: "Had we not better take this individual to a chemist's?"

Professor Barrell replied in a low voice: "To a chemist's? Do so if you wish ...but it is useless ...you would do better to go to the police-station: this unfortunate man is dead — it is a case of sudden death." The medical man added some technical words which this guardian of the peace did not understand.

II
DOCUMENT NUMBER SIX

"Hullo!...Am I speaking to Headquarters of Police?"

"Yes?"

"To the sergeant?...Good!...It is the superintendent of the Wagram Quarter who is telephoning....They have just brought here the body of an officer who has died suddenly, Place de l'Étoile, and I want you to send me one of your inspectors....This officer was the bearer of important documents....I must send them direct to the military authorities....Hullo!...Good....You will send me someone immediately?...An inspector will be here in ten minutes?...Splendid!...Very good!"

The superintendent hung up the telephone receiver and turned to the policeman, who stood motionless awaiting orders. He was visibly embarrassed.

The police superintendent of the Wagram Quarter was a man of decisive action. He possessed in the highest degree the quality, the most precious of all for those of the police force, whose functions call them to intervene continually in the most surprising adventures — presence of mind.

A few minutes before this the taxi with its tragic burden had stopped at his police-station, and the men on duty had carried in the body of the unfortunate captain.

Called in all haste, the sergeant had immediately made a rapid investigation. He examined the documents in the victim's portfolio.

"Here's a go!" he muttered — "'State of munition supplies!' 'Orders for the eastern fortresses!' I do not want to keep such important documents longer than I can help."

He had immediately telephoned to Headquarters. Reassured by the sergeant's reply, the superintendent turned to the policeman.

"You have made out your report?" he asked curtly.

The honest guardian of the peace touched his cap, looked perplexed, and scratched his head.

"Not yet, Monsieur. No time, Monsieur. But I will write it out at once."

The superintendent smiled at his embarrassed subordinate. "Suppose we do it together!"

"Let us see now! The deceased was a captain — isn't that so? The papers found in his portfolio and the name written on it let us know that he was called Brocq, and that he was attached to the Ministry. So much for his identity. We will not trouble about his domicile, the Place will tell us that! Now let us go into the details of the accident — tell me, my man, exactly how his death occurred!"

Again the worthy guardian of the peace scratched his head with an anxious look.

"I saw nothing of it, Monsieur," he replied.

"And the taxi-driver? You have his deposition?"

"He did not see anything either, Monsieur."

"Call this chauffeur."

A few minutes after, the superintendent dismissed the chauffeur. A short interrogation revealed that the taxi-driver had not only seen nothing, but that he could do nothing to help the enquiry.

The superintendent recalled the honest policeman.

"Come now! You are certain that the victim died immediately?"

"Well, you see, Monsieur, while I was dispersing the crowd, a doctor came up, and it was he who told me how the dead man died!"

"This doctor did not point out to you the cause of death?"

"No, Monsieur. But he gave me his card."

The policeman drew from the pocket of his tunic a dirty note-book. He took a card from it and handed it to his chief. "There, Monsieur!"

The magistrate looked at the name. *Professor Barrell, of the School of Medicine.* Turning the card, he read aloud a few words in pencil:

"Sudden death, which seems due to a phenomenon of inhibition."...

"This professor did not explain what he meant by 'death due to inhibition'?"

"No, Monsieur."

"Annoying!...I do not know what that means."

The superintendent was about to continue his enquiry when there was a knock at his office door.

A policeman informed him respectfully: "There is an inspector, Monsieur, from Headquarters detective department who asks to see you on urgent business — he declares you have sent for him."

"Tell him to come in."

No sooner had this personage from "Headquarters detective department" appeared in the doorway, than the superintendent rose, and advanced with outstretched hands.

"You, Juve! I am delighted to see you! How are you?"

It was, in truth, the celebrated detective, Juve.

Juve had altered but little. He was always the same man; rather thick-set, vigorous, astonishingly alive, agile, as youthful as ever, in spite of his moustache turning grey, in spite of his rounded shoulders which, at moments, seemed to bend under the weight of the toils and fatigues of the past.

This magic name evoked memories of terrible stories, stories of dangers encountered, endured, overcome; of brave deeds; of desperate struggles with the worst criminals.

Juve! He was the man who, for ten years, had represented to all, ability, audacity, limitless daring! He was the man who best knew how to employ wiles and stratagems to secure the triumph of society in the incessant combat it had to sustain against the innumerable soldiers of the army of crime.

When the terrible Dollon affair had come to an end, Juve had been blamed officially, and the detective could not help feeling angry and exasperated, for, after all, if he had failed, he ought not to have been treated as a culprit. Not a soul had had the slightest suspicion of how the affair had ended. Not one of them knew the incredible truth — how the marvellous, the redoubtable, the incredible Fantômas had elected to make his escape at the very moment when Juve was preparing to put the handcuffs on him.

And the detective, disheartened, but determined not to give up the fight against this deep-dyed criminal whom he had been pursuing for years, had asked for a few weeks' holiday, had lain snug, then had returned to his post at Headquarters, had made a point of keeping in the background, only awaiting the moment when he could resume his hunt for the ruffian whom he looked on as a personal enemy.

Since then, nothing had happened to put him on the track of Fantômas. No crime had been committed in circumstances which could leave him to think that this elusive murderer was involved in it.

Our detective had begun to ask himself if, not having been fortunate enough to arrest this king of assassins, he had not at any rate succeeded in unmasking him, in compelling him to fly for his life, in putting him out of power to do harm.

Rapidly the superintendent put Juve in possession of the incidents which had led him to telephone to Headquarters.

"You have done well," said Juve. "Have you the portfolio of this dead man?"

"Here it is, my friend."

Juve opened it.

"If you will allow it, Monsieur, I am going to make a complete list of the contents. This list I shall leave with you. I shall take a copy: that I shall deposit at the office of the Chief of Staff, obtaining a receipt for it. This will relieve both you and myself of all further responsibility on this head."

For some moments Juve and the superintendent occupied themselves in going over the papers of the dead man. Suddenly the detective got up, and, holding a paper in his hand, began walking up and down the room.

"You have read that?" he asked, turning to the superintendent.

"What is it? No."

"Read it!"

The superintendent read:

"Inventory of the documents which were submitted to me by the Second Bureau of the Staff Head-quarters, for which I have signed a receipt, and I have undertaken to return and deliver them up to the Second Bureau of the Staff Headquarters, Monday, November 7th, when given a receipt to that effect."

"Well, what of it?"

"Well," replied Juve. "Compare the documents given on this list with those we have found in this portfolio ... they tally."...

"Of course. That only proves, I imagine, that this officer died at the very moment when he was on the way to his office to return the papers entrusted to him. What do you see surprising in that?"

Juve shook his head. "I see, Monsieur, that what I feared is true: yes, this is certainly the list of documents contained in this portfolio, but."...

"But, one is missing!"

The two men checked the papers of Captain Brocq. Juve was right. There was a document missing — Number Six.

"Whew!" murmured the superintendent. "How are we to know whether this document has been dropped in the taxi, or has already been returned by the captain, or whether."...

"Or whether it has been stolen from him," finished Juve.

The supposition which the detective had put into words was so grave, so terrible, so weighty in its consequence that the superintendent cried, in a shaking voice:

"Robbed! Robbed! But by whom? Where? How? On the way from the Place de l'Étoile here? While the body was being brought to the police station?...Juve, it's incredible!"

Juve was walking up and down, up and down. "I don't like affairs of this sort, in which officers are involved, and most particularly officers connected with the Second Bureau of the Military Staff: they require the most careful handling.... You never know where they will lead. These officers are, owing to their functions, the masters of all the military defences of France.... Confound it!"

Juve stopped short. "You had better let me see the body of this poor fellow."

"Certainly!"...

The superintendent led Juve towards one of the rooms, where the corpse of Captain Brocq was: it had been laid down on the floor. Pious hands had lighted a mortuary candle, and, in view of the position held by the dead man, two of the police staff were keeping watch and ward until someone came to claim the body of the deceased.

Juve examined the corpse. "A fine fellow!" he said quietly.

He turned to the superintendent.

"You told me just now that Prof. Barrell chanced to be present at the moment of death?"

"That is so."

"What did he suppose was the cause of death?"

The superintendent smiled. "Now you have it! Possibly you can throw light on it, my dear Juve, for I could hardly make head or tail of his diagnostic. The professor claims that death is due to a *phenomenon of inhibition*. What does that mean exactly?"

Juve shrugged his shoulders.

"Inhibition!...Peuh!...It is a learned word — very learned!"...

"Which means to say?"...pressed the superintendent.

"It does not mean anything."

Juve's tone was a mixture of contempt and anger. The superintendent was staggered. Juve's anger increased.

"It does not mean anything," he repeated. "Inhibition! Inhibition! It is the term reserved for deaths that are unexplained and inexplicable: it is the term with which science covers herself when she does not wish to confess her ignorance."

The magistrate was smiling now.

"So then, Juve, you conclude that Professor Barrell has declared that this officer had died through inhibition because, in fact, he was ignorant of the cause of death?"

"Exactly!" snapped Juve.

He was kneeling on the floor, bending over the body. Slowly, minutely, he was examining it with his keen eyes, by the flickering light of the mortuary candle.

He had examined successively the face of the dead man, then the arms, the trunk, the shoulders, the whole body. He did not utter a word.

"What are you looking for in particular, Juve?"

"The cause of this *inhibition*," replied the detective, who pronounced the word with unconcealed anger and resentment. He seemed to harbour some subtle rancour regarding the doctor. Suddenly he got up and, turning to the policeman, commanded:

"Undress this body!"

The superintendent interposed.

"What for?"

"It will be useful for your report."

"Come, now! In what way?"

"For that," said Juve, pointing a finger at the officer's short coat....

"That? How that?...I don't see anything," protested the superintendent.

Juve knelt down again, and made a sign to the superintendent to do likewise.

"Look, Monsieur! Just bend down and look at this tiny graze on the cloth."

"Yes!...Well?"

"Does that not tell you anything?"

"No it does not."

Juve rose and repeated his order. "Unclothe this corpse!"

Then, turning to the superintendent, he added:

"What that tells me is, that this man has been killed by a shot from a gun or a revolver."

"Oh, come, now!"

"You will see."...

"The garment is not pierced."...

Juve began to smile.

"Monsieur," said he, "you must know that arms of high penetrating power, firing projectiles of small diameter, grooved projectiles, cause only the slightest graze in the materials they pass through: the damage is almost imperceptible. Numerous experiments have demonstrated this. You see the passage of the projectile is so rapid, its gyratory movement so accelerated, that, in some way, the threads of the fabric are not broken: they are only pushed aside. They come together again after the passage of the ball, and unless a very careful examination is made, one would never know that a projectile had perforated the material."

The two policemen were undressing the corpse.

Scarcely had they undone the waistcoat than the shirt of the unfortunate man was seen to have a spot of blood on it, in the region of the heart.

"See," cried Juve. "It is just as I said: a ball of small diameter, propelled by a formidable power of penetration, has caused immediate death, producing a wound which has hardly bled at all, so precise and clean has the wound been!"

Juve again bent over the corpse.

"It is plain to see that this officer's death has been caused by a ball in the heart, right in the centre of the heart."

The superintendent now protested:

"But what you are telling us, Juve, is terrible, it is inadmissible! How could this person have committed suicide without having been seen in the act by someone? Without anyone finding his revolver? And that at the very moment when he leaned out of the window of the vehicle to give the chauffeur his instructions?"

Juve did not seem disposed to answer this. But, after remaining silent for a minute or two, he took the superintendent by the arm in familiar fashion, and drawing him away said: "Let us return to your office, I have a couple of words to say to you."

When the superintendent and the detective had entered the room, when they were alone together, when the detective had made sure that the double door was shut tight, and that not a soul could hear them, Juve, his hands resting on the writing-table, looked the superintendent straight in the face. The latter, having seated himself in his chair, waited for the detective to speak.

Juve spoke.

"We are thoroughly agreed, Monsieur, are we not, regarding the conditions of the accident?... This officer has been shot through the heart, when he was crossing the Place de l'Étoile in a vehicle, and at the precise moment when he leaned over the door of that vehicle, and this, without anyone having seen or heard what happened?"

"Yes, Juve, that is so. This suicide is incomprehensible!"

"It is not a case of suicide, Monsieur."...

"What is it, then?"

"A crime!"

"A crime!!!"

"This man has been killed by a shot from a gun, a shot fired from a distance. No one saw the assassin do the deed: the Place de l'Étoile was crowded with people. It was a shot fired from a distance, because of an important point, Monsieur. The deceased was attached to the Second Bureau of the Ministry of War. At the time of his death he was the bearer of important documents: one of these important documents is missing! I assure you, Monsieur, this not only determines the fact of the crime, but furnishes us with the motive for that crime!"

The superintendent of police stared at Juve, speechless. At last he said:

"But it is impossible! Absolutely impossible, I tell you! What you are inventing now is impossible!... You forget that a shot from a gun, a shot from so powerful a weapon, makes a noise. Why, deuce take it, the detonation must be heard!"

"No, Monsieur! There are now weapons which are perfectly silent. For example, there are guns in which liquefied carbonic acid is used, which fires a projectile at more than 800 yards, and all that can be heard is a sharp snap when the projectile speeds off."...

"But, look here, Juve! Such a crime as this partakes of the nature of a romance! The criminal must have taken aim in the midst of a crowd! Who, do you suppose, would have been mad enough to attempt it? What scoundrel would ever have run such a risk?"

Juve, very calm, very much master of himself, was standing in front of the superintendent. His arms were crossed: he seemed to defy him, as though he knew beforehand that in him he was to encounter the incredulity of the average person.

"You ask me," replied he, "what criminal could be daring enough to do this? What criminal would have carried out such a murder successfully? Sir, that murderer's name is synonymous with all the maddest attempts, with every kind of atrocity, with every species of cruelty, with all the talents!"...

"And, it is."...

Juve suddenly stopped short, as if he were afraid of the word he was about to pronounce.

"By jove!" he declared, "if I knew the name of the guilty person, I would go and arrest him!"...

While the unfortunate Captain Brocq collapsed inside his carriage, mortally struck by the mysterious shot, pretty Bobinette, who could have had no idea of the accident to her lover, following hard in her wake, continued her drive. She ordered her chauffeur to stop at the riding-alley which passes behind the Chinese Pavilion.

A lingering ray of sunshine still illuminated the thickets of the Bois, but already those out for an airing were hastening towards the city, when Bobinette, discharging her taxi, entered the little path which runs beside the equestrian's track.

She seemed full of the joy of life, stepping smartly along, appreciating the pleasure of this quick, free, independent walk. Soon, however, her pace slackened. She spied an unoccupied seat, looked at her watch, and sat down. She cast a sharp glance towards the far end of the path.

"We are both up to time," she murmured, recognising a figure still some distance away.

Bobinette drew from her muff a small roll of papers.

The advancing person was a seedy-looking individual, stooping, seemingly bent under the weight of a bulky accordion. He looked about sixty; his long white beard, untrimmed and badly neglected, disguised the lower half of his face, while his luxuriant moustache, and his long hair, arranged artist fashion, largely hid the upper part of his countenance.

A beggar? Not at all! This personage would most certainly have spurned such an epithet with a gesture of offended disdain. Live by charity? Not he! Was not his accordion there to show that he possessed a regular means of livelihood? He claimed to be a musician.

He was well known throughout one quarter of Paris, was this poor old man who chanced to be passing along that path in the Bois de Boulogne. He was a perfect specimen of the unsettled type of human being, savagely enamoured of liberty, going from court to court playing with wearied arms the ballads of the moment, indifferent to their melodies, to their rhythms, to their beauties, to their ugliness.... No one knew his real name. They called him *Vagualame*; for his plaintive notes inspired sad thoughts and an indefinable trouble of the nerves in those unlucky enough to listen to him for a time. This nickname stuck to him.

He was quite a Parisian type, this Vagualame: one of those faces at once odd and classic, such as one comes across in numbers on the pavements, known to all the world, without anyone knowing exactly who they are, how they live, where they go, or whence they come....

The old man had, on his side, caught sight of Bobinette. He hastened towards her as fast as his legs permitted; and as soon as he was near enough to speak to her without raising his voice, he questioned her:

"Well?" It was the interrogation of a master to a subordinate.

"Well?" he repeated. His tone was anxious.

Bobinette calmed the old man's apprehensions with a nod. "It's done," said she.

Holding out to him the roll of paper, she added: "I could only get them at the last minute; but I've got them, and I don't fancy he suspects anything."

As Bobinette uttered these last words, the old accordion player chuckled sneeringly:

"So that's what you think? As a matter of fact, it is evident that he suspects nothing now!"

The way in which the old man pronounced the word "now" puzzled the girl.

"What do you mean?"

"Captain Brocq is dead."

"Dead!"

Although she did not love her lover much, at this startling piece of news Bobinette had jumped up, wringing her hands in horror. She grew strangely pale.

"Yes, dead!" replied Vagualame coldly. "Kindly sit down please! See to it that you play your part! You are a young woman speaking to an old beggar, and you are not to forget it."

Bobinette sat down mechanically. She questioned him, and her voice was trembling.

"Dead? What has happened, then?"

"What has happened is that you have played the fool! Brocq saw clearly that you had stolen the document from him."

"He saw?"...

"Yes, he saw it! I had my suspicions, fortunately!... Then this cursed captain threw himself into a taxi and followed you.... At the moment when your own auto turned on the Place de l'Étoile, his was going to meet it! Brocq was already hailing you, and you would have been caught without a doubt had I not come to the rescue."

"Great Heavens! What have you done?"

"I have just told you. Clic-clac! A bullet in his heart, and he remains on the spot.".…

Bobinette was dumbfounded. She did not speak for a minute or two. Then she asked anxiously:

"But where were you?"

"That does not concern you!"

"What must I say, then, if, by chance, I am questioned?"

"What must you say! The truth.".…

"I am to confess that I knew him?"

Vagualame tapped his foot impatiently.

"How stupid you are! There is one thing you must understand. At the present moment it is almost certain that this good fellow's identity has been established. The devil's in it if some policeman is not at his domicile already and if enquiry is not being made into the life of Captain Brocq. To learn that he is on terms of acquaintanceship with your patron, de Naarboveck, is child's play! To prove that he has received a visit from you to-day, to prove that you were his mistress — or, at the very least that you had come on an errand from Naarboveck's daughter, Wilhelmine, why anybody can discover that! To-morrow you will read the details in all the papers, for the reporters are going to get hold of this affair: it is inevitable! Consequently, do you not deny anything: it would only compromise you to no good purpose. You will say.".…

Vagualame stopped short. He raised the accordion which he carried slung over his shoulder, saying in a whisper:

"People are coming. I leave you. I will see you again, if necessary. Do not be anxious. I take all on my own shoulders. Attention!" And suddenly changing his tone, he began to speak in a voice calculated to excite pity:

"Grateful thanks, kind lady! The good God will rain blessings on you for it.…I thank you, kind lady!"

Vagualame moved off.

III
BARON NAARBOVECK'S HOUSE

Despite the gusty wind and squalls of icy rain which deluged Paris, despite the early morning hour, although it was one of those first dark days of November which depress humanity,
Jérôme Fandor, the journalist, editorial contributor to the popular evening paper *La Capitale*,
was in a gay mood, and showed it by singing at the top of his voice, at the risk of rousing the
neighbourhood.

In his very comfortable little flat, rue Richer, where he had lived for a number of years, the
young journalist was coming and going busily: cupboards, drawers, wardrobes, were opened
wide, garments, piles of linen, were spread about in all the rooms. On the dining-room table
a large travelling bag lay open: into this, with the aid of his housekeeper, Jérôme Fandor was
feverishly packing the spare things he required, and was talking in joking fashion with his old
servant, Angélique.

Presently she asked, rather anxiously:

"Are you likely to be away a long time, sir?"

The journalist shook his head and murmured:

"I should like to be, but you don't suppose we journalists get holidays of that sort!"

Still anxious, Angélique went on:

"Perhaps you intend to change your housekeeper when you return, Monsieur Fandor? Nevertheless — — "

"You are really mad, Angélique! Have I not told you twenty times that I am going away for
a fortnight's holiday? Never for a moment have I thought of getting rid of you — quite the
contrary! I am delighted with the way you do your work. There now! I shall go by way of
Monaco — I promise to put five francs on the red for you!"

"On the red?" questioned old Angélique.

"Yes. It's a game. If red's the winner there will be a present for you! Hurry off now and
bring up my trousers!"

Whilst his housekeeper hastened downstairs, Fandor went to the window and, with a questioning glance, considered the dull grey sky.

"Disgusting weather!" he murmured. "But what do I care for that? I am going to the sun
of the South — ah, to the sun!" He laughed a great laugh of satisfaction. How he had looked
forward to this holiday, how he had longed for it! — this holiday he was going to take now,
after two-and-twenty months of uninterrupted work! During those months, in his capacity of
chief reporter to *La Capitale*, scarcely a day had passed without his having some move to make,
some strange happening to clear up, even some criminal to pursue; for Jérôme Fandor belonged
to that species of active and restless beings who are ceaselessly at work, ready for action, bent
on doing things: an activity due partly to temperament, partly to conscience. Added to this,
his profession interested him enormously.

At the commencement of his career — and that of journalism is a ticklish one — he had
been greatly helped by Juve, whose knowledge and advice had been invaluable to him. Fandor
had been involved — particularly during the last few years — in the most sensational crimes,
in the most mysterious affairs, and, whether by chance or voluntarily, he had played a real part
in them. He had not been content to take up the position of onlooker and historian only.

Fandor had made his post an important one: he had to be seriously reckoned with. He
had enemies, adversaries far from contemptible, and time and again the journalist who, with
his friend Juve, had taken part in terrible man-hunts, had attracted towards himself venomous
hatreds, all the more disquieting in that his adversaries were of those who keep in the shade
and never come into the open for a face-to-face tussle.

Finally, and above all, Fandor, coupled with his friend, detective Juve, had either distinguished himself gloriously or covered himself with ridicule, but in either case he had attracted

public attention by his epic combats with the most deadly personality of the age — the elusive Fantômas.

But our holiday-making journalist, whistling the latest air, all the rage, gave no thought to all that. He was reveling in the idea that a few hours hence he would be installed in a comfortable sleeping compartment, to awake next morning on the wonderful Côte d'Azur, inundated with light, drenched in the perfume of tropical flowers, bathed in the radiance of eternal summer.

Ah, then, eight hundred miles and more would separate him from the offices of *La Capitale*, of the police stations, of wretched dens and hovels with their pestilential smells, would separate him from this everlasting bad weather, from the cold, the wet, which were the ordinary concomitants of his daily existence. To the devil with all that! No more copy to feed printer and paper with! No more people to be interviewed! Hurrah! Here were the holidays! It was leave of absence, and liberty.

The telephone bell rang.

Fandor hesitated a moment. Should he answer it?

According to custom, the journalist "had left" the evening before: he could plead his leave, which was in order, and say, like Louis XIV, "After me the deluge!"

This famous saying would have suited the moment, for it was at that instant precisely that an inky cloud burst over Paris and emptied torrents of water over the darkened city.

Perhaps a friend had rung him up — or it was a mistake! So arguing, Fandor unhooked the receiver.

Having listened a moment, he instinctively adopted a more respectful attitude, as if his interlocutor at the other end of the line could see him.

Fandor replied in quick monosyllables, closing the conversation with these words:

"Agreed. Presently, then chief."

As the journalist hung up the receiver his expression changed: he frowned, and pulling at his moustache with a nervous hand, fretting and fuming.

"Hang it! It only wanted this," he grumbled.

Fandor had been called up by M. Dupont, of *L'Aube*, the well-known opportunist deputy, who was the manager of *La Capitale* as well. M. Dupont was only a nominal manager, and generally contented himself with writing up his editorial without even taking it to the office. He left the real management to his son-in-law, whose function was that of editor-in-chief. Thus Fandor had been extremely astonished when his "Head," as he was called in the editorial department, had rung him up.

M. Dupont had summoned him to the Chamber of Deputies, for three o'clock in the afternoon: his chief wished to give him some information for an article on a matter which interested him particularly. Fandor was puzzled, anxious.

What could it be? The chief could not know that he was taking his holiday.

"Bah!" said he, "Dupont evidently does not know. I will go to our meeting-place and will explain my approaching departure to him, and the devil's in it if he does not pass on this bit of reporting to one of my colleagues!"

"Madame Angélique," continued Fandor in a joyous voice, turning to the breathless old housekeeper who had just come back laden with parcels, "Get me lunch quickly. Then you must strap up my portmanteau. This evening I am going to make off, whatever happens!"

For two hours, interminable hours they seemed, Fandor had waited for M. Dupont in the Hall des Perdus[1] of the Palais-Bourbon. The deputy was at a sitting of the Chamber. If the ushers were to be believed, the discussion was likely to go on interminably. Several times our young journalist had thought he would simply make off without word said, excusing himself on the score of a misunderstanding when eight hundred odd miles lay between him and the directorial thunders. But he was too scrupulous a journalist, too professionally honest to follow the prompting of his desires.

So, champing his bit, Fandor had stood his ground.

As he was looking at his watch for the hundred and fiftieth time, he quickly rose and hastened towards two men who came out of a corridor: they were M. Dupont and a personage whom Fandor recognised at once. He bowed respectfully to them, shaking hands with the cordial M. Dupont, who said to his companion:

"My dear Minister, let me present to you my young collaborator, Jérôme Fandor."

"It is a name not unknown to me," replied the minister; then, having innumerable calls on his time, he quickly disappeared.

A few minutes after, in one of the little sitting-rooms reserved for Parliamentary Commissions, the manager of *La Capitale* was conversing with his chief reporter.

"It was not to present me to the minister that you sent for me, my dear Chief — unless you intend to get me an appointment as sub-prefect, in which case."...

"In which case?" questioned M. Dupont gently.

Fandor's reply was frank.

"In which case, even before being nominated, I should tender you my resignation: it is not a profession which tempts me much!"

"Reassure yourself, Fandor, I have no intention whatever of sending you to live in the provinces: but if I asked you to see me here, it was with reference to a very delicate affair about which I mean to give you *instructions* — I insist on this word."

"Good," thought Fandor. "It's all up with my holiday!"

He tried to ask this question before his chief went into details, but M. Dupont interrupted him with a movement of his hand.

"You will leave for your holiday a few hours later, my dear fellow, and you can take eight days in addition."

Fandor bowed. He could not dispute his chief's decision — and he had gained by this arrangement.

"My dear Fandor," said his chief, coming to the main point, "we published yesterday evening, as you, of course, know, a short paragraph on the death of an artillery officer, Captain Brocq.... There is something mysterious about his death. Captain Brocq who, owing to his functions, was attached to the Second Bureau of the Staff Headquarters, that is to say, the Intelligence Department, was in touch with different sets of people: it would be interesting to get some information about them. I mentioned this just now to the Minister of War, and to the Minister for Home Affairs: both are agreed, that, without making too much noise about this incident, we should institute enquiries, discreet, of course, but also pretty exhaustive. You are the only man on the paper possessed of the necessary tact and ability to carry the thing through successfully."

An hour later, under the pouring rain, Fandor, with turned-up trousers, his greatcoat collar raised, was walking stoically along the Esplanade des Invalides, which was feebly lighted by a few scarcely visible gas-jets. He reached the other side of the Place à la rue Fabert; looked at the number of the first house in front of him, followed the pavement a moment, turning his back on the Seine, then reached the Avenue de la Tour-Maubourg by way of the rue de l'Université.

Fandor repeated to himself the final words of his chief's instructions.

"Interview Baron de Naarboveck; get into touch with a young person called Bobinette; find out who and what are the frequenters of the house where this well-known diplomat lives."

Our journalist was not anxious as to the result of his interview; it was not his first experience of the kind, and this time his task was rendered especially easy, owing to the letter of introduction which M. Dupont had given him, in order that he might have a talk with M. de Naarboveck, who lived in a sumptuous mansion in the rue Fabert.

Fandor did not go straight ahead to this interview: his method was not so simple. After identifying the front of the house, wishing to know the immediate neighbourhood thoroughly, he went all round the mass of houses which limited the rue de l'Université; he went through the Avenue de la Tour-Maubourg, in order to discover whether the house was double or single, if it had one or two exits. Fandor was too much a detective at heart to neglect the smallest detail.

His inspection was soon done. The house possessed two entrances; that in the Avenue de la Tour-Maubourg was for the use of the servants and common folk only. The front door opened on the rue Fabert. A courtyard at the back separated it from the Avenue de la Tour-Maubourg.

The house consisted of three storeys, and a ground-floor approached by a few steps.

Fandor returned to the Esplanade des Invalides, and walked up and down under the trees for some time, watching the comings and goings of the neighbourhood. At a quarter to seven he had looked at his watch, and, not seeing any light in the first-floor rooms, the shutters of which were not yet closed, he concluded that the inmates had probably not come in.

Just then Fandor saw an automobile, a very elegant limousine, draw up before M. de Naarboveck's house. A man of a certain age descended from it, and vanished in the shadow of a doorway: the door had opened as the carriage stopped.

"That's de Naarboveck," thought Fandor.

Then he saw the carriage turn and move away.

"The carriage goes in: the master does not go out again," deduced Fandor.

A short time after, the chauffeur, having taken off his livery, came out of the house and went away.

"Good," remarked Fandor. "The man I am after will not budge from the house to-night."

The next to enter were two young women: then some twenty minutes passed. The rooms on the first floor were lit up, one after the other. The house was waking up. Fandor was making up his mind to ring when a motor-car brought a fourth person to the door. It was a young man, smart, distinguished-looking, very fair, wearing a long thin drooping moustache: movements and appearance spoke his profession: an officer in mufti, beyond question.

Fandor once more encircled the house; he had reached the door opening on to the Avenue de la Tour-Maubourg when he saw a confectioner's boy slip into the house.

"M. Dupont told me de Naarboveck lived alone with his daughter, therefore he has people dining with him this evening," reasoned the journalist. He then decided to dine himself, and return an hour and a half later. Naarboveck well dined and wined could give him more time, and would be the easier to interview.

Three-quarters of an hour later Fandor left the humble eating-house, where he had dined badly in the company of coachmen and house-servants, but fully informed as to the private and public existence of the person he was going to interview. He had set his host and his table neighbours gossiping to such purpose that he could tell at what time de Naarboveck rose in the morning, what his habits were, if he fasted on Fridays, and what he paid for his cigars.

"Monsieur de Naarboveck, if you please?"

Jérôme Fandor had rung the bell of the front entrance in the rue Fabert. It was just striking nine. A house-porter of the correct stamp appeared.

"He lives here, Monsieur."

Fandor offered his card, and the letter of introduction from M. Dupont.

"Please see that these are handed to Monsieur de Naarboveck, and find out if he can receive me."

The porter, having decided that the visitor was too well dressed to be left waiting on the steps, signed to the young man to follow him. The porter rang, and a footman in undress livery immediately appeared, and took card and letter from the porter.

The servant looked consideringly at Fandor's name engraved on the card, stared at this unknown visitor, hoping he would definitely state the purpose of his visit, but the journalist remained impassive, and as his profession was not indicated on his card the servant had to be satisfied with his own curiosity.

"Kindly wait here a moment," said the footman, in a fairly civil tone of voice. "I will see if my master is at home."

Fandor remained alone in a vast hall, furnished after the Renaissance manner. Costly tapestries covered the walls with their imposing pictures, their sumptuously woven epics.

The footman quickly returned.

"Will Monsieur kindly follow me?"

Relieved of his overcoat, Fandor obeyed.

One side of the hall opened on a great double staircase, the white stone of which, turned grey with the passing of time, softened by a thick carpet and ornamented by a marvellous balustrade of delicately wrought iron-work, a masterpiece of the XVIIth century.

The lackey opened a door which gave access to a magnificent reception-room, sparsely furnished with pieces of the best Louis XIV period. Mirrors reflected the canvases of famous painters, family pictures of immense artistic value, and still more valuable as souvenirs.

Traversing this fine apartment, they passed through other drawing rooms furnished in perfect taste. Fandor reached the smoking-room at last, where Empire furniture was judiciously mingled with pieces made for comfort after the English fashion, the tawny leather of which harmonised marvellously with the blood-red of the ancient mahogany and with its ancient bronzes.

The lackey pointed to a chair and disappeared.

"By jove!" said Fandor, half aloud, "this fine fellow has done himself well in the way of a dwelling-place!"

The journalist's reflections were interrupted by the entrance of an exceedingly elegant young lady.

Fandor rose and saluted this charming apparition.

IV
A CORDIAL RECEPTION

The journalist had naturally expected to see Monsieur de Naarboveck enter the room: in his stead came this pretty girl.

"Be seated, I beg, Monsieur," she entreated.

"She is his daughter," thought Fandor. "I am given the go-by: the diplomatist is not going to see me! I am sorry for that, but, on the other hand, here is this delicious creature."

"You asked to see Monsieur de Naarboveck, did you not? It is for an interview, no doubt. Monsieur de Naarboveck makes it a point of honour never to get himself written about in the newspapers, therefore you must not be surprised."...

The charming girl paused.

Fandor bowed and smiled. He said to himself:

"I shall have to listen for five minutes to this delightful person assuring me that her father does not wish to talk; after that he will come himself, and will tell me all I want to know."...

Thus he listened with divided attention to the pretty creature's words. Then he interjected:

"Monsieur, your father."...

His companion smiled.

"Excuse me!" she said at once. "You have made a mistake: I am not Mademoiselle Wilhelmine de Naarboveck, as you seem to imagine. I am merely her companion: I dare add, a friend of the house. They call me Mademoiselle Berthe."...

"Bobinette!" cried Fandor, almost in spite of himself. He immediately regretted this too familiar interjection; but that young person did not take offence.

"They certainly do call me that — my intimates, at least," she added with a touch of malice.

Fandor made his apology in words at once playful and correct. He must do all in his power to make himself agreeable, fascinating, that he might get into the good graces of this girl; for she was the very person whom it behooved him to interrogate regarding the mysterious adventure, the outcome of which had been the death of Captain Brocq.

Bobinette had answered Fandor's polite remarks by protesting that she was not in the least offended at his familiar mode of address.

"Alas, Monsieur," she had declared, in a tone slightly sad, "I am too much afraid that my name, the pet name my friends use, will become very quickly known to the public; for, I suppose, what you have come to see M. Naarboveck about is to ask him for information regarding this sad affair we have all been thinking so much about."

"Now we have come to it!" thought Fandor.

He was going to take the lead in this conversation, but the young woman did not give him time.

She continued in a rapid tone, on one note, almost as if she had repeated a lesson learned by heart.

"Baron de Naarboveck, Monsieur, cannot tell you anything that you do not already know, except — and there is no secret about it — that Captain Brocq used to come here pretty regularly. He has dined with the Baron frequently, and they have worked at several things together.... Several of his friends, officers, have been received here as well: M. de Naarboveck is very fond of company."...

"And then he has a daughter, has he not?" interrupted Fandor.

"Mademoiselle Wilhelmine, yes."

Fandor nearly added:

"A daughter to get married."

It seemed clear to him, that in spite of her timid and reserved airs, this red-haired beauty seemed to like the idea of playing a part in the drama.

"Mademoiselle," questioned Fandor, "it has been reported that yesterday afternoon you had occasion to meet Captain Brocq, some hours before his sad end?"

The young woman stared fixedly at the journalist, as if to read his thoughts, as if to divine whether or not he knew that not only had she met Captain Brocq, but had spent some time with him alone.

Fandor did know it, but he remained impenetrable.

Bobinette, very much mistress of herself, said quite simply:

"It is a fact Monsieur, that I did see Captain Brocq yesterday. I had to give him a message."

"You will think me very inquisitive," continued Fandor, who pretended not to look at the young woman, in order to put her more at her ease, but who, in reality, did not lose a single change of expression on her pretty face, for he could watch its reflection in a mirror. "You will think me very inquisitive, but could you tell me the nature of ... this communication?"

Bobinette replied, quite naturally:

"To be sure I can, Monsieur. Baron de Naarboveck is giving an entertainment here shortly, and the captain was going to take part in it. As he was very much of an artist we counted on his doing some menus in colour for us: I simply went to see him with a message from Mademoiselle Wilhelmine."...

The conversation stopped short.

Fandor had turned around quickly. Behind him — doubtless he had been there for some moments — a man was standing. Fandor had not heard him enter the room. He was a man of a certain age. His moustache was quite white: he wore the whiskers and imperial of 1850.

Fandor recognised Baron Naarboveck. He was going to apologise for not having noticed his entrance, but de Naarboveck smiled at the journalist with apparent cordiality.

"Pardon me, Monsieur Fandor, for not having received you myself, but I had a guest: moreover, Mademoiselle Berthe must have told you what my views are regarding interviews."...

Fandor made a slight gesture. The baron continued:

"Oh, they are definite, unalterable! But that will not prevent you from taking a cup of coffee with us, I feel sure. I have the highest esteem for Monsieur Dupont, and the terms in which he has recommended you to me are such that, from now on, I have not the slightest hesitation in treating you as one of ourselves, as a friend."

Monsieur Naarboveck put his hand familiarly on the young journalist's shoulder, and led him into the next room.

It was a library: a very lofty room. It was soberly and elegantly furnished. Before a great chimney-piece of wood, two young people were standing, and were chatting very much at their ease.

They paused when Fandor entered.

Close behind followed Mademoiselle Berthe.

Fandor bowed to the two young people.

Naarboveck made the introductions:

"Monsieur Jérôme Fandor — Mademoiselle de Naarboveck, my daughter — Monsieur de Loubersac, lieutenant of cuirassiers."

Silence reigned after these formal introductions. If Fandor was in certain measure satisfied with the turn the conversation had taken, he was really bored by this involuntary intrusion into a family gathering which mattered little to him. He felt he had been caught. How the devil was he going to escape from this wasp's nest? His eye fell on a timepiece. Seeing the hour, he thought:

"Had it not been for this Brocq fellow, and that fool of a Dupont, I should now be in the train asleep, and rolling along towards Dijon!"...

Mademoiselle de Naarboveck, with the ease of a well-bred woman, offered the journalist a cup of boiling hot coffee.

Mademoiselle Berthe suggested sugar.

Monsieur de Naarboveck, as if he had suddenly remembered something, said to him:

"But you bear a name which recalls many things, Monsieur Jérôme Fandor! It was you, of course, famous journalist that you are, who, some time ago, was in constant pursuit of a mysterious ruffian whom they called Fantômas?"

Fandor, a little embarrassed, smiled. It seemed to him something quite abnormal to hear Fantômas mentioned in this gathering, so simple, so natural, so commonplace.

Surely, this criminal, his adventures, the police, and even reporting, must partake of the fantastic, the imaginary — it must all be Greek to such conventional people.

Nevertheless, as Monsieur de Naarboveck spoke, Mademoiselle Berthe drew close to the journalist and gazed at him with curiosity.

"But tell me, Monsieur, may I ask you a question? Perhaps it is my turn to be inquisitive — but then, so were you just now!"

Fandor laughed. Decidedly this young and pretty person was charming.

"I am certainly bound to reply to you as you wish, Mademoiselle!"

Nodding with a mischievous look, and casting a glance at the Baron asking his approval — he signified his consent by a nod — she demanded with an innocently curious air:

"Do tell me, Monsieur, who this Fantômas is?"

Fandor stood speechless.

Ah, this question, which this young woman had asked so naturally, as if it referred to the most simple thing in the world, how often had he asked himself that same question? During how many sleepless nights had his mind not been full of it? And he had never been able to find a satisfactory answer to "Who is Fantômas?"

Fandor had been asking this question for years. He had, after a fashion, vowed his existence to the search for this mysterious individual. How often, and often, in the course of his investigation, in the midst of his struggles with criminals during his long talks and conferences with Juve, had he not thought that he had run the bandit to earth, identified him, was going to drag his personality out into the broad light of day — and then, suddenly, Fantômas had disappeared.

Fantômas had made a mock of him, of Juve, of the police, of everybody!

For weeks, for months, all trace of him was lost completely; then one fine day he would produce a drama, it might be a big drama, which took public opinion captive, it might be a drama in appearance insignificant, and then each one saw and followed traces which were more or less normal and ordinarily probable. Fandor and Juve, Fandor alone, or Juve isolated, following the indications which only their perspicacity enabled them to discover, still and always felt the presence, the trace of this monster, this being so enigmatical, so indefinable, who was terrorising humanity.

Then implacable and dangerous pursuits, redoubtable struggles, were the order of their days and nights.

Juve, Fandor, the representatives of justice, one and all, united to reduce the circle in which this ruffian revolved, and at the moment they were about to catch him, he would fade away, leaving them as their only spoil, the temporary personality with which he had clothed himself, and under which he had momentarily deigned to make himself known.

Now behold, here was this little red-haired creature, Bobinette, who asked for the solution of this formidable, incomprehensible, unprecedented thing, wanted it straight away.

"Who is Fantômas?"

Fandor's attitude, his expression showed how surprised he was at such a question.

M. de Naarboveck emphasised and justified the journalist's astonishment.

Then, in a rather dry, hard voice, Monsieur de Loubersac gave his opinion:

"My dear Baron, don't you think that for several years past we have been made sufficient fools of with all these Fantômas tales? For my part, I don't believe a word of them! Such a powerful criminal has no chance nowadays, that is to say, if he exists. One must see life in its true proportions and recognise that it is very commonplace.".…

"But, Monsieur," interrupted Mademoiselle Berthe, who, covered with blushes, scarcely dared raise her eyes to the handsome lieutenant, "but, Monsieur, for all that, Fantômas has been much talked about!"

The young officer looked the red-haired beauty up and down, bestowing on her but a cursory glance. Fandor noticed that Bobinette was greatly troubled by it. Following this little by-play, he immediately got a very clear impression that if the lieutenant did not consider the pretty girl worthy of much consideration, she, on her side, seemed very much influenced by all that this elegant and handsome young officer said or did.

Fandor had noticed, too, while the talk went on, that Mademoiselle de Naarboveck was deeply moved, and looked sorrowful. She was a graceful girl, in all the freshness and brilliancy of her twenty years, with large eyes, soft and luminous. Her natural disposition was evidently a bright and gay one, but this evening sadness overshadowed her, and to such a point that, in spite of her efforts to be lively and pleasant, she could not hide her sad preoccupation.

M. de Naarboveck, who had been watching Fandor closely, said to him, in a low voice:

"Wilhelmine has been very much upset by this terrible accident which has overtaken our friend, Captain Brocq, and we."...

Just then, the harsh sarcastic tones of de Loubersac broke in afresh:

"In conclusion," exclaimed the lieutenant, "I maintain that Fantômas is an invention, a more or less original one, I am ready to admit, but an invention of not the least practical interest. Just an invention of the detectives, this Fantômas; or, it may be of the journalists only, who have made the gaping public swallow this hocus-pocus pill — this enormous pill!" The lieutenant stared at Fandor defiantly. "And let me add, I speak from knowledge, for, up to a certain point, I know all these individuals!"

Fandor was not in the least impressed by the lieutenant's aggressive declarations. He regarded him calmly — there was a touch of irony in his gaze: at the same time, he did not clearly understand de Loubersac's last phrase.

The excellent Monsieur de Naarboveck murmured in his ear:

"De Loubersac, you know, has to do with the Second Bureau at the Ministry of War: the statistics department."...

It was only at half past eleven that Fandor had been able to tear himself away from the de Naarboveck house.

Fandor wandered on the boulevards a long time before he returned to his flat.

On his table, near his portmanteau ready strapped for departure, he found the Railway Guide lying open at the page showing the lines from Paris to the Côte d'Azur! He would not look at the seductive time-table. He rushed to his portmanteau, undid the straps in furious haste, dragged out his clothes, which he flung to the four quarters of the room. For the moment he was in a towering rage.

"And now, confound it! That Brocq affair is not clear! It's no use my trying to persuade myself to the contrary! There is some mystery about it! Those officers! This diplomat! And then this questionable person, neither servant, nor lady accustomed to good society, who has to me all the appearance of playing not merely a double rôle, but at the least a triple, perhaps a quadruple!... Good old Fandor, there's nothing for it, if you want to go South, but to see friend Juve and get some light on it all."

Having come to this conclusion, Fandor went to bed. He could not sleep. There was one word which ceaselessly formed itself in luminous letters before his mind's eye — a word he dare not articulate. It was a synthetic word which brought into a collected whole facts and ideas; it was the summing up of his presentiments, of his conclusions, of his fears; the word which said all without defining anything, but permitted everything to be inferred: that word was — *Spying*!

V

THEY ARE NOT AGREED

As one who had the privilege of free entry to the house, Fandor opened the front door of Juve's flat with the latchkey he possessed as a special favour, traversed the semi-darkness of the corridor and went towards his friend's study.

He raised the curtain, opened the door half-way, and caught sight of Juve at his desk.

"Don't disturb yourself, it is only Fandor!"

The detective was absorbed in the letter he was writing to such a degree that he had never even heard the journalist enter. At the sound of his voice Juve started.

"What! You! I thought you had flown yesterday, flown South!"

Fandor smiled a woeful smile.

"I did expect to get away yesterday evening. Juve, in my calling, as in yours, it is the height of stupidity to make plans. You see! Here I am still — stuck here!"

Juve nodded assent.

"Well, what then?" he asked.

"Well, what do you think, Juve?"

The detective leaned back in his chair and considered his young friend.

"Well, my dear Fandor, to what do I owe the pleasure of this visit?"

Fandor did not seem much disposed to answer. He had taken off his hat and overcoat. Now he drew from his pocket a cigarette-case. He selected one and lighted it carefully, seeming to find a veritable delight in the first whiffs which he sent towards the ceiling.

"It's a fine day, Juve!"

The detective, more and more astonished, considered the journalist with the utmost attention.

"What's the matter with you, Fandor?" he said at last.

"Why are you carrying on like this? Why are you not on your travels?... Without being inquisitive, I suppose you have your head full of other things than the state of the weather?"

"And you, Juve?"

"How? I?"

"Juve, I ask you why you are so upset?"

The detective folded his arms.

"My word, Fandor, but you are losing your head. You think, then, that I am thoroughly upset?"

"Juve, you look like a death's-head!"

"Really?"

"Juve, you have not been to bed!"

"I have not been to bed, have I not? How do you know that?"

Fandor approached the writing-table and pointed to the corner, where a series of half-smoked cigarettes were ranged side by side.

"Ah, I do not doubt, Juve, but that they tidy up your study every morning; but, here are twenty-five cigarette ends, lying side by side: you certainly have not smoked all those in one morning, consequently you have lighted them during the night, and consequently you have not gone to bed."

Juve's tone was bantering.

"Continue, little one, you interest me."

"And, to cap it all, the ends of your cigarettes have been chewed, bitten, mangled, — an indisputable sign of high nervous tension — therefore."...

"Therefore, Fandor?"

"Therefore, Juve, I ask what is wrong with you — that's all!"

The detective fixed the journalist with a piercing look, trying to guess what he was aiming at. But Fandor was too good a pupil of Juve to let him have the slightest inkling of his feelings. There was an enigmatic smile on his lips whilst he awaited Juve's reply.

The detective quickly decided to speak out.

"I am looking into a very serious affair which interests me greatly."

"Grave?"

"Possibly."

This did not satisfy Fandor. He seated himself on the corner of the writing-table and considered his friend.

"See now, Juve, answer me if you can see your way to it.... Your attitude makes me sure that important things are in the air: you are in a very emotional condition, and that for some reason I have not fathomed. Can I be useful to you? Will you not let me share this secret?"

"Will you tell me yours?"

"In three minutes."

Juve sat for a few minutes deep in thought. Then in a changed voice, a solemn voice with a sharp note in it, he said:

"You know about Captain Brocq's sudden death, of course?... Let me tell you that I have discovered it was an assassination. It's this affair I am giving all my attention to."

When there was mention of the Brocq affair, Fandor started. Here was a strange coincidence. Since last night had not his own mind been distressed by the mysteries he divined in this strange death? And now here was Juve also upset by his examination of this same affair.

Fandor drew up a chair, placed himself astride it, facing Juve, putting his elbows on the back and holding his head between his hands.

"You are looking into this Brocq affair, Juve?... Very well! So am I!... You have read my articles?"

"They are very interesting."

"They lack conclusiveness, however!... But, as things are, I could not do better, not having any precise information and facts to go upon. Are you quite certain about the facts yourself? Do you know who has struck the blow?"

"Don't you suspect, Fandor?"

Juve did not give him time to reply. He half rose from his seat, and, bending close to Fandor, looked him straight in the eyes.

"Tell me, my boy! Suppose that after six months of truce, six months of tranquillity, your whole existence is again violently upset? If you understood that the efforts and dangers and struggles and tenacity of six long years were entirely wasted, and that the results you thought you had achieved did not exist — that you had to begin all over again — that once more you had to play a match with not only your life for stakes, but your honour as well — tell me, Fandor, would you not be stirred to your depths?"

Our journalist feigned indifference: it was the best way to draw Juve on, he well knew.

"What do you mean, Juve?"

"What do I mean, my boy? You shall hear! Do you know who killed Captain Brocq?"

"No! Who?"

"Fantômas!"

At this sinister name Fandor jumped up as though thunderstruck.

"Fantômas?... You accuse Fantômas of having killed Captain Brocq?"

Juve nodded assent.

The two men stared at each other in horror-struck silence.

Fantômas!

What a flood of memories, horrid, menacing, that name evoked! There flashed through Fandor's mind all that he knew of the atrocities which could be imputed to Fantômas. He seemed to live over again the recent years of continual struggle, of almost daily contest with the mysterious criminal — Fantômas!... But had not Juve declared — and not so long ago —

after the drama of rue Norvins,[2] when the elusive monster had been driven to flight — had not Juve declared that Fantômas had vanished for good and all! Now, at this precise moment, he was accusing this criminal of a fresh crime!... Fandor thought, too, of the conclusions he had himself arrived at, whilst studying the Brocq affair from his own point of view: that it was a drama of spies and spying.... Surely either he was mistaken — or Juve was!... Was it a murder, or a political assassination?... No longer pretending indifference, he questioned Juve anxiously:

"You accuse Fantômas? In the name of death and destruction, why?"

Juve had regained his self-possession. By pronouncing the word "Fantômas," by giving utterance to his secret fears, he had relieved his feelings.

"Fandor!" said he, in a quiet voice: "Consider carefully all the details and circumstances of this drama! In open day, on one of the most frequented promenades of Paris, an officer falls mortally wounded when passing in a taxicab, going possibly to some appointed meeting-place in one of the restaurants of the Bois. His taxi is surrounded by a crowd of vehicles, and without having time even to see his attacker, without anyone having seen him, Brocq collapses, mortally wounded, killed as though in battle, by a shot, a mysterious shot, fired from a weapon of the most perfect kind.... Come now, Fandor! Is that not a crime worthy of Fantômas?"

But the journalist was not convinced.

"True, this crime is worthy of Fantômas, but I do not think Fantômas has committed it.... You go too far, Juve! You are the victim of your hobby. Believe me, you exaggerate — you cannot trace every strange and subtle crime to this criminal!"

"If you do not attribute this crime to Fantômas, then at whose door do you lay it?" demanded the detective, who was well aware that he must guard against being the victim of a Fantômas obsession.

"Juve," replied Fandor, "I have been charged by Dupont to look into the Brocq affair, and have had to postpone my holiday to do it — that is how you see me this morning.... Well, I have begun my enquiry, and am trying to find out the exact truth regarding this unfortunate officer's death.... I have visited certain of his relations, interviewed the people who have known him, I have been able to get into touch with this Bobinette, who seems to be the last person who approached him a little before his assassination, and I have also arrived at a conclusion."

"And that is — Fandor?"

"A conclusion, Juve, which does not involve Fantômas in the slightest degree, a conclusion which, I assure you, has the advantage of being more certain, plainer, more absolutely definite than yours."...

"And that is — Fandor?"

"Juve, this officer belonged to the Second Bureau of the Staff Officer's Headquarters."...

"Yes, and?"...

"Juve, when an officer of the Second Bureau disappears in such tragic conditions, do you know what one presumes to be the reason of that disappearance?"

"What?"

"Juve, I assert that if Captain Brocq is dead it is because there is a spy in the pay of a foreign power, who, being under supervision, perhaps on the point of being arrested, has resolved that the captain must die in order to save himself.... A document has been stolen, and it is precisely this fact which makes me disbelieve in the intervention of Fantômas."...

"You do not believe me, Juve?"

The detective shrugged his shoulders.

"No, I do not think you are right.... In the first place, Fantômas is capable of everything — capable of the theft of a document for which a foreign power would pay him very highly, just as there is no other kind of theft he is not capable of.... And then, dear boy, a spy, a traitor in the pay of a foreign power would not dare to attempt the crime to which we are giving all our attention — not in that particular way at any rate. There is only one person who would risk that — Fantômas."

Fandor's laugh had a note of mockery in it. He let Juve see that he thought his ideas on this subject were very simple indeed.

"It is your hobby which always inspires you," he repeated.... "Beyond question I am the first to believe in the audacity of Fantômas ... and if I do not know all the secrets of terror hidden in this word 'spying,' I am ready enough to be convinced.... But, look here, Juve, I know the world of spies, I have studied them, I know what they are capable of attempting, ... and I do not speak lightly when I tell you that the assassination of Brocq is a political crime."

Juve continued to shake his head, quite unconvinced.

Fandor continued:

"Juve, believe me! Who says 'spy,' says 'capable of anything.' The officers of the Second Bureau are, in short, the true directors of the police spy system; they know all the shameful mysteries whereby some individual reputed honest, honourable in appearance, is in the pay of the foreigner. They know the traitors. They know who sells France and who buys France. Every day they are in relation with the agents belonging to all classes of society, lawyers, commercial men, small shopkeepers, commercial travellers, railway servants, women of the world, women of the pavement, thousands of individuals who continually travel about the country, holding it in a network of observations, notes, remarks, the result of all of which might be that some one power would have immediately the advantage over some other, because it knew the weak points where it could launch its attack.... You know, Juve, that they are people who do not shrink from anything when their interest is at stake. You know that the man who betrays, who spies, who is an informer, is always disavowed by the country who employs him.... You know that those who are taken in the act are punished to the utmost, consequently they will stick at nothing to save themselves from being caught. Do you not think that in this spy-world there might be found a man who, driven into a corner by circumstances, would be daring enough to commit the crime which is occupying our attention now? You say: 'It is a crime worthy of Fantômas!' Agreed. But I reply to you: 'There must be spies worthy of being compared to Fantômas!' "...

Fandor stopped short. Suddenly Juve threw himself back in his chair: the detective laughed aloud, a burst of ironic laughter. "My dear boy," said he, "do not be angry with me."

"What nonsense, Juve — You know very well that I would not be that!"

"Well, my dear Fandor, you see in the assassination of Captain Brocq an affair of spying because you have had your hobby for some time past — the hobby of spying."

Fandor smiled. Juve continued:

"Come! Is it not true that six months ago — it was just after the Dollon assassination — you published in *La Capitale* a whole series of papers relating to affairs of treason?"

"True, but."...

"Is it correct that you learned just then that one could define the Second Bureau as the world of spies, and that you were extremely struck by this, extremely surprised?"

"That is so, Juve. It is precisely because I had this information, and was able to get a fair knowledge of the terrible secrets existing in this dark Government department, that I am in a position now to ascribe the Brocq affair to the action of some group of spies."

"Your hobby again, Fandor! The assassination of the captain has occurred under such circumstances that it can only be imputed to Fantômas. Let us look the truth in the face! We are going to enter into a fresh struggle with Fantômas! That is a certainty!"

"It's your hobby now, Juve! There's no Fantômas in this affair. No! We are face to face with a very serious business, there I agree with you; but it is wholly a spy job — nothing else!"

Getting up, the journalist added:

"This very evening I shall publish in *La Capitale* an article in which I shall explain exactly what spies are, the real part they play in the body politic, their terrible power; that it is a mistake to consider them only cowards; that owing to the exigencies of their sinister profession, they very often give proof of an exceptional courage — bravery — and in which I shall."...

With a shrug, Juve interrupted:

"In which you will write nonsense, old boy.... Anyhow, you are free!"

"That's true! Free to spend a fortnight in the Sunny South, where I shall be in a few hours' time! Anyhow, read my article in *La Capitale*; I tell you I am going to take a lot of trouble over it!"...

"A fortnight hence, then, Juve!" He added in a bantering tone:

"Don't dream too much of Fantômas....What!"

VI
CORPORAL VINSON

With one knee resting on his portmanteau, Jérôme Fandor was pulling with all the force of his powerful arms at the straps in order to buckle them up.

It was Sunday, November the thirteenth, and five o'clock in the afternoon. The flat was brilliantly illuminated, and the greatest disorder reigned throughout.

At last Fandor was off for his holiday! Not to risk losing his train, our journalist meant to dine at the Lyons railway station.

"Ouf!" cried he, when he had succeeded in cramming his mass of garments sufficiently tight, and had then closed the portmanteau.

Fandor uttered a sigh of satisfaction. This time there could be no doubt about his departure — the thing was certain. He was casting a final glance round when he stopped short in the middle of the passage.

The door-bell had been rung: evidently someone was at the entrance door. Who was it? What was it? Had something arisen which was going to prevent his departure? He went quickly to the door. He opened it to find a soldier on the landing.

"Monsieur Fandor?" he enquired in a gentle, rather husky voice.

"Yes. What is it you want?" replied the journalist crossly.

The soldier came forward a step: then, as if making an effort, he articulated painfully:

"Will you permit me to enter? I am most anxious to speak to you."

Fandor, with a movement of the hand, signified that the importunate stranger might come inside. He observed the man closely. He was quite young, and wore infantry uniform: his stripes were those of a corporal. His hair was brown, and his light eyes were in marked contrast to the much darker tones of his face. A slight moustache shaded his lip.

The corporal followed Fandor into his study, and stood still with an embarrassed air. The journalist considered him an instant, then asked:

"To whom have I the honour of speaking?"

This question appeared to tear the soldier from a kind of dream. He jumped, then mechanically stood at attention, as if before a superior officer.

"I am Corporal Vinson."

Fandor nodded, tried to remember him, but in vain. The name told him nothing....

"I have not the honour to be known to you, Monsieur, but I know you very well through your articles."

Then he continued in almost a supplicating tone:

"I greatly need speech with you, Monsieur."...

"Another bore," said Fandor to himself, "who wants to get me to give him a recommendation of some sort!"

Our journalist boiled with impatience at the thought of the precious minutes he was losing. He would have to cut his dinner short if he did not wish to miss the night express. Nevertheless, wishing to lessen the unpleasant reception he had given this unwelcome visitor, he murmured in a tone which was cold, all the same:

"Pray be seated, Monsieur: I am listening to you!"

Corporal Vinson seemed greatly agitated.

The invitation was evidently very opportune, for the visitor let himself fall heavily into an arm-chair. Great drops of perspiration were on his forehead, his lips were pallid: at intervals he looked at the journalist, whose impassible countenance did not seem to invite confidences. The poor trooper lost countenance more and more: Fandor remained silent.

At last Vinson managed to say, in a voice strangling with emotion:

"Ah! Monsieur, excuse me for having come to disturb you like this, but I was determined to tell you ... to know you — to express to you ... how I appreciate your talent, your way of writing ... how I like the ideas you express in your paper!... There was your last article, so just, so ... charitable!"

"You are very kind, Monsieur," interrupted Fandor, "and I am much obliged to you; but, if it is the same to you, we might arrange a meeting for another day, because now I am very pressed for time."...

Fandor made as if to rise to emphasise his statement; but Corporal Vinson, far from imitating the movement, sank deeper and deeper in the large arm-chair, into which he had literally fallen a few minutes before, and with an accent of profound anguish, for he understood Fandor's desire to shorten the conversation, he cried with a groan:

"Ah, Monsieur, do not send me away! If I keep silence now, I shall never have the courage to speak — but I must."...

The soldier's countenance was so full of alarm that Fandor regretted his first movement of ill-temper, his show of impatience. Perhaps this man had interesting things to say! He must give the fellow confidence. Fandor smiled.

"Very well," he suggested amiably, "let us have a talk if you really wish it."...

Corporal Vinson considered Fandor a moment, thanking him with a look for his more cordial attitude; then suddenly drawing himself up into a standing position, he shouted:

"Monsieur Fandor ... I am a traitor!"

Though far from expecting so brutal a declaration, Fandor sat tight. He well knew that in such circumstances comments are useless. He rose slowly, approached the soldier, and, placing his hands on the agitated man's shoulders, pushed him back into the arm-chair.

"Control yourself, Monsieur, I beg of you," he said in a kind voice. "You must not upset yourself like this! Be calm!"

Great tears flowed down the corporal's sunburnt cheeks, and Fandor considered him, not knowing how to console so great, so spontaneous a grief.

Amidst his despair, Corporal Vinson stammered out:

"Yes, Monsieur, it's because of a woman — you will understand — you who write articles in which you say that there should be pity for such unfortunates as I am — for one is a miserable wretch when a woman has you in her clutches, and you have no money — and then, with that sort, once you have started getting mixed up in their affairs, you are jolly well caught — you have to do as you are told — and always they ask more and more of you.... Ah, Monsieur, the death of Captain Brocq is a frightful disaster! As for me.... If I have turned traitor — it is their fault."...

The corporal murmured some unintelligible words, pronouncing names unknown to Fandor; but our journalist was rejoicing more and more at this outpouring.

Suddenly he got the impression that the mysterious happenings, the obscure drama he had been on the fringe of for some days past was becoming clear, that the veil of ignorance was being torn away. Fandor had the sensation of being a spectator, before whose eyes a curtain was slowly rising which until then had concealed the scenery of the play.

The corporal continued, stammeringly:

"Ah, Monsieur, you do not know what it is to have for your mistress such a woman as ... she whom I love, ... such a woman as ... Nichoune! Nichoune! Ah, all Châlons knows what she is like. Her wickedness is well known ... but for all that, there is not a man who."...

Fandor interrupted:

"But, my good corporal, why are you telling me all this?"

"Why, Monsieur," replied Vinson, after a pause and a piteous look, "because — it's because ... I have sworn to tell you everything before I die!"

"Hang it all! What do you mean to do?" asked Fandor.

The corporal replied simply, but his tone was decisive:

"I mean to kill myself!"

From this moment it was Fandor who, far from wishing to start off for his train — he had given up any idea of leaving for the South that evening — was bent on getting from the soldier further details about his life.

Fandor now learned that the corporal had been in the service some fifteen months. He had been among the first conscripts affected by the new law of two years' compulsory service, and had been sent to the 214th of the line, in garrison at Châlons. Owing to his qualities he had been much appreciated by all his superior officers. As soon as he had finished his classes, he obtained his corporal's stripes, and in consideration of his very good handwriting, and also owing to the influence of a commandant, he got a snug post as secretary in the offices of the fortress itself.

Vinson was thoroughly satisfied with his new situation; for, having been brought up in his mother's petticoats, and practically the whole of his adolescence having been passed behind the counter of the maternal book-shop, he had much more the temperament of a clerk than of an active out-of-doors man.

The only sport which he enjoyed was riding, riding a bicycle, and the only luxury he allowed himself was photography.

Time passed. Then, one Sunday evening, he went with some comrades to a Châlons music-hall.

Vinson's chief companions were some non-commissioned officers, a little better off than he was....Without being lavish in their expenditure, these young fellows did not reckon up their every penny, and, not wishing to be behindhand, Vinson had sent to his mother for money again and again, and she had kept him in funds.

On this particular evening, after the concert, they had invited some of the performers to supper in a private room, and Vinson, in the course of the entertainment, was attracted, fascinated, by a tall girl with dyed hair, emaciated cheeks, and brilliant eyes, whose flashy manners smacking of some low suburb, had subjugated him completely.

Vinson made an impression on the singer, for she did not respond to the advances of a swaggering sergeant, reputed generous, but turned her attentions to the modest corporal.

They talked, and they discovered they were affinities. The result was they found themselves at daybreak on the deserted boulevard of Châlons. The corporal's leave did not expire till the evening of the following day. Nichoune offered him hospitality: they became lovers.

Vinson's heart was in this liaison: he persuaded himself that the chain that bound them was indissoluble. The singer's idea was to profit by it. Her demands for money were constant: she harried her lover for money.

Little by little, Vinson's mother cut off supplies: the corporal, incapable of breaking with Nichoune, ran up debts in the town.

"But," went on Vinson, "this is only the beginning. I have told you this, Monsieur, with the hope of excusing myself to a certain extent for what I did later on. My actions were the outcome and consequences of my difficulties."

"Something serious?" questioned Fandor.

"You shall judge of that, Monsieur."

Vinson went on with his confession in a firmer tone. Fandor realised that the corporal had decided to make a clean breast of it.

"It sometimes happened after I had had a scene with Nichoune, and had quitted her in a fury, that I would go for a long bicycle ride into the country, taking my shame and rage with me. On a certain Saturday, bestriding my faithful bike, I went for a spin along the dusty high-road which runs past the camp. After going at high speed, I dismounted, seated myself under a tree in the shade, by the side of a ditch, and was falling asleep. It was summer, the sun was pouring down. A cyclist stopped in front of me with a punctured tyre. He asked me to lend him the wherewithal to repair it; and whilst the solution was drying we started talking.

"This individual was about thirty; elegantly dressed; and from the way he expressed himself, one could see that he was a man accustomed to good society.

"He told me he was making a tour, and was now doing the neighbourhood about Reims and Châlons.

"'Not very picturesque country,' I remarked.

"But he retorted;

"It is interesting — the roads, for example, are complicated!'

"I began to laugh at this, and as he insisted on the difficulty he had to find his way in these parts, I offered to let him look at my Staff-office map. I carried a copy in my blazer....Ah, Monsieur — how well Alfred played his little comedy! That is what he called himself, at least, that was the name he was known by — the only name I have ever known. He seemed absolutely stupefied at the sight of this map, ordinary though as it was, and seemed set on buying it from me. I did not want to part with it. He offered five francs for it. I expressed my astonishment that he would not wait till he got to Châlons, where he could procure one like it for the sum of twenty sous.

"Bah!' declared Alfred, 'It gives me pleasure to pay you that sum — it is a way of thanking you for having lent me the use of your cycle outfit.'

"My faith, Monsieur Fandor, I was too beggared to say 'No!' so I accepted the money, while making excuses for myself: my plea being that a soldier is not a rich man.

"I pass over details. It is sufficient to say that when we returned to Châlons together, we were such good friends that he asked me to dine with him. When he saw me back to barracks, Alfred pressed a loan on me. I had told him about Nichoune, and about the pecuniary difficulties I was in, for by this time, I had full confidence in him. He slipped a twenty-franc piece into my hand with an air of authority: 'When you become a civilian again,' said he, 'you will easily be able to pay me back; and besides, to salve your pride, I am going to ask you shortly to do me a few services. I often have little things done. I shall entrust the doing of them to you, and shall pay you accordingly.'...

"You understand, Monsieur Fandor, that there was no reason for refusing, that I could see, especially as he made the offer very nicely, and that it came in the nick of time, at the very moment when — I have to admit it — I would have done anything for money....

"After this we met frequently. Alfred used to send me invitations, and often he included Nichoune. He never would let me pay for anything; and, I must confess, that the greater part of the time I should have found it very difficult indeed to pay a sou!

"We always met at some appointed place outside the town: he would not stay in Châlons longer than he could help, because he said the air there was bad for his delicate lungs. He was particularly interested in aviation, and he was for ever getting me to pilot him about the aviation camp.

"'You who draw so well,' he would say; 'make me a plan of this apparatus!...Explain to me how these huts are constructed!'

"He would question me as to the effectives of the regiments, ask me details as to estimates, statements, and returns which passed through my hands in the offices.

"Finally, one day, as I had no inkling of what he was really aiming at, Alfred put me on to it!"...

The corporal stopped. His throat was strained and dry.

Fandor brought him a glass of water, which he swallowed at a gulp. With a grateful look he continued:

"'Vinson,' said Alfred to me, 'I have confidence in you, and you know how discreet I am! Very well, I have a superb piece of business in hand which ought to bring us in a great deal of money. A stranger with whom I came into contact recently, who is a very good fellow, who has been obliged to leave his country owing to troubles that were brought on him, possesses a document, a very interesting one, which would be much valued at the Staff Headquarters of the Sixth Corps. He needs money and would be willing to sell it. I tried to buy it from him, but I have not the necessary funds. I was seeking a solution of the difficulty, when this stranger asked me to procure him some photographs of the Châlons barracks, in exchange for which he would give me his document. He needs these photographs for postcard purposes. If we could supply him with them in three days, not only will he give us his important paper, but he will pay twenty francs for each proof as well!'

"Ah, Monsieur Fandor, this story did not hang together, but I was actually weak enough to believe it! Or at least I tried to make myself believe it. Besides, this proposal of Alfred's came just in time: I had not a sou to my name! Nichoune was making a terrible row, and I hardly dared venture into the streets, I had so many creditors.

"I tried to square matters with my conscience: telling myself that there was nothing compromising connected with these photographs: in fact, views of our barracks are to be found in any album on sale, however small.

"Later on, I learned that this was a method *they* employed to decoy the guides, to draw them securely into their toils. *They* first of all give them very insignificant things to do, in order not to frighten them, and pay a high price: it is afterwards that they fasten you up tight. You shall see how."...

Fandor nodded. It was nearly time to catch the train, but he thought no more of the Côte d'Azur! He was too interested in the corporal's confession, and felt that by letting him speak he would learn more, he would learn much. He therefore encouraged Vinson to continue. The corporal asked nothing better.

"The photographs taken, I rejoined Alfred, who had told me to be sure to get leave for forty-eight hours, whatever happened. Alfred dragged me to the railway station; he had two tickets. We went off to Nancy, where, said he, we should find the purchaser. At Nancy, no one; whoever it was, had gone to a street in one of the suburbs. We waited in a little flat. Towards four in the afternoon Alfred said to me: 'Bah! Don't let us hesitate any longer. If the stranger has not come, it is because he is waiting for us elsewhere — I know where — let us go to meet him — at Metz!"

"'At Metz!' I cried. 'But we should have to cross the frontier, and I have not...'

"Alfred interrupted me, laughing. He opened a press and brought out civilian clothes, then he took wigs from a drawer, and a false beard. At the end of half-an-hour we were disguised; an hour later we were in Lorraine. We left the train there. It was there that, for the first time, I began to be afraid, for it seemed to me that when leaving the station at Metz, Alfred exchanged a quick glance with the policeman on duty. Ah, Monsieur Fandor, how I have regretted this journey! Directly we were in a foreign country, Alfred's attitude towards me changed: he was no longer the friend, he was the master. He had got me, the rogue, and jolly tight too!

"'Where are we going?' I asked.

"Alfred chuckled.

"'By jove! can't you guess?' he replied. 'Why, we are going to the Wornerstrasse, to visit Major Schwartz of the Intelligence Department.'

"'I shall not go!' I declared.

"Alfred's look was a menace.

"'You will come,' said he, in a low voice. 'Consider! If you refuse, at the end of five minutes the police will have unmasked you!'...

"There was nothing else to be done. I knew this Intelligence Department already, by reputation. Alfred had spoken to me about it. It was a vast suite of rooms on the first floor of a middle-class house, where a number of men in civilian clothes were at work. They all bore the military stamp. We had to wait in a large room filled with draughtsmen and typewriters, and on the wall hung a map, on a huge scale, of the frontier of the Vosges.

"Alfred sent in his name.

"A few minutes afterwards we were ushered into an office. A big man, seated behind a table heaped with bundles of papers, scrutinised us over his spectacles: he was bald, and wore a thick square-cut fair beard. He examined the photographs without a word, threw them carelessly on a set of shelves, and took from his drawer ten louis in French money, which he counted out to me. Of any document in exchange there was, of course, no question! I thought everything was finished, and I was preparing to leave this abominable place when the big man put his hand on my arm. It was Major Schwartz himself, the chief of the spy system there — I learned that later. He said to me in very correct French, with hardly a trace of accent to betray his origin:

"'Corporal Vinson, we have paid you lavishly for information of no value, but you will have to serve us better than that, and we shall continue to treat you well.'

"I thought I should have fainted when I heard my name pronounced by this man. It was clear he already knew my rank and name....He knew much more than that — as the conversation which followed let me see. He informed me that he wished to obtain a complete statement of the organisation of the dirigibles and aeroplanes; he must have the characteristics of all the apparatus; a list of the Flying Service Corps: he exacted even more confidential information still — where the aviators and the aircraft were to be moved if mobilisation took place — the whole bag of tricks, in fact!"

"And," asked Fandor, hesitating a little, "you have ...supplied him with all this?"

In a voice so low as to be barely audible, and blushing to the roots of his hair, Vinson confessed:

"I supplied it all!"

"Is that all you have to say?"

"Not yet, Monsieur — listen:

"Alfred had gone back with me as far as Nancy, where I had put on my uniform again; then I returned to Châlons quite by myself.

"I asked myself if it would be possible to get clear away from the terrible set I was mixed up with. Try as I might, I could not manage it. Every day Alfred harried me, threatened me: I had to obey him. Then almost on the top of this came the affair of Captain Brocq."

Fandor had been waiting for this. He had foreseen that he was going to learn what the connecting link was, which united the adventures of Corporal Vinson with the drama of the Place de l'Étoile, but his expectations were not fulfilled....True enough, Vinson, through the mysterious intervention of his redoubtful friends, was to enter into relations with Captain Brocq, to whom he had been recommended, how or in what terms he did not know.

The business hung fire for several weeks, and this was owing to Vinson himself, whose moods alternated from one of shrinking disgust to one of bravado courage.

"At times," said he, "I wished to break with them at any cost, and become honest once more; but, alas, I was always under the evil influence of Nichoune, who was a very close friend of Alfred, and the pair of them encouraged me to tread the traitor's path without faltering. Then, without breathing a word, I put in a request through the proper channel for a change of garrison. I hoped to get sent either to the West or the South; above all, I was bent on leaving the Sixth Corps, on flying from the frontier neighbourhood, and finishing my service in some district or region where it would be impossible for them to make me their spy tool. But, I do not know how — was it through Nichoune? — I expect so, because I had unluckily confided this secret to her one evening — Alfred got wind of what I was up to. He flew into a fearful rage. Suddenly he quieted down, and began to laugh.

"'Ah, my boy, I am going to play a good joke on you!'

"It was a terrible joke — it is that still, Monsieur! Listen to what happened! I got my exchange all right: it is on that account I have eight days' leave; but next Monday, November 21st, before midday, I must report to my new regiment. But this regiment, the 257th Infantry, is in garrison at Verdun!...You grasp it?"

"I begin to," murmured Fandor.

"At Verdun," continued Vinson, who had risen, and was walking to and fro, pressing his head between his hands, a prey to an indescribable anguish...."At Verdun! That is to say at the frontier itself! That means I shall be in the thick of all that lot — at their mercy!...Oh, the trick had been well thought out, carefully contrived! I have got away from the wasp's nest only to tumble into the middle of the swarm! Oh, Monsieur, I am losing my head absolutely! I feel that they have me tight, that it is impossible to get free of them and, what is more, I am afraid of being taken up ...yes. These last few days at Châlons I have been terrified: I believe that they suspect me, that they suspect Nichoune, that my superiors have me under supervision! Directly after the announcement of Captain Brocq's assassination appeared in the papers, all this descended on me as swiftly as a tempest. Oh, I am lost! Lost!!...I wished to come and make an open confession of all my shame to you that, by means of an article in your paper, you may put young soldiers on their guard, those who, owing to a mad infatuation for some abominable women, or through need of money, should be disposed to follow my wretched example some cursed day or other — yes, my damnable example!"

The corporal fell down in the middle of the room, fell down like a crumpled rag: he sobbed. Fandor pitied this miserable creature who had sunk so low. He raised him gently.

"Vinson," he declared, "you must not die. Remember you have a mother! Listen! Be brave! Summon your courage! Tell your chiefs everything — everything!"

The wretched man shook his head.

"Never! Never, Monsieur — I could not do it. Think, Monsieur: it is the vilest of vile things I have done — I, a soldier of France — of France, Monsieur!... You spoke of my mother! It is because of her I wish to kill myself! You must know that she is an Alsatian!... She would go mad — mad, Monsieur, if she learned that her son has betrayed France!... This evening Corporal Vinson will no longer exist — it will be well finished with him!"

There was a great silence.

Fandor, with his arms folded and anxious brow, was pacing up and down his study, seeking a solution of this frightful problem, asking himself what was to be done....He saw that this miserable Vinson was caught in the wheels of a terrible machine, from which it was almost impossible to snatch him into safety. Nevertheless, his conscience revolted at the idea that he should do nothing to avert this wretched lad's suicide. He must stop Vinson — he must certainly save him from himself at any price, save him doubly!

Then Fandor saw further than this.

He perceived that good may come out of evil: perhaps through Vinson and his relations with this nefarious nest of spies, they would succeed in clearing up the dark mystery surrounding the death of Captain Brocq. Evidently all these happenings were interconnected!...

With his mind's eye, Fandor saw this foreign spy system under the form of an immense — a vast spider's web. Could one but lay hands on the originator of the initial thread, or the master-spider himself, then they could strike at the extreme ends of this evil tissue.

Fandor admonished Vinson for a long time. Our journalist was now eloquent, now persuasive: he heaped argument on argument, he appealed to his self-respect, to duty! When at last he saw that the young corporal hesitated, that a faint gleam of hope appeared, that a vague desire for rehabilitation was born in him, he stopped short and demanded abruptly:

"Vinson, are you still bent on killing yourself?"

The corporal communed with himself a moment, closed his eyes, and, without a touch of insincerity, replied in a steady voice:

"Yes, I have decided to do it."

"In that case," said Fandor, "will you look on the deed as done, and take it that you are no longer in existence?"

The corporal stared at Fandor, speechless, absolutely dumbfounded. Fandor made his idea more definite.

"From this moment you do not exist any more, you are nothing, you are no longer Corporal Vinson."...

"And then?"...

But Fandor must have a definite promise.

"Is this agreed to?"...

"I agree."

"Swear it!"

"I swear it!"

"Very well, Vinson, you now belong to me, you are my property, my chattel; I am going to give you my instructions, and they must be strictly obeyed, carried out!"

The miserable soldier seemed crushed to the earth; but with a movement of his head he signified that he was prepared to do whatever the journalist ordered.

VII

THE SECOND BUREAU

As early as nine o'clock that morning, there was unusual activity in the Second Bureau of the Headquarters Staff.

The Second Bureau!

This formidable office, whose official designation, *Bureau of Statistics*, did not deceive anyone, occupied premises in the Ministry of War. Modest as to appearance, this Bureau was located on the third floor of one of the oldest buildings in the rue Saint Dominique. The departments of the Second Bureau impinged on a long corridor, and had taken possession of quite half the floor in the right wing of the building.

Anyone authorised to enter here would find a fairly large outer room, where about a dozen secretaries would be working at wooden desks. These secretaries are changed frequently, so that they may not get to know too much about the work passing through their hands, though they are seldom given anything of an important confidential nature to deal with. There is a vast square room adjoining, reserved for the so-called "*statistics.*" This immense apartment is abundantly lighted by two large windows and a large table of white wood stands in the centre of the room. Occasionally it is heaped with papers, but generally it is clear, and only maps are to be seen, maps of all parts of France and of foreign countries also, marked with red pencil, ornamented with cabalistic signs, thickly sprinkled with notes. Placed against the walls are the desks of the officers of this department, two captains and two lieutenants. Next to this room is the small office where Commandant Dumoulin, the chief assistant, is generally to be found. Fixed into the wall, on the right-hand side, is the one remarkable thing in this most ordinary looking office: here is the famous steel press, of which Commandant Dumoulin alone possesses the key, and in which are enclosed, they say, the most secret instructions relating to National Defence and Mobilisation.

This office communicates on one side with the office of statistics, and on the opposite side with a sitting-room, soberly furnished with arm-chairs and sofas covered with green velvet; on the walls is a green paper; one picture only adorns this solemn reception-room, whose doors are tightly closed to air and sound — the portrait of the president of the Republic. Here are received visitors of mark, who have information of the highest importance to communicate. Here conversations can be freely carried on, for thick window curtains, door curtains and carpet deaden sound.

At the extreme end of the corridor is the office of the commander-in-chief, Colonel Hoffer-man. At once elegantly and comfortably furnished, this office is quite unlike the others: there is more of the individual than the official here. An array of telephones keeps the colonel in touch with the various departments of the Ministry, with the Municipality, with the Governor of Paris. In a recess is a telegraphic installation.

This able infantry officer is a man of great distinction. He has directed the delicate service of "statistics" with much tact and discretion for the past three years. His fair complexion, blue eyes, blonde hair betray his Alsatian origin. This handsome bachelor, verging on the fifties, is very much a man of the world, is received in the most exclusive sets, and has been known to carry on the most intimate conversations with charming ladies in his office. Was the subject of these talks National Defence? Who knows?

In the officers' room there was animated talk.

"Then it is an artilleryman again?" asked Lieutenant Armandelle, a regular colossus with a brick-red complexion, who had passed long years in Africa at the head of a detachment of Zouaves.

Captain Loreuil was sharpening a pencil. He stopped, and, throwing himself back in his chair, replied with a smile:

"No, my dear fellow, this time it is to be a sapper." Looking over his spectacles he softly hummed the old refrain of Thérèse:

"Nothing is as sacred to a sapper!"

Armandelle burst out laughing.

"Ah, my boy, come what will, you meet it with a smile!"

"By Jove, old man, why be gloomy?" answered the lively captain. "We can only live once! Let us make the best use of our time, then! Why not be jolly?"

Judging by his looks, Captain Loreuil had followed his own advice. Clean-shaven, plump of face, stout of figure, he wore glasses, large round glasses set in gold frames, for he was exceptionally short-sighted. His colleagues had nicknamed him "The Lawyer." It was easy to see that he was much more at home in mufti than in uniform. He would say, laughing:

"I have all the looks of a territorial, and that is unfortunate, considering I belong to the active contingent."

Loreuil was one of the most highly appreciated officers of the Second Bureau. Had anyone examined the hands of "The Lawyer" just then, he would have seen that they were roughened and had horny lumps on them of recent formation. His fingers, all twisted out of shape at the tips, seamed with scars, led one to suppose that the captain was not entirely a man of sedentary office life. In fact, he had just returned after a fairly long absence. He had disappeared for six months. It was rumoured in the departments that he had been one of a gang of masons who were constructing a fort on a foreign frontier, a fort, the plans of which he had got down to the smallest detail. But questions had not been asked, and the captain had not, of course, given his colleagues the slightest hint, the smallest indication of how those six months had been passed. Besides, unforeseen journeys, sudden disappearances, unexpected returns, mysterious missions, made up the ordinary lot of those attached to the Second Bureau.

The old keeper of the records, Gaudin, who was methodically sorting a voluminous correspondence which was to be laid before Commandant Dumoulin, put a question to Armandelle:

"Lieutenant, is it not a captain of the engineers who is to take the place of this poor Captain Brocq?"

"True enough, Gaudin! His nomination was signed by the minister yesterday. We expect him this morning at half-past nine. What time is it now?

"A quarter past nine, lieutenant!"

"He will be punctual."

"Why, of course!" cried Captain Loreuil. "That is why I caught sight of the chief just now. He is earlier than usual. What is the name of the new-comer?"

"Muller," said Armandelle. "He comes from Belfort," cried Loreuil:

"I know what Hofferman will say to him — 'My dear Captain, you enter this day the house of silence and discretion.'"

Loreuil turned to Gaudin.

"Where is Lieutenant de Loubersac this morning?"

"Why, Captain," explained the old keeper of records, "you must know very well that he has been ordered to act as escort to the King of Greece."

"Confound Loubersac! He goes to all the entertainments."

Steps were heard, some brief words were spoken in the adjacent corridor, an orderly opened the door and saluted.

"Captain Muller has arrived, Monsieur!"

Extended very much at his ease on a comfortable couch, Colonel Hofferman was polishing his nails, whilst Commandant Dumoulin stood respectfully before him tightly encased in his sober light infantry uniform. Dumoulin was fully alive to the importance of his position: was he not the repository of the famous key which unlocked the steel press?

The colonel looked up at his subordinate.

"You are going to put Captain Muller in the way of things here, Commandant, are you not?"

"Yes, Colonel!"

"It will be a good thing to have a talk with Captain Muller. He comes just at the moment when we have some very nasty business in hand — difficult — very worrying.... That's so, Dumoulin?"

"True, Colonel! That's a fact."

Hofferman pressed a bell. An orderly appeared.

"Ask Captain Muller to kindly step in here."

Almost at once Captain Muller entered, saluted, and remained standing at some distance from his chief.

"Take this arm-chair, Captain." Hofferman was amiable politeness itself. Dumoulin, rather scandalised that the colonel should encourage such familiarity in a subordinate, was on the point of retiring discreetly. The colonel made him sit down also.

Hofferman turned to Captain Muller.

"You come amongst us, Monsieur, at a sad moment. You know, of course, that you are Captain Brocq's successor? A most valuable officer, to whom we were greatly attached."

Captain Muller bent his head. He murmured:

"We were men of the same year, comrades at the school — Brocq and I."

Hofferman continued:

"Ah, well, you are to take on the work begun by Captain Brocq.... Now tell me, Captain, what importance do you attach to the orders regarding the roll-call, the mustering and distribution of the mechanics and operatives of the artillery in the various corps — from the point of view of mobilisation, that is?"

"It is of the very greatest importance, Colonel."

"Good!"

Hofferman paused. He continued, in a low tone and with a grave air:

"In the newspapers — oh, in ambiguous terms, but clear enough to the initiated — the public has been given to understand that not only has an important document been stolen from Captain Brocq before, or at the time of his assassination, or after it, but that this document was none other than the distribution chart of the concealed works in and about the girdle of forts on the east of Paris.... This is inaccurate. Captain, what has disappeared is the distribution list of our artillery mechanics! That is much more serious!... However, for some time past we have had under consideration a rearrangement scheme. We are going to take advantage of the disappearance of the document in question, Document Number 6 — keep that number in mind — we are going to draw up a new plan for the mobilisation of the rear-guards. You are to be entrusted with this, and I count on your devoting your whole time and attention to it."

Captain Muller understood that the conversation was at an end. He rose, saying quietly:

"You may count on me, Colonel."

He was then given his official instructions.

Hofferman left the couch, and, dropping his nail polisher, came towards the captain with outstretched hands.

"My father knew yours in bygone days," he cried genially; "both were natives of Colmar."

"Why, is that so, indeed, Colonel?" cried the captain, delighted to find himself among friends.

Hofferman nodded.

"All will go well, be sure of it. I know you take your work seriously.... We have excellent reports of you — you are married, are you not?"

Muller nodded in the affirmative.

"Excellent!" declared the colonel. Pointing a threatening finger at Muller.

"You know our standing orders here! Many acquaintances — very few intimates: no mistress."

The colonel did not remain alone in his office long. He sent for Lieutenant de Loubersac. With a soldier's punctuality he appeared before his chief. He was in uniform.

"Nothing unusual this morning, Loubersac?" questioned Hofferman, gazing complacently at the soldier, superb in his magnificent uniform, an elegant and splendid specimen of a cavalry officer.

"Nothing, Colonel. The arrival of the King of Greece has been perfectly carried out."

"The crowd?"

"Oh, indifferent on the whole; come to have a look at him out of curiosity."

"Ah, no King of Spain affair?"

"No, no! Out of that I got this scar on my forehead."

"Well," cried the colonel, "it's an ill wind that blows nobody any good! You will get the cross all the quicker!"

Lieutenant de Loubersac smiled.

Hofferman continued:

"My dear fellow, ...you know ...the vanished document!...It's extremely important — it will have to be found!"

"Good, Colonel!"

"Have you just now a particularly sharp agent?...Shrewd?"

"Yes, Colonel," said de Loubersac, after a moment's reflection.

"Who is he?"

"The man engaged on the V — — affair."

"When shall you see him?"

"This afternoon, Colonel. We have an appointment for three-thirty."

"The worst of it is this affair is making no end of talk — scandal — it's the very devil and all! Some fools of papers who deal in scandal are scaring the public with rumours of war: they speak of the eventual rupture of diplomatic relations. The financial market is unsteady — the Jews are selling as hard as they can, and that is disquieting, for those fellows have a quicker scent than any one....Lieutenant, it is urgent: set your agent to work at once! He must act with discretion, of course, but he must act as quickly as possible — it is urgent!"

"And what are the conditions, Colonel?"

After a moment's reflection, Hofferman replied:

"You must make and get the best conditions you can."

It was noon, and twelve was striking. The vast ministerial premises, where silence had reigned till then, were filled with murmurs and the sharp sound of voices: there were hurrying footsteps on the stairs, doors banged: the offices were emptying for a couple or hours.

"Ah, ha!" cried Captain Loreuil, jamming an enormous soft hat down on his head till it all but covered his eyes. This gave him the appearance, either of an artist of sorts or of a seller of chestnuts! Now behold the handsomest cavalier of France and Navarre!...

And he struck up, in a clear voice:

"Ah, how I would love this cuirassier
If I were still a demoiselle."

Henri de Loubersac, who had just collided with the captain, burst into laughter, and warmly shook hands with him.

A limited number of people, some curious, others merely idle, were standing motionless in the Zoological Gardens. They were lining the palisade which surrounds the rocky basin where half a dozen crocodiles were performing their evolutions.

Besides children and nursemaids and governesses, there were also poverty-stricken creatures in rags, some students, a workman or two, the inevitable telegraph boy who was loitering on the way instead of hastening onwards with the telegrams, and, noticeably, a fair young man, smart, in tight-fitting overcoat and wearing a bowler hat. He had been standing there some ten minutes, and was giving but scant attention to the saurians. He was casting furtive glances around him, as though looking for someone.

If he were awaiting the arrival of some member of the fair sex, it hardly seemed the place for a love-tryst, this melancholy Zoological Gardens, misty, with the leaves falling, gradually baring the trees at the approach of winter.

A uniform suddenly appeared in one of the paths: it was a sergeant belonging to the commissariat department, who was passing rapidly, bent on business.

Directly the fair young man saw him he left his place by the palisade and hid himself behind a tree, muttering:

"Decidedly one has to be constantly on the defensive!" He unbuttoned his coat and looked at his watch.

"Twenty-five minutes past three! He will not be long now!"

Two hundred yards from this spot, before the chief entrance to the Gardens, a crowd had gathered; inveterate idlers jostling one another in the circle they had formed round a sordid individual, a miserable old man with a long white beard, who was drawing discordant sounds from an old accordion.

Some kindly housewives, some shock-headed errand-boys, were exercising their lungs to the utmost, trying to help the musician to play according to time and tune.

But, in spite of the goodwill about him, the poor man could not manage to play one single bar correctly, and his helpers bawled in vain.

At the end of a few minutes the accordion player gave up his attempts, and, taking his soft and ancient hat in his hand, he put in practice a much easier exercise: he made the round of the company to collect their offerings. The crowd melted like magic, leaving him solitary, hat in hand, and with only a few sous in it for his pains. With a resigned air, the man pocketed his meagre takings, then, pushing the accordion up on his back where it was held in place by a strap, he walked, bent, staggering, towards the gate. He passed through it and entered the Gardens.

The old man went to a secluded seat behind the museum. Almost immediately he saw a well-dressed young man approaching, the very same who some ten minutes before had been staring at the crocodiles with but lukewarm interest.

The young man seated himself beside the old accordion player without seeming to notice him. Then, in an almost inaudible voice, as if speaking to himself, the young man uttered these words:

"Fine weather! The daisy is going to bloom."

At once the accordion player added.

"And the potatoes are going to sprout!"

They identified each other.

The two men were alone in this deserted corner of the garden; they drew closer together and began to converse.

"Are things still going well, Vagualame?"

"My faith, Monsieur Henri, that depends."...

The old accordion player cast a rapid penetrating glance at the countenance of his companion: it was done with the instinctive ease of habit.

The young man was leaning forward, tracing circles in the sand with his stick.

"What is the position, Vagualame?" he asked briefly.

"I have no more money, Lieutenant."

The young man sat upright and looked at the old man angrily.

"What has come to you? There is no lieutenant here — I am M. Henri, and nothing else! Do I trouble myself to find out who you are, Vagualame?"

"Oh," protested the old man, "that's enough! Do not be afraid, I understand my business: you know my devotion! Unfortunately it costs a great deal!"

"Yes," replied Henri de Loubersac — for he it was — "Yes, I know you are always hard up."

"Shall I have money soon?" insisted Vagualame.

"That depends....How are things going?"

"Which things?"

The lieutenant showed impatience. Was Vagualame's stupid, silly manner intentional?

Assuredly, that handsome fellow, that dashing soldier, Henri de Loubersac, knew nothing of this same Vagualame's relations with Bobinette, nor his attitude towards that mysterious accomplice of his whom he had just assassinated, or pretended to have assassinated, Captain Brocq. Thus Vagualame had two strings to his bow, serving at one and the same time the Second Bureau and, most probably, its bitterest adversaries.

"Vagualame, you really are a fool," went on de Loubersac. "What I refer to is the V. affair: how does it stand — what has been done?"

The old man began to laugh.

"Peuh! Nothing at all! Another rigmarole in which women are mixed up! You know the little singer of Châlons, called Nichoune? She made her first appearance at La Fère, and since then the creature has roved through the rowdy dancing-saloons of Picardy, of the Ardennes — you must know her well, Monsieur Henri."

The lieutenant interrupted him.

"All this does not mean anything, Vagualame!"

"Pardon! Nichoune is the mistress of Corporal V. — he is on leave, the corporal is.".…

"I know, he is in Paris."

"Well, then, what do you wish me to do?"

"You must go to Châlons and make an exhaustive enquiry into the relations of V.... with Nichoune. V. was eaten up with debts."

"He has settled them," remarked Vagualame.

"Ah!" Lieutenant de Loubersac was rather taken aback.

"Well, find out how and why. Get me information also about someone called Alfred."

"I know him, Lieutenant, — pardon — Monsieur Henri — a — letter-box — a go-between."

"We must know exactly the nature of the relations between Corporal V. and the late Captain Brocq."

These last words particularly interested Vagualame: he drew nearer still to de Loubersac, tapping him on the knee.

"Tell me, has anything new come to light in that affair?"

Henri de Loubersac moved away, and looked the old accordion player up and down.

"Do not meddle with what does not concern you."

"Good! Good! That's all right!" The old fellow pretended to be confused, nevertheless a gleam of joy shone beneath his eyelids.

There was a moment's silence. Henri de Loubersac was gnawing his moustache. Vagualame, who was stealthily watching him, said to himself:

"As for you, my fine fellow, I am waiting for you! You have a fine big morsel for me! I see what you are driving at!".…

True enough! Suddenly, between him and the lieutenant there was an exchange of hurried words in a low tone.

"Vagualame, would you like a highly paid commission?"

"Yes, Monsieur Henri. Is it difficult to earn?"

"Naturally."

Vagualame insisted:

"Dangerous, as well?"

"Perhaps!"

"How much will you pay?"

Without hesitation, the officer said:

"Twenty-five thousand francs.".…

Equally without hesitation, but putting on an offended air, Vagualame retorted.

"Nothing doing!"

"Thirty thousand?"

The old man murmured: "What the devil is it a question of?"

Lowering his voice still more, de Loubersac added:

"It is a lost document!... Perhaps it is a case of theft ... a list of the distribution of artillery operatives — Document Number Six!"

"But," cried Vagualame, who feigned sudden comprehension of this document's importance, "but that is equivalent to a complete plan of mobilisation?"...

Exasperated, Lieutenant Henri interrupted the old fellow:

"I do not ask for your opinion as to its signification and value. Can you recover it?"

Vagualame murmured some incomprehensible words.

"What are you saying?" questioned de Loubersac, who, growing more and more exasperated, shook him by the sleeve.

"Gently, Monsieur Henri, gently, if you please," whined the old man, "I was only thinking what is always the case: 'Look for the woman!'"

"The disappearance of the document," continued de Loubersac, "is coincident with the death of Captain Brocq — so it is supposed."...

He stopped and stared at Vagualame, who was rubbing his hands, simulating an extreme satisfaction, and mumbling with an air of enjoyment:

"Women! Always the dear women!... Ah, these dear and damnable women!"

He resumed his serious expression: his manner was decided.

"Monsieur Henri," he declared, "I will find it; but the price is fifty thousand francs."

"What!" De Loubersac was startled.

Vagualame raised his hand as if taking heaven to witness that his statement was final.

"Not a sou more! Not a sou less! Fifty thousand is the price: fifty thousand!"

Henri de Loubersac hesitated a second, then concluded the interview.

"Agreed to!... Be quick about it!... Adieu!"

VIII
A SINGER OF THE HALLS

"Nichoune!... Nichoune!... Nichoune!"

"Be off with you, Léonce! To the door!"

It was a regular hubbub! An uproar! It increased!

Léonce the comedian had to cut short his monologue!

The little concert-hall at Châlons was at its liveliest. There was not a single seat to be had. It was a mixed audience of soldiers and civilians, and the uniform did not fraternise too well with the garb of the working-man!

This low-class concert-hall was frequented by soldiers, who, out on leave, would visit the taverns, the beer-houses, and finish the evening on the squalid benches of this Eldorado of the provinces.

On this particular evening these critical gentlemen of the Army were less satisfied than ever. There had been three "first appearances," of poor quality, and they accused the management of having filled the hall with civilians in order to secure a good reception for these mediocre performers. Hussars and cuirassiers joined forces and made a frightful uproar.

"Take the comic man away!"

"He shall not sing!"

Then the entire audience shouted one name, demanded one performer only.

"Nichoune!... Nichoune!... Nichoune!"

Nichoune was indeed the star of the company!

She was rather pretty, her face was intelligent, and what was rare enough in that hall, her tone was almost pure and true, and, above all, she sang popular ditties so that the audience could join in the chorus. As usual, after every singer, male or female, there were loud demands for Nichoune. Her admirers were merciless: they had no consideration for her fatigue: they would have kept her on the platform from eight o'clock till midnight!

The manager rushed to Nichoune's dressing-room.

"Come! Come at once! They will smash up everything if you do not hurry on."

Nichoune got up.

"Ah, ha! If I don't get a rise after this — well, I shall be off! You will see! They will have to have me back, too!"

The manager showed by a shrug of the shoulders that this was a matter of profound indifference to him.

"Come on to the platform, my dear! And be quick about it!"

Nichoune raced down the stairs and appeared before the clamouring crowd panting. At sight of her, calm succeeded storm: the idol was going to sing!

Nichoune swaggered down the stage and, planting herself close to the footlights, flung the title of her song at the delighted audience in strident tones.

"*Les Inquiets!*... Music by Delmet.... Words also.... It is I who sing it!"

Whilst Nichoune began her song, hands on hips, she scrutinised her audience, bestowing little smiles on her particular admirers. She could not have been in her best form, because when about to start her third verse she suffered a lapse of memory, hesitated, and started the fourth. This passed unnoticed by her audience, who gave her a vociferous ovation at the close.

"The programme! the programme!" they yelled.

As a rule Nichoune would disdainfully refuse to go down among the audience. This evening, however, she nodded a "Yes," and, taking a pile of little programmes from the wings, she descended the few steps which led from the stage to the body of the hall. Twenty hands were outstretched to help her down. She pushed them aside with mocking looks. Shouts of admiration, compliments, clamourous declarations of love were rained on her by the soldiers she had charmed and now swung past with a provocative swish of her skirt and a smile of disdain.

Nichoune went on her way, bent on getting rid of her burden of programmes with all speed.

Just as another singer appeared on the platform, Nichoune reached the last row of chairs, and was about to leave, when she heard her name uttered in a low voice by a man enveloped in a large cloak.

He was standing, and was leaning against the wall at the extreme end of the concert-room: he was an aged man.

Nichoune hesitated, searching with her eyes for the person who had called her in a low, penetrating voice. She was about to continue on her way, when the old fellow half opened his cloak for an instant to give her a glimpse of a bulky kind of a box which was slung across his chest.

Immediately the singer went straight towards him.

"A programme?" she asked him in a loud voice.

He gave an affirmative nod for all the world to see: then whispered low.

"Go home directly the concert is over! I must speak to you!"

"Very good," replied the singer in a submissive tone.

Then aloud she queried:

"You are a musician, are you?"

The man in the cloak gave answer audibly:

"Yes, my dear, I am a musician also, but not of your sort! It's not gaiety I deal in!" With that, the unknown displayed an accordion which was slung across his chest.

Nichoune hurried to her dressing-room. She must get away before her admirers demanded her reappearance on the platform. The old man quitted the establishment. Stepping out of the vestibule, dimly lighted by a flickering jet of gas, he strode along the narrow and tortuous streets of Châlons at a great pace. This pedestrian seemed out of humour: he marched along, bent beneath the weight of his accordion, tapping the road violently with the point of his long climbing stick. Taking a circuitous route, he at last reached a sort of little inn. It appeared a poor kind of a place, but clean. The old fellow entered with a resolute air. The porter, half asleep, offered him a candle which he lit with a twist of paper, kindled at the gas-jet. The old man mounted the stairs to his room and closed the door carefully. Having satisfied himself that the window shutters were fastened, he took off his cloak, lit his lamp, drew up a chair, and leaned his elbow on the table. The light fell on his face, and it was easy to recognise the man who had spoken to the mistress of Corporal Vinson: he was none other than Vagualame, the beggar-assassin.

Before long there was a knock at the door.

"Who is there?"

"I ... Nichoune!"

Vagualame rose and opened to her.

"Come in, my dear!" Vagualame was now the amiable friend.

He looked with delight at the pretty little face of his visitor.

"As pretty as ever, my dear! Prettier than ever!" he cried.

He stopped flattery: the singer evidently disliked it. She seated herself on the edge of a sofa and stared at him.

"I don't suppose you have come to Châlons just to tell me that! Nothing serious?"

Vagualame shrugged his shoulders.

"No, no! Why, in Heaven's name, are you always so frightened?"

"That's all very well. It's jolly dangerous, let me tell you."

"Dangerous!" repeated Vagualame contemptuously. "Absurd! You are joking! It's dangerous for imbeciles — not for anyone else! Not a soul would ever suspect that pretty Nichoune is the 'letter-box' — the intermediary between me and 'Roubaix.'"

"You are going to give me something for Roubaix again?" Nichoune did not look as if Vagualame's assertion had relieved her fears.

Vagualame evaded a direct answer.

"You have not seen him for a week?"

54

"Roubaix? No."...

"And Nancy?"

"Nor Nancy."

"Well," said he, after a moment's reflection, "that does not matter in the least! I can now tell you that Belfort will certainly pass this way to-morrow morning."...

"Belfort? But he is not due then!"

"Belfort has no fixed time," replied Vagualame sharply. "I have already told you that Belfort is his own master: his is a divisional."

"A divisional? What exactly is a divisional?" demanded the singer.

"Now you are asking questions," objected Vagualame. His tone was harsh. "That is not allowed, Nichoune! I have told you so before....What you do not know you must not try to discover....I myself do not know all the ins and outs of the organisation!"

He continued in a less severe tone:

"In any case Belfort passes this way to-morrow between eleven o'clock and noon....He does not know me — is not aware of my existence....It is through an indirect course that I learned he was coming; also that he would have something to say to you....Will you, therefore, hand him this envelope?"

Vagualame drew from the inside pocket of his short coat a large packet sealed with red wax.

"Be very careful! This document is important — has been difficult to obtain — extremely difficult!...On no account must it go astray!...Tell Belfort that it must be handed over as quickly as possible....Well?"

Nichoune did not take the packet Vagualame was holding out to her. She remained seated, her gaze fixed on the tips of her shoes, her hands buried in her muff.

"Well, what is it? What are you waiting for?" Vagualame repeated.

At this Nichoune blazed out:

"What the matter is? Why, that I have had enough of all this: I don't want any more of it! Not if I know it! It's too dangerous!"

Vagualame appeared stupefied.

"What, little one?" he asked very gently. "You do not wish to be our faithful letter-box any more?"

"No!"

"You do not want to hand this over to Belfort?"

"No, no! A hundred times no!" Nichoune shook her head vigorously.

"But why?"

"Because ...because I don't want to do it any more! There!"

"Come now, Nichoune, what is your reason? You must have one."

This time the singer got up as though she would go off at once.

"Reasons?" she cried. "Look here, Vagualame, it's better to tell you the truth! Very well, then, spying is not my strong point! It is three months since I began it — since you enticed me into it ...and life is not worth living....I am in a constant state of terror — I am afraid of being caught at it. They say: 'Do this — Do that!' I am always seeing new agents ...you come — you go — you disappear — it's maddening! I have already broken with my lover ...with Vinson! I don't want to be on such terms with anyone mixed up in your spying, I can tell you!...In the first place, there's something wrong with my heart, and to live in such a perpetual state of terror is very bad for me ...so you have got to understand, Vagualame — I say it straight out — I don't go on with it....I would rather go to the magistrate and put myself completely outside this abominable business — there! That's all about it!"

It was impossible to mistake the meaning of these decisive words. Here was not the spy who sought to increase his pay by threatening to reveal everything; it was the spy who is obsessed with the fear of being taken, who no longer wishes to continue his dreadful work — to follow his nefarious calling.

Vagualame gave no sign of surprise.

"Listen, my pretty one! You are at perfect liberty to do what seems good to you, and if you have just come in for some money!"...

"No one has left me any money," interrupted Nichoune.

"Oh, well," replied Vagualame, "if you despise the nice sum I bring you every month, that's your business! But I don't suppose you want to leave your old comrade in a fix, do you?"

Nichoune hesitated.

"What do you want me to do now?" she asked.

"A very little thing, my pretty one! If you will not go in with us any longer, you are perfectly free to leave us, I repeat it, but don't leave us in the lurch just at this moment! This paper is of the very greatest importance ... be nice — take it, and give it to Belfort — I will not bother you again after this."...

Nichoune held out her hand, but it was with an ill grace.

"Oh, all right!" said she. "Give me the thing! All the same, you know now that it is the very last time you are to apply to me!"

Then she added, laughing in her usual hail-fellow-well-met way, and pressing the old fellow's hand as she moved towards the door:

"I don't mean to be the letter-box of Châlons any more: that's ended — the last collection has been made!"

Nichoune departed. Vagualame wished her a cordial "Good night"; then, locking the door, he became absorbed in his reflections.

Towards five o'clock in the afternoon of the day following his private talk with Nichoune, Vagualame accosted the proprietor of a little inn situated at the extreme end of the town, and far removed from the tavern where he had passed the night.

"Mademoiselle Nichoune is not in, is she?"

"No, my good man — what do you want with her?"

Vagualame gave a little laugh.

"Has she not told you, then, that she was expecting someone from her part of the country to call on her?"

The innkeeper was leaning carelessly against the wall. He straightened himself a little.

"Yes, Mademoiselle Nichoune has told us that an old musician would call to see her this afternoon, and that we must ask him to wait."...

"Ah, she's a good, kind little thing! How courageous! What a worker!" Vagualame seemed to be speaking to himself.

"You know her very well, then?" asked the puzzled innkeeper.

"I should think I did!" protested the old fellow. "Why, it was I who taught her to sing!... Do you think she will be long, my little Nichoune?"

"I don't fancy so! If you would like to come in and wait for her in her room, you will find it at the end of the corridor. It's not locked....You will find some picture papers on her table."

"Thank you, kind sir," said Vagualame after a moment's hesitation. "I will go in and rest for a few minutes," and, hobbling along, he gained the singer's room. The moment he was inside, and the door safely shut, his whole attitude changed. He looked eagerly about him.

"If there is anything, where is it likely to be?"...He considered. "Why, in the mattress, of course!"

He drew from some hiding-place in his garments a long needle, and began to probe the mattress of Nichoune's bed very carefully.

"Ha, ha!" cried he, suddenly. The needle had come in contact with something difficult to penetrate. "I wager it's what I am after!"

Vagualame slipped his hand, spare and delicately formed, under the counterpane.

"Little idiot!" he exclaimed in a satisfied tone. "She has not even hidden it inside the mattress! She has just slipped it in between the palliasse, and the hair mattress on top — why, she's a child!"

He drew out two envelopes and eagerly read the addresses.

"Oh," cried he, "this is more serious than I thought!... Action must be taken at once!... Nichoune! Nichoune! you are about to play a dangerous game, a game which is likely to cost you dear!"

On the first of the envelopes Vagualame had read one word:

"Belfort."

This was the document he had handed over to the actress the night before. After all, he was not much astonished to find that Nichoune had not passed the letter on. But the other envelope bore an address which Vagualame gazed at reflectively.

"Monsieur Bonnett,
Police Magistrate."

"She is selling us, by Jove!" he murmured. "There's not a doubt of it! The little wretch!... She has scruples, has she!... Her conscience reproaches her! I am going to give her a lesson — one of my own sort!"

Vagualame was turning the letter over and over.

"I must know its contents," he went on...."Ah, I shall manage to get hold of this little paper, to-morrow morning, when."...

Vagualame's murmured monologue came to an abrupt conclusion.

"That's her voice!" he exclaimed. With the nimbleness of youth he put back the two letters, rapidly drew from his pocket a bundle of letters; with marvellous ability forced open a table drawer, and mixed them with others Nichoune had placed there.

"There, my little dear!" said he, aloud. "There's something to do honour to your memory!"

He closed the drawer in a second. He had barely time to seat himself in an arm-chair near his accordion, lying on the floor, when Nichoune entered.

"Good day!" cried she.

Vagualame pretended to wake up with a start.

"Ha, ha! Good day, Nichoune! Tell me, you have not seen Belfort? Eh?"

"How do you know that?" demanded Nichoune, on the defensive. She looked surprised.

"I have just met him....He told me that he had not come across you at the usual meeting-place."

Nichoune lowered her head.

"I thought I was being followed ...so, as you can understand, I did not go."

Vagualame nodded approval.

"Good! Quite right! After all, it is not otherwise of importance. You must give me back my envelope now!"

"You want it?"

"Why, of course!"

Nichoune hesitated a second.

"Just fancy, Vagualame, I took the precaution to hide it between my two mattresses! Wait!... Here it is!"

Nichoune held out his letter.

"Thank you, my dear!"

Vagualame looked as if the returning of the document was a matter of the most perfect indifference to him. He gazed hard at Nichoune — stared so fixedly at her that she demanded:

"Whatever possesses you to stare at me like that?"

"I am thinking how pretty you are!"

"Well, I never! You are becoming quite complimentary!"

"It's no flattery. I think you are very pretty, Nichoune, but your hands! They are not pretty!"

The singer laughed and held out her little hands.

"What is there about them you have to find fault with?"

"They are red....It astonishes me that a woman like you does not know how to make them white!...Don't you know what to do to them?"

"No! What must I do?"

"Why," retorted the old musician, "the very first thing you have to do is as simple as A B C! All you have to do is to tie up your hands every night with a ribbon, and so keep them raised above your head!"...

"How? I don't understand!"

"It's like this! You stick a nail into the wall ...and then you manage things so that you keep your hands up-raised the whole night through....You will see then ...your hands will be as white as lilies in the morning....White as lilies!"

Nichoune was extremely interested.

"Is that true? I shall try it this very night! White, like lilies, you say?...And you have to sleep with your hands stuck up in the air!...I shall try it — shall begin to-night."

A few minutes later Vagualame left Nichoune, after promising that he would not give her any more spy work to do, and declaring that she should never again be mixed up in any dangerous business. As he went along the streets of Châlons, the dreadful old man chuckled and sniggered.

"Hands in the air, my beauty!...Just try that, this very night! With that little heart mischief of yours! Ha! ha! We shall not be kept waiting for the consequences of that performance! It will serve as an example to all and sundry when they wish to write to the magistrate!"

Vagualame's face took on a wicked look.

"I shall have to be as careful as can be when I hide myself in that little fool's room to-night! At all costs I must get hold of that compromising letter before anyone in the hotel hears of the death! Not a soul must catch a glimpse of me — that's certain!"

Those who passed Vagualame simply thought he was an old beggar, an old accordion player....

IX

WITH THE UNDER-SECRETARY OF STATE

"Come in!" cried Hofferman, who was writing hard.

An orderly stepped gingerly into the room.

"An usher, Colonel, with a message, begging you to be so good as to step downstairs at once to see the Under-Secretary of State."

Hofferman looked up.

"Are you sure the message is for me?"

"Yes, Colonel."

"Very well. I am coming immediately."

The orderly vanished. Hofferman remained in thought for a minute or so, rose abruptly, half opened the door of the adjoining room, and addressed Commandant Dumoulin:

"The Under-Secretary of State wishes to see me. I am going down now."

The colonel passed rapidly along the interminable corridors separating him from the building in which the Under-Secretary's offices were situated.

"What can he want to see me about?" Colonel Hofferman asked himself as he entered the Under-Secretary's room.

Monsieur Maranjévol, an exceedingly active and immensely popular deputy from la Gironde, to whom had been entrusted the delicate task of serving as buffer between the civil and the military sections. Monsieur Maranjévol was not alone in his vast reception-room, with its gilding and pictures of battle scenes; seated opposite, and with his back to the light, was a civilian, of middle height, clean-shaven, whose thin hair, turning grey, curled slightly at the nape of the neck.

The Under-Secretary rose, shook hands with the colonel, and went straight to the point.

"Monsieur Juve of the detective force: Colonel Hofferman, head of the Second Bureau."

The policeman and the soldier bowed gravely. They awaited the beginning of the conference in a somewhat chilly silence.

Monsieur Maranjévol explained that after a short talk with Juve regarding Captain Brocq's death, he had considered it necessary to put him in touch with Colonel Hofferman.

The colonel, who had been showing signs of impatience for the last few minutes, suddenly broke out:

"My faith, Monsieur," declared he, in a sharp abrupt voice, staring straight into Juve's eyes, "I am very glad to have the opportunity of meeting you. I shall not disguise from you that I am astonished, even very disagreeably astonished, at your attitude during the past few days regarding this wretched drama. Up to now, I have always considered that the private personality of an officer, above all, of an officer on the Headquarters' Staff, was a thing which was almost inviolable....But it has come to my knowledge that at the death of Captain Brocq, you have devoted yourself not only to making the most minute investigations — that, perhaps, was your right and your duty — into the circumstances accompanying the death, but that you have searched the domicile of the defunct as well, and this without giving us the required preliminary notice. I cannot and will not sanction this method of procedure, and I congratulate myself on having this opportunity of telling you so."

During this speech of the colonel's Monsieur Maranjévol stared with astonished eyes, first at the soldier and then at the detective. The good-natured and peaceable Under-Secretary was surprised at the colonel's violent attack, and asked himself how Juve was going to take it.

Juve took it with an unmoved countenance. He said, in his turn:

"I would point out to you, Colonel, that had it been only a question of a natural death, I should have contented myself with restoring to you the documents which had been collected at our headquarters; but, as you probably knew, Captain Brocq was killed — killed in a mysterious fashion. I thus found myself in the presence of a crime, a common law crime: the inquest has restored it to the civil law jurisdiction, and not to the military: believe me, I understand my business, I know my duty."

Juve had uttered these words with the greatest composure; but the slight tremble in his voice would have made it clear to anyone who knew him well, that the detective was maintaining his self-control only by a violent effort.

The colonel replied in a tone stiff with offence:

"I persist in my opinion: you have no right to meddle in an affair which concerns us alone. The death of Captain Brocq coincides with the loss of a certain secret document: is it for you or for us to institute an enquiry into it?"

After a pause, Juve's retort was:

"You must permit me to leave that question unanswered."

With all the bluntness of a military man, Colonel Hofferman had put his finger on the open wound which for long years had been a source of irritation to the detective force and the intelligence department alike, when, owing to circumstances, both were called on to intervene at one and the same time. In cases of theft and of spying the conflict was ceaseless.

Monsieur Havard, Juve's chief, had talked this matter over the night before, and his last words of command were:

"Above all, Juve, manage matters so that there is no fuss!... There must not be a fuss!"

Colonel Hofferman, misinterpreting the detective's attitude, turned triumphantly to the Under-Secretary:

"Not only that," he continued, "I think there has been far too much talk made about the death of Captain Brocq. This officer was the victim of an accident. We cannot discuss it. That is all there is to be said. It really does not matter much. We of the Intelligence Department are soldiers, and believe in a policy of results: at the present moment we have lost a document: we are searching for it: action must be left to us.... And, Monsieur, I revert to my first question — what the devil was the police doing at Captain Brocq's — what business was it of theirs? Really, the detective service is arrogating to itself more and more powers — powers that cannot be sanctioned, that will not be granted or permitted."

Juve had so far contained himself, though with difficulty, but now Colonel Hofferman was going too far. It was Juve's turn to break out.

"Monsieur," he cried, in a voice vibrating with passion, turning to the Under-Secretary: "I cannot accept such observations — not for a moment! I have among my papers on the case important proofs that the assassination of Captain Brocq is surrounded with mysterious occurrences, and also of the gravest nature. The theory Colonel Hofferman has just put forward will not hold water — it does not hang together! To gain a full understanding of a thing one must begin at the beginning. This beginning I have brought, and I make you judge, Monsieur, of whether or no it is worth the most careful consideration."

Caught between two fires, the Under-Secretary looked exceedingly sorry for himself. Above everything, he dreaded being forced to act as umpire between Hofferman and Juve. There was no escape, however, so, with a weary air, he asked Juve to make his case clear.

"Well, gentlemen," began our detective, who had fully regained his self-possession, "you know what the circumstances were which led me to the discovery that Captain Brocq had been mysteriously assassinated? It was, obviously, of the first importance that I should learn every detail regarding his private life, get to know with whom he had intercourse, who his correspondents were, find out where he was accustomed to go, so that, being thoroughly posted up regarding his personality, I could discover to whose interest it would be that he should disappear.... I went to Brocq's flat in the rue de Lille to collect evidence from various sources. I have it all written down in my case papers. One fact stands out clearly: Captain Brocq was regularly visited by a woman whom we have not as yet been able to identify beyond a doubt, but we shall soon know who she is. I am certain she is a lady of fashion. She was his mistress: the commencement of a letter written to her by the deceased shows this; but, unfortunately, he has not addressed her by name. The letter was begun, according to the experts, some hours before the drama of assassination was enacted....It is the mauve document, number 42. It commences: *"'My darling'."*...

Juve showed this sheet of mauve letter paper to his listeners. Colonel Hofferman seemed to attach no importance whatever to it.

Juve continued:

"I should greatly value Colonel Hofferman's opinion regarding the suppositions I am about to formulate. Well, gentlemen, here is what I deduce from my investigations....Captain Brocq was a simple, modest fellow; a hard worker; reasonable, temperate, serious-minded officer: a good middle-class citizen, in fact. If Captain Brocq had an irregular love affair, it was assuredly with the best intentions; Brocq, who perhaps had not been able to resist his senses, was too straight a man to willingly entertain the idea of not regularising the union later on. Is that your opinion, Colonel?"

Hofferman frankly replied:

"It is my opinion, Monsieur Juve. That was certainly Captain Brocq's character. But I do not see what you are driving at."

"At this," replied the detective. "Captain Brocq's mistress must be looked for, not among women of the lower orders, but among those of a higher class, who are more outwardly correct, at any rate, more women of the world. Among those with whom Brocq was on friendly terms, was the family of an old diplomat of Austrian extraction, a Monsieur de Naarboveck. This de Naarboveck has a daughter: she is twenty. This Mademoiselle Wilhelmine was terribly distressed, and in a state of profound grief, the day after Brocq's death. I am not going so far as to pretend that Mademoiselle de Naarboveck was Brocq's mistress; but one might easily think so."

"How do you know that Mademoiselle de Naarboveck showed grief at the death of Captain Brocq?"

"Through a journalist who was received in the de Naarboveck family circle the day after the drama."

"Oh, a journalist!" protested the colonel.

Juve smiled slily.

"A journalist not like the others — it was Jérôme Fandor, Colonel!...He went to de Naarboveck's to fulfill a mission entrusted to him by those in high places. The Minister of War."...

The Under-Secretary cut the inspector short.

"We know all about that, Monsieur Juve ...besides the person whom the Minister wished to learn something about was not Monsieur de Naarboveck's daughter, but her companion — a young woman named Berthe."...

"And nicknamed Bobinette!" finished Juve.

"What do you think of her?" asked the Under-Secretary.

Juve's reply was an indirect one.

"The more I think about it, the more I am tempted to believe that Wilhelmine de Naarboveck was Brocq's mistress — oh, in the right way, in all honour! — and that in the background, surreptitiously, a third person pushed herself into their confidence was the recipient of their secret, and on this account she could take a good many liberties with them. Berthe, or Bobinette, was this third person, of course!...She is known to have visited Brocq repeatedly....Now, what was she doing there — what was her object? Well, we have to get a clear idea of what happened and draw our conclusions. Remember, Brocq left his flat in great haste on the afternoon of his assassination; he took a taxi at the des Saints-Pères, and drove off in pursuit of someone.... Why, we do not know, yet; but this someone was a woman, and I am convinced the woman was Bobinette."

"What is Bobinette's social position?"

"Gentlemen, I wish I could define it in a single word, but it is here that I enter the region of enigmas. Here is mystery on mystery. Without breaking the seal of professional secrecy, I may tell you that this woman should be known to me; I say 'should' because I still lack precise information about her; I await this information with impatience — I fear it also, for, gentlemen."...

Juve stopped short, got up, and began pacing the immense room. Drawing up before the Under-Secretary and Colonel Hofferman, he gazed at them. His manner was impressive.

"Gentlemen," said he, in a quiet penetrating voice, and with an air of intense conviction: "Gentlemen, if my conjectures are correct, Bobinette is naught but a girl of low birth — of the lowest — a creature who will stick at nothing, who has been mixed up with a band of criminals, the most cunning, the most artful, the most unscrupulous, the most dangerous band of criminals in all this round world — a band I have, time and again, pursued, decimated, broken up, dispersed ... only to see them spring to an associated evil life again, a ceaseless rebirth of maleficent forces, forming and reforming, a malevolent, hydra-headed monster, a band, gentlemen, of incarnated evil — the band of Fantômas!"

Juve became silent. He wiped his forehead.

The harsh voice of Colonel Hofferman broke the silence:

"Hypotheses! True to this extent, Monsieur Juve, that Brocq may very well have had a mistress — we are all agreed about that — but, in reality, it is simply romance!"

There was a discreet knock at the door.

"What is it?" demanded the Under-Secretary. The form of an usher showed itself in the half-opened doorway.

He entered, and, turning towards the Under-Secretary, said: "Excuse me, sir." Then, addressing Colonel Hofferman: "Captain Loreuil sends me to tell Colonel Hofferman that he has returned, and has a communication of extreme urgency to lay before him."

"The captain must wait!" cried Hofferman, in a harsh, authoritative tone.

But the usher, fulfilling his orders, replied:

"The captain anticipated this answer, Colonel, and told me to add that the communication cannot wait."

The usher withdrew. Hofferman glanced questioningly at the Under-Secretary.

"Go to him, Colonel, and return as soon as possible."

The Under-Secretary addressed Juve:

"The Government is greatly annoyed by all these incidents, which are assuming enormous proportions....Are you aware that rumours of war are becoming wide-spread?...Public opinion is in a most unsettled state....Things are bad on the Bourse, too — going from bad to worse!... Really, it is all most distressing!"

With a movement of sympathetic acquiescence, Juve said gently:

"I cannot help it, Monsieur!"

It was noon. Twelve was striking.

X
AUNT PALMYRA

Early in the morning of the day on which the meeting took place in the private office of the Under-Secretary of State, the proprietor of *The Three Moons* at Châlons was busy bottling his wine. Dawn was just breaking, and the good man had a spirit lamp in his cellar to throw light upon his task.

Suddenly his bottling operations were disturbed by an unknown voice calling him insistently from the top of the steps.

"Hey, there! Father Louis! Where is Father Louis?"

Fuming and grumbling, the innkeeper mounted his cellar-steps, and appeared on the porch.

"I am Father Louis! What am I wanted for?"

The publican found himself face to face with an enormously stout woman: a grotesque figure clad in light-coloured garments, so cut that they exaggerated her stoutness; a large, many-coloured shawl was thrown round her shoulders; on her head was a big round hat, tied with strings in a bow under her chin. This odd head-gear was topped with a bunch of gaudy feathers, ragged and out of curl. A veil of flowery design half hid this woman's features: though far from her first youth, she no doubt wished to appear young still. The skin of her face was covered with powder and paint, so badly laid on, that daubs of white, of red, and blue, lay side by side in all their crudity: there was no soft blending of tints: it was the make-up of no artist's hand.

"What an object!" thought the publican, staring at this oddity, who had seated herself on the porch seat and had placed on the ground a great wicker basket filled with vegetables.

"Ouf!" she cried. "It is a long step to your canteen, Father Louis! My word, I never thought I should get here! Well now, how is my little pet of a girl?"

Nonplussed, suspicious, Father Louis looked hard at this strange visitor: never had he seen anyone like her! What astonished him was to hear her calling him by the name used only by his familiars.

"Whoever are you?" he asked in a surly tone. "I don't remember you!"

"That's not surprising," cried the visitor, who seemed of a gay disposition, for she always laughed at the close of every sentence. "My goodness! It would be queer if you did not recognise me, considering you have never seen me before!...I am Aunt Palmyra, let me tell you!"

The innkeeper, more and more out of countenance, searched his memory in vain.

"Aunt Palmyra?" he echoed.

"Why, of course, you big stupid! Nichoune's aunt — a customer of yours, she is! She must have mentioned me often — I adore the little pet!"

Father Louis had not the slightest recollection of any such mention, but, out of politeness, he murmured:

"Of course! Why, of course!"

"Well, then, old dear, you must tell me where she hangs out here! I must go and give her a hug and a kiss!"

Mechanically, the innkeeper directed Aunt Palmyra.

"On the ground floor — end of the passage!...But you're never thinking of waking Nichoune at this early hour! She'll make a pretty noise if you do!"

"Bah!" cried Aunt Palmyra: "Wait till the little dear sees who it is!...Just look at the nice things I've brought her!" and, showing him the vegetables in her basket, she began to drawl in a sing-song voice:

"Will you have turnips and leeks? Here's stuff to make broth of the best! It will make her think of bygone days when she lived with us in the country!"

"My faith!" thought Father Louis, "if Nichoune opens her mouth!"

Aunt Palmyra was knocking repeatedly at Nichoune's door, but there was no response.

"Well, what a sleep she's having!"

"Likely enough," replied Father Louis, "considering she was not in bed till four o'clock!"

All the same, this persistent silence puzzled the innkeeper. He tried to peep through the keyhole, but the key was in it. Then he quietly drew a gimlet from his pocket and bored a hole in the door. Aunt Palmyra watched him smiling: she winked and jogged his elbow.

"Ho, ho, my boy! I'll wager you don't stick at having a look at your customers this way, when it suits you!"

With the ease of practice the innkeeper glued his eye to the hole he had just made. He uttered an exclamation:

"Good heavens!"

"What is it?" cried Nichoune's aunt in a tone of alarm. "Is her room empty?"

"Empty? No! But."...

Father Louis was white as paper. He searched his pocket in feverish haste, drew from it a screwdriver, rapidly detached the lock, and rushed into the room, followed by Aunt Palmyra, who bawled:

"Oh, my good lord! Whatever is the matter with her?"

Nichoune was stretched out on her bed, and might have seemed asleep to an onlooker were it not for two things which at once struck the eye: her face was all purple, and her arms, sticking straight up in the air, were terrifyingly white and rigid. Approaching the bed, the innkeeper and Aunt Palmyra saw that Nichoune's arms were maintained in this vertical position by means of string tied round her wrists and fastened to the canopy over the bed.

"She is dead!" cried Father Louis. "This is awful! Good heavens! What a thing to happen!"

Aunt Palmyra, for all her previous protestations of affection for her charming niece, did not seem in any way moved by the tragic discovery. She glanced rapidly round the room without a sign of emotion. This attitude only lasted a moment. Suddenly she broke out into loud lamentations uttering piercing cries: she threw herself into an arm-chair, then sank in a heap on the sofa, then returned to the table! She was making a regular nuisance of herself. The innkeeper, scared and bewildered, did not know how to act: he was staring fixedly at the unfortunate Nichoune, who gave no sign of life. Involuntarily the man had touched the dead girl's shoulder: the body was quite cold.

The innkeeper, who had been driven into a state of distracted bewilderment by Aunt Palmyra's behaviour, now bethought him of his obvious duty: of course he must call in the police, and also avoid scandal. Also he must stop this old woman's outrageous goings-on.

"Be quiet!" he commanded. "You are not to make such a noise! Stay where you are! Don't stir from that corner until I return …and, above all, you must not touch a single thing before the arrival of the police."

"The police!" moaned Aunt Palmyra. "It is frightful! Oh, my poor Nichoune, however could this have happened?"

Nevertheless, scarcely had the innkeeper retired than the old woman, with remarkable dexterity, rummaged about among the disordered furniture, and seized a certain number of papers, which she hid in her bodice.

Hardly had she pushed them out of sight when the innkeeper returned, accompanied by a policeman. It was in vain that Father Louis endeavoured to get the policeman into the tragic room. He did not wish to do anything.

"I tell you," he repeated in his big voice, "it's not worth my while looking at this corpse … for the superintendent will be here shortly, and he will take charge of the legal procedure."

At the end of about ten minutes the magistrate appeared, accompanied by his secretary, and immediately proceeded to a summary interrogation of the innkeeper; but, in the presence of Aunt Palmyra, it was impossible to do any serious work. This insupportable old woman could not make head or tail of the questions, and answered at random.

"Leave the room, Madame, leave the room, and I will hear what you have to say presently."

"But where must I go?" whined Aunt Palmyra.

"Go where you like! Go to the devil!" shouted the exasperated inspector.

"Oh, well, I suppose I ought not to say so," replied the old woman, looking seriously offended, "but, though you are an inspector, you have a very rude tongue in your head!"

To emphasise her majestic exit, Aunt Palmyra added:

"Fancy now! Not one of you have thought of it! I am going as far as the corner to look for flowers for this poor little thing."

Either florists were difficult to find, or Aunt Palmyra had no wish to see them as she passed by, for the old woman walked right through the town without stopping. When she reached the railway station she looked at the clock.

"By the saints! I have barely time," she ejaculated.

The old termagant traversed the waiting-room, got her ticket punched — it was a return ticket — and stepped on to the platform at the precise moment a porter was crying in an ear-piercing voice:

"Passengers for Paris take your seats!"

Aunt Palmyra installed herself in a second-class compartment: *"For ladies only."*

The train rolled out of the station.

An inspector was examining the tickets at the stopping-place at Château-Thierry.

"Excuse me, sir," said he, waking a passenger who had fallen fast asleep — a stout man, with a smooth face and scanty hair — "Excuse me, Monsieur, but you are in a *'For ladies only!'*"

The man leapt up and rubbed his eyes; instinctively, with the gesture of a short-sighted man, he took from his waistcoat pocket a large pair of spectacles in gold frames, and stared at the inspector.

"I am sorry! It's a mistake! I will change into another compartment!"

The stranger passed along the connecting corridor, carrying a small bundle of clothes wrapped in a shawl of many colours!... An hour later, the train from Châlons arrived at Paris, ten minutes behind time. Directly he stood on the platform the traveller looked at his watch.

"Twenty-five past eleven! I can do it!"

He jumped into a taxi, giving his orders:

"Rue Saint Dominique — Ministry of War!... and quick!"

Shortly after the unexpected departure of Colonel Hofferman, Juve, judging it useless to prolong the conversation, had quitted the Under-Secretary of State's office. Instead of mounting to the Second Bureau, he sent in his name to Commandant Dumoulin. Although their acquaintance was but slight, the two men were in sympathy: each realised that the other was courageous and devoted to duty; both were enamoured of an active life and open air.

Juve was hoping that at all events he would hear something new, if not facts about the affair he had in hand, at least with regard to the attitude which the military authorities meant to take up. Commandant Dumoulin, however, knew nothing or did not wish to say anything, and Juve was about to leave, when Colonel Hofferman entered.

Hofferman looked radiant. Catching sight of Juve, he smiled.

"Ah! Upon my word! I did not expect to find you here, Monsieur ... but, since you are, you will be glad to get some news of the Brocq affair."...

Juve's eyes were shining notes of interrogation.

"I rendered due homage to your perspicacity just now," continued the colonel: "you were absolutely right in your prognostication that Brocq had a mistress; unfortunately — I am sorry for the wound to your self-esteem — the correctness of your version stops there! Brocq's mistress was not a society woman, as you thought: on the contrary, she was a girl of the lower orders ... a music-hall singer, called Nichoune ... of Châlons!"

"You have proof of it?"

The colonel, with a superior air, held out a packet of letters to Juve.

"Here is the correspondence — letters written by Brocq to the girl! One of my collaborators seized them at girl's place."...

Juve scrutinised the letters.

"It's curious," he said, half to himself.... "An annoying coincidence ... but the name of Nichoune does not appear once in these letters!"

"No other name appears," observed the colonel: "Consequently, taking into consideration the place where these letters have been found ... we must conclude."...

"These letters had no envelopes with them?" questioned Juve.

"No, there were none, but what matters that?" cried the colonel.

"Very queer," said Juve, in a meditative tone. Then raising his voice:

"I suppose, Colonel, that your ... collaborator, before taking possession of these letters, had a talk with the person who had received them. Did he manage to extract any information?"

Hofferman interrupted Juve with a gesture.

"Monsieur Juve," said he, crossing his arms, "I am going to give you another surprise: my collaborator could not get the person in question to talk, and for a very good reason: he found her dead!"

"Dead?" echoed Juve.

"That is as I say."

The detective, though he strove to hide it, was more and more taken aback. What could this mean? No doubt he would soon secure additional information; but what was the connecting link? where, and who was the mysterious person who was really pulling the strings? The sarcastic voice of the colonel tore Juve from his reflections and questionings.

"Monsieur Juve, I think it is high time we had some lunch ... but before we separate allow me to give you a word of advice.

"When, in the course of your career, you have occasion to deal with matters relating to spies and spying, leave us to deal with them, that is what we are here for!... As for you, content yourself with ordinary police work, that is your business, and, if it gives you pleasure, continue your hunt for Fantômas, that will give you all the occupation you require!... Yes," continued the colonel, while Juve was clenching his fists with exasperation at this irony which was like so many flicks of a whip on his face, "Yes, leave these serious affairs to us — and occupy yourself with Fantômas!"

XI
THE HOODED CLOAK OF FANTÔMAS

Leaning on his window-sill, Jérôme Fandor was apparently keeping a strict watch on the comings and goings of the passers-by, who, having finished their Sunday walk, were bending their steps towards dinner, a quiet evening, and a reposeful night. Seven o'clock sounded from a neighbouring clock, its strokes borne through the misty atmosphere, darkened by fog: it was a peaceful moment, made for pleasurable relaxation ofter the activities of the day. Jérôme Fandor, however, was not enjoying the charm of the hour. Although his attitude was apparently tranquil, listless even, inwardly he was in a state of fury, a condition of feverish enervation.

"To be so near success," he thought; "to be on the point of bringing in a magnificent haul, and then to get myself locked up, like a fool! No! Not if I can help it! Why it would be enough to make me strangle myself with my handkerchief as they believed that wretched Dollon, of sinister memory, did in the past!"

He smoked cigarette after cigarette, raving to himself, yet never taking his eyes off the pavements, where tirelessly, ceaselessly, a stream of pedestrians passed up and down the street.

"Was I mistaken, I wonder!" he went on. "Still, I cannot help fancying that youth — he was fifteen at the most — that sickly young blackguard of the Paris pavements who followed me into the tube, then took the same train as I did, who was behind me as I crossed the Place de la Concorde, who was continually and persistently on my tracks — I cannot think he was there by chance!... Well, it is no use worrying myself into a fever over it!"

Fandor found it almost impossible to recover his tranquillity of mind. Again and again, in the course of the day, he had come across the same individuals during his peregrinations, which took him from one end of Paris to the other: was it accident, coincidence, fatality, or was a very strict watch being kept over his movements? Thus Fandor had asked himself whether the Second Bureau had been warned of the part he had played with regard to Vinson? Was he not being watched and shadowed in the hope of running the treacherous corporal to earth? If the Second Bureau had decided to arrest Fandor, he certainly would not escape. "I shall be jailed within twenty-four hours," thought our journalist. "This branch of the detective service is so marvellously organised, that should the heads of it look upon me as Vinson's accomplice they will arrest me before I have time to parry the blow. In that case, the band of traitors I pursue, and am on the point of unearthing, will gain enough time to take their bearings, make all their arrangements, and disappear, without counting that this miserable Vinson, who relies on my help, will be caught at once."

Suddenly Fandor left his post of observation, shut his window, and went to the telephone.

"I must put Juve in possession of all the facts up to now, then, if I am caught, Juve will see to it that I am set free — he will put his heart into it, I know."

Unfortunately, it was not Juve who was at the other end of the line. He had gone out; his old servant took Fandor's message.

"Tell Monsieur Juve directly he comes in that I cannot go out, but that I absolutely must see him. Tell him the matter is most urgent."

It was ten o'clock at night. Corporal Vinson was dressing in haste.

"Plague take it!" he cried. "I mustn't lose a moment if I don't want to miss my train."

Vinson was dressing in Fandor's bedroom. There must have been a time when Corporal Vinson was very proud of putting on the uniform of a French soldier; but at this particular moment his feelings were the very opposite. However, he clad himself in this same uniform with lightning rapidity. Careful of his smart appearance, the corporal examined himself in the glass: the reflection was so satisfactory that he broke into smiles — undoubtedly his uniform suited him.

There was a violent ring at the door-bell. Vinson jumped: he began to tremble.

"Who can it be at this hour?" he asked himself. "I was sure something would happen! I was bound to catch it somehow!"

Vinson dared not risk a movement: he stood rigid, motionless. Whoever was at the door must be led to think that there was not a living soul in Fandor's flat.

Again the bell rang, a violent ring: it was the ring of someone who does not mean to go away, who knows that the delay in opening the door is deliberate.

"Plague take that porter!" murmured the corporal. "I'll wager."...

Again the bell rang violently.

Something had to be done. Drops of sweat rolled down the corporal's face.

"By jingo, this business is going to end very badly!"

The young soldier rapidly drew off his shoes and tiptoed to the vestibule. Through the key-hole he looked to see who was ringing for the fourth time, and more violently than ever.

No sooner had Vinson looked than he swore softly.

"Good Heavens! What I feared! It's an agent from the Second Bureau!...I recognise him!... I am sold — there's not a doubt of it!"

Ghastly from terror, Vinson watched the visitor put his hand in his pocket, then choose a key from his bunch.

"Ah! This individual has a master-key! And I — I have an idea!"

Vinson leaped backwards, just as the agent was putting his key in the lock, and rushed towards Fandor's study. He locked the door at the precise moment the agent entered the flat.

"Halt!" cried he: Vinson's movements had been heard.

The corporal's answer was to double-lock the door. "What you are doing there is childish!" cried the agent. "I have master-keys! Give yourself up!" Taking a fresh key, he unlocked the door Vinson had just closed. The corporal was not in the room. The agent rushed to another door which led from the study to the dining-room. He opened that door, entered the dining-room; it was empty also: Vinson had fled to the room adjoining.

"You cannot keep at it!" cried the agent. "You see the doors cannot offer a moment's resistance! I shall corner you!"

But Vinson, retreating from room to room, aimed at drawing on his pursuer to the last room of the flat. Directly the agent entered the dining-room, Vinson, quick as lightning, leapt into the corridor, crossed the vestibule at a bound, opened the door leading to the staircase, slamming it behind him.

On the landing he hesitated a second.

"Must he go down the stairs?"

The agent would follow in his track, the pursuit would develop, for, seeing a soldier in uniform racing along, the passers-by would join in the running: it would be fatal — Vinson would be caught.

"I'll double back," thought he, "back and up!"

Hurriedly he mounted the next flight of stairs, gaining the third story. No sooner had he reached the landing which dominated Fandor's flat than the agent, in his turn, reached the staircase and ran to the balustrade to try and catch sight of Vinson on his way down to the street. He did not doubt that this was the soldier's way of escape. The agent could not see a soul.

"Got off, by Jove!" He was furious.

He was about to descend, when someone, belonging to the house probably, began to mount the first flight of stairs in leisurely fashion, someone who could have no suspicion of the pursuit going on in the house. Very likely the agent neither intended nor desired to be recognised for what he was: it was quite probable that he did not wish to be seen, for, on hearing this someone coming up towards him, he stopped short in his descent....It was his turn to hesitate a moment. Then it suddenly occurred to him that this new-comer might be a resident on one of the lower floors and so would not come higher. With this, the agent retraced his steps, crossed the landing on to which Fandor's flat opened, and began to mount the next flight leading to the third floor.

This did not suit Vinson: he was on tenterhooks.

"If he keeps coming up," thought the corporal, "much use it will be for me to retreat upwards! He will nip me on the sixth floor! It's a dead cert!"

Then he had a brilliant idea. He began to walk on the landing with heavy steps, imitating someone coming downstairs. Forthwith, the agent, who was coming up, stopped short. He had no wish to be seen by the person descending either! The only thing left for him to do was to take refuge in the journalist's flat! Easy enough with his master-key! He reopened the door, closing it just in time to escape being seen by the resident coming upstairs.

Vinson, who had not lost a single movement of the agent's, gave a sigh of satisfaction. He had perfectly understood the why and wherefore of his pursuer's hesitations; he seemed now in high good-humour; had he not caught sight of the new arrival! He was immensely amused!

The person who had just come upstairs was now ringing Fandor's bell. Not getting any answer, he selected a key on his bunch, and it was his turn to let himself in to the journalist's flat.

As he was closing the door, Corporal Vinson, from the landing above, gave him an ironical salute.

"I much regret that I am unable to introduce you to each other! But, by way of return, I thank you for the service you have unwittingly done me."

The way was open: Vinson rapidly descended, gained the street, hailed a cab.

"To the Eastern Station!"

"I have missed the express," he muttered; "but I shall catch the first train for those on leave."

Whilst Corporal Vinson was congratulating himself on the turn of events, the agent remained in Fandor's flat, feeling as if he were the victim of an abominable nightmare. No sooner had he hurriedly let himself into the flat in order to escape the resident coming upstairs, than he heard the bell ring: he felt desperate: "Who the devil was it!" Assuredly not the unknown who had fled so mysteriously — "Who then?"

When the bell rang a second time, the man cried: "What's to be done?" Well, the best thing was to wait in the journalist's study: it was more than probable that, not obtaining any response, the visitor would go away!...This was not at all what happened.

With the same assurance which he himself had had a few minutes before, the agent of the Second Bureau heard the new arrival slip his key into the lock, open the door, close it as confidently as though he were entering his own home; and now, yes, he was coming towards the study!

There was no light burning in Fandor's study: some gleams from the gas-lamps in the street dimly illumined the room. The agent, who was leaning with his elbow on the mantelpiece, could not clearly distinguish the features of the person who now stood in the doorway.

It was certainly not the journalist. The intruder was a man of quite forty; he wore a soft hat turned down at the edges, thus partially concealing the upper half of his face, which was sunk in the raised collar of an overcoat.

The intruder bowed slightly to the agent, then taking a few steps into the room, went to the window, looked about outside. He seemed to be someone on intimate terms with the master of the flat, and might be going to await his return.

"He must be a friend of Jérôme Fandor's," thought the agent. "He must think the journalist will be here shortly, perhaps that he is actually in the flat somewhere, and that I too am waiting for him." Evidently the best thing to do was to stay where he was, and not to make any remark which might attract attention.

Some minutes passed thus. Presently, the two men, tired with standing, seated themselves.

"The old boy will get sick of waiting," thought the agent. "He will go away, and I shall take my departure when he has cleared out."

But the new-comer, making himself very much at home, now relieved himself of his greatcoat, removed his hat, and, having caught sight of a lamp on the mantelpiece, took a box of matches from his pocket, and proceeded to light it. At the moment when the match flared up, the man, turning his back on the agent, could not see him: but the agent could see the man distinctly. There could be no question that the man lighting the lamp was someone the agent had not expected to meet, for the emissary from the Second Board did the very reverse of what the new-comer had done: he turned up the collar of his greatcoat!

The two men were now face to face in the lighted room....There was a silence which lasted some minutes: the agent broke it.

"You await Monsieur Fandor?" asked the agent.

"Yes, Monsieur, and you also, no doubt?"

"Quite so ...and I have more than an idea that we shall have to wait a long time for him....I saw him a short while ago, he had a piece of pressing business on hand, and I do not think he will be back before."...The agent was quite obviously trying to get the new-comer to retire.

"Bah!" retorted the latter: "I am in no hurry." Whilst speaking the unknown visitor stared strangely at the emissary of the Second Bureau: he was thinking.

"Where have I seen that long beard — that remarkably heavy moustache?...And then this bundle he has put down!...If I am not jolly well mistaken, I know this individual!"

"Well, now," he said pleasantly, "since chance has thrown us into each other's company, allow me to introduce myself, Monsieur! I am Brigadier Juve of the detective force, from Police Headquarters."

"In that case, we might almost count ourselves colleagues, Monsieur! I am the agent Vagualame, attached to the vigilance department of the Secret Service!"

With that, Vagualame held out his hand to his colleague, Juve! It was done with an unmistakable air of constraint.

It really seemed as if Juve had been awaiting this very action; for, at the precise moment Vagualame held out his hand, the detective extended his, and prolonged the hand-clasp as if he never meant to let go — a regular hand-grip!

Juve was thinking hard.

"Vagualame! Here is this Vagualame at Fandor's!...It's significant!...and then?...No, there's no doubt about it! This beard is false! That moustache is artificial!...This individual is made up!"

Perceiving that he was face to face with a disguised man, Juve was about to hurl himself on this masquerader, when that individual, forestalling the detective's movement, seized the initiative with lightning rapidity. He tore his hand from Juve's tenacious grip, bounded to the mantelpiece, threw down the lamp with a jerk of his elbow, thrust Juve violently aside, and rushed to the door.

Like lightning Juve tore off in pursuit.

The masquerader had the advantage by some yards. Banging door after door in Juve's face, he rushed towards the entrance hall, gained the staircase, racing down it by leaps and bounds, four steps at a time!...Juve at his heels, risked breaking his neck in hot pursuit....

Vagualame reached the porch of the house door: Juve was close on his quarry....

"I shall get him!" thought Juve: "In the street the people will lend me a helping hand!"

Vagualame fled through the doorway: in passing, he seized the massive door and pulled it to with a resounding bang....

Juve, borne forward by the impetus of his dashing pursuit, staggered backwards and rolled to the ground....

Instantly Juve sprang to the porter's lodge and demanded the string! In the twinkling of an eye and Juve was out in the street! He was furious, he was breathless....The whole length of the pavements not a soul was in sight! Vagualame had vanished!

Taking advantage of the fact that Fandor's concierge knew him well, and was aware of his standing as an officer of the detective force, Juve, after having explained in a few words to the honest creature the cause of the commotion mounted to Fandor's flat once more.

"What the deuce is the meaning of all this?" he was asking himself. "Two hours ago, Fandor telephones me that he must see me on a matter of the utmost urgency ...he telephones me that he cannot go out, that he is waiting for me....And now, not only is he not here, but I stumble on an agent from the Second Bureau....I encounter a Vagualame disguised, who runs as if all the devils of hell were after him ...who makes off with extraordinary agility, whose presence of mind in burking pursuit is marvellous!...Who is this fellow?...What was he up to in Fandor's flat?...Where is Fandor?"

Our detective had just re-entered the journalist's study. There, on the floor, lay the bundle which had excited his curiosity when Vagualame was present.

"The enemy," thought he, "has retired, but has abandoned his baggage!"

Juve relighted the lamp, and undid the black serge covering of the bundle.

"Ah! I might have guessed as much, it is an accordion, Vagualame's accordion!"

Mechanically turning and returning the instrument of music, Juve slipped his hands into the leather holders, wishing to relax the bellows, which were at full stretch.... To his surprise the bellows resisted.

"Why, there must be something inside the accordion!" he exclaimed.

Juve drew from his pocket a dagger knife and slit open the bellows with one sharp cut.... Something black fell out — a piece of stuff, Juve picked it up, spread it out, and considered it.... He grew pale as he looked, staggered like a drunken man, and sank on a chair, overcome. What he held in his hand was a hooded cloak, long and black, such as Italian bandits wear — a species of mask.

Sunk in his chair, his eyes staring at this sinister garment, Juve seemed to see rising before him a form at once mysterious and clearly defined — the form of an unknown man enveloped in this cloak as in a sheath, his face hidden by the hooded mask, disguised, by just such a cloak as he had exposed to view when he slashed open the bellows of this accordion!

This form, mysterious, nameless, tragic, thus evoked, Juve had rarely seen; but each time that figure in hooded black had appeared, it was in circumstances so serious, under conditions so tragic, that it was graven on his memory — graven beyond mistake — graven ineffaceably!

Had not Juve been haunted by this form, this figure so mysteriously indicated, haunted by this invisible face hidden by its hooded cloak of black — haunted for years! Never had he been able to get close to it!

Never had he been able to seize it in his hands, outstretched to grasp it!

Whenever this sinister garment had met his eyes, it had been the sign of some frightful deception! He did not know the countenance it masked so darkly, but that same cloak that he knew!... So well did he know it, that never could he confuse it with another hooded cloak of black — never! Its shape was peculiar; its cut singular — unmistakable! It was the impenetrable mask of one of those counterfeit personalities assumed at the pleasure of that enigmatic, sinister, formidable bandit, whom Juve had pursued for ten years, without cessation, without mercy; there had been no truce to this hunting.

Now he turned, and returned, this cloak of dark significance with trembling hands, as if he would tear its secret from its sinister folds. This hooded cloak which his knife had revealed, which he had torn from its hiding place in the accordion of Vagualame, was none other than the cloak of Fantômas.

Suddenly there was brought home to Juve the comprehension of all this adventure signified — a distracting, a maddening adventure!

"Fantômas! Fantômas!" Juve murmured. "Great Heavens! I saw Fantômas before me!... Vagualame! He is Fantômas!... Curse it! He has slipped through my hands, thrice fool that I am! Never again will he appear as this beggarly accordion player — never will he dare to show himself in that make-up!... What new form will he take?... Fantômas! Fantômas! Once again you have escaped me!"

Our detective remained in Fandor's flat all night. He awaited the journalist's return.

Fandor did not come.

XII
A TRICK ACCORDING TO FANDOR

It was a November Sunday evening. A crowd of leave-expired soldiers were entraining at the Eastern Station. They would be dropped at their respective garrisons along the line of some 400 kilometres separating the capital from the frontier.

They had dined, supped, feasted with friends and relatives: now they were voicing regretful farewells by medley of songs and ear-splitting serenades. They scrambled into the third-class compartments, fifteen, sixteen at a time, filling the seats and overflowing on to the floor. Little by little the deafening din of the "wild beasts," as they were jokingly called, diminished; their enthusiasm died down as the night advanced, while the train rushed full steam ahead for the frontier of France.

They fell asleep, knowing that kind comrades would awaken them when the train drew up at their various garrisons. At Reims, the compartments disgorged the dragoons pell-mell; at Châlons, so many gunners and infantry had got out that the train was half emptied. At Sainte-Menehould, a large contingent of cuirassiers and infantry had cleared out. Towards four in the morning the express was nearing Verdun.

As the train steamed out of Sainte-Menehould, a corporal of the line, who had been forced to sit up as stiff as a poker for several hours, stretched himself at length on the compartment seat with a sigh of relief. But the jerks and jolts of the carriage, the hard seat, made sleep impossible: the epaulettes of his uniform were an added source of discomfort. The corporal sat up, rubbed the musty glass of the window, and watched for the coming day. On the far horizon, beyond a shadowy stretch of country, a pallid dawn was breaking. Trees were swaying in a gusty wind. At intervals, when the clatter of the onrushing train lessened, the heavy pattering of rain on the roof became audible.

"Confound it!" growled the corporal. "Detestable weather! Hateful country!"

Whilst attempting some muscular exercises to unstiffen his aching limbs, he muttered:

"And only to think of that wretch Vinson enjoying the benefit of my first-class permit!... Started off to-night under my name, and is now rolling along in a comfortable sleeping-car towards the sunny South with a nice bit of money in his purse!"

The corporal in the inhospitable third-class of the Verdun train made mental pictures of Vinson's progress south. He talked to himself aloud.

"Good journey to you, you jolly dog!...In six weeks' time, if you have a thought to spare for me, you will send your news as we arranged!"

The corporal began breathing warm breaths on his numbed fingers.

"By Jove! The company is not prodigal of foot-warmers, that's certain! It's an ice-house in here!"

He continued to soliloquise:

"It's a deuce of a risky business I have let myself in for!...To take Vinson's place, and set off for Verdun, where his regiment is doing garrison duty, the regiment to which he has just been attached!...It would run as smooth as oil if I had done my military service, but, owing to circumstances, I have never been called up!...A pretty sort of fool I may make of myself!"...

After a reflective silence, he went on:

"Bah! I shall pull through all right! Have I not crammed my head with theory the last eight days, and pumped Vinson for all he was worth about the rules and regulations, and the ways of camp life!...All the same ...to make my début in an Eastern garrison, in the 'Iron Division,' straight off the reel takes some nerve!...What cheek!...It's the limit!...But, my dear little Fandor, don't forget you are at Verdun not to play the complete soldier but to gather exact information about a band of traitors, and to unmask them at the first opportunity — a work of national importance, little Fandor, and don't you forget it!"

Thus our adventurous Vinson-Fandor lay shivering in the night train on the point of drawing up at Verdun.

Having saved the wretched Vinson from suicide, Fandor had made him promise to leave France and await developments, whilst Fandor, posing as Vinson, studied at close quarters the spies who had drawn the miserable corporal into their net. Fandor could personate Vinson with every chance of success, because the 257th of the line had never set eyes on the corporal.

After a week of perplexity, Fandor had come to a decision the previous night. Wishing to let his "dear master" know of his audacious project, he had telephoned to Juve on the Sunday evening to ask him to come to the flat. Then Vagualame had appeared on the scene. Fandor knew him to be an agent of the Second Bureau. Evidently Vagualame was after Vinson. If Fandor had let himself be caught in the corporal's uniform, which he had just put on, his spy plans would have been ruined, and the corporal, to whom he had promised his protection, would have been caught.

Fandor fled. The situation would have to be made clear when opportunity offered.

"Certainly," said Fandor to himself, with a smile: "things are pretty well mixed up at present! That meeting between Vagualame and Juve at the flat must have been a queer one! Two birds of a feather, though differing in glory, who would not make head or tail of so unexpected a conference!"

To clear up the imbroglio, Fandor had meant to send Juve a wire on his arrival at Verdun; on second thoughts he had decided against it. Probably the spies, or the Second Bureau, or both, were keeping a sharp watch on Vinson: it would be wiser to refrain from any communication which might reveal the fact that the corporal Vinson, who joined the 257th of the line at Verdun, was none other than Jérôme Fandor, journalist.

Though stiff with cold and fatigue, Fandor's brain was clear and active.

It is all right! Juve would be surprised, anxious, would make enquiries at the Company's offices, would learn that on the Sunday evening Fandor had occupied the place reserved for him in the sleeping-car, would be reassured, would not worry about Fandor's abrupt departure and silence — Fandor was holiday making!

"Yes, it is all right!" reiterated Fandor. "What I have to do is to throw myself wholeheartedly into my part, and play it as jovially as possible!"

The train whistled, slowed down, entered the station of Verdun.

Fandor let the crowd of soldiers precede him, as well as one or two civilians whom the night express had brought to this important frontier fortress. Having readjusted his coat, the fringes of his epaulettes, and put on his cap correctly, this corporal of the 257th line, stepped on to the platform, reached the exit, passed out on to a vast flat space, and found himself floundering in a sea of mud.

The men who had arrived with him had hurried off: Fandor was alone on the outskirts of the silent town.

What to do? Which way to go?

Under the flame of a gas-jet struggling against the onslaughts of the wind, Fandor caught sight of the honest face of a constable enveloped in a thick hooded coat. He eyed Fandor.

"Excuse me," said Corporal Vinson-Fandor, rolling his r's, in imitation of a rustic fresh from the country, "but could you tell me where I shall find the 257th of the line?"

"What do you want with the 257th of the line?" queried the constable.

"It is like this, Monsieur: I was in the 214th, garrisoned at Châlons. I have had eight days' leave, and they inform me I am attached to the 257th."

The constable nodded.

"And now you want to get to your new regiment?"

"Precisely."

"Well, the 257th is in three places: at bastion 14; at the Saint Benoit barracks; and at Fort Vieux — which are you bound for, Corporal?"

"I don't know — I've no preference," murmured Corporal Vinson-Fandor.

The two men stood staring at each other in the rain.

Despite the chill and melancholy dawn, with its darkly reddening skies, Fandor felt he was on the very verge of bursting into wild laughter.

"Let us see your route instructions," quoth the constable.

Corporal Vinson-Fandor showed his paper.

"That's it!" cried the constable triumphantly. "You are down to report yourself at the Saint Benoit barracks. You're in luck, my lad! It's only fifty yards or so from here!...Go down the road, and you will see the barrack wall on the left. The entrance is in the middle."

Fandor saluted the friendly constable, hurried off, and reached the Saint Benoit gate in a few minutes.

"The 257th?" he asked the sentry.

"Here!...You will find the sergeant in the guard-room."

Fandor entered a smoke-filled room; several soldiers were stretched at full length on a bench, slumbering: a snoring non-commissioned officer was lying on three straw bottomed chairs close to a stove.

At Fandor's entrance he was wide awake in a moment: he swore: it was the sergeant.

"What do you want?" he demanded roughly.

Adopting a military manner, Fandor announced:

"Corporal Vinson, just arrived from Châlons, exchanged from the 214th, sergeant!"

"Ah! Quite so. Wait! I will show you your company."

Stretching himself, the sergeant marched to the end of the room, turned up a gas-jet, opened a book, looked through the pages slowly. His finger stopped at a name.

"Orderly!"

A man presented himself.

"Conduct Corporal Vinson to A block, second floor."

Turning to Fandor, the sergeant informed him:

"You are attached to the third of the second."

While plodding through the mud of the courtyard, Fandor said to himself:

"The third of the second means, I suppose, that I have the honour of belonging to the third company of the second battalion."

Fandor gazed with lively curiosity at the immense building in which he was to pass his days and nights for he did not know how long a time. As he scrutinised this enormous pile, standing harsh and stark in its uncompromising and ordered strength, as he took stock of the vast courtyards and the stony lengths of imprisoning walls, he got an idea of that formidable organisation called a regiment, which itself is but an infinitesimal part of that great whole we call an army. Appreciating as he now did the importance, the immutability, the regularity of the movements of the military machine, with its wheels within wheels, Fandor asked himself if it were possible to carry through the programme he had drawn up for himself. Could he, at one and the same time, trick the French Army and save it?...He had taken his precautions: he had read and reread Vinson's manual, now *his* manual. Mentally he had put himself in the skin of a corporal: he was letter perfect, and now he must cover himself with the mantle of Vinson —for the greater glory of France!

He could not help laughing when he read the list of his facial characteristics: chin, round; nose, medium; face, oval; eyes, grey. Vague enough this to be safe! Fandor's hair was dark chestnut: Vinson's was brown. Vinson and Fandor were sufficiently alike as to height and figure: besides, soldiers' uniforms were not an exact fit.

"Here you are, Corporal!" announced the orderly. He pointed to a vast room at the end of a corridor. The bugle had just sounded the reveille and the barrack-room was humming like a hive of awakened bees. The orderly had vanished. Fandor stood at the threshold, hesitating: his self-confidence had gone down with a run. It was a momentary lapse. Pulling himself together he walked into the room.

When giving him his instructions, Vinson had warned Fandor, that when it came to settling down in barracks he would find nothing to hand.

"Among other little items, your bed will be missing. As corporal you have a right to round on them. Row them hot and good — start reprisals straight away. The men will pretend not to understand, but insist — don't take no for an answer; take whatever you want right and left — in the end you will get properly settled in."

Fandor carried out these instructions. Before he had been ten minutes in the room, men were rushing in all directions, fussing, jostling one another, coming, going, demanding of all the echoes in that huge white-washed barn of a barrack-room dormitory:

"Where is the palliasse of Corporal Vinson!"

"Find me the bolster of Corporal Vinson!"

XIII
JUVE'S STRATAGEM

Whilst Jérôme Fandor was commencing his apprenticeship as a soldier at the Saint Benoit barracks, Verdun, a sordid individual was following an elegant pedestrian who, descending the rue Solférino, went in the direction of the Seine. It was about seven in the evening.

"Pstt!"

This sound issued from the ragged individual, but the passer-by did not turn his head.

"Monsieur!" insisted the sordid one.

As the elegant pedestrian did not seem to know he was being followed, the sordid individual stepped to his side, and murmured in his white beard distinctly enough to be heard:

"Lieutenant! Do listen!...Look here, Monsieur de Loubersac ...Henri!"

The young man turned: he gave the importunate speaker a withering stare: he was furious. The speaker was Vagualame.

"I shall fine you five hundred francs! How dare you accost me like this? Are you mad?" De Loubersac's voice shook with rage.

Lieutenant de Loubersac had just quitted the Second Bureau after an unusually hard day's work. Fatigued by the over-heated offices, he was enjoying the fresh air and exercise in spite of the chilling mist overhanging Paris. When his thoughts were not connected on his work, he would dwell tenderly on every little detail of his meetings with pretty Mademoiselle de Naarboveck. Had she not given him permission to call her Wilhelmine, and did he not cherish the hope of soon making her his wife?

But this Vagualame was insupportable! That he should dare to accost him without observing the customary precautions — hail him by his style and title in a most public thoroughfare — should so imprudently compromise himself and an attaché of the Second Bureau! Well, he knew how to attack informers and such gentry in their most vulnerable spot — their purse; hence the fine of five hundred francs he had imposed on Vagualame!

The old fellow shuffled along beside the enraged lieutenant, whining, complaining of the precarious state of his finances, but de Loubersac was adamant. Perceiving this, Vagualame desisted.

"I want to talk to you," said he.

"To-morrow!" suggested de Loubersac.

"No, at once. It is urgent."

De Loubersac could hardly hear what Vagualame said. Twice he cried, in an irritated voice:

"What is the matter with you? I cannot understand what you say. I can hardly hear you."

"I have a severe cold on the chest, lieutenant."

Certainly Vagualame's voice was remarkably hoarse.

"If the Government does not give me something regular to live on, I shall die in hospital."

De Loubersac looked about him anxiously. If his colonel should catch sight of him conferring with an agent so near the headquarters of the Second Bureau he would incur a sharp reprimand. The interview must take place; therefore they must conceal themselves. Vagualame, as though reading the lieutenant's thought, pointed to the steep flight of steps leading to the banks of the Seine.

"Let us go down by the river! We shall be undisturbed there!"

De Loubersac acquiesced. So the smart young officer and the old beggar in his ragged coat, with the accordion hanging over his shoulder, who might have been mistaken for Quasimodo himself, descended the steps in company. Vagualame's eyes gleamed with joy. They were piercing eyes, full of life and intelligence, not the fierce furtive eyes of Vagualame, for this Vagualame was Juve!

The day following the famous evening he had passed in Fandor's flat, Juve, as we know, had discovered that Vagualame, agent of the Second Bureau, was cleverly disguised, and was none other than Fantômas! Juve appropriated the accordion left by the fleeing bandit: Juve also decided to personate Vagualame and spy on the various persons who had relations with this sinister being. As far as Juve was concerned, Vagualame-Fantômas was done for, therefore it was highly improbable that the criminal, daring to the last degree though he was, would show himself in his Vagualame guise for some time to come. Therefore Juve must act at once. His first move must be to meet and talk with the Second Bureau officer most in touch with Vagualame, and make him talk without arousing his suspicions. Juve also meant to mix with Vagualame's associates, trusting to luck and his own perspicacity to get on to various trails, trails that would lead him to the solution of grave problems.

Juve had felt anxious as he accosted de Loubersac: no doubt the lieutenant and his secret agent had some set form of greeting, some agreed on method of imparting information. By incurring the fine, Juve realised that he had made a wrong start — perhaps omitted a password. Still, he had obtained the essential thing — a private talk with this particular official of the Second Bureau.

The talk began with an abrupt question from de Loubersac:

"And the V. affair?"

"The V. affair?... Peuh!"

"What the deuce does he refer to?" Juve was asking himself.

Unsuspecting, de Loubersac came to his aid.

"Our corporal must have returned to Verdun to-day?"

"Ah!" thought Juve, "our corporal is Vinson!" The further he proceeded in his present investigations the clearer grew the connection between the Brocq affair and those of Bobinette, Wilhelmine, de Loubersac: surely they were all interpreters of the tragic drama conceived by Vagualame-Fantômas!

"His leave expired this morning," continued de Loubersac.

"He left yesterday evening. I have proof of it," asserted Juve-Vagualame.

"Anything new?"

"Not so far."

"Are you going to Verdun?"

"Possibly."

"How about the document?"

"Hum!" murmured Juve-Vagualame. Here was another conundrum he must go warily.

"You are constantly looking for it, of course? You know it is the most urgent of all!"...

Juve nodded agreement.

"Place it in my hands, and I shall give you fifty thousand francs in exchange for it — you know that!"

"Less the fine," put in Juve-Vagualame with a comical grimace.

De Loubersac smiled.

"We will speak of that again." There was a pause.

"A good deal has happened since the death of Captain Brocq's mistress." Juve-Vagualame remarked.

"Is Captain Brocq's mistress dead, too?... Poor girl!"

De Loubersac stared hard at the accordion player.

"Oh come now, Vagualame! Where are your wits — wool-gathering?"

"Wits wool-gathering, lieutenant!" echoed Juve-Vagualame.

"There is no lieutenant, I tell you!" cried de Loubersac, with a stamp of his foot. "It is Monsieur Henri — just Henri, if you like. How many more times am I to tell you this?"

Juve-Vagualame's reply was an equivocal gesture.

"You do not know about the Châlons affair — the assassination of the singer, Nichoune?"

"No — that is to say."...

"Well, then?" De Loubersac was staring at Vagualame with puzzled eyes.

"Well, then — as to that — no!... I had better hold my tongue."

"Speak out!" commanded de Loubersac.

"No," growled Juve-Vagualame.

"I order you to do so."

"Well, then," conceded Juve-Vagualame, "since you must know what I think, I consider Nichoune was in no sense the mistress of Captain Brocq."

"They found letters from Captain Brocq on her." De Loubersac's laugh had a sneer in it.

"Bah!" said the old accordion player, punctuating his remark with some piercing sounds from his ancient instrument of discordant music. "It was a got-up business!"

"What is that you say?" objected de Loubersac. After a moment's reflection he added:

"But of course, you must know more about it than anyone, Vagualame, because you saw her just before the end. Didn't you have a talk with Nichoune on the Friday, the eve of her death?"

Juve-Vagualame was about to speak. De Loubersac added:

"The innkeeper saw you!"

"Did he now? What is this?" thought Juve. This statement opened up a fresh view of things. De Loubersac did not give him time for reflection.

"Who, then, do you think killed Nichoune?"

Juve would not for the world voice his suspicions just then. With a side-glance at the lieutenant, he remarked:

"Faith, what I am inclined to think is, that the guilty person is that Aunt Palmyra."

"Aunt Palmyra!" repeated de Loubersac. "Decidedly my poor Vagualame, you are stupid as an owl to-day! Well, there is no harm in telling you this — Aunt Palmyra was one of my colleagues!"

"I suspected as much," thought Juve, "but I wanted him to confirm it."

De Loubersac was again the questioner.

"Vagualame! You spoke just now of Brocq's mistress: if, as you seem to think, Nichoune had no such relation with the captain, where are we to look for his mistress?"

"Hah!... Look in another direction ... among his friends ... in the great world ... the diplomatic set, for preference ... Think of those in the de Naarboveck circle"....

"Look out, Vagualame!" exclaimed de Loubersac. "Weigh your words well!"

"Do not be afraid, lieu ... pardon — Monsieur Henri!"

"Perhaps you think it is Bobinette?" queried de Loubersac.

"No."

"Who then?"

Juve shot his answer at the lieutenant, like a stone from a catapult.

"Wilhelmine de Naarboveck!"

A shout of indignant protest burst from de Loubersac. He could not contain his fury: he kicked the supposed Vagualame with such force that he sent him rolling in the greasy mud of the Seine bank.

"Beast!" growled Juve, as he picked himself up. "If I were not Vagualame, I should know how to answer him," he muttered. "As it is!"...

Juve rose, stumbling and staggering like a badly shaken old man, and leaned against the hand railing of the steps.

Meanwhile de Loubersac was walking up and down, talking aloud, in a state of extreme agitation.

"Disgusting creatures!... Low-minded wretches!... Degrading occupation!... They respect nothing, and no one!... Insinuating such abominations!... Wilhelmine de Naarboveck the mistress of Brocq!... How vile!... Loathsome creatures!"

It was now obvious to the alert Juve, who drank in every word, each gesture of de Loubersac's that the enraged lieutenant adored Wilhelmine ... no doubt on that score!

When de Loubersac had calmed down somewhat, Juve cried softly:

"Oh, Monsieur Henri!"...

Roused from his reflections, de Loubersac shouted:

"Hold your tongue, you sicken me!"

"But," insisted Juve-Vagualame, "I have only done my duty. If I spoke as I did, it was because my conscience."...

"Have you got consciences — your sort?" cried de Loubersac, casting a glance of withering contempt at the supposed old man.

There was a silence. Then de Loubersac walked up to the old accordion player and asked anxiously:

"Can you give me proofs of the truth of what you have just asserted?"

"Perhaps," was the evasive answer.

"You will have to give me proofs," insisted de Loubersac.

"Proofs?...I have none," replied the mysterious old fellow. "But I have intuitions; better still, my confidence is grounded on a strong probability."

This statement came to de Loubersac with the force of a stunning blow: it came from one whom he considered his best agent: he knew Vagualame always weighed his words: his information was generally correct.

"We cannot continue this conversation here," he said. "To-morrow we must meet as usual — and remember — do not attempt to accost me without using the password."

"Now, how the deuce am I to know what this famous word is?" Juve asked himself. Then he had an inspiration.

"We must not use it again," he announced. "I have reason to think our customary password is known ...I will explain another time ...it is a regular story — a long one."

"All right," agreed de Loubersac. "What should it be?...Suppose I say *monoplane?*"

"I will answer *dirigible,*" said Juve-Vagualame.

"Agreed."

De Loubersac rapidly mounted the steps leading to the quay, glad to close a detestable interview.

Juve-Vagualame remained below. He struck his forehead.

"Monsieur Henri!" he called.

"What?"

"The meeting place to-morrow?"

De Loubersac had just signalled to a taxi: he leaned over the parapet and called to Juve-Vagualame, who had got no farther than the middle of the steps:

"Why at half past three, in the garden, as usual!"

"Oh, ho!" said the old accordion player. "He will be furious! I shall play him false — bound to — for how can I keep the appointment — confound it! What garden? Whereabouts in it?" Then, as he regained the quay, Juve laughed in his false white beard.

"What do I care? I snap my fingers at that rendezvous. I have extracted from him what I wanted to know — it matters not a jot if I never set eyes on him again! And ...now ...it is we two, Bobinette!"

XIV
BEFORE A TOMB

"This is a surprise!"

Mademoiselle de Naarboveck stopped. She smiled up at Henri de Loubersac.

"Do you know, I saw in this glass that you were following us," she said, pointing to a mirror placed at an angle in a confectioner's shop at the corner of rue Biot.

These artless remarks put the handsome lieutenant out of countenance: he blushed hotly, but he pressed the little hand held out to him so simply, and with such a look of frank pleasure. He stammered some excuse for not having recognised her. He bowed pleasantly to Wilhelmine's companion, Mademoiselle Berthe.

Wilhelmine turned to her.

"This meeting was not prearranged: it is one of pure chance." The tone was defensive without a touch of the apologetic.

Mademoiselle Berthe smiled, and declared that she had not for a moment supposed that the meeting had been prearranged.

De Loubersac gazed considerably at the two girls. Wilhelmine was looking particularly pretty. Beneath her fur toque shone masses of her pale gold hair, framing a charming little face. A long velvet coat with ermine stole suggested the youthful contours of her slender figure. Mademoiselle Berthe wore rough blue cloth, and a large hat trimmed with wings, which set off her piquant face with its irregular features and ruddy locks.

Wilhelmine and Henri de Loubersac strolled on together in the direction of the Hippodrome. Mutual protestations of love were, exchanged. Presently Wilhelmine asked:

"But what brought you in this direction?"

"Oh, I was going ... to pay a visit ... it is a piece of very good luck my coming across you like this."

De Loubersac seemed to have something on his mind. Despite his protestations he did not look as if he were enjoying this chance meeting.

"Where were you bound for, Wilhelmine?" he asked.

She looked up at her lover with sad eyes. Pointing in the direction of the cemetery of Montemartre, she replied in a low tone:

"I am going to visit the dear dead."

"Would you allow me to accompany you?" begged de Loubersac.

Wilhelmine shook her head.

"I must ask you to allow me to go there alone. It is my custom to pray there without witnesses."

De Loubersac turned towards Mademoiselle Berthe with a questioning look — a gesture of interrogation.

Wilhelmine replied to it:

"As a rule I go to the cemetery alone. You see me with my companion to-day because my father wished it. Since the sad affair which has thrown a shadow over our life, he is in a constant state of anxiety about my safety: he does not wish me to go about unaccompanied. I shall be waited for at the cemetery."

Wilhelmine's candid eyes gazed at de Loubersac, who was gnawing his moustache with a preoccupied air.

"What is the matter, Henri?" she asked.

De Loubersac came closer to Wilhelmine, grew red as fire, and without daring to look her in the face, burst out:

"Listen, Wilhelmine! I would rather tell you everything....Oh, you are going to think badly of me....The truth is — our meeting is not accidental ... it is of set purpose on my part....For the last two days I have been worried — preoccupied — jealous....I am afraid of not being loved by you as I love you ... afraid that there is ... or was ... something between us — dividing us — someone."...

Wilhelmine looked at her lover with the eyes of an astonished child.

"I do not understand you," she murmured.

Mastering his emotion, de Loubersac decided to make a clean breast of it.

"I will be frank, Wilhelmine.... Your last words have increased my torture.... Have you not spoken of *your* dear dead, and must I learn that you are perhaps going to pray ... at the tomb of Captain Brocq?"

More and more astonished, Wilhelmine replied:

"And suppose I were going to do so? Should I be doing wrong to pray for the repose of the soul of the unfortunate Captain Brocq, who was one of my best friends?"

"Ah!" cried Henri de Loubersac: "Is it love you feel for him, then?" He looked so despairing that Wilhelmine, offended, hurt though she was by her lover's suspicions, pitied his anguish and reassured him:

"If you had been following me for some time past, you would have seen that I have been in the habit of going to this cemetery — have gone there regularly long before Captain Brocq's death — consequently."...

Wilhelmine, with a look of sorrowful disappointment, closed her lips: she was resolutely mute.

Henri de Loubersac brightened up, thanked her with a frankness so spontaneous, so sincere, that it would have touched the hardest woman's heart, and Wilhelmine's was a supremely tender and sensitive one. Yet, when he again asked for whom she was going to pray, for whom was the delicious bouquet of violets she was carrying, half hidden in her muff, she murmured:

"That is my secret.... If I told you the name of the person at whose tomb I am going to pray, it would have no significance for you."

"Wilhelmine! Let me accompany you!" implored de Loubersac.... "I love you so much — you must forgive my blundering!"

The lovers discussed the question: finally, Wilhelmine's hesitations were overcome: de Loubersac carried the day triumphantly.

Mademoiselle Berthe had fallen behind: she had kept a discreet distance between the lovers and herself, but had watched them with the eyes of a lynx. Now Wilhelmine waited for her to come up with them; then she requested her companion to stay in the quiet avenue Rachel while she and Lieutenant de Loubersac went into the cemetery.

No sooner had they disappeared than Bobinette set off as fast as she could go in the direction of the boulevard de Clichy. Yes, there was the sordid figure of Old Vagualame, bent under the weight of years and of his ancient accordion: he seemed to be stooping more than usual.

Had he also followed them? He had. Thus Juve-Vagualame was continuing his quest with the hope of getting further light on the series of mysteries he was seeking to solve. He must learn more of Bobinette's relations with Fantômas, whom she apparently knew only under the guise of Vagualame. Juve had made himself up so carefully that he felt confident even the bandit's intimates would not suspect they had to do with a police officer. Its quality was soon proved: Bobinette came towards him with not a sign of uneasiness.

"There you are, then!" she cried.

In spite of her familiar address, Juve noticed the touch of respect in Bobinette's voice — Vagualame played the part of master to this red-haired girl.

"What a long time it is since one had the pleasure of seeing you, my dear Monsieur Vagualame!" There was a touch of malicious irony in Bobinette's tone.

Juve-Vagualame nodded. He would have liked to know what Wilhelmine and Henri were doing in the cemetery, but Bobinette was his query for the moment. Her next remark was startling.

"It looks as though you were afraid to show yourself since your last crime."

Juve repressed any sign of the satisfaction this declaration gave him.

"My last crime?"

"Don't play the blockhead," she went on. "Have you forgotten that you told me how you had assassinated Captain Brocq?"

"That is ancient history," muttered Juve, "...and I am not afraid of anyone....Besides ...did I tell you that now?" he hinted, with the hope of obtaining further details. But Bobinette seemed to think she had had enough of the subject. She laughed.

"What a way of walking you have!" she exclaimed.

Juve was purposely exaggerating Vagualame's attitude: it enabled him to conceal his face better.

"I stoop so much because my age weighs me down....When you grow old.".....

Bobinette burst into peals of laughter.

"You don't think, do you, Vagualame, that I take you for an old man? Ha, ha! I know you are disguised; made up admirably, I dare say, but you are a young man....I am quite, quite sure of it!"

Juve was saying to himself:

"This grows better and better!"

Juve's conviction was that this old Vagualame, secret agent of the Second Bureau, murderer of Captain Brocq, the Vagualame he had encountered at Fandor's flat, could only be a young man in the flower of his age — could be none other than Fantômas.

Juve was about to put more questions to Bobinette, but two figures came into view, and they were nearing the avenue Rachel.

"Make off with you!" cried Bobinette. "There they are coming back!"

Juve did not wish de Loubersac to catch a glimpse of him: he would be surprised, suspicious, and would question him about the missed rendezvous. Juve had not gained sufficient information, however.

"I must see you again, Bobinette." His tone was pressing, insistent.

"When?"

"This evening."

"Impossible."

"To-morrow, then."

Bobinette shook her head.

"You know very well that to-morrow I shall be gone."

"Where?"

"Where?"

The red-haired beauty cried impatiently:

"It's you ask me that?...Why ...I go to the frontier."

"Correct," said Juve. He would have welcomed further details. "Well, then, when can we meet?" pressed this determined accordion player.

"How about next Wednesday?" suggested Bobinette.

"That will do. We will go to the theatre — a moving picture show!"

"Always to places in the dark, eh!" observed Bobinette maliciously.

Wilhelmine and Henri were coming nearer.

Juve-Vagualame turned as he was making off.

"Nine o'clock, before the moving picture place, rue des Poissonniers." With that, Juve-Vagualame disappeared into a smoky wine shop.

De Loubersac, very pale, and Wilhelmine, whose eyes were red, rejoined Bobinette, whose face became expressionless.

They went slowly off together.

When the coast was clear, Juve-Vagualame left the wine shop and proceeded towards the cemetery. Amid the cypresses and tombs of the necropolis, looming sad and shadowy in the fading light, he made his way slowly along the principal path, questing for traces of the lovers' footsteps in the sand. He was fortunate enough to come on them at once; the soil being moist, the lovers' footmarks could be clearly distinguished in the sand of the alleys. Guided by them,

Juve turned into a little pathway on the right, passing the mausoleums, and pausing before a new-made grave, that of Captain Brocq, a humble tomb. A few fresh violets were scattered around it, from Wilhelmine's bunch, no doubt. The lovers had but tarried there. Juve continued to follow their footmarks, by many twists and turns, almost to the end of the cemetery. As he advanced he felt more and more certain that he had come this way some years ago, when his detective work had led him into a mysterious network of robberies and murders, the moving spirit of them all being Fantômas — the enigmatic Fantômas.

Juve was going over in memory those past days of mysterious doings and strange adventures, when he found himself facing a vault richly decorated with unusually beautiful sculpture. A bronze plaque was affixed to this tomb, and on it, engraved in letters of gold, was a name Juve had had occasion to utter many a time and oft:

Lady Beltham

Lady Beltham!
Lady Beltham?
A name Juve associated with strange and terrible events.[3] Lady Beltham had been a sensational creature.

After adventures, one more extraordinary than another, Juve had succeeded in identifying this English great lady as the mistress of a formidable criminal, relentlessly hunted down, for ever escaping — the elusive Fantômas!

Juve had lost track of both, when the discovery of an extraordinary crime had led to the identification of the victim, a woman: she was declared to be — Lady Beltham. The corpse had been buried in this very cemetery; distant relatives in England had guaranteed all expenses connected with the burial and erection of this costly tomb.

The public had believed this to be the end of Lady Beltham. Juve presently discovered that Lady Beltham was not dead: another woman had been buried in her place. He preserved absolute silence convinced that sooner or later this criminal great lady — for, in conjunction with Fantômas, she had committed abominable crimes — would reappear, and he could then arrest her. Time had passed, but for all his efforts Juve could not discover the hiding-place of this strangely guilty woman.

When he saw a large bunch of violets lying before the door of Lady Beltham's vault, he divined them to be the offering of Wilhelmine.

Juve now asked himself if he had not come across this Wilhelmine in the past, this girl with pale gold hair, and clear deep eyes; if he had not, in the long ago, met under painful circumstances a little child who was now this pretty girl, beloved of Henri de Loubersac. Juve did not dwell on these vague, floating impressions. He turned his attention to more definite points.

There were people who believed in the death of Lady Beltham; they were in the majority: among these was Wilhelmine de Naarboveck. Why did she come to pray at Lady Beltham's tomb and bring offerings of fragrant flowers?

A mere handful of people knew Lady Beltham was not dead; knew that another woman had been interred in her stead. Lady Beltham herself knew it; her accomplice and lover — Fantômas — must know it. Besides, these two there was Jérôme Fandor who knew of the substitution, and there was Juve himself. What others could there be?

Twilight was deepening into darkness. The cemetery guardians were clearing it of visitors. Juve became once more the old accordion player.

As he made his way home on foot, he asked himself:

"What are they looking for?"

The military authorities, represented by the Second Bureau, want to recover a stolen document.... The civil authority, represented by Police Headquarters, wish to discover a murderer guilty of two crimes: the murder of Brocq — the murder of Nichoune.

The murderer of Brocq is assuredly Vagualame: as to the murderer of Nichoune: I do not yet know under what guise he committed his crime, but of one thing I am certain — the author of this double crime is none other than — Fantômas!

XV
THE TRAITOR'S APPRENTICESHIP

Although for the past four days Fandor had shown himself the most punctual, the most correct, the most brilliant of French corporals, although he had replaced the unfortunate Vinson with striking ability, it was never without a feeling of bewildered terror that he awoke each morning in the vast barrack-room at Saint-Benoit, Verdun.

No sooner was he dressed than he found himself in the thick of a life made up of fears, of ever-recurring alarms, a nightmare life, the strain of which was concealed by an alert confident manner, a gallant bearing. Never having done his military service, since legally he did not exist — it was the cruelest mystery in our journalist's life — Fandor had played his corporal's rôle by intuition, combined with a trained power of observation, Vinson's manual, and Vinson's verbal instructions. Vinson, for his own sake most of all, had utilised every minute, and had put the eager Fandor through several turns of the military mill.

Nevertheless, whenever he gave an order to the men of his squad, he asked himself with terror, whether he had not inadvertently committed some gross blunder, whether some inferior might not call out ironically:

"I say, Corporal Vinson, where the devil have you come from to be carrying on like that?"

"Suppose I were found out," he thought, "I wonder if they would shoot me forthwith, to teach me not to run such mad risks in search of information for police reports?"

On this particular morning, Fandor awoke with a stronger feeling of uneasiness than ever. The previous evening, the adjutant for the week had drawn him apart at roll-call, and had handed him a slip of paper.

"You have a day's leave! You have joined only four days, yet you have managed to obtain your evening! Smart work! Congratulations! By jove, you must have some powerful backing!"

Fandor had smiled, saluted, marched off to bed — but not to sleep.

"A day's leave! The devil's in it! Who signed for me? What is the next move to be?" he thought.

This very morning, at ten o'clock delivery, the post sergeant had handed him a card. It bore the Paris postmark: on it was drawn the route from Verdun to the frontier. That was all.

He remembered what Vinson had said to him in the flat:

"What is so terrifying about this spying business is that one never knows whom one is obeying, whose orders one ought to follow, who is your friend, who is your chief: one fine day you learn that you have had leave granted you: you then receive, in some way or another, directions to go to some place or another.... You go there ... you meet people you do not know, who ask you questions, sometimes seemingly trivial, sometimes obviously of the gravest importance.... It is up to you to find out whether you are face to face with your spy chiefs, or if, on the contrary, you have not fallen into a trap set by the police to catch spies.... You cannot go to a rendezvous with a quiet mind: how do you know that you will not be returned between two gendarmes!... It is impossible to ask for information: equally impossible to ask for help, should you be in imminent danger.... Spies do not know one another: they are disowned by whoever employs them: they are humble wheels hidden in an immense mechanism.... It matters little if they are broken to pieces, they can so easily be replaced!"

Fandor's recollection of these statements did not tend to make him cheerful. He summed up the situation, and came to a decision.

"I have been given leave I did not ask for: somebody must have asked it for me. This 'someone' is the chief spy, already in touch with Vinson, or the chief spy at Verdun, who has been warned of Vinson's arrival: the post card I received from an unknown individual has nothing on it but the indications of a route already known to me, that from Verdun to the frontier. I shall follow that route as a pedestrian, and I look forward to meeting some interesting persons on the way."

Surrounded by the noisy disorder of the barrack room, amidst men rising hastily that they might not be reported missing at the morning muster, which would shortly take place in the courtyard, Fandor-Vinson dressed quickly. He put on his sword-belt, ascertained that his servant had sufficiently polished the brass buttons on his tunic, his sabre, and other trappings. The adjutant for the week entered.

"You are off at once, Vinson?"

"Yes, sir."

"Good! I will arrange for the fatigues — very pleased to! Ah, you are new here, are you not? Well, I will give you a bit of good advice. Be in the barracks on the stroke of the hour. Remember, men on leave must not play tricks with punctuality."

"Right, sir!"

The adjutant turned sharp about and went off.

"He is jolly amiable, that's sure!" was Fandor's comment.... "I wonder, if by chance."...

Since Fandor had so rashly mixed himself up in this spy business, he was inclined to see everywhere traitors and accomplices; but he reminded himself that he must beware of preconceived ideas.

It was on the stroke of seven when Fandor showed his permit to the sergeant at the gate of the barracks.

"Here's one who's going to amuse himself," grumbled the sergeant. "Pass, Corporal!"

Fandor smiled joyously: but the smile did not express his real feelings.

Instead of making directly for the road to the frontier, he strolled about the town, went by roundabout ways, returned on his steps, assuring himself that he was not being shadowed.

The day was fine; a slight violet haze lingered in the hollows; the air, fresh but not chill, was deliciously pure. Fandor walked along the high road at a smart pace. He turned over in his mind certain warnings given him by Vinson.

"When an individual knows he is going to a rendezvous he makes a point of talking to every person he meets whom he thinks likely to be the individual he is to have dealings with."

But Fandor did not see a soul to speak to. The highway was deserted, and the fields lay empty and desolate as far as an eye could reach. Not a toiling peasant was to be seen.

He had been walking for over an hour, quite determined to carry this adventure through to the end, when, from the top of a hill he caught sight of a motor-car drawn up on one of the lower slopes of the road.

"They may, or may not, be the individuals I am out to meet," he thought: "but I am glad enough to meet some human beings....I shall stroll near their car, which seems out of action: it will help pass the time."

He went up to the motor-car. There were two people in it; a man clad in an immensely valuable fur coat, and a young priest, so muffled up in rugs and wraps and cloaks that only his two eyes could be seen.

Just as he got up to them, he heard the priest say in a tart voice to the man in the fur coat, now standing in the road:

"Whatever is the matter? What has gone wrong with your car now?"

The priest's smart companion exclaimed in a tone of comic despair:

"It is not the right front tire this time: it is the back tire, the left one, that is punctured!"

"Ought I to get out?"

"By no means! Do not stir! I am going to put the lifting-jack under the car, and shall replace the damaged tire in no time."

Fandor was only a few yards off.

The man in the fur coat, evidently his own chauffeur, half turned towards the soldier, adding:

"Unfortunately, my jack does not work very well, I doubt if I can succeed unaided in getting it under the wheel-base."

"Can I give you a lift?" asked Fandor.

The chauffeur turned with a smile.

"That is very kind of you, Corporal....I will not refuse your help."

From a box he extracted a lifting-jack which, to Fandor's expert eye, did not seem to function so badly as all that. The chauffeur slipped it under the car. Fandor lent an experienced hand, and lifted the wheel, whose tire had just given up the ghost.

"There, Monsieur! These punctures are the cause of endless delays," remarked Fandor, for the sake of saying something. The priest shrugged, and said in a disagreeable tone:

"Our tires have come to grief twice already this morning!"

The chauffeur was busied with his car fiddling with the machinery. He shot a question at Fandor:

"Are we far from Verdun?"

"Five or six kilometres."

"No more?"

"About that, Monsieur."

The chauffeur stood upright.

"It is Verdun, then, we can see over there?"

"What do you mean?" queried Fandor.

"That belfry in the mist."

"That is not a belfry: it is a chimney, the bakehouse chimney."

"Of the new bakehouse, then?"

"Yes, Monsieur."

"I had an idea it was not finished."...

"It is not finished, but it soon will be — in a matter of six months."...

"Ah! Good!...Now tell me is there no railway along the route we are following?"

"No. They intend laying down a line for strategic purposes, but they have not started on it yet."

The chauffeur smiled approval, while continuing to tinker at his machine.

"Ah, these projects!" he remarked. "They are long in coming to anything — these French administrative projects!"

"Well!... Yes."

There was a pregnant silence.

Fandor thought: "This grows interesting: it is quite on the cards that this tourist may be."...

"Ouf!" exclaimed the chauffeur, suddenly jumping up. "A stiff job this, Corporal! Will you be good enough to lend me a hand again?"

"Certainly."

"Oh, not just at once!...Let me rest a few moments! Doubled up as I have been, my back feels positively broken."

The stranger took a few steps along the road. He pointed to the horizon.

"One has a pretty view here!...You know this part of the country, Corporal?"

"So, so!...Fairly well."

"Ah! Then you can give me some information!...What is that other big chimney down there?...Do you see it?...Between those trees! Those two trees — there!"

"It is the chimney of the bell foundry."

"Ah, yes, I have heard that foundry mentioned, it is true....It seems to be quite near!"

Fandor shook his head.

"It seems to be — but, by the road, it is a good eleven kilometres away."

"As much as that? As the crow flies it is close to."

"Yes. It seems so."

The chauffeur insisted:

"But, how far do you think it is, Corporal, from here to it, in a straight line?...They ought to teach you to measure distances in your regiment!"

Fandor was no longer in doubt: this man was the spy he was out to meet! Fandor once again recalled Vinson's words: "When one has to do with a fresh spy chief, it is a certain thing that he will make you pass a little kind of examination ... will put you through a regular cross-examination to ascertain your capacities — what you are made of!"

Corporal Fandor-Vinson replied instantly:

"As the crow flies, I calculate it is not more than four kilometres. The road winds a great deal."

"Good! Good!" cried the chauffeur. "I should have said so, also."

It seemed to Fandor that the man in the costly fur coat hesitated, was on the point of asking a question, thought better of it, turned away, went back to his car. He called out:

"Look here, Corporal! Since you are so kind, help me with this lever!"

That was soon done. The inquisition recommenced.

"Have you been long with the Verdun garrison?"

"Oh, no! Only a few days!"

"You are not bored?"

"Why should I be?"

"I mean — you do not find the discipline severe?"

Fandor tried to find out what the man in the fur coat was driving at.

"Oh, I have not much to complain of: I can get leave pretty easily."

"And that is always pleasant," remarked the man in the fur coat. "Young soldiers in garrison towns have a deuced poor time of it — is that not so?...And they do not know how to amuse themselves when they have leave....But, no doubt you have friends here, Corporal?"

"I do not know a soul in Verdun."

"Ah, well, since you have been so obliging, it would give me pleasure to introduce you to some people, if you would care for it?...You would find them amusing."

"You have friends in Verdun, sir?" asked Fandor in his turn.

"I know a few people: so does the abbé who accompanies me. I have it!...an idea ...Corporal, come at six o'clock this evening ... no, seven o'clock, and very punctually, and ask for me at the printing office of the Noret Brothers. They are real good fellows! You will find some youngsters of your own age there. You will find you have much in common. I am sure they will prove useful acquaintances."

The man in the fur coat accented the word "useful."

This told Fandor that there was business on hand at the printing works — and he was to be involved in it.

"You are really too kind, sir!...I do not wish to."...

"Not at all! Not at all! It is nothing! And you have been so obliging!...Come to the Noret's at seven without fear of being considered an intruder!"

The man in the fur coat accentuated the word "fear" significantly. He set his motor going and jumped into the car.

"Again, many thanks, Corporal! I do not offer to take you back to Verdun, as my car has only two seats! Till this evening, then!"

The car moved off, rapidly putting on speed.

"There goes the chief spy!" thought Fandor. "Never set eyes on the fellow before, nor heard his voice, either! Now, whom shall I meet to-night at this cursed rendezvous, and what is the business? Some traitorous deviltry, of course!"

It was striking seven when Fandor presented himself at the Noret printing works.

He rang: he was admitted, and shown into a waiting-room. There was a touch of the convent parlour about it. The man who had opened to him asked:

"What name shall I give to the gentlemen, Monsieur?"

"Tell them it is Corporal Vinson."

Fandor's heart was beating like a sledge hammer as the minutes dragged by: it was an eternity of waiting! A flock of suspicions crowded his mind: might he not have fallen into a trap?

At last a tall, thin, red-bearded young man walked into the room: he greeted Fandor-Vinson with:

"Good evening, Corporal. Our mutual friends have informed us that we might expect you. They have not arrived yet; but there is no need to wait for a regular introduction — what do you think?"

"You are too kind, Monsieur. A simple corporal like myself is very fortunate to find friends in a garrison town."

"To pass the time till our friends arrive, what do you say to visiting the workshops?... You will find it interesting ... and useful."

"That word 'useful' again!" thought Fandor. "Decidedly there is business afoot to-night!"

His guide expanded.

"In Paris they despise provincial industries! They pretend to believe that no good work is done — can be done — in country districts....It is a mistaken notion! Examine our machines!"

The red-bearded young man ushered Fandor into the workshops. They were extensive, spacious.

"Here is the machine which prints off *The Beacon of Verdun*!" he explained. "You can see for yourself that it is the latest model! Do you know anything about the working of these machines?"

Fandor could hardly restrain his laughter.

"What would this guide of mine think if he knew that for a good many years I have had to cross the machine-room of *La Capitale* every evening, and consequently have been able to see and admire printing machines of a very different quality of perfection to this one he has praised so emphatically?"

Fandor-Vinson played up.

"It seems to me a marvellous machine! I should like to see it working!"

The red-bearded young man smiled.

"Come here some afternoon, and I will show you the machine in full work!...Come soon!"

He led Fandor to another part of the printing-room.

"Do you know anything about linotypes?"

Again Fandor-Vinson played the admirer's part, though he knew these machines were out-of-date.

"What is his game?" was our journalist's mental query.

The answer soon came. His guide led him to a strange-looking object concealed by some grey material. It might well be a cabinet for storing odds and ends, but Fandor felt sure the grey stuff covered something metallic.

"See, Corporal, this will please you!" said the red-bearded young man. He uncovered the object.

"You know what it is, do you, Corporal?"

"Not in the least!"

"A machine for making bank-notes!"

"Really! You manufacture bank-notes, do you?" remarked Fandor. His tone was non-committal.

"You shall see for yourself, Corporal! Of course they are only made for the fun of the thing — still, they might happen to prove useful — one never knows!"

Again the marked accent on "useful."

Again Fandor-Vinson played up.

"I should like to have a squint at those holy-joke notes!"

"I was going to suggest it!"

Turning a handle, the red-bearded young man put the machine in motion.

"Place yourself there, Corporal! Put your hands to it! You shall see what will happen!"

Fandor did as directed.

"Hold out your hands!"

Fandor-Vinson held out his hands.

A new fifty-franc note fell into them.

"What do you say to that? Is it not a good — a perfect imitation?" The red-bearded young man's tone was triumphant.

Fandor-Vinson examined it.

"That it certainly is," he acquiesced.

"Here are more!... Look!... Take them!"

Nine notes fell into the outstretched hands of Corporal Fandor-Vinson of the 257th of the line, stationed at Verdun.

Our journalist had sharp eyes. He was no longer puzzling over this performance.

"Look here, Corporal! Keep these notes if they amuse you!" said the red-bearded young man, smiling.

"You might even try to pass them off, if the joke appeals to you!"

Fandor's replies were monosyllables: he was watching the machine.

"What a childish trick!" he said to himself: "Why, these notes dropped into my hands are real!... This machine does not print anything!... My new friend has slipped these notes under the rollers as payment for future treachery, expected betrayals — it is a way of paying me!"

Corporal Fandor-Vinson found the necessary words to show he fully understood the quality of the payment — its real value. Supposing that no more would be required of him, he tried to get free of this spy, and leave the premises, but his red-bearded paymaster had other views.

"Now, Corporal," said he, "shall we empty a bottle together in honour of our meeting?"

Fandor was far from wishing to clink glasses with the spy: still, needs must when the devil drives you into a tight corner of your own choosing! The offer was accepted with feigned pleasure. Corporal Fandor-Vinson kept a smiling face, whilst, glass in hand, he talked trivialities with his host.

At last Corporal Fandor-Vinson rose:

"My leave has not expired, it is true, Monsieur," he said, "but I have some rounds to make. Pray excuse me!"

The thin, red-bearded young man did not seek to detain him. The interview was at an end: the business done for that evening.

"You will return, will you not, Corporal?" asked his host. "We are at your disposal, I and my brother, whenever you have need of us — our friends also. They will regret having arrived too late to meet you!... And, Corporal ...we know some officers — if you want leave now and again — you must let us know — will you not?"

Corporal Fandor-Vinson said the expected things, and hastened away, glad to be quit of this red-bearded young spy of a printer. He hurried off towards the centre of the town, covering his tracks as Juve had taught him how to do. He had time to spare before returning to barracks. He entered a small café and ordered a drink.

"Behold me one of the precious spy circle of Verdun," thought he. "I must make the most of my privileges."

His glass remained untouched while he sat thinking long and deeply.

XVI
AT THE ELYSÉE BALL

The ball was in full swing. There was a crush in the brilliantly lighted reception-rooms of the Elysée. Prominent members of Parliament, diplomats, officers naval and military, representatives of the higher circles of commerce, and finance, rubbed shoulders with the undistinguished, at the official reception given in honour of Japan's new ambassador, Prince Ito. The prince was stationed in the centre of the inmost drawing-room, gorgeously arrayed in his national costume, a delicate smile on his lips as he watched the President's guests with bright shrewd eyes, while music from an invisible Hungarian band floated on the air.

In this particular room two men were in earnest conversation: Colonel Hofferman and Lieutenant de Loubersac.

"Well, Lieutenant, I have been too pressed for time to-day to see you … but, Heaven knows, I have not forgotten for a moment the matter I entrusted to you…. They are causing me the greatest anxiety."…

"I can well understand that, Colonel."…

"Anything new?"

"No, Colonel…. That is to say — I ought to say 'No' to you."…

"What the devil do you mean?" The colonel stared at his junior a moment; then, taking him by the arm, said in a confidential tone:

"Let us take a turn in the garden, it is not cold…. We had better have our talk away from such a collection as this … one does not know who or what one's neighbours may be."

"Right, Colonel, prudence is the mother of surety."

The colonel shrugged.

"I have no desire to pun, but since you speak of La Sûreté,[4] I cannot help noticing that they are blundering terribly over these very affairs. Confound those clumsy fools and their meddling! They will interfere with things which are no concern of theirs — not in the slightest!"

"Are they still investigating?"

"No. The warning I myself administered to their famous Juve has taught them a lesson. They are keeping quiet at present. Plague take the lot of them!… It makes me furious when I think what happened the other day — creating a scandal about things the public ought to be kept in ignorance of — ought never to hear of — never!… Those confounded meddlers complicate our task abominably."

Colonel Hofferman paused: de Loubersac kept a discreet silence.

The two men were walking down the little path which encircles the principal lawn of the Elysée Gardens, now almost deserted.

The colonel turned to his companion.

"What was that you were saying just now?… You had something fresh to tell me, and you had not…. That is the Norman way of putting it!… Not like you, de Loubersac!"

"It is merely the answer of one who hesitates to speak out," replied de Loubersac, laughing, "… who hesitates to give a definite opinion, who, nevertheless."…

"Who nevertheless what?… De Loubersac, just forget I am your colonel — speak out, man!… Have you an idea of where the document was lost?"

"That?… No."…

"Then what conclusion have you arrived at? Have you further information about Brocq's death?"

"Hum!"…

"About Nichoune's death, perhaps?"

"Colonel! Have you noticed that for some time past I have not handed you any report from the agent Vagualame?"

"The deuce…. What do you imagine that means?"

"I do not imagine anything, Colonel — I state facts!... Nichoune is dead, murdered: there is not a shadow of a doubt about that.... Nichoune was the mistress of Corporal Vinson.... This Vinson was on the point of playing the traitor, if he had not already done so; he was also a friend of Captain Brocq, and Brocq died just when the document disappeared — the document confided to him by our service ... so much for facts."

The colonel was staring fixedly at de Loubersac.

"I do not see what you are driving at!" said he.

"I am coming to it, Colonel.... Nichoune was found dead on Saturday, November 19th, but on the evening of November 18th Nichoune received a visit from our agent, Vagualame, whom I had sent to Châlons by your own orders to occupy himself with the V. affair."

"Well?"

"Well, Colonel, I do not much like that, but what I like still less is, that, a few days ago, I had occasion to see Vagualame ... and this agent far from bringing me details of Nichoune's death, at first go off wanted to deny that he had been at Châlons! I could swear he was going to declare he had not been there, when a reply of my own — a blunder, I confess it — I did not take time to think — informed him that I knew of his visit to Nichoune."

Colonel Hofferman weighed the gravity of de Loubersac's words; he strode along, head bent, hands clasped behind his back, gazing with unseeing eyes at the pebbles on the path. At last he spoke.

"Tell me how you knew for certain that Nichoune had received a visit from Vagualame!"

"For some time past, Colonel, Vagualame has been under the eye of the officer charged with the supervision of our spies, de Loreuil. Under the guise of Aunt Palmyra he discovered that Nichoune had been murdered. This was the morning after her interview with Vagualame. The discovery, I may tell you, did not take de Loreuil altogether by surprise. He had observed Vagualame's attitude towards the girl, and had considered it queer — suspiciously so."

"This is serious, but it is not sufficiently definite," pronounced Colonel Hofferman.... "Let us admit that Vagualame has played a double game, has been at once traitor and spy. That being so, he may have murdered Nichoune; but as to incriminating this agent whom we have known a long time... well... you have merely a vague indication to go upon... the kind of reticence, or what you thought was reticence, he wished to maintain regarding his journey to Châlons."

"Yes," admitted de Loubersac, "if that were all I had to go upon, it would amount to little."

"You know something else?"

"I know that I arranged to meet this agent yesterday in the Garden, as our custom is, that I waited there, that he never turned up."

Colonel Hofferman took de Loubersac's arm as they walked slowly back to the reception-rooms.

"What you have just told me is exceedingly serious: we must enquire into this at once — without loss of time. If Vagualame has really fled, the probability is that he is Nichoune's murderer.... In that case, there is nothing to prevent our suspecting him of no end of things which I need not particularise."...

The colonel pointed to an individual standing by a buffet near the entrance to the great reception-room.

"Let us go the other way," said he. "There is Monsieur Havard! I do not at all want to meet him!... If we have to arrest Vagualame, it would be unnecessary to take Police Headquarters into our confidence."

"Undoubtedly, Colonel."

"Then let us keep clear of Monsieur Havard! Devote your whole attention to clearing up the questions raised by your talk. Find Vagualame for me in three days. If you have not run him to earth, then set our special enquiry men on his track.... I shall see you to-morrow at the Ministry — six sharp."

Whilst Colonel Hofferman and Lieutenant de Loubersac were having their talk, Jérôme Fandor, who was also at the Elysée ball, in his own proper person, was busying himself with the affairs which had led him to consider that the murder of Captain Brocq was a crime which must be imputed to one of those foreign spies with which France was now swarming. At Verdun, along the entire frontier, there were nests of these noxious vermin.

Fandor was, of course, still stationed at Verdun. He had arrived early at the ball, hoping to pick up information from some friend as to how the Second Bureau was taking the disappearance of Corporal Vinson. Did the Second Bureau suspect anything?... What?... Had Nichoune's murder been explained?

Fandor stationed himself near the entrance to the first reception-room, watching all who entered, seeking the welcome face of friend or acquaintance.

Someone slapped him on the shoulder.

"Hullo, Fandor! Are you reporting the official fêtes nowadays?"

"You, Bonnet? What a jolly surprise! I have heard nothing of you for ages. How goes it?"

"My dear fellow, good luck has come my way at last!... I am police magistrate at Châlons! There's news for you!"

"By Jove, Bonnet! That is good hearing! You arrive here in the very nick of time!"

"Old Bonnet at Châlons and police magistrate!" thought Fandor. "What a bit of luck for me!"

"I want to ask the police magistrate of Châlons most interesting things," said Fandor, smiling at his friend.

"Information for a report?" queried Bonnet.

"Just so."

Fandor drew his "old Bonnet" away from the crowd of eyes and ears around them. They came on an empty little smoking-room. The very place!

"Now tell me, my dear Bonnet, have you not been engaged on a recent case — the death of a little singer, called."...

"Nichoune?... That is so. My first case at Châlons."

"Ah!... Now, just tell me!"

The examining magistrate shook his head.

"I cannot tell you much, for the good reason that this affair is as mysterious as can be, and is giving me no end of trouble.... You knew Nichoune, Fandor?"

"Yes — and no.... I would give a good deal, though, to know who her murderer is!"

"I also," said Bonnet, smiling. "Would I not like to put my hand on the collar of that individual!... Naturally, I want to carry through the enquiry with flying colours!"

"Have you no idea as to who the murderer might be?"

Police Magistrate Bonnet rose.

"That is as may be!... It seems that on the eve of her death, this Nichoune received a visit from an old man — a beggar — whom I am unable to identify — who has vanished into thin air.... Would you like me to keep you informed? Rue Richer is still your address?"

"Yes. It would be awfully kind of you to write when you have any fresh facts to disclose about this case. I cannot explain to you all the importance I attach to that, but it is enormous!"

"It is understood, then! Count on me. I shall tell you all I can without breaking professional secrecy.... Shall we take a turn through the rooms, old boy?"

"If you like, my dear Bonnet."

The two men strolled through the thinning rooms, talking of what all the world might hear.

"Dear boy, I must leave you," said Fandor suddenly.... "An interview!... Till our next meeting!"

Fandor went up to a man standing in a doorway, gazing disdainfully at the couples revolving in the centre of the room.

"Will you grant me a word or two, Monsieur Havard?" asked Fandor respectfully.

The chief of police brightened.

"Four, if you like, my good Fandor, I am bored to death. I would rather submit to your indiscreet questioning than stick here in a brown study — black, I might say — with only my own thoughts for company."

"Good heavens, Chief! What is troubling you to such an extent?"

Monsieur Havard laughed.

"Oh, I will tell you the reason of this melancholy mood!...You are on pretty intimate terms with Juve, are you not?"

"You have heard from him, Chief?"

"No, it is precisely."...

"You are anxious, then?"

"No, no! Be easy!" smiled Monsieur Havard.

He caught Fandor by the lapel of his coat.

"Look here, my dear fellow! It is precisely because you and Juve are on such intimate terms — this friendship between you is a fine thing — that I should like you to use your influence with Juve."

"With Juve?"

"Yes. With Juve. You know how highly I esteem him? He is our best detective. Very well he is making a thorough mess of his career: he prevents his own promotion, because he is so obstinately set on searching for his elusive, fugitive, never-to-be-caught Fantômas!"

"I do not understand you, Chief."

"You soon will. Do you know where Juve is at this moment?"

"No."

"I am as ignorant of his whereabouts as you are!...It is beyond bearing!...Juve goes his own way beyond what is allowable. He declared to me, the other day, that he was certain the death of Captain Brocq must be credited to — whose account do you think?...Why to Fantômas! And clac! Since then I have not heard a word from him! Juve is pursuing Fantômas! Now, Fandor, how can I tolerate this?"

Fandor considered Juve had a perfect right to take his own initiative in this particular matter — he had earned the right if ever a man had. He answered his aggrieved chief with a question.

"But suppose Juve is right?"

"Right?...But he deceives himself....I have proof of it!"

"You have proof of it?...But who then, according to you, Chief, has killed Brocq?"

"My dear fellow," said Monsieur Havard, in a positive tone, "for a logical mind that reasons coolly, for one who does not bewilder himself in a network of Fantômas hypotheses, he who killed Brocq is assuredly he who has killed Nichoune! Brocq, I imagine, was killed by someone lying in wait on the top of the Arc de Triomphe. An accomplice, during this time, or some hours before — it matters little — had stolen the document the Ministry are looking for.... Brocq knew Corporal Vinson ...you are aware of that, Fandor?"

"Yes, yes! Please continue!"

"Good. Vinson had the murdered Nichoune as his mistress....Do you not think the link between these two names is evident?...Brocq and Nichoune have died by the same hand."...

"But all this does not exclude Fantômas as the guilty person!"

"You go too fast, Fandor. I know who killed Nichoune!"

"Oh! I say!"

"But I do. Deuce take it, you do not suppose I go by what these officers of the Second Bureau are doing in the way of a search, do you?...They fancy they are detectives!"

"Oh, that is going too far, surely!" expostulated Fandor.

"No," asserted Monsieur Havard. "Who did the deeds?...I know. The investigations of my own agents, the information obtained through the Public Prosecutor and the magistrates, point to one person — Vagualame — an old sham beggar, who has relations of sorts with the Second Bureau."

Fandor could scarcely keep his countenance: he nearly burst into derisive laughter. Vagualame guilty! Monsieur Havard evidently had not all the facts. Could he possibly realise that Vagualame was one of Colonel Hofferman's most trusted men?

Jealous of the Second Bureau and all its works, Monsieur Havard meant to carry off the honours this time: he was going to arrest Vagualame as the murderer of both Captain Brocq and Nichoune! And then what a jolly blunder Police Headquarters would make! What a fine joke! Fandor really must help it on! He said to himself:

"Only let the police paralyse the action of the Second Bureau agent, old Vagualame, and I, the false Corporal Vinson, will be all the more free to act."

"You have serious circumstantial evidence against this person?" Fandor asked with a grave face.

"Very serious. I know for certain that he saw Nichoune the evening before her death: he was even the last person known to have spoken to the singer. I know that he then left Châlons, and has not returned there!...I know that he was on good terms with very shady people, some of whom are suspected of spying; and all that.".…

Fandor interrupted:

"If I were in your place, Chief, and knew what you seem to know, I would not hesitate a moment....I should arrest Vagualame!"

Monsieur Havard's glance was ironical.

"Who told you that I had not so decided?...At this moment my best trackers are out on Vagualame's trail.…If I run him to earth, he will not be at large long, I can promise you! It would end a bothersome affair, and would open the eyes of Colonel Hofferman who must be a hundred leagues from imagining that Vagualame is the murderer of Captain Brocq and Nichoune."

On this Fandor and Monsieur Havard parted. Dancing went gaily on in the warm, perfumed atmosphere of the ball-rooms; but Fandor and Monsieur Havard, Colonel Hofferman and Lieutenant de Loubersac had had their serious interviews and had gone their respective ways.

XVII
IN THE STRONGHOLD OF THE ENEMY

The curtain with its pictured red cock was down, lights were up in the modern Cinema Concert Hall, rue des Poissonniers. Most of the spectators were on the move. An old white-bearded man of poverty-stricken appearance rose from his seat beside a pretty, red-haired girl, elegantly dressed. He murmured:

"I am going out for a smoke."

The girl nodded. She stared at the spectators with indifferent eyes. They were mostly women and girls. There was a mingled odour of hot coffee and orange peel. Drinks and refreshments, for the good of the house, were now the order of the evening.

The odd-looking old fellow, with a shabby accordion slung over his bent shoulders, making his way to the exit, was detective Juve, Juve-Vagualame in fact. He had kept the appointment made with Bobinette a week ago. This cinema entertainment in an unfashionable quarter suited his purpose exactly. In such an audience his appearance would attract but little attention, and the long intervals of darkness were all in his favour. Bobinette must not have her suspicions aroused.

Juve-Vagualame marched up and down outside the hall, rubbing his hands with satisfaction. Things were going well. Bobinette had been with him less than an hour, but she had given him an almost complete account of her doings during the past week. She announced that her trip to the frontier had been crowned with success: that the plan arranged with Corporal Vinson had proved astonishingly successful. She could not praise this wonderful Vinson enough. How intelligent he was? Say but half a word and he understood everything. As cynical as you please, he would stick at nothing, declaring himself ready for anything, regardless of consequences!

From this, Juve-Vagualame gathered that Corporal Vinson was a daring traitor, was the most out-and-out scoundrel imaginable.

Bobinette also told her supposed chief that the moment for the great stroke was at hand. She whispered low: "To-morrow Vinson will be in Paris!"

Juve had already learned that Vinson was stationed at Verdun, was granted frequent leave, and that on the morning of December 1st he would be in Paris. This was the evening of November 30th! Bobinette had not said exactly what he was coming to do, and Juve feared to ask questions that might arouse the red-haired girl's suspicions.

A shrill-sounding bell warned spectators that the interval was over. Juve-Vagualame returned to his seat. He was saying to himself:

"I must know exactly what Vinson is coming to Paris for."

After several attempts, he drew an important statement from Bobinette. He played the part of sceptic. The more enthusiastically convinced Bobinette was that the "great affair" would be successful, the more sceptical he grew.

She committed herself to a statement of extreme importance.

"Don't I tell you, old unbeliever that you are, that Corporal Vinson is to bring the plan of the piece in question?"

"The plan!" objected Juve-Vagualame. "That is good, as far as it goes; but that is not sufficient!"

Bobinette shrugged her plump shoulders. She was exasperated. The noise of the orchestra covered the sound of her imprudently loud answers.

"Since I tell you I have in my hands the piece of the gun which is to go to the Havre agent! I expect you have forgotten the details concerning this object? The manufacture of it is so complicated that, without the design for its construction, the piece would be much like any other.... We have the piece — I tell you it is in our hands.... To-morrow we shall possess the design of it, thanks to Vinson — can we possibly expect anything more complete than that?"

There was a pause. Then Bobinette announced:

"If, after that, you do not pay me what you owe me, you can be sure I shall not serve you ever again!"

Juve-Vagualame promised immediate payment.

"But," said he to himself, "her remuneration will not take the form she expects!"

To mislead the curious, the serious talk of this incongruous pair was punctuated by loud-voiced remarks having no connection with the real matter in hand.

Juve's one idea now was to see this piece of a gun for himself. When Bobinette, at last, grasped this, she stared at him with bewildered eyes.

"But what are you thinking of, Vagualame? I do not carry the thing about with me."

"I think, on the contrary, that you keep it well hidden in your own room."

"Assuredly," confirmed Bobinette.

"I mean to see it. I expect you to agree to that," declared Juve-Vagualame.

"You intend to come to?"... Bobinette looked terrified.

"Exactly."

"But when? Do you recollect, Vagualame, that I shall have to hand it over early to-morrow morning?"

"There is time for me to see it between then and now! See it, I must! Examine it, hold it in my hands, I will! I have my most excellent reasons for this!"

Juve meant to seize the piece of a gun and arrest the guilty girl.

Bobinette dared not openly kick against her chief's iron determination; but she made another attempt to turn him from his purpose.

"You know quite well that I am living in the Baron de Naarboveck's house. The least noise, an alarm raised, and I would not answer for the consequences: we should almost certainly be caught!"

"We have nothing to fear. An hour from now I wish to be in your room!"

"But — how shall you get into it?" asked Bobinette, who was giving way before this persistent attack.

"You will return alone. You will go up to your room. I know whereabouts it is: you will leave the window half open. I will enter your room by the window."

Bobinette saw this was possible, though risky. A large gutter pipe ran up the whole height of the house; it was fastened to the wall by projecting clamp-hooks of solid iron. For an agile man this was simply a staircase. Bobinette was aware of this. In the course of her adventurous life, she had been initiated into all sorts of tricks and stratagems; she was practiced in every form of gymnastic exercise. Vagualame could and would reach her room by the gutter-pipe ladder, it was not too difficult; but it was a risky undertaking, for, and particularly from the Esplanade des Invalides, a climber might be seen, an alarm raised, and the police would intervene.

Juve-Vagualame and Bobinette left the "movies" hall at half-past ten. In a taxi they discussed how best to effect an entrance into the de Naarboveck mansion. Juve-Vagualame stuck to his original idea.

The taxi drew up at the bridge. Juve-Vagualame paid the driver. Bobinette hurried away, slipped into the house, and went straight up to her room. She busied herself with the preparations agreed on, whereby Vagualame could the more easily effect an entrance in his turn.

Safe in her room, Bobinette experienced a strange, a penetrating emotion. She felt as though something around her in which she had moved safely, was cracking; with a sudden and terrible lucidity she saw herself marching forward, powerless to draw back, marching helplessly towards an abyss — an abyss which was about to engulf her! She trembled, trembled violently. She was encompassed by vague and agonizing terrors.

Out in the night Juve, wandering restlessly, awaited his hour! This time! Ah, this time! He murmured:

"I shall be in the stronghold of the enemy at last!"

XVIII
IN THE NAME OF THE LAW!

The Baron de Naarboveck and his daughter, Wilhelmine, were comfortably seated before a wood fire in the library. So numerous were their social engagements they rarely had time for a quiet talk together. Wilhelmine was in good spirits. De Naarboveck listened with an indulgent smile to her vivacious account of the little happenings and doings of her day. Presently a more serious subject came up for discussion. The word "marriage" was mentioned. Wilhelmine blushed and lowered her eyes, while the baron sounded her teasingly on her feelings for de Loubersac.

"My dear child," said the baron; "this young officer has a fine future before him; he is charming; is sufficiently well connected; adequately endowed with this world's goods; bears a known name; you would find him a suitable match."

Wilhelmine kept silence. An anxious, preoccupied look replaced her bright expression: her animation had died down. At last she murmured:

"Dear father, I have nothing to hide from you, and I willingly confess that I love Henri with my whole heart. I know he loves me also; but I ask myself whether he will not raise objections when he learns my life's secret!"

"My dear child, there is nothing in this secret which impugns your honor: you are not the responsible party. If, up to the present, I have thought it well to introduce you to my friends as my dau."...

De Naarboveck stopped short; the library door had opened. A footman appeared and announced:

"A woman has just arrived with her son, and wishes to see Mademoiselle or Monsieur. She says it is the new groom she has brought."

The baron looked puzzled. Wilhelmine rose.

"I forgot to tell you I was expecting the stable boy this evening. He replaces Charles."

She turned to the impassive footman.

"Please ask Mademoiselle Berthe to attend to these persons. They come late — much too late!"

"Mademoiselle will please excuse me for troubling her," replied the footman, "but Mademoiselle is still out, and."...

"In that case I will see them myself, though it is an unconscionable hour — not at all a good beginning."...

The woman and her son had been shown into the smoking-room. When Wilhelmine entered, the pair bowed respectfully.

The would-be groom was a nice-looking lad, and gave the impression of being superior to the common run of his class and calling. Agreeably surprised, Wilhelmine asked to see his references: she wished to make sure that they were in order; preliminaries, through the medium of an agent, had been gone into some days before. The woman displayed them, announcing in a loud, harsh voice:

"I am his mother!"

This mother was as unpleasant to behold as her son was the contrary, thought Wilhelmine.

She was a stout, vulgar, clumsy creature, enveloped in a large shawl of many colours which did not hide her obesity. The old termagant's face seemed all paint and large gold-rimmed spectacles, and peering eyes. This grotesque visage was shaded by a flowered veil.

"What a horrid old creature!" thought Wilhelmine, as she listened with scarcely concealed distaste to the woman's voluble praises of her son's qualities....According to her, he was a marvel of marvels.

Monsieur de Naarboveck remained in the library pacing up and down, smoking an expensive cigar. Wilhelmine did not return. Feeling sleepy, he quitted the room and went down the long gallery at a leisurely pace. The reception rooms opened on to it. The spacious entrance hall was visible from the wrought-iron balustrade bordering this gallery.

The baron stopped. He listened. Surely there were voices in animated discussion in the vestibule! Yes. Men were arguing with the porter — insisting.... The porter was coming up. The baron went down to meet him. Two men, in derby hats and tightly buttoned overcoats, confronted him. They carried neither stick nor umbrella, their hands were gloveless. There was an air of suppressed haste about them. They saluted. One of the two offered his card. The baron read:

Inspector Michel,
Detective Force,
Police Headquarters.

"Kindly follow me, gentlemen!"

De Naarboveck walked quietly up the grand staircase, his hand on its superb wrought-iron balustrade.

The two men followed in silence.

The baron opened the smoking-room door, saw it was empty, entered, signed to the policemen to follow, and closed the door.

"To what do I owe the honour of your visit, gentlemen?"

De Naarboveck's tone was icy.

Inspector Michel spoke.

"You must pardon us, Monsieur. Only a matter of the most serious importance — exceptionally serious — could have brought us to your house at so late an hour.... We hold a warrant, and, with your permission, we shall proceed to make an arrest."

De Naarboveck looked fixedly at the policemen.

"Gentlemen, that you should invade my house at such an hour, this matter must indeed be of singular importance," he said stiffly. Then, in a voice quivering with sarcasm, he enquired:

"Am I to be permitted to know what it is all about?"

"There is no harm in asking that, Monsieur," replied Inspector Michel, in a matter-of-fact tone. "The individual we have come to arrest here is a ruffian, wanted for a couple of murders: that of a Captain Brocq, and that of a little music-hall singer called Nichoune."

That this statement had upset the baron was evident: he had grown white to the lips. Inspector Michel realised that the idea of this double-dyed murderer having taken refuge in his house must have given the rich diplomat a horrid surprise. He continued his statement.

"The individual we have come to arrest is known under the name of Vagualame!"

"Vagualame!" stammered de Naarboveck. He staggered slightly and caught at the mantelpiece for support.

"How upset the baron is!" thought Inspector Michel. "Hardly to be wondered at!" He hurried on with his statement.

"We were on the watch on the Esplanade des Invalides, about half an hour ago — nothing to do with this affair — when we saw Vagualame approaching this house."

"You saw Vagualame!" exclaimed the baron, with the amazed, incredulous look of a man who finds himself suddenly faced by a set of lunatics. "But — it's — it is.".... he gasped.

"It is so, Monsieur," asserted Inspector Michel. "This old ruffian, after lingering about a few minutes to assure himself that he was not being followed — we managed to conceal ourselves sufficiently behind the trees — Vagualame effected a most suspicious entry into your house, Monsieur. He climbed the wall with the help of a gutter-pipe, and entered the house through a half-opened window on the third floor! You permit, Monsieur, that we take action at once!"

Without waiting for the baron's authorisation, Inspector Michel made a sign to his colleagues. They removed their overcoats, placed them on a chair, drew out their revolvers, and left the room.

The detectives were on the first steps of the flight of stairs leading to the third story, when they heard voices just above them. The piercing notes of the new groom's mother mingled with the refined accents of Wilhelmine de Naarboveck, who, in the absence of her companion, was about to show the new groom the room allotted to him. In such matters Wilhelmine was more punctilious than most.

"Did you hear, Vagualame?"

Bobinette paled. Could her overstrung nerves be playing her tricks? No.... There certainly were voices, voices on the floor below, strange voices!... Whose?... Why?

Vagualame was seated at the foot of the bed, much at his ease. His accordion lay on the floor. He met Bobinette's urgency with a shrug.

"Bah!"

With a despairing gesture, the terrified girl moved close to the old man.

"Don't you understand?... They have seen you! They are after you!... Master!" Bobinette bent forward, looked Vagualame in the eyes ... started ... drew back with a jerk.

This was not the Vagualame she knew!... Not her master!... Who, then?... Who but an enemy?... A police spy?... Horror!... She was trapped!... Lost!

Her heart was beating frightfully — beating to bursting point. Were her knees going to give way?... They should not!... Play the poltroon?... Never!... Rage boiled up in her; brain and will were afire.... She submit to the humiliation of arrest, the long-drawn-out agonies of cross-examinations, the tortures of imprisonment in Noumea?... Not Bobinette!... Never, never, never!

Almost simultaneously with her backward jerk from the stranger eyes of this Vagualame, Bobinette darted to a chiffonier, slipped her hand into a drawer among ribbons and laces, seized a revolver, and snatched it out....

Agile as a panther, Vagualame leaped at the girl, caught her wrist in a grip like a vice. The pain of it was intense — Bobinette dropped her weapon.

"No more of this nonsense!" commanded Vagualame in a hard voice.

"Keep cool, I tell you!... Go on to the landing. Look over. See what is happening. You are not to be afraid."

Struck speechless, Bobinette stared at the old man, who commanded her as a master, and might stand by her as an accomplice — but — those terrifying eyes were not the eyes of her own Vagualame — no! How to act?

She was left no choice. The old man was pushing her relentlessly towards the door. He must be obeyed.

Listening, on the alert, Juve-Vagualame remained in the room, ready to conceal himself behind the curtains. Who were these mounting the stairs? Some of the household? Suppose Bobinette's agitation was so marked that it aroused their suspicions, and his presence was revealed?... Should the position become untenable, he would leave by the window, close to which he was standing, make his way over the roofs to a neighbouring house — but — confound it!... neither the gun piece would be in his hands, nor would he have learned where Bobinette had her rendezvous with Corporal Vinson next morning!...

Bobinette was swaying in the doorway, as though the landing were red-hot ploughshares to be walked on! The ordeal was beyond her!

Four persons set foot on the landing. (A peremptory order from de Naarboveck had caused Wilhelmine to descend.)

Inspector Michel and his colleague stared at the individuals in whose company they found themselves — the young groom and his amazing mother!

With a caricatural gesture of disdain, and an off-handed air, this corpulent personage demanded stridently:

"Who are these gentlemen?"

Inspector Michel looked the outrageous creature up and down.

"Who are you, Madame?... What are you doing here?"

The inspector's tone was severity itself.

Juve, behind his window-curtains, breathed a sigh of relief.

"Ah, Michel has it in hand! That's all right!"

The groom's mother was taken aback — she hesitated; thereupon, Inspector Michel stated his name and rank! On that, the large body of this irrepressible personage made straight for him, caught him familiarly by the neck, and whispered in his ear.

The effect of the whispered words was to put Inspector Michel out of countenance: he looked abashed. He was annoyed: his tone was one of protest.

"I recognise you now, certainly — Monsieur!... But since when have you taken it upon yourself to — to start operations of the kind we have in hand — we, the representatives of Police Headquarters?"

The woman's retort was haughty.

"I belong to the information department of the Second Bureau."

"The Second Bureau does not make arrests — not that I am aware of — Captain!"

The obstreperous mother of the pretended groom was — Captain Loreuil!

Pointing to his young companion, Captain Loreuil announced:

"This gentleman belongs to the secret service department of the Home Office!... But what really matters, Inspector, is that we are losing time! Let us effect a capture — the capture is the thing!"

The distracted Bobinette, still swaying in the doorway, failed to grasp the full meaning of what these intruders were saying. Inspector Michel marched up to the trembling girl.

"Mademoiselle! Are you alone in your room?"

Bobinette nodded. She was incapable of speech. The inspector ignored the nod, brushed past her, stepped into the room and glanced rapidly round.

Bobinette, wild-eyed with fear, watched the proceedings. She saw the stout woman moving the chairs, looking under the bed, shaking the hangings. The fussy, obnoxious creature tore apart the window-curtains.... Vagualame was exposed to view!... He had not escaped, then!

They dragged the old fellow from his hiding-place: they promptly handcuffed him.

"Vagualame! In the name of the law I arrest you!" declared Inspector Michel.

Captain Loreuil shouted in his natural voice, which, issuing from this apparent woman, had a ludicrous effect:

"Ha! at last we have got him!"

Juve-Vagualame did not budge. With inward joy, he awaited the arrest of Bobinette.

"Things go well," he thought: "if not so well as old Michel believes. Comrade Juve in the bracelets, and Vagualame free! But he holds Bobinette in his hand — the old ruffian's accomplice, unmasked!"

What was this? Could Juve believe his ears?... Michel apologising to this guilty creature! Felicitating her on her escape from Vagualame's clutches! What the deuce?...

"Ah, Mademoiselle! You never suspected who was so near you, now did you?" Inspector Michel was saying to Bobinette, whose self-confidence was beginning to return.

"You have certainly had a narrow escape," he went on with a congratulatory smile. "This old ruffian meant to murder you, I am convinced."

Pointing triumphantly to Juve-Vagualame, he added:

"But Vagualame cannot harm you now! The law has got him! The law has saved you, Mademoiselle!"

Inspector Michel made a sign. His colleague and the Home Office detective dragged Juve from the room. Juve offered no resistance.

"That Michel is an idiot — the completest of idiots," he thought.

"Come along, now! We are off to the Dépôt!" commanded Michel, shaking Juve-Vagualame by the shoulder.

Juve was about to tear off his false beard, make himself known, and get Bobinette arrested. He thought better of it. He was pretty sure the girl doubted his genuineness. This arrest under her eyes would persuade her that the Vagualame they were taking to prison was the real Vagualame.... Better that she should cherish this delusion for the present. Once out of the de Naarboveck house, he could explain matters to his colleagues.

Thinking thus, Juve-Vagualame, encircled by watchful policemen, descended the stairs. On the first floor he caught a glimpse of the baron and his daughter in the ante-room. De Naarboveck's bearing was dignified: Wilhelmine seemed terribly frightened. There was a scared, hunted look on her pallid face.

Behind Juve-Vagualame in his handcuffs followed the pseudo-mother. Judging it unwise to make himself known to the master and mistress of the house, Captain Loreuil played his part vigorously to the last. Close on Juve's heels he came, shouting:

"This is a nice kind of shop, this is!... You shall not remain here, Sosthène, my child! Come, then, with your mother! She will find you a very different situation to this! My poor Sosthène!"...

Majestically, with a wave of her arm signifying disdainful rejection, the pseudo-mother drew her shawl of many colours about her corpulent person and sailed out of the de Naarboveck mansion.

Meanwhile, up on the third floor, a puzzled, confused, battered Bobinette was recovering from the shocks and terrors of the evening. She lay back in an arm-chair trying to piece things together.

Two things were clear: Vagualame was arrested; she was free, and with the famous gun piece still in her possession.... To-morrow, she would obey orders received: she would take the piece to Havre, accompanied by Corporal Vinson, who would bring the plan of the apparatus.

Bobinette had bent her head to the storm: she now raised it proudly.

XIX
THE MYSTERIOUS ABBÉ

Fandor half opened his eyes. Was he dreaming? This was not the barrack dormitory, with its gaunt white-washed walls and morning clamour....Of course! He was in a bedroom of a cheap hotel in Paris. Cretonne curtains shaded the window. A ray of light was reflected in a hanging mirror of scant dimensions, decidedly the worse for wear. Below it stood a washstand. On its cracked and dirty marble top could be seen a chipped and ill-matched basin and soapdish. A lopsided table occupied the middle of the room. On a chair by his bed lay Fandor-Vinson's uniform. His valise reposed on a rickety chest of drawers. Fandor was loath to rouse himself. His bed was warm, while about the room icy draughts from ill-fitting door and window were circulating freely.

He would have to get up presently, dress, and keep his appointment. His appointment! Ah! Wide awake now, our journalist considered the situation.

A couple of days ago the adjutant had announced:

"Corporal Vinson, you have eight days' leave: you can quit barracks at noon to-morrow."

Fandor had been given leave several times already: he merely replied:

"Thanks, Lieutenant."

He then looked out for a post card from the spies, appointing a rendezvous. A letter was handed to him by the post sergeant.

The letter commenced:

"*My dearest darling*"....

"Ah!" thought Fandor. "Now I am indeed a soldier. I receive a love letter!"

His unknown correspondent wrote:

"*It is so long since I saw you, but as you have eight days' leave I can make up for lost time! Would you not like to arrange a meeting for your first morning in Paris? You will go as usual, will you not, to the Army and Navy Hotel, boulevard Barbès? You will find me at half-past eleven to the minute, in the rue de Rivoli, at the corner of the rue Castiglione. We might breakfast together. To our early meeting, then! I send you all my kisses.*"

The signature was illegible.

Fandor understood the hidden meaning. He was to hand over the design as he had promised; but he had decided to put them off with a concocted design of his own! He must hasten now to the appointed meeting place.

Fandor rose at once. Whilst dressing he decided:

"I shall go in mufti — be Jérôme Fandor, undisguised. Better be on the safe side — this may be an anti-spy trap. Of course I shall miss my rendezvous; but *they* will not be put off so easily. They will write at once, making a new appointment. Then I shall go as Corporal Vinson, if I think it the wisest thing to do."

Fandor ran down the rickety stairs. He learned from Octave, the hotel porter, that his room had been paid for three days in advance. Saying he would not be back until the evening, probably, Fandor stepped on to the boulevard Barbès, and hailed a cab.

"Take me to the foot of the Vendôme column," he ordered.

Arrived at the rendezvous, Fandor sauntered along, awaiting developments. Presently he noticed in the distance a figure he seemed to know. It was moving towards him.

"My word! I was not mistaken," thought Fandor, watching the young woman. She also was sauntering under the arcades of the rue de Rivoli, glancing at the fascinating display of feminine apparel in the shop windows. Fandor drew aside, watching her every movement, and swearing softly.

The girl came nearer. Fandor's curiosity made him make himself known, that he might see what she would do. He showed himself, and saluted with an impressive wave of his hat, exclaiming:

"Why, it is Mademoiselle Berthe!"

The girl stopped.

"Why — yes — it is Monsieur Fandor!... How are you?"

"Flourishing, thanks! I need not ask how you are, Mademoiselle!... You bloom!"

Bobinette smiled.

"How is it I find you here at this time of day?"

"Why, Mademoiselle, just in the same way as you happen to be here — the fancy took me to pass this way!... I often do."

"Oh!" cried Bobinette in an apologetic tone. "Now, I am going to ask you how it is you have never responded to Monsieur de Naarboveck's invitation to take a cup of tea with us now and then! We were speaking of you only the other day. Monsieur de Naarboveck said he never saw your signature in *La Capitale* now — that most probably you were travelling."

"I have, in fact, just returned to Paris. Are all well at Monsieur de Naarboveck's? Has Mademoiselle Wilhelmine recovered from the sad shock of Captain Brocq's death?... His end was so sudden!"

"Oh, yes, Monsieur."

Fandor would have liked to find out the exact nature of Bobinette's intimacy with the ill-fated officer, also to what extent she was in love with Henri de Loubersac; but, as she showed by her manner that she did not relish this talk, either because of the turn it had taken, or because it was held in a public place, Fandor had to take his leave. Bobinette went off. Fandor noted the time as he continued his saunter. It was a quarter to twelve. Of the few passers-by there was not one who merited a second glance or thought!... Impatiently he waited, five, ten minutes: at one o'clock he betook himself to his hotel. There he found an express message, unsigned. It ran:

"My darling, my dear love, forgive me for not meeting you this morning in the rue de Rivoli, as arranged. It was impossible. Return to the same place at two o'clock, I will be punctual, I promise you.... Of course you will wear your uniform. I want to see how handsome you look in it!"

"I do not like this," thought Fandor, rereading the message. "Why ask me to come in uniform?... Do they know I came in mufti this morning?... I shall go again; but I think it is high time I returned to civilian life!"

It was two by the clock on the refuge, in the rue de Rivoli. Fandor-Vinson emerged from the Metropolitan and crossed to the corner of the rue Castiglione. He took a few steps under the arcade, saying to himself:

"Punctual to the tick and in uniform! The meeting should come off all right this time!"

A delicately gloved hand was placed on his shoulder, and a voice said:

"My dear Corporal! How are you?"

Fandor-Vinson turned sharply and faced — a priest!... He recognised the abbé. It was he of the Verdun motor-car.

"Very well! And you, Monsieur l'Abbé?... Your friend? Is he with you?"

"He is not, my dear Corporal!"

"Is he at Verdun?"

The abbé's reply was a look of displeasure.

"I do not know where he is," he said sharply, after a pause.... "But that is neither here nor there, Corporal," he went on in a more amiable tone. "We are going to take a little journey together."

This news perturbed Fandor-Vinson: it was not to his liking.

The abbé took him by the arm.

"You will excuse my absence this morning? To keep the appointment was impossible.... Ah! Hand me the promised document, will you?... That is it?... Very good.... Thank you!... By the by, Corporal — there you see our special train." The priest pointed to a superb motor-car drawn up alongside the pavement. A superior-looking chauffeur was seated at the wheel.

"Shall we get in? We have a fairly long way to go, and it is important that we arrive punctually."

Fandor could do nothing but agree. They seated themselves. The abbé shared a heavy travelling rug.

"We will wrap ourselves up well," said he. "It is far from warm, and there is no need to catch cold — it is not part of our programme!... You can start now, chauffeur! We are ready."

Once in motion, the abbé pointed to a voluminous package which prevented Fandor from stretching his legs.

"We can change places from time to time, for you cannot be comfortable with this package encumbering the floor of the car like this."

"Oh," replied Fandor-Vinson, "one takes things as they come!... But we should be much more comfortable if we fastened this rather clumsy piece of baggage to the front seat, beside the chauffeur, who can keep an eye on it!"

"Corporal! You cannot be thinking of what you are saying!" The priest's reply was delivered in a dry authoritative voice.

"I have put my foot in it," thought Fandor. "I should just like to know how!" He was about to speak: the abbé cut in:

"I am very tired, Corporal, so excuse me if I doze a little! In an hour or so, I shall be quite refreshed. There will be ample time for a talk after that."

Fandor could but agree.

The car was speeding up the Avenue des Champs-Elysées. They were leaving Paris — for what destination?

"Does your chauffeur know the route, Monsieur l'Abbé?"

"I hope so — why?"

"Because I could direct him. I could find my way about any of these suburbs with my eyes shut."

"Very well. See that he keeps on the right road. We are going towards Rouen." With that the abbé wrapped himself in his share of the ample rug and closed his eyes.

Fandor sat still as a mouse, with all the food for thought he required.

"Why Rouen? Why were they taking him there?... What is this mysterious package which must remain out of sight at the bottom of the car?"

Fandor tried to follow its outline with the toe of his boot. It was protected by a thick wrapping of straw.

"Then who was this abbé?" His speech showed he was French. He wore his cassock with the ease of long habit: he was young. His hand was the delicate hand of a Churchman — not coarsened by manual labour. Fandor, plunged in reflections, lost all sense of time.

The car sped on its way, devouring the miles fleetly. No sooner out of Paris than Saint-Germain was cleared — Mantes left behind! As they were approaching Bonniéres, Fandor, whose eyes had been fixed on the interminable route, as though at some turn of the road he might catch sight of their real destination, now felt that the abbé was watching the landscape through half-closed eyes.

"You are awake, then, Monsieur l'Abbé?" observed Fandor-Vinson.

"I was wondering where we were."

"We are coming to Bonniéres."

"Good!" The abbé sat up, flung his rug aside.

"Do as I do, Corporal. Do not fold up the rug. Throw it over our package. Prying eyes will not suspect its presence."

With the most stupid air in the world, Fandor asked:

"Must it not be seen, then?"

"Of course not! And at Bonniéres we must be on guard: the police there are merciless: they arrest everyone who exceeds the speed limit.... Nor do we wish to arouse their curiosity about us personally. There is a number of troops stationed here: the colonel is notorious for his strictness: he is correctness personified."

Fandor-Vinson stared questionably at the abbé.

"But you do not seem to understand anything, Corporal Vinson!" he cried in an irritated tone. "Whatever I say seems to send you into a state of stupefaction!... I shall never do anything with you, you are hopeless!... Ah, here is Bonniéres! Once outside the town, I will give you some useful explanations."

A bare three minutes after leaving Bonniéres behind, the Abbè turned to Fandor and asked in a low voice:

"What do you think is in that package, Corporal?"

"Good heavens! Monsieur l'Abbé."...

"Corporal, that contains a fortune for you and for me ... a piece of artillery ... the mouth-piece of 155-R ... rapid firer!... You see its importance?... To-night we sleep in the outskirts of Rouen ... to-morrow, we leave early for Havre.... As I am known there, Corporal, we shall have to separate.... You will go with the driver to the Nez d'Antifer.... There you will find a fishing-boat in charge of a friendly sailor ... all you have to do is to hand over this package to him.... He will make for the open sea, where he will deliver it — into the right hands."...

Involuntarily Fandor drew away from the priestly spy. The statements just made to him were of so grave a nature; the adventure in which he found himself involved was so dangerous, so nefarious, that Fandor thrilled with terror and disgust. He kept silence: he was thinking. Suddenly he saw his way clear.

"Between Havre and the Nez d'Antifer I must get rid of this gun piece. However interesting my investigations are I cannot possibly deliver such a thing to the enemy, to a foreign power! Death for preference!"...

His companion broke in.

"And now, Corporal, I fancy you fully understand how awkward it would be for you, much more so than for me, if this package were opened, because you are a soldier, and in uniform."

Fandor showed an unflinching front, but a wave of positive anguish rushed over him.

"This cursed abbé has me in his net!" he thought. "Like it, or not, I must follow him now. I am regularly let in!... As a civilian, as Fandor the journalist, I might go to the first military dépôt I can come at, and state that I had discovered a priest who was going to hand over to a foreign power an important piece of artillery!... The pretended Vinson would have done the trick and would then vanish.... But in uniform!... They would certainly accuse me of suspicious traffic with spies.... They would confine me — cell me.... I should have the work of the world to obtain a release under six months!... Another point.... Why had they chosen him, Corporal Vinson as they believed, for such a mission?... Assuredly the spies possessed a thousand other agents, capable of carrying triumphantly through this dangerous mission, this delivery of a stolen piece of ordnance to a sailor spy in the pay of a foreign power inimical to France!"

It was horrible! Abominable! This spy traffic! Only to think of it soiled one's soul! Fandor sickened at the realisation of what was involved — that this betrayal of France was not a solitary instance — that there must be a hundred betrayals going on at that very moment! That France was being bought and sold in a hundred ways for Judas money — France!

His thoughts turned shudderingly away from such hell depths of treachery.

He brought his mind to bear on other points.

"Why, after so much mystery, such precautions, does this Judas of an abbé disclose the contents of that damnable package before its delivery? Why this halt in the outskirts of Rouen when a quick run, a quick handing over of the package is so essential?... With such a powerful machine, why this stop in a journey of some 225 kilometres?"

Fandor felt a cold shiver run down his spine.

"Suppose this abbé is playing a trick on me?... If yesterday, to-day, ... no matter when ... I have betrayed myself? If these people have discovered my identity? If, knowing that I am not Vinson, but Fandor, they have made me put on uniform, placed in the car with me a compromising portion of a gun, and are going to hand me over to the military authorities, either at Rouen, or elsewhere?"

The abbé, comfortably ensconced in the corner, was slumbering again.

Fandor cast stealthy glances at his companion, considering him carefully.

Now he came to examine him, surely this priest's face had a queer look?... The eyebrows were too regular ... painted?... How delicate his skin?... Not the slightest trace of a beard?... A shoe — the traditional silver-buckled shoe of the priest — was visible below the cassock.... That was all right ... but, how slender his ankle?...

Fandor pulled himself up. What would he imagine next? True, he was wise to suspect everything, everybody — test them, try them — in this terrible position he had got himself into, nevertheless, he must keep a clear head.

The car was passing through a village. The abbé opened his eyes.

"Monsieur l'Abbé," declared Fandor, "I am frozen to death. Would you object to our stopping a minute so that I might swallow a glass of rum?"

The abbé signalled the driver. The car stopped before a little inn. The innkeeper appeared.

"Bring the driver a cognac!" ordered the priest. "Give Monsieur a glass of rum. You may pour me out a glass of aniseed cordial."

"Aniseed cordial!" thought Fandor. "That is a liqueur for priests, youths, and women!"

"In an hour," said the abbé, "we shall be at Rouen. We shall pass through the town; a few kilometres further on, at Barentin, we shall halt for the night.... I know a very good little hotel there!"

Fandor refrained from comment. What he thought was:

"A fig for Barentin!... If I see the least sign that this little fellow is going to give me the slip, leave me for a minute — if it looks as though he were going to warn the authorities — I know someone who will take to flight ... and how!"...

XX
MAN OR WOMAN

Kilometres succeeded kilometres in endless procession. Ceaselessly the landscapes unrolled themselves like views on a cinema film. Swiftly, regularly, relentlessly, the car sped forward. Again the priest, with half-closed eyes, snuggled into his cushions.

Fandor felt strangely drowsy. This was due, he thought, to the long journey in the open air, and to a nervous fatigue induced by the tense emotions of the day.

"The nuisance is," thought he, "that no sooner shall I lay my head on the pillow to-night than I shall be snoring like the Seven Sleepers."

The car continued to advance.

After a sharp descent, the car turned to the right: the road now wound along the side of a hill, bordered by the Seine on one side, and on the other by perpendicular cliffs. High in the grey distance, dominating the countryside, rose the venerated sanctuary of Rouen — Nôtre Dame de Bon Secours.

"We have only six more kilometres to cover," remarked the abbé.

Soon they were moving at a slower pace through the outskirts of Rouen.

Jolted on the cobbles of the little street, thrown against each other every time the car side-slipped on the two rails running along the middle of the roadway, Fandor and the little abbé were knocked wide awake.

"We are not going to stop?" asked Fandor.

"Yes. We must recruit ourselves: besides, I have to call at a certain garage."

"Attention!" said Fandor to himself. "The doings of this little priest are likely to have a peculiar interest for me! At the least sign of danger, my Fandor, I give thee two minutes to cut and run!"

Our journalist knew Rouen well. He knew that to reach Barentin, the car, passing out of the great square, surrounded by the new barracks, would follow the quay, traverse the town from end to end, pass near the famous transshipping bridge, and join the high road again.

"If we pull up at one of the garages along the quays, all will be well," thought Fandor....."In case of an alarm, a run of a hundred yards or so would bring me to one of the many electric tramways....I should board a tram — devil take them, if they dared to chase and catch me!"

The car had reached the bridge which prolongs the rue Jeanne d'Arc across the Seine. They were now in the heart of Rouen. The chauffeur turned:

"Can I stop, Monsieur? I need petrol and water."

The priest pointed to a garage.

"Stop there!"

The chauffeur began to supply the wants of his machine with the help of an apprentice. The priest jumped out and entered the garage. Fandor followed on his heels, saying:

"It does one good to stretch one's legs!"

The abbé seemed in no wise disturbed. He walked up to the owner of the place.

"Tell me, my friend, have you, by chance, received a telegram addressed to the Abbé Gendron?"

"That is so, Monsieur. It will be for you?"...

"Yes, for me. I asked that a message should be sent to me here, if necessary."

Whilst the priest tore open his telegram, Fandor lit a cigarette....By hook or by crook, he must see the contents of this telegram which his travelling companion was reading with frowning brows. But Fandor might squint in the glass for the reflection of the message, pass behind the abbé to peep over his shoulder while pretending to examine the posters decorating the garage walls: he had his pains for his reward: it was impossible to decipher the text....He must await developments.

When the car was ready to start he decided to speak.

"You have not received vexatious instructions, I hope, Monsieur l'Abbé?"

"Not at all!"

"There is always something disquieting about a telegram!"

"This one tells me nothing I did not know already — at least, suspected! The only result is that instead of going to Havre we shall now go to Dieppe."

"Why this change of destination?" was Fandor's mental query. "And what did this precious priest suspect?"

The abbé was giving the chauffeur instructions.

"You will leave Rouen by the new route....You will draw up at an hotel which you will find on the right, named, if my memory does not play me false, *The Flowery Crossways*."

"A pretty name!" remarked Fandor.

"A stupid name," replied the abbé. "The house does not stand at any cross-roads, and the place is as flowerless as it is possible to be!" There was a pause. "That matters little, however, Corporal: the quarters are good — the table sufficient. You shall judge for yourself now: here is the inn!"

Under the skillful guidance of the chauffeur, the car turned sharply, and passed under a little arch which served as a courtyard entrance. The car came to a stand-still in a great yard, crowded with unharnessed carts, stablemen, and Normandy peasants in their Sunday best.

A stout man came forward. His head was as hairless as a billiard ball. This was the hotel-keeper. To every question put by the little abbé he replied with a broad grin which displayed his toothless gums. His voice was as odd as his appearance, it was high-pitched and quavering.

"You can give us dinner?"

"Why, certainly, Monsieur le Curé."

"You have a coach-house where the car can be put up?"

With a comprehensive sweep of his arm, mine host of *The Flowery Crossways* indicated the courtyard. The carts of his regular clients were left there in his charge: he could not see why the motor-car of these strangers could not pass the night there also.

"And you can reserve three rooms for us?" was the little abbé's final demand.

This time the face of mine host lost its jovial assurance.

"Three rooms? Ah, no, Monsieur le Curé — that is quite impossible!...But we can manage all the same....I have an attic for your chauffeur, and a fine double-bedded room for you and Monsieur the corporal....That will suit you — I think?"

"Yes, quite well! Very well, indeed!" declared Fandor, delighted at this opportunity of keeping his queer travelling companion under his eye.

The little abbé was far from satisfied.

"What! You have not two rooms for us?" he expostulated. "I have a horror of sharing a room with anyone whatever! I am not accustomed to it; and I cannot sleep under those conditions!"

"Monsieur le Curé, it's full up here! I have a wedding party on my hands!"

"Well, then is there no hotel near by, where I can."...

"No, Monsieur le Curé: I am the only hotel-keeper about here!"

"Is it far to the parsonage?"

"But, my dear Abbé!" protested Fandor: "I beg of you to take the room! I can sleep anywhere ...on two chairs in the dining-room!"

"Certainly not!" declared the little priest. He turned to the hotel-keeper: "Tell me just how far the parsonage is from here?"

"At least eight kilometres."

"Oh, then, it is out of the question! What a disagreeable business this is!...We shall pass a dreadful night!"

The abbé was greatly put out.

"No, no! I will leave the room to you!" again protested Fandor.

"Do not talk so childishly, Corporal! We have to be on the road again to-morrow. What good purpose will it serve if we allow ourselves to be over-fatigued and so fit for nothing?... After all, a bad night will not last forever!...We must manage to put up with the inconvenience."

Fandor nodded acquiescence. Things were going as he wished.

"Dinner at once!" ordered the abbé.

An affable Normandy girl laid their table in a small room: a profusion of black cocks with scarlet combs decorated the paper on its walls. The effect was at once bewildering and weirdly funereal.

Meanwhile the abbé walked up and down in the courtyard; to judge by his expression he was in no pleasant frame of mind.

When he came to table, Fandor noticed that he forgot to pronounce the Benedicite. He was still more interested when the ecclesiastic attacked a tasty chicken with great gusto.

"This is certainly the 1st of December, therefore a fast day according to the episcopal mandate, which I have read ... and behold my little priest is devouring meat! The hotel-keeper offered us fish just now, and I quite understood why, but it seems fasting is not obligatory for this priest — unless this priest is not a priest!"

Whilst the abbé was enjoying his chicken in silence, with eyes fixed on his plate, Fandor once again subjected him to a minute examination. He noted his delicate features, his slim hands, his graceful attitudes: he was so impressed by this and various little details, that when the abbé, after dessert and a last glass of cider, rose and proposed that they should go up to their room for the night, Fandor declared to himself:

"My head on a charger for it! I bet that little abbé is a woman, then more mystery, and a probable husband or lover who may come on the scene presently! Fandor, my boy, beware of this baggage! Not an eye must you close this night!"

The priest had had the famous package taken upstairs and placed at the foot of his bed.

Fandor and the abbé wished each other good night.

"As for me," declared Fandor, unlacing his boots, "I cannot keep my eyes open!"

"I can say the same," replied his companion.

Fandor's next remark had malice in it.

"I pity you, Monsieur l'Abbé! No doubt you have long prayers to recite — especially if you have not finished your breviary!"

"You are mistaken," answered the abbé, with a slight smile: "I am dispensed from a certain number of religious exercises!"

"A fig for you, my fine fellow!" said Fandor to himself. "The deuce is in if I do not catch you out over one of your lies!"

The little abbé was seated on a chair attending to his nails.

Fandor walked to the door, explaining:

"I have a horror of sleeping in an hotel bedroom with an unlocked door!... You will allow me to turn the key?"

"Turn it, then!"

Locking the door, Fandor drew the key and threw it on to the priest's lap.

"There, Monsieur l'Abbé, if you like to put it on your bedside table!"

Fandor's action had a purpose. Ten to one you settle the sex of a doubtful individual by such a test. A man instinctively draws his knees together when an object is thrown on them: a woman draws them apart, to make a wider surface of the skirt for the reception of an article and thus prevent its fall to the ground.

Fandor was not surprised to see the little priest instinctively act as would a woman.... But, would not a priest, accustomed to wear a cassock, act as a woman would? Fandor realised that, in this instance, the riddle of sex was still unsolved.

Fandor-Vinson began to undress: the priest continued to polish his nails.

"You are not going to bed, Monsieur l'Abbé?"

"Yes, I am."

The ecclesiastic took off his shoes; then his collar. Then he lay down on the bed.

"You will sleep with all your clothes on?" asked Fandor-Vinson.

"Yes, when I have to sleep in a bed I am not accustomed to!... Should I blow out the candle, Corporal?"

"Blow it out, Monsieur l'Abbé."

Fandor felt sure the little priest was a woman disguised. He dare not take off his cassock because he was she!

Wishing his strange companion a good night's rest, Fandor snuggled under the bedclothes. Determined to keep awake and alert, he tried to pass the dark hours by mentally reciting *Le Cid*!

XXI
A CORDIAL UNDERSTANDING

"Let us make peace!"

Juve held out his hand — a firm, strong hand — the hand of a trusty man.

"Let us make peace frankly, sincerely, wholeheartedly!"

Lieutenant de Loubersac signed the pact, without a moment's hesitation: he put his hand into the hand of Juve, and shook it warmly.

"Agreed, Monsieur: we are of one mind on that point!"

The two men stood silent, considering each other, despite the violence of the west wind sweeping across the end of the stockade, bringing with it enormous foam-tipped waves, rising from a rough, grey sea.

The detective and the officer were on the jetty of Dieppe harbour. This chill December afternoon, the sea looked dark and threatening.

Since their arrival at Dieppe, Juve and de Loubersac had mutually avoided each other. Time and again they had come face to face, each more bored, more cross-looking than the other. This mutual, sulky avoidance was over: they had made it up.

The evening before, following his arrest under the guise of Vagualame, Juve had been conducted to the Dépôt by his colleagues. No sooner were they seated in the taxi, under the charge of Inspector Michel and his companion, than Juve made himself known to his gratified, unsuspecting colleagues. It was a humiliating surprise for the two policemen: they felt fooled.

Juve, realising that neither Michel nor his colleagues were at present likely to lend him their generous aid in the carrying out of certain plans, decided to keep silence: nor would he let them into the secret of his discoveries regarding Bobinette's highly suspicious character and conduct: that she was an accomplice, a tool of the real Vagualame was established beyond a doubt.

The crestfallen Michel had to unhandcuff Juve and restore him to liberty; but he extracted a promise from his amazing colleague that he would see Monsieur Havard next morning, and give him an account of all that had passed.

Accordingly, at seven o'clock next morning, Juve was received by Monsieur Havard.

Juve had hoped for a few minutes' interview, then a rush to the East Station, there to await the arrival of Corporal Vinson. The interview was a long one: Juve was too late.

But he had not lost time at Headquarters. The Second Bureau had telephoned, warning Police Headquarters that Corporal Vinson, arrived in Paris, was going to Dieppe very shortly, where a foreign pleasure-boat would take possession of a piece of artillery, stolen, and probably being taken care of by the corporal.

This information coincided with what Juve had learned from Bobinette, and completed it. He must start for Dieppe instanter. If he had any luck he would arrest the soldier, and Bobinette as well. She would convey the piece to Vinson in the morning, and would accompany him to Dieppe. She was daring enough to do it.

At the Saint Lazare station Juve had caught the train for Dieppe which meets the one o'clock boat, bound for England. He had just settled himself in a first-class compartment, of which he was the solitary occupant, when he recognised an officer of the Second Bureau walking in the corridor — Lieutenant Henri de Loubersac!

The train was barely in motion when de Loubersac seated himself opposite Juve. The recognition had been mutual.

A few hours before, Henri de Loubersac had learned of the extraordinary arrest of the false Vagualame. He then understood that it was with Juve he had talked on the quay near the rue de Solférino. The officer of the Second Bureau was profoundly mortified: he had been taken in by a civilian!

He declared:

"It is the sort of thing one does not do! It is unworthy of an honourable man!"

In the Batignolles tunnel Juve and he began discussing this point: de Loubersac angry, excited; Juve immovably calm.

The discussion lasted until their train ran into Dieppe station. They had exhausted the subject, but had scarcely touched on the motives of their journey to this seaport. The two men separated with a stiff salute.

Obviously both were keeping a watch on the approaches to the quay: they encountered each other repeatedly; it became ridiculous. Being intelligent men devoted to their duty, they determined to act in concert for the better fulfillment of this same duty — duty to their respective chiefs — duty to the State — duty to France!

So they made it up!

After their cordial handshake, Juve, wishing to define the situation, asked:

"Now what are we after exactly — you and I? What is the common aim of the Second Bureau and Police Headquarters?"

De Loubersac's reply was:

"A document has been stolen from us: we want to find it."

Juve said:

"Two crimes have been committed: we wish to seize the assassin."

"And," continued de Loubersac, with a smile, "as it is probable the murderer of Captain Brocq and Nichoune is none other than the individual who stole our document.".…

"By uniting our efforts," finished Juve, "we have every chance of discovering the one and the other."

There was a pause. Then Juve asked:

"Nevertheless, Lieutenant, since I find you here, I fancy there is some side development — some incident?… In reality, have you not come to Dieppe to intercept a certain corporal who is to deliver to a foreign power a piece of artillery of the highest importance?"

"You have hit it!" was de Loubersac's reply. "I see you know about this gun affair!"

Juve nodded.

The two men were slowly returning towards the town by way of the outer harbour quays. They approached a dock, in which was anchored a pretty little yacht flying the Dutch flag. Juve stared hard at this elegant craft. De Loubersac enquired if yachting was his favourite sport. Juve smiled.

"Far from it! Nevertheless, when that yacht weighs anchor, it would be my delight to inspect her from stem to stern, accompanied by the Custom House officials. It is my conviction that Corporal Vinson will soon turn up, slip aboard with the stolen gun-piece, conceal it in some prepared hiding-hole below: his otherwise uninteresting person will be hidden also."

"I am of the same mind," declared de Loubersac.

As the two men strolled they exchanged information.

De Loubersac told Juve that, according to the latest messages from the Second Bureau, Vinson had left Paris with a priest, in a hired motor-car, and had taken the road to Rouen, that in all probability they would reach Dieppe before nightfall, and when they arrived!…

"It is precisely at that moment we shall arrest them. I have made all arrangements with the local police," finished de Loubersac.

"Ah!" murmured Juve. "What a pity Captain Loreuil and Inspector Michel came on the scenes last night and arrested me prematurely, thinking they had got the real Vagualame, for now I can never make use of the ruffian's disguise to pump the different members of the great spy organisation we are on the track of!"

"But what prevents you now from masquerading as Vagualame?" demanded de Loubersac.

"Why, when no one knew I was a false Vagualame, I could make up in his likeness: now they know the truth; not only is it known by the followers of Vagualame by this time, but — I am certain of it — I was recognised by the real Vagualame himself!"

"Did he see you then?"

"I would stake my life on it!" asserted Juve.

"Just when?...Where?...In the street?" de Loubersac was keenly interested.

"No — just when I was arrested."

"But, from what I have heard, there were very few of you!" cried de Loubersac. "Then the real Vagualame must have been at the Baron de Naarboveck's?"

"Hah!" was Juve's non-committal exclamation.

"Whom do you suspect?"

Juve kept silence.

Suddenly he concealed himself behind a deserted goods waggon. De Loubersac did the same. Both fixed examining eyes on a couple coming in their direction. They were not the expected pair of traitors.

"Who?" again asked de Loubersac.

Juve was impenetrable.

"I am inclined to think that the companion, Mademoiselle Berthe, otherwise Bobinette, has played, and perhaps still plays, an incomprehensible part in these affairs."

"You find it incomprehensible?" Juve burst into laughter. "I do not!"

"Well then, were I in your place, I should not hesitate to arrest her!"

"And then?"

"Oh, explanations could follow."

Juve considered his companion a minute: then, taking his arm in friendly fashion, continued their walk along the quay.

"I have a theory," said Juve; "that when dealing with such complex affairs as these we are now engaged on, affairs in which the actors are but puppets, acting on behalf of the prime mover, a master-mind, ungetatable, or almost so, we should aim at first securing the prime mover. To secure the puppets and leave the prime mover free is to obtain but a partial success: the victory is then more apparent than real.... I might have arrested Bobinette as we shall probably arrest Corporal Vinson before long; but would her arrest furnish us with the master key to this problem? Have we not a better chance of discovering the powerful head of this band if we allow his collaborators to perform their manœuvres in a fancied security?"

The prime mover of these mysteries? Juve was convinced that the prime mover of these nefarious mysteries, the murderous master mind was, and could be, none other than — Fantômas!

Juve paused abruptly.

A man was coming to meet them — an investigating agent attached to the general commissariat department at Dieppe.

"They are asking for Monsieur Henri on the telephone," he announced.

De Loubersac rushed to the police station. Over the telephone, a War Office colleague informed him that the fugitive corporal, accompanied by a priest, had during the last hour arrived at a garage in Rouen.

Meanwhile Juve had received a cypher telegram at the police station, confirming the news, with the addition that, after replenishing the motor with petrol, they had set off again at once — they had received a telegram.

Juve and de Loubersac returned to the quay.

"Our beauties will not be so long now," said he.

With twilight the tempest had died down, night was falling fast. The waters in the docks reflected the light from the quay lamps on their shining, heaving, surface.

Now, for some time, Henri de Loubersac had been longing to ask Juve a question, longing yet fearing to voice it — a question relating to his personal affairs. Had not Juve, as Vagualame, clearly insinuated that Wilhelmine de Naarboveck must have been the mistress of Captain Brocq? Had not de Loubersac protested vehemently against such an odious calumny? But now that he knew this statement was Juve's, he was in a state of torment — his love was bleeding with the torture of it!

At last he summoned up courage to put the question to Juve.

Juve frowned, looked embarrassed. He had foreseen the question. He did not believe that Wilhelmine de Naarboveck had been Captain Brocq's mistress; but he knew there was an undecipherable mystery in this girl's life, and he had an intuition that the discovery of this secret would probably throw light on certain points which, as far as he was concerned, had remained obscure. Was this fair-haired girl really the baron's daughter? Since he had learned that Wilhelmine visited Lady Beltham's tomb regularly — this notorious Lady Beltham, mistress of Fantômas — he had been saying to himself:

"No — Mademoiselle Wilhelmine is not the daughter of de Naarboveck, the rich diplomat! But who, then, is she?"

Juve knew it was useless to say this to de Loubersac, blinded by love as he was; but his aim — a rather Machiavellian one — was to sow seeds of suspicion in the heart of this lover, which would drive him to provoke an explanation, and force Wilhelmine to speak out, for she must surely know the facts relating to her identity!

This Machiavellian Juve did not hesitate to say to de Loubersac:

"You remember what the false Vagualame told you when you talked with him on the banks of the Seine?... You are to-day in the presence of this false Vagualame — of me, Juve — as you know.... Well, I am sorry to tell you that, whatever outside appearance I adopt, my way of thinking, my way of seeing things seldom changes."

Henri de Loubersac understood: he grew pale: his lips were pressed tightly together: he clenched his fists.

Satisfied with this result, Juve repeated to himself this celebrated aphorism of the Bastille:

"Slander! Slander! Some of it always sticks!"

It was dark. In a little restaurant near by, the two men dined frugally: it was a mediocre repast, not too well cooked. Anxious questionings tormented them. The fugitives were long in coming: had they got wind of what was afoot? Had Vinson and the priest been warned that detectives were hot on their trail? If so, it was all up with the arrest!

De Loubersac remained on the watch. Juve returned to the police station. He was crossing the threshold when the telephone shrilled. News from the police sergeant at Rouen!

The corporal and the abbé, leaving Rouen, had taken the road to Barentin, had dined at *The Flowery Crossways Hotel*, and, according to the chauffeur's statement, they would pass the night there: they would reach Dieppe next morning at the earliest possible moment.

Juve hurried with the news to de Loubersac. After a short consultation they separated: each pretended he was going to his own particular hotel to get some rest.

Juve did not quit the neighbourhood of the quay. Installed in a custom house official's sentry box, he stolidly set himself to pass the night with only his thoughts for company. An hour passed. Juve cocked a listening ear; there were furtive footsteps — stealthy movements close by!... Juve thrilled!... If it were the traitor Vinson? The steps came nearer, nearer. Juve slipped out of his shelter. Someone rose up before him — and ... mutual recognition, and laughter!

De Loubersac was on the watch as well!

Jovially, Juve summed up the situation:

"Lieutenant, we can truly declare that, civilian or soldier, in pursuit of our duty we are ever on a war footing!"

Philosophically resigned to a wakeful night, the pair marched stolidly, persistently, doggedly up and down the Dieppe quay — up and down — up and down — an interminable up-and-down!

XXII

HAVE THEY BOLTED?

Whilst Juve and Henri de Loubersac were watching through the midnight hours for the arrival of the traitors, Fandor in his hotel was also on the alert. He did not mean to sleep a wink. The noise of the merry-making below helped him in that.... The revellers retired at last, and silence fell on *The Flowery Crossways*. Fandor, feigning sleep, lay as still as a mouse; but how interminable seemed the hours!

"Ah!" thought Fandor, "if only my abbé were sleeping, I should decamp; but that little bundle of mystery is wide awake: I can sense his wakefulness!"

Fandor lay listening for the next eternity of an hour to strike and pass into limbo.... At last dawn began to break: the window curtains became transparent, a cock crowed in the yard below, the voice of a stable-boy sounded loud in the stillness of early day.

"You are awake, Corporal?" asked the priest in a low voice.

"Quite, Monsieur l'Abbé. You feel rested?"

"I only dosed off a little."

"Liar!" thought Fandor. He replied:

"That is just what I did!" Fandor yawned loudly.

"Will you get up first, Corporal? When you have finished dressing I will start.... In that way we shall not interfere with each other."

"But, Monsieur l'Abbé, I do not want to keep you waiting.... Do get up first!"

"Certainly not! No, no! Do not let us stand on ceremony."

Fandor did not insist. He was too pleased with his room-mate's request.

In next to no time — with a kind of barrack-room lick and polish — Fandor-Vinson had washed his face, had dressed, was ready.

"My dear Abbé," said he, "if you would like me to, I will ascertain whether your chauffeur is up, and will tell him to get ready to start."

"I was going to ask you to do that very thing, Corporal."

As the door closed on him, Fandor turned with an ironic salute towards the little priest.

"Much pleased!" said he to himself. "And with the hope of never meeting you on my road without Juve on my heels to offer you a pair of handcuffs — the right bracelets for you, and richly deserved."

Fandor did not awaken the chauffeur. He went into the yard: there he encountered the hotel-keeper. A brazen lie was the safe way, he decided.

"We have passed a very good night," declared he. "My companions are getting ready.... I am going to see if the car is in order for our start."

To himself Fandor added: "As my little priest's window looks in the opposite direction he cannot see what I am up to."

Fandor was an expert chauffeur. The car was fully supplied with petrol and water — was in admirable order. The hotel-keeper was watching him.

"If they ask for me," said Fandor-Vinson, "tell them I have gone for a test run, and will be back in three minutes."

With that he jumped into his seat, set the car in motion, passed beneath the archway and on to the high road. He turned in the direction of Barentin.

Fandor felt the charm of this early drive through the pastoral lands of Normandy. Hope rose in him: was he not escaping from the terrifying consequences of his Vinson masquerade!

"Evidently," thought he, "I must definitely abandon the rôle of soldier: the risks are too great: if the military authorities laid me by the heels, it would be all up with Fandor-Vinson!... The real Vinson is certainly in foreign parts by now, and safe from arrest.... I know by sight the head spies at Verdun, the Norbet brothers: the elegant tourist and his car, and that false priest!... I can continue my investigations better in my own shoes, and I can get Juve to help me!"

His thoughts dwelt on the mysterious abbé.

"I would give a jolly lot to know who this pretended abbé really is!"

He tore through the village of Barentin at racing speed.

A covered cart full of peasants stopped the way. Fandor drew up. He addressed the driver:

"Monsieur, I have rather lost my bearings: will you kindly tell me in which direction the nearest railway station lies?"

The driver, who was the mail carrier for Maronne, answered civilly:

"You must go to Motteville, Corporal. At the first cross-roads you come to, turn to the right — keep straight on — that will bring you to the station."

Corporal Fandor-Vinson thanked the man, and started off in the direction indicated.

"All I have to do now," thought he, "is to discover some nice, lonely spot for."...

Shortly after this he sighted a grove with a thick undergrowth. It bordered the road. Fandor rushed his machine into a field, and brought it to a stand-still in the centre of a clump of trees. He alighted.

"That motor is a good goer," said he, "but it is too dangerous a companion — too conspicuous a mark."

As he thought of the stranded bundle of mystery at *The Flowery Crossways* he laughed. Then he started for the station at a steady pace.

The chauffeur woke. He saw it was nine o'clock.

"Good lord!...I shall catch it hot! We were to start at eight!"

He dressed hastily; ran down to the yard; stared about him: his car had vanished. Was he still dreaming?...He ran round to the front of the hotel — no car! Was the car stolen?...Had they set off without him?...The hotel-keeper was marketing in Rouen....The stablemen could throw no light on this mystery.

"Probably one of your masters has gone for a turn," suggested a man.

The chauffeur's anger grew.

"If they've dared to!" he shouted. "It is not their car!...I'm not in their service!...That curé came to my garage yesterday and hired my car for an outing....What business has this curé or his soldier to move my car?...I'll teach them who and what I am!"...

The farm boys, stable lads and men were shouting with laughter at the chauffeur's fury. Said one:

"You know their room, don't you?...Why not see if they are in it?...Make sure you have cause for all this dust up!"

The chauffeur rushed upstairs four at a time! He banged on the door of the room taken by his temporary employer and the corporal — banged and thumped!...No response!...He tried the door — unlocked!...He opened it, looked in — empty!

Cursing and raging, the chauffeur clattered downstairs and collided with the hotel-keeper.

"Where is my curé?" shouted the chauffeur.

"Your curé?" echoed the good fellow, staring.

"Yes, my curé. Or his corporal!...Where are they?...Where, I say?"

"Where are they?" gaped the hotel-keeper.

The entire hotel staff was grouped in the background, laughing.

"It's my car! I can't find it!...Do you know where it is?"

"Your car!" exclaimed the hotel-keeper. "But the corporal went off two hours ago and more! He was going for a 'trial spin,' was what he told me!"

"Was the curé with him?"

"No. The curé left just after him, saying he was going to send off a telegram. Was it not true?"

The chauffeur sank on a chair.

"Here's a low-down trick!...Those dirty thieves have cut off with my car! Let me catch them! I'll give them beans and a bit!"

The hotel was in an uproar; the wildest suggestions rained on the distracted chauffeur. He pulled himself together; rose; called to the hotel-keeper, who was mechanically searching the yard for the vanished car:

"Where is the police station? I must warn the police. That priest and corporal cannot have got so very far in two hours! They did not leave together: they had to meet somewhere: they may not know how to manage the car ... that means delay — a breakdown, perhaps!"

Mine host of *The Flowery Crossways* was all the more ready to help the chauffeur in that he had been cheated! Such fugitives would never pay him the eighteen francs they owed him for bed and board unless they were caught and made to disgorge.

"I will come with you to the police station," he announced. "I have my complaint to make also!"

At the police station they saw the police sergeant himself. The chauffeur had barely begun his tale of woe when the sergeant interrupted with the smile of one imparting good news:

"You state that you have lost a motor-car. Does it happen to be red, and will seat four persons?"

"Yes. That's it! Have you seen it?"

"Does it happen to have for number 1430 G-7?"

"Exact!... Has it passed this way?"

"Wait!... Were there not goatskin wraps inside?"

"Yes!... Yes!"

The sergeant laughed silently.

"Very well, then! I should say you were in luck! Now I am going to tell you where your car is!"

The chauffeur beamed. "You know where my car is?"

"I do — a bare fifteen minutes ago it was found in the — open fields, on Father Flory's land, some seventeen hundred yards from the Motteville station.... Father Flory saw it when driving his cattle to pasture: he asked himself if the car had not fallen from the skies during the night!"

The hotel-keeper and chauffeur stared at each other. What had possessed the fugitives to steal the car and then cast it away in the open fields, so near the scene of their theft?... The devil was in it?

The hotel-keeper had an idea they had fled to avoid paying his bill. The chauffeur cared only to get to the car as quickly as possible, to assure himself that it was his car, and was not injured beyond repair.

After much haggling it was arranged that a little cart and horse should take him to the desired spot. Meanwhile the hotel-keeper was to go about his duties at *The Flowery Crossways*. The chauffeur must needs return and telegraph to his garage in Paris for funds: he declared he had not a sou on him.

Finally the chauffeur set off; perched on a big white mare which had been rejected time and again by the Remount Department, he took the road at a galloping trot. When he reached Father Flory's field he gave a sigh of satisfaction. He recognised his car. It proved to be in good condition. Whoever had driven it knew what he was about.

"It was the corporal," decided the joyful chauffeur. "That little curé would be afraid of spoiling his little white hands!"

Surrounded by a crowd of peasants who had hurried from all the farms in the neighbourhood, to see the motor-car which had grown up in a single night in Father Flory's field, the chauffeur set his car in motion. Hard work! The car had been driven deep into the soft soil.... At last he got to the road.

"A very good evening to you, ladies and gentlemen!" he shouted to the peasants who, with ironic grins and hands in pockets, had watched him at work. Not one had come forward to help him!

He set off at top speed for *The Flowery Crossways*.

Meanwhile the police sergeant, important, in full official uniform, had started for *The Flowery Crossways*, accompanied by the hotel-keeper.

"This affair requires looking into," he announced. "The law will have more than a word to say about it. I must get further information and make notes."

He, with the hotel-keeper at his heels, mounted to the little room where Fandor and the little priest had passed the night. The policeman uncovered on entering what he considered a sumptuous, superbly decorated room. He had not the least idea how to set about his investigations in order to get the best results. He seated himself in an arm-chair. He fixed his eyes on the hotel-keeper.

"Do you know the name of these individuals?"

The hotel-keeper, thinking of the eighteen francs he had lost, and of how he could indemnify himself, paid scant attention to the sergeant's so-called investigations.

"Look here!" he cried. "That's a good thing! In their haste they have forgotten to take this package!...There may be things of value in it!...I may be able to pay myself out of them!"

The policeman rose: he also examined the package.

"In the name of the law I shall open this package to ascertain exactly what is in it."

The two men undid the rope tightly bound round the covering; but whilst mine host of *The Flowery Crossways* had no idea of what the contents of the package signified, the sergeant, who had formerly served in the artillery, went white: his voice was stern.

"This is serious — very serious — it is the mouthpiece of a large gun — larger than any I have come across!"

The recovered motor-car drew up before *The Flowery Crossways* with a flourish. The beaming chauffeur jumped down and went towards the hotel-keeper and the police sergeant.

"It was my car all right!" he cried. "And I believed that never again should I set eyes on it!...When I think."...

The chauffeur stopped short; the unresponsive hotel-keeper and the police sergeant were staring at him fixedly. Not a word did they utter.

The chauffeur stared in turn: then he asked:

"Well?...What is it?...Are you frozen, you two?...What's the matter with you?...I inform you that I have found my motor, and that's how you take it!"

The police sergeant answered:

"I must ask you to give us some highly necessary information and explanations....Do you know anything about the priest and the soldier who hired your car and you?"

There was a questioning pause. The chauffeur broke it.

"I have already told you that I do not know them....If I did, things would not have happened as they have!...Now, why have you asked me that question?"

The policeman's reply was another question: his tone was stern.

"Then you declare you had no idea of what they were taking with them in your car?"

"What they were taking with them in my car?" repeated the chauffeur in a tone of bewildered interrogation.

The police sergeant marched up to him.

"Look here, now! It is incredible that you do not know what is in that corded-up package you carried in your car! And now your masters have disappeared; we are to believe that you know nothing about that either!...And now you return!...What is the reason of that?...And is it to be supposed that I am going to allow you to make off again without asking you to explain yourself and this extraordinary situation?"

The chauffeur saw that the hotel-keeper sided with the police sergeant: there was no support to be got in that quarter.

"Explain yourself, policeman!" burst out the chauffeur. "What's all this humbugging claptrap you are giving me?"

"In the name of the law!" declared the offended police officer, in solemn tones: "I think it advisable to arrest you!...You may consider yourself my prisoner!"...

As the astounded chauffeur could not find words to answer this, the sergeant added:

"Ah! My fine fellow! This is the way, then, you steal guns to help the Germans to shoot the French? It's a mercy I spotted you!"

"But you are mad! — mad! — mad!" protested the chauffeur...."You."...

The police sergeant cut him short.

"That is enough!... I am going to take you to Rouen!... You can account for yourself to the magistrates!"

XXIII

LONDON AND PARIS

Juve and Henri de Loubersac passed the night on the quay. Daybreak found them marching side by side, keeping their weary watch and ward. De Loubersac had fallen silent; monosyllabic replies to Juve's remarks had given place to no remarks at all. Juve looked at Henri and smiled.

"He has gone to the country of dreams: he sleeps standing."

In brotherly fashion, the policeman guided the young man towards the shelter: settled him in, and left him. He was within call if needed; meanwhile, he could have his sleep out.

Filling his pipe afresh, Juve resumed his walk along the quay. He was uneasy; he was also in a bad humour. Why did Vinson and this priest tarry on the way? Why should Corporal Vinson, bearer of this compromising artillery piece, plant himself at a little hotel in Rouen for the night? Had they been warned and stopped? Juve feared so.

"Evidently these men are acting for Fantômas," said he to himself: "Fantômas must be watching the police: he knows them, but they do not know him.... Suppose he knows of our arrival at Dieppe?... Suppose the two traitors, being warned, have given our men the slip on the way? Suppose this stop at Rouen was caused by the telegram they received at the garage?... If our arrival here has been signalled, our watch will be fruitless: neither Vinson nor the priest will show themselves on this quay!"

As he kept his tireless vigil. Juve eyed the yacht swinging gently on the rising tide. Could he find a pretext which would take him aboard — justify a thorough investigation of boat and crew?... The answer to more than one tormenting problem might lie hidden there!

Then Juve recalled his talk with de Loubersac. Had he been happily inspired to speak so to him of the girl he loved, the enigmatic Wilhelmine? Suppose de Loubersac, instead of questioning her, broke with her?

"It would be abominable of me to spoil this child's love affair for what are less than suspicions on my part — only the vaguest hypothesis!"

Juve smoked and ruminated as he paced the lonely quay.

"I need not worry," concluded he at last. "Granting that we shall clear up all these mysteries, Wilhelmine's innocence, her candour, will be made manifest; that being so, Henri de Loubersac will be the first to acknowledge it, the first to beg her forgiveness!... Lovers' quarrels are not serious quarrels — so!"...

Juve continued his tireless promenade.

Sailors seeking their fishing-boats swung past him in the growing light of day.

Juve looked at his watch.

"I told them to put on a special for the night, and they have instructions to send me any telegrams.... Still, it is six o'clock.... I will see if there is anything fresh!"

Juve found de Loubersac fast asleep in the sentry box, and shook him by the shoulder.

"Lieutenant!... Lieutenant!" he shouted: "Wake up! I want you to keep watch while I run to Headquarters here.... There may be news!"

De Loubersac jumped up, wide awake in a moment. He took his turn on the quay at once. Juve hurried to the police station. He was on the doorstep when a telegraph boy rode up with a telegram. It was for our detective. The paper shook in Juve's hands as his eyes devoured the message: it was in cypher.

> *"Corporal Vinson taken refuge in London — recognised and identified by me this morning at four o'clock when leaving Victoria Station. I followed him and know where he is. What to be done next? Awaiting your orders."*

Juve wondered whether he was on his head or his heels. Vinson in London! Left Victoria Station this morning! What did it mean?

"The wire is precise in its details. The man who sends it is a sharp police spy — never hesitates, never makes a blunder!... It seems evident that Vinson has given us the slip! He must have reached the coast at some point, and, in an unnoticed boat, has passed under our noses this very night!... Here's a go! The very deuce of a go!"

Intensely irritated, excited, Juve read and reread the telegram, fussed and fumed about the police station under the scared eyes of the policeman on guard duty. That worthy began to think the detective from Paris was an unmitigated nuisance.

Juve did not take this humble colleague into his confidence. He issued orders.

"You must not stir from here till the superintendent arrives. You will hand him this telegram addressed to me here. I will wire instructions in the morning where they are to be forwarded to me in England."

"In England!"

"Yes, I am crossing immediately by a Cook's excursion steamer, which goes in an hour, unless I am mistaken!"

Juve found de Loubersac pacing the quay. He had been smoking cigar after cigar to clear his head. Juve handed him a sheet of paper; on it he had copied the text of the telegram.

"Read that!" he cried.... "These confounded spies have found means to escape our attentions — but this is not the end of the game!"

Lieutenant Henri was thunderstruck.

"What are you going to do, Juve?"

"Reach London with all speed. Will you come, Lieutenant?"

De Loubersac considered.

"No," he decided.... "In the first place, I have no right to leave the country unless authorised to do so. I am not free to act according to my own good will and pleasure: besides, I have an idea there is work for me in Paris.... To watch that little intriguer, Bobinette, will be an interesting task: from what you told me yesterday, she is up to the neck in those villainous plots and plans! While you investigate in London, Paris shall be my field of operations. You approve of this, Juve?"

"I think you are right."

Juve accompanied the lieutenant to the station: de Loubersac was in a hurry to be off. He would not wait for the noon express: he took the slow train. As it began to move, he and Juve exchanged a cordial handshake.

"Good luck!" cried he.

"Thanks, Lieutenant. Good courage!"

The latter admonition was given with a purpose; for Juve was under no illusion as to de Loubersac's feelings.

"At any other time," thought he, "de Loubersac would have seen it to be his duty to accompany me to London: he could have secured an authorisation from his headquarters if required; besides, attached to the Second Bureau as he is, no doubt the ordinary military rules and regulations would hardly apply to him: to a large extent he must be allowed a free hand in emergencies. This is an emergency — an important one!... No, he wishes to see Wilhelmine: he is in love, is worried, suspicious: he wishes to clear up the mystery surrounding Wilhelmine's identity: he is determined to know what exactly were her relations with Captain Brocq: also, he wants to find out all there is to find regarding Bobinette and her doings.... To get to the bottom of these dark mysteries, unravel the tangled threads needs a clear head and a brave heart, for his feelings are deeply involved, and they may yet be cut to the quick!... He is a straight goer, that young man!" was Juve's concluding thought.... "He will do his duty: and when one does one's duty, with rare exceptions, the result is happiness."

Whilst Juve returned to the jetty to await the departure of the excursion steamer, Henri de Loubersac, alone in his compartment, reflected sadly on his relations with Wilhelmine.... He had loved her a long time. A frank, a sincere affection for her had gradually grown into a love which filled his whole heart and mind. Juve's words had troubled him profoundly. This spy chase had been a momentary distraction, but now his anxieties, his suspicions, his fears, swarmed and buzzed among his thoughts: he could not banish them!

His reflections so absorbed him that he lost consciousness of time and place: when the train came to a stand-still in Rouen station, he could have vowed they had left Dieppe but a few miles behind!

He would stretch his limbs on the platform. He jumped out; but, as he strolled past the kiosks, gazing at the papers and magazines exhibited in them, his mind was haunted but by one vision: Wilhelmine....

The train was about to leave: the porters were shouting: he hastened to his compartment: his foot was on the mounting board: it might have been nailed there, for the moment!...A young woman was seated in the further corner. She had lowered her window, and, with head out, was either saying good-bye to someone or was watching the comings and goings of the station.

Her attitude, the lines of her figure, were familiar to de Loubersac. He felt sure he knew her. He took his seat and awaited the turning of her head.

A piercing whistle and the train began to move. The young woman drew back, pulled up the window, and sat back in her seat.

Henri de Loubersac saw her.

She made a movement of surprise.

"You! Monsieur Henri!"

"You! Mademoiselle Bobinette!"

"By what chance?" began de Loubersac.

Bobinette interrupted:

"It is rather I who might ask you that, Monsieur Henri!...As for me, I have been spending four days with my family at Rouen....I asked for a holiday and Monsieur de Naarboveck very kindly granted it ...but you?"

De Loubersac was nervously chewing the end of his blonde moustache. With a shrug he replied:

"Oh, I! It is never surprising to meet me in a train: I am constantly on the move: here — there — everywhere!...You have news of Mademoiselle Wilhelmine?"

"Excellent news. You are coming to Monsieur de Naarboveck's soon?"

"I think of calling on the baron this evening."

Talk continued, commonplace, desultory. What questions crowded to his lips, sternly repressed!

"She lies," thought he, while listening to the details of her family visit. "She certainly lies!... I must pretend to be her dupe — the miserable creature!"

His whole soul revolted at the thought that this Bobinette, involved as she must be in disgraceful adventures, abominable tragedies, shared Wilhelmine's home, was her so-called friend! He was seized by a mad desire to grip Bobinette by the throat — silence her lying tongue — arrest, handcuff her on the spot — render her powerless!

He had noticed a vague line of black showing below her light coloured taffeta skirt. It might be the frill of a petticoat just too long. Thinking no more of it he continued to chat of indifferent things....Presently, a quick movement of Bobinette's raised her skirt a little more. This time the watchful de Loubersac could not be mistaken: he had seen clearly that what showed beneath Bobinette's skirt, every now and again, was a priest's cassock!

Bobinette's dress concealed the disguise of a priest.

Too well he understood the part this perverse creature had been playing! Now he could account for their meeting in this train coming from Rouen!...She had recently associated with Corporal Vinson as a priest. She had seen him off, no doubt, and, anxious to rid herself of her ecclesiastical exterior as quickly as might be, she had slipped on a dress over her ecclesiastical garment.

What was all this but a painful confirmation of Juve's words?...How could Wilhelmine be entirely ignorant of this dreadful creature's character? How could Wilhelmine be wholly innocent of the terribly compromising actions of her daily companion? Did Wilhelmine lack intuition? Was she without that delicate sensitiveness which is the birthright of all nice women? How could a pure girl breathe the miasmic atmosphere which must emanate from the soul of this abominable woman?

It was terrible!

The desultory commonplace chat went on, whilst de Loubersac was considering how best to act.

Arrest Bobinette?

Yes. He must not, dare not, hesitate. It was his duty. If he held this young woman at his mercy, it was, perhaps, the only way, painful as it was, to ultimately clear up the position of Wilhelmine.

How proceed?

Whilst still chattering of this and that, Henri de Loubersac made up his mind.

"Being a soldier, and not a policeman, I cannot myself arrest this woman. The scandal would be tremendous! I should get into the hottest of hot water with my chiefs: it is not my job.... Directly we arrive at the Saint Lazare station I will manage to signal one of the plain clothes men always on the watch there! Two of them will have her fast before she knows where she is!"

This seemed the easier because Bobinette had a heavy valise with her: she would have to call a porter and give him instructions — this would give him time to act.

Reassured, Henri de Loubersac continued to laugh and joke, though it went sorely against the grain....

At last! Saint Lazare station! The train stopped.

"I will say good-bye, Mademoiselle Bobinette....I must hurry away!...You will excuse me?"

De Loubersac leaped on to the platform, jostling the passengers crowding his path. He must reach the platform exit without a second's delay!...As he handed his ticket to the collecter, a hubbub arose. Passengers were stopping, turning back, running — something sensational must have happened!

He paused. He heard a porter at his elbow say in a low voice:

"Don't stop, Monsieur Henri — you may be noticed."

De Loubersac identified the speaker as a man in the employ of the Second Bureau. He handed his wraps to this detective, dressed as an ordinary porter.

"What is happening, then?" he asked.

"An arrest, ordered by the Second Bureau. There was a man, or a woman, in your train."

"Ah, Bobinette must have been identified at Rouen when she got into the train — Juve's men must have wired from there!" Henri de Loubersac rejoiced. How he hated this creature, whose detestable influence must harm Wilhelmine, whose wickedness might work woe to the girl he loved! This traitorous wretch would be under lock and key now!

Splendid!

With mind relieved, he thanked the informer and prepared to leave the station. But, as he descended the steps leading to the Cour du Havre he stopped. Two police detectives whom he knew well were walking on either side a soldier in corporal's uniform — Vinson, of course! They must be taking him to the Cherche Midi prison.

De Loubersac realised what had happened.

"By-Jove! The telegram Juve had received at Dieppe must have been false!...Vinson and Bobinette, discovering that they were under observation, had found means to send Juve a telegram announcing that Vinson had been met in London: having thus drawn Juve over to England they had returned to Paris....The traitors must have separated: this would lessen their chances of being recognised....They must have arrested Vinson as he was leaving the train....Bobinette, become unrecognisable when her cassock was hidden, must have escaped!"

De Loubersac ran back. He hunted the station all over. He jumped into a taxi and drove up and down all the adjoining streets; but the chase was a useless one! Bobinette was invisible — Bobinette had seized her opportunity. She had disappeared!

XXIV
AN APPETISER AT ROBERT'S BAR

"Have another whisky, old sport?"

"Not I! We have taken too much on board as it is."

"You must! You must! Seen through the gold of old Scotch, life seems more beautiful, and the barmaids more fetching."

Perched on the high stools which allowed them to lean on the rail of the bar the two topers solemnly clinked glasses.

The younger of the two, a lean, dark fellow, emptied his glass at one go, but his companion, a big fair man about thirty-five, clean shaven, and slightly bald, handled his glass so awkwardly that the contents escaped on to the floor.

The big fair man called for fresh drinks. Their glasses were refilled so quickly that the dark young man failed to notice it: he drank on and on automatically, as though wound up to do so, but his companion barely wetted his lips with the intoxicating liquor.

It was six o'clock and a dismal December evening; but there was an animated cosmopolitan crowd in Robert's bar.

Robert's of London is the equivalent of Maxim's of Paris. The great place for luxurious entertainments, it opens its doors at twilight, and does not close them till the small hours are well advanced. When evening falls, the scene grows animated: business men and women of pleasure crowd the rooms. Gradually the crowd assumes a cosmopolitan character. A band of Hungarian gipsies plays inspiriting and seductive music. The crush increases, the noise grows louder, and amidst this babel of voices, the racket, the din, the barmaids ply their trade with calm determination: they flirt with their customers and egg them on to drink glass after glass of wine and spirits for the good of the house, in an atmosphere thick with tobacco smoke.

Every ten minutes or so, a newspaper boy slips in with the latest evening editions, to be chased out by one of the managers of mixed nationality who, for the most part, talk in a strangely mixed tongue, partly French, partly English.

In this noisy crowded place the two drinkers were talking together familiarly.

The dark young man, after having listened with curiosity to the confidences of his companion, which must have been of an extraordinary nature, judging by the exclamations of surprise they evoked, asked:

"But what is your profession, then?"

"But I have already told you," replied the fat man. "I am a clown — a musical clown.... I interpret comic romances.... I dress up as a negro, I play the banjo!" This jovial individual began humming an air which was the rage of the moment.

The dark young man interrupted with another question:

"What is your native country, Tommy?"

"Oh, I am a Belgian.... And you, Butler?"

The dark young man, who answered to the name of Butler, gave what had to pass for an account of himself.

"I.... I'm Canadian — just come from Canada — hardly three months ago."

"As much as that?" remarked fat Tommy.

Butler seemed upset by this question.

"Yes, yes!... And I feel very anxious, because I don't know my way about, and I don't know English very well, and I can't find work, try as I will... it seems no use."...

"What can you do?"

"A little of everything."

"That is to say — nothing!"

Butler said slowly:

"I can do book-keeping."

The clown burst out laughing.

"That will not take you far! There are hundreds and hundreds of stick-in-the-muds at that job!"

"What do you want me to do, then?" asked Butler.

His plump acquaintance put a hand on his shoulder.

"There is only one career in the world — the theatre!... There is only one profession worth following, that of artiste!... See how I have succeeded! And without having received the least instruction, for my parents never cared a hang for my future — I soon earned plenty money; now, though still in the full flush of young man-hood, I am on the point of making a fortune!"

The clown evidently fancied himself, for he was of a ripe age — no chicken.

His companion gazed at him admiringly.

Certainly the clown looked wealthy: his thick watch-chain was gold, English sovereigns, ostentatiously displayed, were stuffed in a bulging purse: his appearance justified his boasts.

"I would ask nothing better than to get into a theatre," said Butler with a simple air, "but I don't know how to do anything!"

The clown shot a shrewd glance at his companion: Butler's face was flushed, his eyes were wandering: his wits seemed dulled: the glasses of whisky were having their effect.

Tommy murmured into Butler's ear:

"I have known you but a short time, but we are in sympathy, and already I feel a very great friendship for you. Tell me, is it the same on your side?"

Touched by this cordiality, Butler raised a shaky hand above his glass and declared:

"I swear it!"

"Good! My dear Butler, I think things will arrange themselves marvellously well....Just fancy! When walking on the Thames Embankment to-day, I met a theatrical manager whom I have known this long while ...a very good fellow, called Paul....Naturally we had a glass together.... Then I asked him what he was doing. His answer was 'I am looking for an artiste!' Of course, I suggested myself! Paul explained that he did not need a clown, but a professor....I promised to find him one if I could....Would you like to be this professor?"

"Professor of what?" questioned Butler, who, in spite of his growing intoxication, was lending an attentive ear to clown Tommy, who laughed at the question.

"You would never guess who would be your pupils!...You would have to teach Japanese canaries to sing!"

Butler considered this a joke in the worst of taste. The clown declared there was nothing ridiculous about teaching Japanese canaries to sing....The important point was that the professor of singing Japanese canary birds would receive immediate payment.

Whilst Butler was turning over this offer in his muddled mind — for he had persuaded himself that the offer was a genuine one — the clown fidgeted on his high stool, and hummed an air from *Faust* in a falsetto voice. The clown stopped.

"Come, Butler, is it settled?"

Butler hesitated.

"I am not sure that I had better."

"But yes, certainly you had better," insisted the clown. "And, as it happens, I have agreed to dine with this manager he must be in the room downstairs....I will go and look for him!... We three could meet and talk the thing over."

"Where should I have to go?" asked Butler. "To what country?"

"To Belgium, of course," replied Tommy. "The manager is a Belgian, like myself — we are compatriots."

The clown, judging that his companion had decided to accept the offer, left him, saying:

"I am going to find the manager and tell him my friend Butler will be his professor of Japanese singing canaries."

Butler sighed, then swallowed another glass of whisky.

Pushing his way among the crowded tables of the front downstairs room, the clown reached the end of the room. He approached a clean-shaven man seated before a full glass: it was untouched.

"Monsieur Juve?" asked Tommy in a low voice.

Juve nodded.

"Captain Loreuil?"

"That is so: at present, Tommy, musical Belgian clown. And you are Monsieur Paul, theatrical manager.... That is according to our arrangement, is it not?"

"Quite so.... Anything fresh?"

Loreuil smiled. "I have got your man."

"Sure of it?"

Loreuil seated himself next Juve. He spoke low.

"He calls himself Butler... says he is Canadian.... He declares he has been in London some time: it is a falsehood. I recognise him perfectly. I had already seen him at Châlons, when he had a connection with the singer Nichoune, and we suspected him of being the author of the leakages in the offices of the Headquarters Staff."

"That is Corporal Vinson, then?"

"Consequently you must intervene," said Loreuil.

Juve reflected. After a short silence he said:

"Intervene! You go too fast. Remember we are in a foreign country, and there is no question of a common law crime: Vinson is not accused of murder, simply of treason.

"I like that word 'simply,'" remarked Loreuil ironically.

"Don't take that in bad part," smiled Juve; "but it has its importance from an international point of view. I cannot arrest Vinson in England on the pretext that he is a spy."

"Happily we have foreseen that difficulty," said Loreuil. "Butler will accompany us to Belgium. He believes we are Belgians. Belgium means France, as far as we are concerned — the three of us!"

Juve had reached London the evening before. He had found at Scotland Yard several telegrams and a private note from a detective friend, informing him of the arrival of an individual known to be an officer of the Second Bureau.

Juve met Loreuil. The two men, on the same quest, put their heads together. They were soon on the track of Vinson. A man answering to his description had been in London several weeks. This was the truth. Juve would not admit it. He believed Vinson had arrived in England only a few hours ahead of him.

Loreuil, whose mission did not include the arrest of Vinson, considered he had done his part as soon as he had identified the corporal. Juve would do the rest.

"We are agreed, then!" said Loreuil. "If I introduce you to Butler as Paul, the theatrical manager, who wishes to engage him as trainer of canaries ... the rest you can manage for yourself.... Be circumspect! The fellow is on the lookout!"

"He must leave with me to-night — it is urgent!" insisted Juve.... "You must help me, Captain!"

Captain Loreuil frowned.

"I must confess I don't like this sort of thing!" said he.

"But this affair is more serious even than you know," said Juve. "This Vinson business does not stand alone: it is but a strand in a vast network of mystery and wickedness of the most malignant kind."

Still the captain was reluctant. To take part in such a sinister comedy; to make a poor wretch tipsy in order to deliver him to the authorities for punishment, wounded the captain's self-respect. Juve overcame his hesitations with the words:

"It is not merely a secret service matter, Monsieur: it is a question of National Defence."

"I will help you, Monsieur," was the captain's answer to this, adding:

"Let us go up! Our man's patience must be giving out."

XXV
THE ARREST

The Dover Express, the Continental Mail, was moving out of Charing Cross station.

Three travellers were seated in a first-class compartment. They were smoking big cigars: their eyes were bright, their cheeks flushed; they looked like big men who had dined well. These were Butler, Tommy and Paul, leaving for Belgium: otherwise Juve, Loreuil and Vinson bound for France! Copious libations of generous wines and strong liqueurs had reduced Butler-Vinson to the condition of a maudlin puppet: Tommy and Paul had made Butler most conveniently drunk.

The train rushed forward through station after station, brilliantly lighted, then plunged into the obscurity of the country. A stupefying warmth from the heating apparatus impelled slumber. Unfortunate Butler-Vinson, lulled by the regular movement of the train, was soon fast asleep.

Juve and Loreuil kept vigil. They were sitting side by side facing their captive.

"Dover will be the difficulty," whispered Juve, who had drawn closer to the captain.

"Yes, that is the crucial point," agreed Loreuil....

The express was entering the tunnels pierced in the precipitous coastline of the Channel near Dover. There was a short stop at Dover Town station before it drew up on the Pier. There the travellers would embark. Of these there were two distant streams: those crossing to Belgium: those bound for France. Butler-Vinson still slept soundly. Juve was waiting till the last minute. Then he would awaken his prisoner as he already considered him and shepherd him aboard the Calais boat.

Captain Loreuil got out and went on ahead.

"Come along, Butler!" Juve cried suddenly. He shook the slumbering traitor sharply.

Butler-Vinson leaped to his feet with frightened eyes and gaping mouth.

"What is it?" he stuttered. "What do you want with me?"

Juve's smile was a masterpiece of hypocrisy.

"Why, old fellow, you must wake up! We must go aboard our boat!"

The corporal heard men shouting:

"Steamer *Victoria* for Ostend! Steamer *Empress* for Calais!"

"We must hurry!" cried Juve, pushing the bemused Butler-Vinson out of the compartment.

There was a sea fog growing denser every minute. Without their powerful electric lights it would have been impossible to recognise the boats or the gangways leading to them.

Juve had Butler by the arm: a necessary precaution, for the wretched man could scarcely keep on his feet. Juve propelled him towards a gangway: a minute later both were on the boat.

Vinson caught sight of the inscription *Empress* on the lifebuoys. A flash of reason illumined Butler-Vinson's drink-soddened mind. He hesitated, drew back with a frightened look.

"Didn't I hear just now that this boat goes to Calais?"

A passing sailor heard this question. He was about to enlighten Butler-Vinson, but Juve pushed him aside — this imbecile was going to spoil everything!

"No, old fellow, you are quite mistaken! It is the *Victoria* that goes to Calais: we go to Ostend with the *Empress*."

Butler-Vinson accepted this statement as true.

An ear-piercing whistle sounded; the cables were drawn up: a vibratory motion told the passengers they were off.

The mast-head light was extinguished: the mail-boat silently made its way out to sea.

There was a dense fog in the Channel. The fog-horn sounded its lugubrious note.

The sea was rough: a strong wind from the south-west had been blowing all the afternoon. The boat began to pitch and toss: the passengers were drenched.

Though nothing of a sailor in the nautical sense, Juve took his duckings with equanimity: a bit of a pitch and toss would keep Vinson occupied.

The fog was Juve's friend: it lent an air of vagueness, of confusion, to Butler-Vinson's sur-roundings. The vagaries of the steamer would further distract what thoughts he was capable of. Still, they were on an English boat, and should the corporal grasp what was happening and refuse to disembark, Juve would be in a fix. Butler-Vinson must be kept in ignorance of the truth till they were on French soil.

Captain Loreuil had remained at Dover, declaring he still had much to do in England. Be-sides, he could not be brought to consider that to arrest criminals came within the scope of his duties: to mark them down, point them out, yes. Thus he had tracked down the traitor and left him in good hands.

Meanwhile, Butler-Vinson was suffering from a severe attack of sea-sickness. His head seemed splitting with throbbing pain.

"How long shall we be getting across?" he asked in a faint voice.

"Three hours," said Juve: this was the crossing time between Dover and Ostend.

Heavy cross-seas were running. Those who braved the buffetings and drenchings above deck were now few: it was a villainous crossing!

At the end of an hour and a half the odious waltz of the steamer slowed down. The fog-horn was silent: the *Empress* moved alongside the jetties of Calais.

The gangways were let down; porters invaded the deck, carrying away luggage to the trains awaiting the travellers in the terminus station.

"Now for it!" thought Juve.

Once on French soil it was all up with the liberty of Corporal Vinson! His arrest would be immediate.

Juve considered the miserable heap collapsed on a side bench: this traitorous rag of humanity had once been an upright man — a true soldier of France! It was terrible! It was piteous!

Juve raised Butler-Vinson. The wretched fellow could hardly stand up. Juve signed to a sailor, who took the corporal's left arm while Juve supported him on the right. Vinson disembarked. He set his feet on the soil — the sacred soil of France!

The crowd was pouring into the great hall, where customs officers were examining the small baggage.

Juve drew Butler-Vinson to the left: the traitor must not catch sight of the French uniforms. An individual seemed to rise out of the ground in front of them: Juve said to him in a low voice:

"Our man!"

Revived by a cordial, Vinson gradually recovered his senses. Painfully he raised his heavy eye-lids: he looked about him curiously, anxiously. He was in a large, square room, dimly lighted, almost empty, with bare white walls.

"Where am I?" he asked Juve. Three men surrounded him. Juve's was the sole face he knew.

Juve wore a solemn look: his words were gently spoken.

"You are at Calais, in the special police quarters connected with the station. Corporal Vinson, I am sorry to have to tell you that you are under arrest."

"My God!" exclaimed the traitor. He attempted to rise, but fell back on his seat: his eyes were staring at the handcuffs on his wrists! He burst into tears.

Juve felt pity for this miserable being, huddled up there in the depths of humiliation and ter-ror. But the dreadful fact remained — Vinson was a criminal, a traitor! Perhaps his errors were due to a bad bringing-up, to deplorable examples, alas!... Juve was not there to pass judgment, but to deliver the guilty wretch into the hands of the authorities.

"Come now!" he said, tapping Vinson on the shoulder. "Come, we are leaving for Paris!"

Corporal Vinson, traitor, raised supplicating eyes to Juve: then, realising all resistance was vain, he rose painfully: he assumed an air of indifference.

A policeman from Headquarters had joined Juve. The three men got into an empty second-class compartment.

In a voice quivering with shame, Vinson begged Juve not to allow anyone to enter. "I should be so ashamed," he muttered, with hanging head and hunched shoulders.

"We shall do our best to prevent it," Juve assured him. After an explanation with the station-master, the compartment was labelled *"Reserved."*

The train started. Vinson was wide awake now, and dejected to the last degree. After a hand-to-mouth existence, but still a free one, in England, he had allowed himself to be nabbed by the police, like the veriest simpleton! The papers would be full of it!

Vinson, who had been led into criminal ways by his love for a bad woman, troubled himself much less regarding the punishment to be meted out to him than about the dreadful distress his arrest would cause his mother. The old Alsatian mother, when she learned that her son was in prison charged with treason to France, would die of grief. Vinson wished with all his heart that he had stuck to his first decision — that he had killed himself rather than make confession to the journalist, Jérôme Fandor, who had wished to save him, and had helped him to escape, but who had really done him a bad service, since, deserter as he was, he had been caught like the most vulgar of criminals!

The train stopped at a station.

"I am dying of thirst," mumbled Vinson.

Juve sent his second in command for a bottle of water from the refreshment buffet.

Vinson thanked Juve with a grateful nod.

Refreshed, Vinson pulled his wits together.

Juve, noticing this, began questioning him, promising to treat him as well as he possibly could, if he would speak out, in confidence; assuring him of the leniency of the judges if he consented to denounce his accomplices.

When Vinson realised that he was to stand his trial for spying, for betraying his country, as well as for desertion, he was only too glad to obey Juve's suggestion.

"Ah!" murmured he, while tears rolled down his cheeks, "Cursed be the day when I first agreed to enter into relations with the band of criminals who have made of me what I am to-day!"

Vinson gave Juve a full account of his temptation, his errors; nevertheless he did not tell the detective of his relations with Jérôme Fandor. Had he not promised absolute secrecy? Traitor and spy as he was, Vinson had given his word of honour, and this journalist had been kind to him in return, had given him a chance to escape and start afresh: not for anything in the world would he have betrayed his oath!

Juve was a hundred leagues from suspecting the substitution which had taken place between Vinson and Fandor. He was convinced he had Corporal Vinson before his eyes; but he also thought he had his grip on the individual who had left Paris the night before, accompanied by an ecclesiastic, for the purpose of handing over to a foreign power a most important piece of a gun stolen from the Arsenal, as well as the descriptive plan that went with it.

But when he cross-questioned Vinson on this point, the corporal did not in the least understand what he was driving at! Juve, who had been congratulating himself on his prisoner's frankness, grew angry with what he believed was a culpable reservation. Why did the corporal, who, up to this, had spoken so freely, now feign ignorance of the gun piece affair?... Well, he would find out his prisoner's reasons presently....Not wishing to scare him, Juve changed the subject....He had any number of questions to ask the culprit. Did he not know Vagualame, the real Vagualame?

Vinson told him many things about the old accordion player with the patriarchal white beard which he already knew; but one remark particularly impressed him.

"If only the police knew all that goes on in the house in the rue Monge!"...Vinson stopped short.

This remark opened new horizons to Juve. When they arrived at the North station, some hours later, and Juve had transferred his prisoner to a cab, giving the driver the address of the Cherche-Midi prison, our detective had learned that Vagualame-Fantômas was in the habit of visiting a mysterious house in rue Monge. Here he met many of his accomplices. It was here the band of spies and traitors, of which he seemed chief, disguised themselves, issuing forth to ply their nefarious trade and mock the police.

Juve made a compact with himself.

"As soon as I have handed my corporal over to the military jailors, I know where I shall go to smoke a cigarette!"

XXVI

WILHELMINE'S SECRET

"You are alone, Wilhelmine?"

Mademoiselle de Naarboveck had just left the house in the rue Fabert. It was three in the afternoon, and she was going shopping. At the corner of the rue de l'Université she came on Henri de Loubersac.

It was a delightful surprise. She had not seen him for several days. She was aware of the difficult and dangerous nature of her future fiancé's duties; that they frequently took him from Paris for days at a time; that they forbade him writing even a post card to let her know where he was!...Now she felt delightedly sure that he had taken advantage of his first free moment to pay her a visit. How charming of him!

The truth was that de Loubersac, whose anxieties and suspicions had increased hour by hour, till he was suffering the tortures of the damned, had made up his mind to have a decisive talk with Wilhelmine. A clear and final explanation he would have, cost what it might!

Full of joy at the meeting, Wilhelmine did not seem to notice his anxious looks, his strained expression. She answered his question with a welcoming smile.

"I am alone."

"Your father?"

"Went away this morning: the calls of diplomacy are numerous, and frequently sudden, you know!"

"And Mademoiselle Berthe?"

Wilhelmine raised her beautiful bright eyes and met her fiancé's questioning glance.

"No news of her for several days. Berthe seems to have disappeared." Her tone was grave.

De Loubersac did not speak: mechanically he fitted his step to Wilhelmine's. Presently he asked:

"Where do you think of going?"

"I was going to do a little shopping ... nothing much ... there is no sort of hurry!"

She felt that Henri wished to discuss something important with her: hers was too direct a nature to put him off with flimsy excuses when he desired a serious talk.

"Should we walk on a little, talking as we go?" she suggested, with a charming smile. To walk and talk with Henri was such a pleasure!

De Loubersac agreed.

The young couple crossed the Esplanade des Invalides, and by way of the rue Saint-Dominique, the boulevard Saint-Germain, and rue Buonaparte, reached the Luxembourg Gardens. Here they could talk at ease.

A few casual remarks, and Henri de Loubersac came to his point.

"Dear Wilhelmine, there is a series of mysteries in your life which I cannot help thinking about: mysteries which trouble me greatly!...Forgive me for speaking to you so frankly!...You know how sincere my feeling for you is!...My love for you is strong and deep....My one desire in life is to join my fate, my existence, to yours....But before that, there are some things we must speak of together, serious things perhaps, about which we must have a clear understanding."

Wilhelmine had grown strangely pale. Despite the protestations of love in which her future fiancé had wrapped his questions, she was greatly troubled. The painful moment she had waited for had come: she must tell Henri de Loubersac the secret of her life: no very grave secret if considered by itself; but the consequences of it, and the innumerable deductions that could be drawn from it, might react unfavourably on their relations to each other!

Wilhelmine must speak out.

They were just outside the church of Saint-Sulpice. Some large drops of rain fell.

"Let us go into the church!" said Wilhelmine: "It will be quiet there. If what I have to say to you is said in that holy place, you will feel that I am speaking the truth. It is almost a confession." The poor girl's voice trembled slightly as she uttered these decisive words — words that frightened de Loubersac. What shocking revelations did they foreshadow?

He acquiesced: the lovers entered the porch.

As he stepped aside to let Wilhelmine pass, he noticed a cab with drawn blinds which had that minute drawn up not far from the space in front of the church. He examined it anxiously.

"It seemed to me we were being followed — shadowed," replied de Loubersac. "It is of little importance, however — we must expect that in our service."

"Yes, you also have secrets," remarked Wilhelmine.

"They are only professional ones: there is nothing about my personality to hide: my life is an open book for all the world to read!"

De Loubersac's tone was hard.

It hurt Wilhelmine.

For some while they had been seated behind a pillar, in the shadow: Wilhelmine had been speaking: Henri had been listening.

She told him she was not the daughter of the baron de Naarboveck, that her real name was Thérèse Auvernois.[5]

This told de Loubersac nothing.

Wilhelmine explained that her childhood had been passed in an ancient château, on the banks of the Dordogne, with her grandmother, the Marquise de Langrune. One fatal December day the Marquise had been assassinated. They were led to believe the assassin was a young man, son of a friend of the family, by name, Charles Rambert. This tragedy had altered the whole course of the orphan girl's life. She was taken care of by the father of the supposed murderer, a worthy old man, Monsieur Etionne Rambert. He recommended her to Lady Beltham, whose husband had been murdered some months before; thus the bereaved girl came to live under Lady Beltham's wing, and grew very fond of her. Then Monsieur Etionne Rambert disappeared in a shipwreck, and Wilhelmine went with Lady Beltham to her castle in Scotland.

Two peaceful years passed. Among other friends and visitors, Wilhelmine met the Baron de Naarboveck, a foreign diplomat. Then Lady Beltham went to France, and one sad day the orphan girl learned that her mother by adoption had died there![6]

Six dreary, anxious months followed. Then the baron, the only person in the whole world who seemed to care whether she lived or died, came to find her. He took her to Paris. There he decided to pass her off as his daughter, declaring he had very grave reasons for doing so.

Though making her the centre of a mystery, for undeclared reasons of his own, de Naarboveck was very good to her, helped her to unravel her financial affairs, and informed her that she was the owner of a large fortune. He told her that some day she would have to go to a foreign country to take possession of this fortune — the baron did not say where.

Wilhelmine stopped her narrative, jumped up, pointing to a shadow moving across an altar.

"Did you see?" she questioned anxiously.

"I think I did," answered Henri de Loubersac. "It is the shadow of some passer-by thrown into relief on the light background."

"Oh, I hope we are not being spied on!"

"Of whom are you afraid?" asked de Loubersac.

Wilhelmine — or Thérèse Auvernois, as she had confessed herself to be — glanced about her. There was not a soul within hearing! Now she would speak her mind to Henri — her dear Henri — and tell him all.

"You want to know, dear one, why my existence has been surrounded with so many mysterious precautions of late years! You wish to know why the baron is so determined that my real identity should remain hidden! You are right; for I have long asked myself the same question. When I spoke to the baron about this for the first time — it was only a few weeks ago, and told him that I wished to appear as what I really am, Thérèse Auvernois, my father by adoption — I may call him that, seeing how good, how kind he has been to me — began by telling me it was impossible — that the most terrible misfortunes would result from such a revelation....I insisted. I wanted to know what these dreadful misfortunes would be, and why they would follow as a matter of course, were it made known that I am Thérèse Auvernois. Thereupon the baron told me astonishing things.

"According to him, from the time of my poor grandmother's death, I, and those near to me, all those about me, were pursued, not only by a terrible fatality, but also by a being, who, for unknown motives, wished to sow perpetual death and terror among those intimately connected with us.

"The baron did not want to talk of all this, but I made him speak out. Bit by bit, I learned the details of one of those tragedies which touched my life when a child. I went to the National Library, secretly, and looked through the newspapers of that period. I noticed that in whatever concerned us, whether legally or privately, closely or distantly, one name appeared and reappeared, a terrifying and legendary name, the name of a being we think of but dare not mention — the name of Fantômas!"

Henri de Loubersac was staggered. This statement of the girl he knew as Wilhelmine de Naarboveck, far from impressing him favourably, seemed to him an improbable story invented, every bit of it, for the sole purpose of putting him on the wrong track.

He had learned to love this charming girl, believing her to be sincere, honest, pure, brought up as a young girl should be, amidst elegant and distinguished surroundings: now, behold an abyss opened before his eyes, separating him from one whom he was now inclined to consider an adventuress.

He remembered Juve's words!

Granting the truth of her statement, that a tragedy had shadowed her young life and altered her existence, this did not prevent her from having been seduced by Captain Brocq! Rather, her early experiences would tend to break down the barriers, behind which nice girls lived and moved!...There were things that called for an explanation! For instance, how explain the intimacy existing between de Naarboveck, his so-called daughter, and this Mademoiselle Berthe, whose part in the affair engaging de Loubersac's attention was open to the gravest suspicions?...

Wilhelmine continued what she called her confession, thinking aloud, opening her heart, confiding in her dear Henri, whose silence she took for sympathy and encouragement.

"Fantômas," she murmured: "I cannot tell you how often I have thought over this maddening, this puzzling personality, terrifying beyond words, who seems implacably bent on our destruction!...Again and again I have had reason to fear that his ill-omened influence has been directed against my humble self!...As if he guessed something of this, the baron has frequently sought to reassure me; yet, through some singular coincidence, each time we have spoken of Fantômas a tragedy has occurred, a dreadful tragedy, which has reminded us of monstrous crimes committed by him in the past!"

Wilhelmine's statements were impressing de Loubersac less and less favourably.

"Play acting — and clumsy play acting at that!" decided Henri: "Done to avert my suspicions, imagined to feed my curiosity!...She thinks herself a capable player at the game! She does not know the person she is playing with!"

De Loubersac came to a decision. He rose, stood close to Wilhelmine, who also rose, instinctively, looked her straight in the face, and asked, point-blank:

"Wilhelmine de Naarboveck, or Thérèse Auvernois — it matters little to me — I wish to know the real truth....Confess, then, that you were Captain Brocq's mistress!"

"Monsieur!" exclaimed the startled girl. She met de Loubersac's inquisitorial look proudly. His penetrating stare did not falter.

Suddenly Wilhelmine's lips began to tremble. She grew deadly pale: she might have been on the verge of a fainting fit. She had realised the incredulity of the man to whom, in her chaste innocence, she had given her heart. In the pure soul of this loving girl an immense void made itself felt. It was as though a flashlight had revealed to her the lamentable truth: that the strange position in which destiny had placed her — a position strange but not infamous — had made of her a being apart, had put her outside the ordinary life of humanity, outside the law of love!... A desire to explain, to convince, to justify herself, the desire of a desperate creature at bay, burned up in her like a flame: it flashed and died. Henri had no confidence in her! He believed this odious thing of her — this abominable, incredible thing!... Her heart was full to bursting with an agony of grief, of outraged innocence.... She looked him straight in the eyes — her own flashing fury.

"You insult me!" she cried...."Withdraw what you have just said!... You will apologise!"

De Loubersac said in a low, distinct voice:

"I maintain my accusation, Mademoiselle, until you have furnished me with absolute, undeniable proofs!"...

De Loubersac's voice failed him. Wilhelmine had turned from him. She hurried to the door, descended the church steps, and threw herself into a passing cab.

De Loubersac had followed her.

In tones of contempt she had flung at him the words:

"Farewell, monsieur — and for ever!"

Henri's answer was a shrug of the shoulder.

As he stood there, an outline, a shadow, appeared under the church porch: a something, a being, indescribable, appeared, disappeared, running with spirit-like swiftness, vanishing. Henri de Loubersac had a clear conviction that during his conversation with her who might have been his fiancée in days to come, they had been shadowed, spied upon!

XXVII

THE TWO VINSONS

There were strange happenings elsewhere on the day Henri de Loubersac and Wilhelmine de Naarboveck had parted in grief and anger.

It was on the stroke of noon when Corporal Vinson heard a key turn in the lock of his cell. Two military jailors confronted him.

"Butler?"

The traitor answered to that name.

Juve, for reasons of his own, had not revealed the prisoner's true quality. Vinson had therefore been entered in the jail book as Butler.

One of the jailors, an old veteran, whose uniform was a mixture of the civil and the military, took the word.

"Butler, you are to be transferred to a building belonging to the Council of War: there you will occupy cell 27....Our prison here is for the condemned only, so you cannot remain. You belong to the accused section."

All that mattered to Butler-Vinson for the moment was — he had to reach his new quarters by crossing the rue Cherche-Midi between two jailors....He would be exposed to the curious glances of the public! He shuddered at the thought!...And there was worse to come! This was but the commencement of his purgatory....As he had not known how to die at the right moment, he must arm himself with courage to expiate his cowardice!...He must leave the shelter of his cell!...With an intense effort of will he stretched out his arms, was handcuffed without a murmur, and, marching between his two jailors, he quitted the prison.

The bright light of noonday made him blink. On reaching the pavement he recoiled with a convulsive movement: the jailors pulled him forward.

It was the crowded hour, when men leave offices and shops for a midday meal. But the public of these parts, accustomed to such comings and goings of prisoners and their jailors, paid no attention to this pitiful trio.

The prisoner seemed so overcome with emotion that, after uttering a long sigh like a death rattle, he sank, a dead weight, into the arms of his jailors.

They were forced to support him. They carried him to the courtyard of the Council of War. Some, whose curiosity was aroused by the unusual pallor of the prisoner, wished to follow, but the jailors closed the great doors of the courtyard.

Before leading him to his cell, they dumped their inanimate prisoner on a chair in the porter's lodge....The porter brought vinegar. They rubbed Butler-Vinson's temples with it. A jailor slapped his hands. In vain! The prisoner showed no signs of life!

"You had better take him to his cell," advised the porter. "Perhaps he will come to his senses if laid on his palliasse? In any case, run for the medical officer."

The jailors, who could make nothing of their prisoner's mysterious condition, transported him to cell 27. They laid him on his palliasse.

"Lieutenant Servin?"

"Commandant?"

"Will you help me to reduce these papers to order? It is half-past eleven: I want to go to breakfast!"

The lieutenant brought a pile of documents to his superior's table and rapidly classified them.

His superior, Commandant Dumoulin, had been chief assistant at the Second Bureau. He had passed long years at his post there. Previous to that, he had acted as Government Commissioner on the Councils of War in the various garrisons where he had been stationed....Some six months ago Dumoulin had sent in his request to the Minister of War for a change of billet. His record being an excellent one, the Minister had appointed him Government Chief-commissioner attached to the Principal Council of War, sitting in Paris.

Dumoulin had recently taken up his new duties, and was counting on getting peacefully into the run of things, when, the evening before, he had been warned at his own home by a private note from the Minister, that a deserter, accused of treason, had been arrested, and that Corporal Vinson was the man in question.

At the sight of this name Commandant Dumoulin thrilled with excitement. As former Under-Secretary at the Second Bureau he had the affair at his finger ends, and well knew how tangled, how obscure it was, how bristling with dangers, how rich in complications.... The Vinson affair, it was the Captain Brocq affair, the singer Nichoune affair ... the story of a plan of mobilisation stolen, of a gun piece lifted from the Arsenal!... He was in for a big affair — a sensational case!...

The commandant passed a wakeful night and arrived early at his office. He must get to work! Fortunately, among his deputies he had found a competent and zealous helper in Lieutenant Servin. He turned to him now.

"Our next proceeding will be to establish the identity of Corporal Vinson. We must examine him on that point without delay.... Send for him immediately, Lieutenant!... According to the prison register, he occupies cell 26."

"Excuse me, Commandant; Vinson, who was registered this morning at the Cherche-Midi prison, must actually be in the Council buildings, where he occupied cell 27."

The commandant adjusted his eye-glasses, looked closely at a yellow paper, and corrected in his turn:

"That is an error: in cell 27 is an individual named Butler."

"Yes, Commandant: Butler — he is Vinson!"

"I do not understand," objected Dumoulin. "You must have made a mistake. Corporal Vinson was arrested yesterday at the Saint Lazare station: he was brought here and was registered for cell 26; besides, I was immediately informed of this arrest by a private telegram."

"Commandant," persisted the lieutenant: "Corporal Vinson, who hid himself under the name of Butler, was arrested early this morning at the Calais station, when he landed from England. The arrest was effected by Inspector Juve, who took his prisoner to Cherche-Midi about six o'clock; and this Vinson occupied cell 27."

"Come, now, Lieutenant, you have lost your head!" grumbled the commandant: "Since Vinson was arrested yesterday at the Saint Lazare station, it is evident that he was not arrested last night at Calais! Vinson and Butler — that makes two."

"I beg your pardon, Commandant: that makes only one!"

The commandant looked severely at his subordinate.

"That is enough, Lieutenant!... Send for Corporal Vinson who occupied cell 26."

"Right, Commandant!"

Some minutes later there was a knock at the door: two warders with a prisoner stood on the threshold.

The commandant assured himself with a glance that the non-commissioned officer, acting as reporter, was at his post, and that Lieutenant Servin was seated at the desk next his own.

"Enter!" he commanded.

Dumoulin solemnly opened the voluminous bundle of papers set before him, looked through the documents, affecting not to see the prisoner stationed before him.... Ready at length to begin the interrogation, the commandant raised his head, straightened himself, and ordered:

"Approach!"

The prisoner, a warder on each side of him, took a step forward.

"You are truly Corporal Vinson?"

"No, Commandant!"

Dumoulin was silent a moment, choking with anger, his hand trembling slightly — did the fellow mean to mock him?... He frowned. He did not like the manner of this fellow, with his bright, piercing eyes, his scornful looks. He repeated:

"Are you Corporal Vinson?"

"No, Commandant."

Dumoulin was boiling with rage: he was about to explode. Lieutenant Servin approached: in a low voice he said:

"Commandant! Someone wishes you to see him immediately."

Servin handed his superior a card. On it the commandant read:

Inspector Juve,
Detective Force,
Police Headquarters.

"What does he want?"

"He is the detective who arrested Vinson."

"Well," exclaimed the exasperated Dumoulin, "he arrives at the right moment! Let him come in!"

Juve entered and saluted Dumoulin with an amiable smile. He did not take any notice of the prisoner, who was standing with his back to the light.

"It is I, Commandant, who arrested Corporal Vinson; consequently, I have come to place myself at your disposal."

"You have done the right thing!" cried Dumoulin. "Now, will you get this prisoner to own up? Make him tell us whether or no he is Corporal Vinson!"

Dumoulin pointed an irate finger at the prisoner.

Our detective stood rooted to the ground!... The prisoner moved quickly towards him.

"Fandor!"

"Juve!"

"What does this mean, Fandor?"

"It means, Juve, that I am arrested in the place of Corporal Vinson!"

"Nothing of the sort!... I arrive from London. I arrested Vinson yesterday evening at Calais!"

Fandor laughed: he could have roared with laughter.

"My dear Juve," said he, "I should have to talk to you for two mortal hours before you would understand a word of this business!"

Fandor turned to the thunderstruck Dumoulin, and said in a voice of the most exquisite politeness:

"Commandant, I must state once for all that I am not Corporal Vinson!... I am a journalist, whom you perhaps know by name: Jérôme Fandor, on the staff of *La Capitale*.... If you see me in this uniform, this disguise, that relates to a series of events, details of which I will give you with pleasure, as soon as I have reduced my own ideas to order.... As things stand, I am fortunate in meeting my friend Juve, who, if you desire it, will confirm the truth of my statement."

Dumoulin, more and more nonplussed, started in turn at the detective, at the journalist, at his reporter.... With face red as a boiled lobster, he turned to Lieutenant Servin....

When this farcical scene began, Servin had gone into his own office, and had given his secretary an order. The secretary had just returned. The lieutenant, having recorded the answer brought him, had just that moment returned to the commandant's office.

Lieutenant Servin looked upset.

"Commandant!" he gasped out.

He turned to our detective.

"Monsieur Juve!"

He continued staring first at one man, then at the other.

"An incredible thing has happened!... I have just heard of it!... I had given the order to have Corporal Vinson brought here immediately — the real Corporal Vinson — he whom Monsieur Juve arrested under the name of Butler: well, Commandant, it appears that on entering his cell they found him — dead!"

"What is that you say?" asked Dumoulin and Juve together.

"I say that he is dead," repeated the lieutenant.

"But how?" questioned Juve.

The lieutenant made a sign to the sergeant in charge.

"Go for the medical officer."

Some minutes passed in a silence that hummed with questions.

A young assistant surgeon appeared.

"Kindly explain what is wrong, Monsieur!" commanded Dumoulin.

The surgeon spoke.

"My commandant sent for me, about an hour ago. I was to attend to a prisoner who had fainted. This man, when crossing the rue du Cherche-Midi, had suddenly lost consciousness. His warders could not revive him. They carried him to his cell. They laid him on his palliasse. When I arrived the man was dead."

"Dead of what?" demanded Dumoulin.

"A bullet in his heart," replied the surgeon.... "I ascertained this when undressing him. The bullet will be found at the post-mortem: it has probably lodged in the vertebral column."

Dumoulin rose: paced the floor: he was greatly agitated.

"Oh, come, come!" he cried. "People are not killed like that in the open street!... It is un-heard of! Unbelievable!... A bullet presupposes a revolver — a weapon of percussion of some description — a detonation!... There is a noise, a sound!"

Dumoulin went up to the young surgeon. There was a note of suspicious contempt in his question:

"Are you quite sure of what you say?"

"I am quite sure, Commandant."

During this discussion Juve had approached Fandor. When the surgeon made his statement, Juve murmured in Fandor's ear:

"Vinson shot through the heart by a bullet!... Like Captain Brocq!... Killed undoubtedly by a noiseless weapon ... when crossing the street!... Here, again, is — Fantômas!"

Things calmed down somewhat. Fandor addressed Dumoulin:

"Excuse me, Commandant, for having troubled you. I should be most grateful if you would set me at liberty. One tragedy follows hard on another! It is phenomenal!... I shall have to."...

Commandant Dumoulin burst out:

"By Heaven!" he shouted, thumping the table with his fist: "You are the limit!... The take-the-cake limit!... You flout me! You practise on my credulity!... Now you would steal a march on me! Try it on — will you?... Ah! You are not Corporal Vinson!... No?... You are a journalist!... You have got to prove that!... Even if you do prove it, you have got yourself into a pretty pickle by your fooling, by making a laughing-stock of the entire army in your own preposterous person — by assuming that uniform!...

"Guards!" shouted Dumoulin. "Take this man back to his cell! Be sharp about it!... Double his guard!"

Fandor was not allowed time to protest: he was marched off at the double.

Juve tried to get in a word of explanation.

"I assure you, Commandant, it is certainly Jérôme Fandor you are deal — — "

"You!" yelled the commandant. "Get out! Foot it!... Leave me in peace, can't you!... Out with you, or I'll know the reason why!... Begone!"...

Dumoulin was apoplectic with rage.

XXVIII
AT "THE CRYING CALF"

"What's your drink?"

"What's your offer?"

Hogshead Geoffrey, also nicknamed "The Barrel," thumped the table with a formidable fist, at the risk of upsetting a pile of saucers, which, at this advanced hour of the evening, showed clearly how he had spent the hours passed in the wine-shop.

"What do I offer?" he retorted. "I offer what's wanted. I don't haggle. When I ask a fellow: 'Old man, what do you want to wet your gullet?' that means: 'Choose.' There now!"

Hogshead Geoffrey's companion merely said:

"Pass the programme!"

Once in possession of the wine-list — if such could be called the crumpled, dirty paper on which the owner of the house had scribbled in pencil the fresh drinks, composed of indescribable mixtures specially recommended to his clients — the guest of Hogshead Geoffrey became absorbed in the list of strange beverages.

So mean-looking an individual was this guest that he had been nicknamed "The Scrub." He also answered to the more aristocratic title of "Sacristan." Once he had been sacristan at the church of Saint-Sulpice, but intemperate habits had led to his dismissal. What odd link there was between this sorry little fellow and the robust Geoffrey?[7]

The Scrub ordered: "A thick 'un — jolly thick!" He eyed his host.

"What's been your lay? I haven't clapped eyes on you for days!"

Hogshead Geoffrey emptied his glass at one go. Leaning his head against the wall, his fists on the table, his legs stretched out, he stared at the ceiling.

The atmosphere of this den in the rue Monge was poisonous with the odours of stale wine and rank tobacco. The musty air was thick, the shop was ill-lighted by one jet of gas in the centre of the room.

"Well, old Scrub," said Geoffrey at last. "You haven't seen me because you haven't!... You remember I passed the Markets' test and was nominated market porter?"

"Jolly well I do!... We had a famous drinking bout that time!"

"That's so, Scrub!... And my sister Bobinette paid the piper!... You remember I was rejected?... Well, I got into the Markets all the same!... Then — one fine day I gave a tallykeeper a regular knock-down-and-outer!"

"You did?"

"Just didn't I?... I gave him such a oner — just like this!"...

Lifting his enormous hairy fist, Hogshead Geoffrey brought it down on the table with disastrous results: the ancient worm-eaten board was split from end to end!

Flattering remarks were showered on this colossus from all sides.

"Ho! ho! Nothing can resist me!" shouted Hogshead Geoffrey.... "Give me anything you choose!... Every table in the room! No matter what! I'll break it in two — man or woman! Wood or stone!... It's all one to me!"

True or not, Hogshead Geoffrey, when not too much in liquor, was a gentle soul, a simple, kind creature; quick-tempered, kind-hearted. Liable to sudden gusts of anger, he was equally capable of knocking the life out of a comrade with his gigantic fist or of comforting some sniveling street urchin crossing his path.

Well did the Scrub know it. He too was a contradictory mixture. This mean little human specimen had been newsboy, seller of post cards, opener of cab doors, Jack of any little trade, the companion of pickpockets and other light-fingered gentry, also adored the good manners of bygone vestry days, the polished phrases, the benedictory gestures!

When in hospital, chance had given him Hogshead Geoffrey for bed-neighbour. It did not take him long to realise that he would be the gainer by a friendship with this kindly giant: it would be a partnership of brain and muscle.... The Scrub commanded: Geoffrey executed.

When the admiration for his prowess had died down, Hogshead Geoffrey continued his story:

"When I had given the chief the knock-out, the next day they gave me the order of the boot, if you would believe me!... I was properly down and out! I hadn't saved a sou — was in debt right and left, to the wine-shops — was all but run in!"...

"What did you do?" enquired the Scrub.

"Bobinette helped me."

"Your sister?"

"Oh, she's a sharp one!... She's studied, too!... She did the bandages at Lariboise!... She had the sous!... I told her my troubles!... She let me have the dibs, so I could hang on!"

"Until you got a billet at *The Big Tun*?"

"No!... Bobine said: 'Here's gold, little brother! It's all I have ... don't come for more!... You must find a way out of the mess!'"

"And you did?... How?"

Hogshead Geoffrey hesitated: he sipped his absinthe.

"Oh ... well ... I found a way out."...

"How? I ask you."...

"I tell you I managed all right! And then I got my job at *The Big Tun*."

"Where you are now?"

"Where I am."

"You paid back your sister?"

Hogshead Geoffrey roared with laughter.

"I paid her back so little that I didn't know what had become of her!... She had turned her back on Lariboise without leaving an address.... Thought she must have kicked the bucket!... I would have been sorry for that!... She's a good sort!... But yesterday I had word from her.... Bobinette asked me to meet her."...

"You told her to come here?"

"Sure!"

"And how did she know your address?"

Hogshead Geoffrey scratched his big head.

"Lordy! I don't know!... Probably she saw my name quoted the other day in the *Petit Journal*, among the conquerors in the Who's Strongest Competition. She wrote putting the number of my old shanty, rue de la Harpe!... No good being astonished at what she does!... I tell you she has education — she has!"...

It was half an hour after midnight. The owner of *The Crying Calf* shouted in a stentorian voice:

"Now, boys! It's only seven sous drinks now!"

It was the accustomed warning, taken as a matter of course.

Protesting in a squeaky voice that his constitution was weakly, that his doctor had ordered him not to sit up late, the Scrub, who feared a meeting with Bobinette, knowing she had little liking for him, now took himself off.

Geoffrey ordered two drinks. He was bored. Bobinette was behind her promised time. He would have left, but Bobinette would pay for his drinks — a nice little total!

At last she appeared: an out-of-breath Bobinette, and somewhat flustered.

She was quietly dressed — almost shabby. This was no place for one of the elegant toilettes affected by Mademoiselle de Naarboveck's companion!... After her Rouen journey, after her meeting with Lieutenant de Loubersac in the train, she had thought it wiser not to go back to the baron's house. She had written to say she was ill. Then she had taken refuge in a quiet little inn in la Chapelle neighbourhood, there to await events.

Vagualame's arrest had made a terrible impression on her.... Vagualame had not betrayed her; but she sensed snares, pitfalls all about her: she might be trapped any minute: she must disappear! After Vagualame's arrest she had had but one idea: to get rid of the gun piece, hand it to the foreign power, and receive the promised reward.... When, instead of Corporal Vinson, whom she had summoned in accordance with her orders, she had perceived Fandor, she was puzzled, suspicious.

If Bobinette went to the meeting place in her own undisguised person, and met Fandor as Fandor, it was because she had had the same idea as the journalist.

"I will walk through the arcades as Bobinette, and I shall see if Corporal Vinson is there, or if, by chance, he is not alone!"

That same day at Rouen she had had a bad shock. The telegram she had received at the garage was from Vagualame!... How could an arrested Vagualame send her a telegram, and such a telegram?

This telegram, in their usual cypher, informed her that at all costs, and at once, she must separate herself from Corporal Vinson, who was not the real Vinson, but a counter-spy!... Bobinette all but fainted from fright.... She must escape from this counter-spy!... Yet, owing to the false Vinson's insistence, she had been forced to share his room!... He did not mean to let her out of his sight, that was plain!...

No sooner had the false Vinson gone down to the car in the morning than Bobinette had slipped off, hot foot for Rouen. The gun piece was left behind! The chauffeur would bear the brunt of that, thought Bobinette, as she sped on her way. Later, she read of his arrest and release.

Her meeting with Lieutenant de Loubersac and the sight of the false Vinson's arrest at the Saint Lazare station showed the terrified girl that things had gone mysteriously, hopelessly wrong!...

Without resources, Bobinette had pawned her few jewels. Then a letter from Vagualame had reached her. She had obeyed the instructions it contained.... That he had learned her address did not surprise her: she knew he never lost track of those it was to his interest to keep an eye on.

Before Vagualame's note reached her she had been worried and bored.

"I must make sure of shelter and protection if needs be," she reflected: "I will look up Geoffrey. We will meet at *The Crying Calf*, it is safe there!"

"Sit you down here, little Bobine!" suggested Hogshead Geoffrey...."And now, what will you take?"

Bobinette ordered a gooseberry syrup.

"Quite the lady's drink," remarked mine host of the wine-shop with a humorous air.

Brother and sister exchanged confidences.... The good Geoffrey told of his fight, of situations obtained and lost, of fisticuff encounters, of quarrels and blows.... Bobinette went so far as to say that she was very happy, very much at her ease.

"Just imagine," said she: "I am companion to an old lady, a Russian, who in her time has had trouble with the police of her country, I think."

"The police? I don't like the police!" interrupted her brother.

"Who does?" ejaculated Bobinette. "Lots of people come to her house. I go to all the dinners, all the parties!"

"Ah, then, you'll foot the bill, Bobine, if you have such a rich situation?"

"I will pay, Geoffrey," said Bobinette: "This old lady, I think."... Bobinette stopped. She went white as a sheet.... An old man had just entered the wine-shop. His steps were uncertain, his back was bent under the weight of an old accordion.

It was Vagualame....

XXIX
I AM TROKOFF

Bobinette's astonishment was so evident that Hogshead Geoffrey, whose powers of observation were small, was struck by his sister's expression.

"You know that old fellow?" he asked. "If he bothers you you've but to pass the word, you know, and I'll soon put him on the other side of the door!"

This amiable offer terrified the girl. She felt sure Vagualame was not at *The Crying Calf* by chance. He had probably followed her — wished to have a word with her.... She must fall in with his wishes. She must cut short this interview with her brother. After all, it was only to pass the time she had come.

"Keep quiet, Geoffrey," she said: "I do not know the old boy, and you deceive yourself if you think he annoys me!... Besides, my dear Geoffrey, I must be off!"

"Be off!... Whatever's come to you, Bobine?"

"I have business on hand elsewhere.... And now that I know you are quite well, Geoffrey, I shall continue my walk."

"True?" protested the bewildered giant: "You're going to cut your stick already?"

"Call the governor!... There's a twenty-franc piece for you! Pay for your drinks and keep the rest," was Bobinette's effective reply.

Hogshead calmed down at once.

"As long as you pay up, Bobine, I've nothing to say; but, all the same, you have queer ideas.... You bring me here to keep an appointment, and then, we're not five minutes together, when up you get on the trot again!"

Bobinette caught her brother's huge fist in a quick handshake, made for the door of *The Crying Calf*, turned out of rue Monge at a slow pace, convinced that Vagualame would join her.

The street was deserted. Bobinette kept in the shadow, avoiding the bright patches cast on the silent roadway from the wine-shops and taverns still open and alight.

She had been walking about five minutes when she felt that someone was walking behind her, hastening to overtake her.... A hand was laid on her shoulder: Vagualame was beside her, regulating his steps by hers.

"Is that species of giant your brother?" he asked.

Bobinette nodded.

"You are free, then?" she asked, breathing hard.

"It looks like it!"

"Who released you?"

"Let us hurry!" said Vagualame: "Let us seek shelter."

"Where?"

"You will see — with friends."

What did it matter to Bobinette where they were going while strange doubts and horrid fears filled her mind?

"Who released you?"

They were passing beneath a street lamp. Vagualame noted that Bobinette was regarding him with defiant eyes. Was this really Vagualame? Was he an impostor?

Vagualame read her thoughts.

"Bobinette, you are nothing but a fool!" announced the old accordion player: "The man arrested at your place was a detective, who had got himself up like me to take you in!... You let him trick you! You are an imbecile!"

Bobinette stopped.

"But then ... if a detective made himself up to resemble you, it means they know you are guilty! It means they are after you! Why, it's a mad thing you are doing, coming to meet me in that rig out! Why have you not disguised yourself?"

Vagualame smiled.

"Possibly I have reason for it, a plan you know nothing about, Bobinette!...But, let us return to the false Vagualame. How was it you did not detect the fraud, if only by the voice?...How is it you have not guessed the truth since?...When you received my telegram at Rouen it should have been as clear as daylight to you!...Eh!"

Bobinette kept silence.

"Well, we will not dwell on the past," declared Vagualame, with an air of magnanimity: "Fortunately your extraordinary simplicity has not had any particular consequences — save the stupid way you let them get hold of the gun piece, and allowed the false Corporal Vinson to escape!"... In a menacing tone he said: "We will return to that question later."

"But," faltered Bobinette: "How could I act otherwise?"

Vagualame threw her such a look, a look so charged with fierce contempt that she could no longer doubt that she was face to face with her master. This master would not allow argument, discussion: well she knew that!

She screwed up her courage to ask:

"How did you learn my address?"

"That is my business!" he declared: "What I want to know I get to know — you must have seen that by this time!"

"How is it, then, you called at *The Crying Calf* to-day?...Geoffrey did not know you: he alone knew I was coming to see him!...You followed me?"

"Suppose I did follow you?"...Vagualame's tone changed: it became imperious.

"Have you quite finished asking me silly questions?...I consider it is my turn to put a question or two to you — What are you doing?"

Bobinette bent her head.

"You have a right to know," she murmured: "When you sent me that letter, after I took refuge in La Chapelle, telling me to go to the house of a Madame Olga Dimitroff and present myself for the post of companion, I went. She engaged me. I am still with her."

"To take refuge in an hotel was an idiotic thing to do, Bobinette....The police could easily have nabbed you there if they had had a mind to. That is why I sent you to one of my old friends — to a person to whom I could recommend you!...Well, Bobinette, you will have to leave that house!"

The young woman bent her head, mastered, ready to accept any orders of Vagualame's before they were issued. All she asked, in a timid voice, was: "Where am I to go then?"

"Far from here."

"Why?"

Vagualame's smile was evil. His reply was like a series of sword thrusts.

"Because Juve has good eyes; because Fandor also begins to see clear....The net begins to tighten....I shall find means to slip through it!...I am not of those who are caught like a mouse in a trap....But, as for you — you with your simplicity — it is high time to put you out of reach of the police!...I am going to give you some money. Five days hence, disguised as a gipsy, you are to be on the road from Sceaux to Versailles, at eleven o'clock at night, by the first milestone on the left side after the aeroplane garage....You have followed me?"

Bobinette was trembling.

"Disguised as a gipsy, Vagualame? Why?"

"That is no concern of yours!...You have only to do as I tell you. I give orders, but not explanations!"

Vagualame felt in his pockets. He held out a note-book.

"You will find two fifty-franc notes in this. It is more than you need for a suitable disguise. I will give you more money when you start off, because I am going to send you to a foreign country."

Whilst talking, Vagualame and Bobinette had gone a long way from *The Crying Calf*. By a labyrinth of little streets, all darkness and mystery, Vagualame had led his companion to a kind of blind alley: a tall house blocked the end of it. A large shop on the ground floor occupied half the front of it. Although the iron shutters had been drawn down, light from the interior penetrated through apertures to the street — thin rays of light.

Vagualame laid a brutal hand on Bobinette.

"Attend to what I say: it is no joking matter. You are coming in with me. I am going to introduce you to my many friends here, whom I have recently got to know: they may say things that will astonish you, but do not show surprise.... I bring you here that you may know where to find me during the five days you remain in Paris.... You have only to write a letter and bring it to the woman who keeps this library. Address to Vagualame: it will reach me."

"Yes," replied Bobinette.

Vagualame knocked three separate times, then twice quickly, on the iron shutters. A key turned in the lock: the door opened. Vagualame thrust Bobinette across the threshold. Out of the obscurity of the streets whipped by an icy wind and torrents of rain, Bobinette found herself in a brilliantly lighted book-shop.

She stood dazzled.

A young woman came forward.

"Good evening, Sophie," said Vagualame: "Anything new?"

"Nothing new, Vagualame!"

Bobinette looked about her. She saw piles of books and collections of magazines and papers. The shop was crowded with them.

"Sophie, I bring a new friend — a sure friend — who may have to bring you a letter for me one of these days," said Vagualame.

The proprietress looked curiously at Bobinette. All she said was:

"Have our brothers been warned, Vagualame?"

"They have not been told yet; but I shall present my friend to them at the first opportunity."

There was loud knocking at the shutters! Voices were heard shouting:

"Open! Open! Open! The police!"

Bobinette grew ashen with terror.

"It is all up!" thought the desperate girl: "They will see Vagualame is free! They will find me with him! We are caught!"

She turned frantically to Vagualame. He stood calm and collected.

"Ah!" said he with a touch of raillery, looking at the proprietress: "They have been warned that you are again breaking the work law!"

Shaking a threatening finger at the rigid Sophie, Vagualame went to the shop entrance. He looked through the large keyhole to see who was demanding admittance at this late hour.... A look, and Vagualame turned, caught Sophie by the arm, and whispered:

"Detective Juve!... Inspector Michel!... Keep cool, Sophie! They cannot know all the ins and outs of your place."

Two strides and Vagualame joined Bobinette. He dragged her to the end of the shop, reached a corner, turned it, and they were standing on boards clear of books: it was hidden from the main part of the shop and from the entrance.

"Draw your skirts between your legs!" he commanded. "Don't utter a sound!... Don't be afraid!"

Vagualame was right. The police had surrounded the mysterious shop.

Noiselessly, gliding past the houses like shadows, revolver in hand, dark lantern at waist, fifteen detectives in plain clothes had converged on the tall house in the blind alley.

Juve was speaking low.

"Careful, Michel! We have seen our birds enter. They are inside.... I shall follow them!... Meanwhile, do not stir from this door.... There is no other issue.... Do not allow a soul to pass — not one!"

"Never fear, Juve!"

Information dropped by Corporal Vinson, who had been taken to *The Crying Calf* by Vagualame, more than once had caused Juve to keep a strict watch on the wine-shop for some days. He had seen first Bobinette and then Vagualame enter the place....When Bobinette came out, almost immediately, he felt sure she had not had time for a talk with Vagualame.... When Vagualame soon followed, Juve had shadowed the old accordion player in the darkness: behind him followed his men on the trail of both.

When he saw Vagualame and Bobinette enter the library he exclaimed, in thought:

"I have them!...I know the house! I am going to arrest Fantômas and his accomplice!"

Cool as a cucumber now that the decisive, ardently-longed-for moment was at hand, Juve repeated his instructions: he did not mean to leave anything to chance.

"You understand then, Michel, not one single person is to leave these premises. Even I can only be permitted to pass when I say to you: 'It is I, Juve,...Let me pass!' You thoroughly understand?"

"Perfectly," replied Michel.

Juve turned to his four picked men:

"Gentlemen! Are you ready?"

Revolver in one hand, lantern in the other, Juve knocked loudly on the shuttered shop door.

"In the name of the law! Open! Open! Open!...The police!"

A bare three minutes had elapsed between Juve's first summons and the opening of the library door.

Vagualame had made profitable use of the three minutes.

"Don't utter a sound! Don't be afraid!" Vagualame had repeated to Bobinette: "They will not take us this time!"

Hustled, dragged to the spot already described, Bobinette now felt the ground giving way beneath her. She rolled on to a steeply inclined plane. Gliding down into the void, clutching Vagualame, she heard a dull sound: it was the trap falling to.

"Quiet!" repeated Vagualame, as Bobinette rolled on to the wood flooring of a sort of cellar piled high with books. He signed to the girl to listen.

"Yes! They are searching the shop, knocking the books about, imagining we are hidden among them!...But, from what I know of Juve, in a very short time he will have ferreted out the trap door and will descend as we have done. He will never be such a fool as to think we have gone down the shop stairs."

"Oh!" groaned Bobinette: "Whatever shall we do?"

Vagualame calmly turned on his pocket electric torch, approached an immense pile of illustrated magazines stacked in a corner. He struck three blows on it, saying in a low clear voice:

"Open! Open to brothers!"

Bobinette, frightened past speech, saw the immense pile of volumes oscillate, then noiselessly divide, disclosing a secret door.

Vagualame pulled her towards it, saying in a joking tone:

"You see how useful it is to have friends of all sorts! Your employer, Olga Damitroff, was well advised when she once told me when and where the Nihilists gather together in Paris to plot against the Czar!"

Vagualame brought her into a large room, lit by torches, where a score of young men were assembled. They rose and reverently saluted Vagualame, who approached them with outstretched hand.

When Juve entered, he soon satisfied himself that only Sophie remained in the library. He gave orders to keep strict guard over the proprietress, notwithstanding her loud protestations.

"Do not permit anyone to leave the premises," he repeated to the men stationed at the door — "except myself, of course."

He turned to others.

"Move all these volumes! There may be a hide-hole concealed behind them....Keep guard at the top of the little staircase. It is the only way of escape ...I am going to make a tour of the cellars and expect to run my game to earth by this staircase."...

Sophie again protested.

"There is nothing in my cellars that ought not to be there! I don't understand what the police want here!"

Juve paid no attention to these protestations. He went towards the corner at the farther end of the shop.

Juve knew all the dens in Paris; there was not a secret society he did not know of — societies, political and otherwise, holding mysterious meetings in these places: he knew of the existence of this trap-door and slide which led to the cellars below this library.

"We will go down to the Nihilists," said he.

Before the interested eyes of his subordinates, Juve set the trap in motion. A counter weight closed it over his head.

Juve rolled into the cellar but a few seconds after Vagualame and Bobinette had escaped from it!... To tell the truth, Juve did not know of the hidden entrance to the secret room. Dizzy from his rapid glide downwards, Juve raised his lantern. He was not surprised to find this retreat empty. He knew the slide led to second and lower series of cellars....

His eye caught a movement. The huge stack of magazines, looking as if it would topple over, so much on the slant was it, was slowly moving into an upright position again! He leaped forward, thrusting his revolver between the opening of the two portions, and prevented them from joining completely!...

What was going on behind this tricky collection of magazines, which had undoubtedly just opened to give passage to Vagualame and Bobinette?

Juve glued his ear to the fissure which marked the edge of the hidden door.... Ah!... Voices of men in discussion!... Juve could not distinguish all that the voices were saying, but a word reached his ear, clear, unmistakable — *Fantômas*!

He listened intently.

"You are right," remarked an invisible speaker: "It is to Fantômas we owe all these police visits and annoyances — his crimes exasperate the police — and to justify themselves in the opinion of the public they track us down more vigorously than ever!"

Another voice answered:

"I know for certain that these coppers are after Fantômas to-night!"

Shouts and hoots resounded.

Menacing voices repeated:

"Since Fantômas is indirectly our persecutor, let us avenge ourselves on Fantômas!... What matters one life compared with the cause we defend — the cause of a whole people!... If Fantômas is in our way, troubles us, let us kill him!... Trokoff will be here to-morrow, this evening perhaps! Trokoff will guide us! Trokoff will find this mysterious bandit who does us so much harm! Trokoff is a valiant man!... We do not know him, but we know what he has done!"

Juve smiled a sardonic smile. He thrust his hand into the opening wedged apart by his revolver, widened the space, opened the secret door, and entered the assembly room of the Nihilists.

"God save Russia!"

Juve pronounced these words with unction, in a solemn voice.

"God save Poland," was the reply. The oldest man present, who had thus been spokesman for the assembly advanced towards the stranger.

"Who are you?" he demanded.

Without the quiver of an eyelid, an eyelash, Juve answered: "I am he whom you have awaited.... He who will direct your arms — guide you! I am Trokoff!"

"Let but one of these inspired fanatics, who hold life cheap, guess that I belong to the police, and they would kill me without mercy or pity," thought Juve, as he faced the assembly of revolutionaries with a serene countenance.

There were no threatening looks. They believed themselves to be in the presence of Trokoff. Had he not opened the door?... Only Trokoff, the expected, the longed for, could have done that!

The assembly acclaimed him:

"Trokoff! We for Russia welcome you! God be with you, Trokoff! Heaven guard you!"

"God be with you, brothers!"

Juve advanced, scrutinising each in turn: neither Vagualame nor Bobinette were among them. Juve addressed them:

"My brothers! You know that the police are now searching the shop overhead: it is a serious moment!"

One of the Nihilists stepped forward.

"We know it, Trokoff! Our brother, Vagualame, accompanied by a young disciple, came to warn us but a minute ago. Be assured, brother! The police are not searching for us this evening....It is the vile wretch Fantômas they are after!...A criminal ruffian, foe of all liberty, whom we have condemned to death....Therefore we are not disquieted. Vagualame has just left us....He will direct the suspicions of the police into another channel. He told us he knew a way of quieting their suspicions."...

"If only Michel does not allow this arch-bandit to slip through his fingers!" reflected Juve, as he listened with unmoved countenance to these remarkable statements. Before the Nihilist could say more, Juve made a declaration:

"Vagualame deceives himself, brother. I must go up at once to give him the aid of my strong arm, otherwise we are finished!...I know only the secret entrance here: guide me to the other exit, so that I may not attract the attention of the police: we do not want our secret entrance discovered!"

"It shall be as you desire, brother. Follow me; but be prudent."

Marching at the Nihilist's heels, after many twists and turns, Juve arrived at the foot of a quite ordinary staircase.

"You have only to mount, brother Trokoff. These stairs lead straight into the shop. If the police ask where you come from, you have only to say that you were looking in the first cellar for a book!...But what matters it if they do visit the cellars! They will never find the hidden door!"

Juve bent his head.

"Thanks, brother! Peace be with you!"

The Nihilist turned away. No sooner was he out of sight than Juve tore up the stairs to complete the arrest of Vagualame and Bobinette!

Inspector Michel had not stirred from his appointed place by the door leading to the street.

He had been on guard about half an hour when Juve, livid, frantic, rushed towards him.

"You have let them go out, Michel!" he shouted: "They are not here!"

"No one has gone out at this door, Chief! I give you my word on it!...But, may I ask how you managed to slip back again without my having noticed you! Deuced clever, I call it!...No one, I say, has left these premises either before or after you!"

"What's that you say?" Juve stared at Michel as if he had taken leave of his senses.

"What I say, Chief, is — the only individuals whom I have allowed to pass out are you and your woman prisoner."

"I and my woman prisoner?" Juve could have howled with rage. He caught the calm, collected Michel by the coat collar, and dragged him outside the shop. Juve looked so desperate, so at his wit's end, that Michel wondered.

"Come now, Chief!" he remonstrated; "I am not dreaming, am I?...Ten minutes ago you came to me here, and you said:

"'Don't move, Michel! Let me pass. I am Juve! I take a prisoner to the station and will return.'"

Juve had grown deadly calm.

"I was disguised, Michel, was I not?"

"Yes. You had put on your Vagualame disguise."

Juve bit his lip till the blood came. That arch-bandit had done him again! Juve could not but admire his coolness and resource. He had known how to take in Michel, because Michel had arrested Juve when disguised as Vagualame at de Naarboveck's house....Michel would naturally think his chief had again assumed the Vagualame disguise for a purpose! Oh, it was the devil's own cleverness!

Juve glared at Michel.

"It was the real Vagualame, I tell you!" shouted Juve.... "It was not I disguised as Vagualame!... It was Vagualame in person, I tell you!... It is Vagualame himself whom you have allowed to escape!"

There was a pause — terrible, heart-sickening.

Michel drew himself up.

"What then, Chief?"

Juve's anger gave place to compassion.

"It is really not your fault, my poor Michel. How could you imagine the infernal trick this bandit was playing on you?... I bear you no grudge for it, Michel!"

But Michel was inconsolable. He had committed an irreparable blunder!

Juve slipped his arm through that of his miserable subordinate. The pair made their way to Headquarters at the head of the little column of subordinates who, understanding that Juve had not found what he sought, were cursing inwardly at the failure of their expedition....

The moment Juve realised that Michel had allowed Vagualame-Fantômas to escape, he had called off his men. He did not wish the Russian revolutionaries cornered and arrested at present.... Possibly Vagualame believed Juve and his men had come to find the Nihilists, and, having failed, had left the premises in a rage!

Sophie would report to the bandit — but she had not heard everything! Thought Juve:

"He will hardly guess that I entered the assembly below by the secret door and made them believe I was Trokoff!... It leaves a way open for future transactions!... Some day, not so far ahead, I may return, may find that devil's Will o' the Wisp of a bandit there and nab him at last!"... Did Michel suspect there were Nihilists on the premises?

"Tell me," questioned Juve: "Did you overhear any suspicious talk?... This Sophie did not say anything interesting?"

"Nothing whatever, Chief."

"Your men, Michel, do not know what individual we are after?"

Michel laughed.

"Oh, they are a hundred leagues off the truth!... That they were out to arrest Fantômas!... Just imagine, Chief! This afternoon, a complaint was lodged at Headquarters with reference to the theft of a bear! The theft was committed at Troyes, at the fair.... Our men are persuaded that to-night's search has to do with this bear-stealing case!... All the more so because, just as we started on this expedition, one of my men, whose home is at Sceaux, told us that his brother, a driver down there, had been ordered to go in five days' time, with two horses, and at five in the morning, on the road to Robinson, and take a gipsy van twenty kilometres from there!... He thought there was something very queer about such a rendezvous as that!"

Juve's interest in this piece of news was keen!

XXX
APPALLING ACCUSATIONS

"But, Commandant, you cannot possibly maintain that I am not Jérôme Fandor, journalist!"

The interview between Commandant Dumoulin and Fandor had already lasted an hour. It was unlike that which had taken place six days before, when Dumoulin had dealt summarily with the Fandor-Vinson case. Since then Fandor had occupied cell 27, and had had no communication with the outside world. Fandor had raged furiously against things in general, against Dumoulin in particular, and against himself most of all. He acknowledged that Juve had done his utmost to extricate him from the tangled web he had involved himself in as Fandor-Vinson.

Each day brought him one distraction which he would willingly have foregone: he passed long exhausting hours in Commandant Dumoulin's office. He found the commandant detestable. Dumoulin was hot-blooded, noisy, unmethodical, always in a state of fuss and fume! He would begin his interrogations calmly, would weigh his words, would be logical, but little by little, his real nature — a tempestuous one — would get the upper hand.

For the twentieth time Fandor had insisted on his identity, and Dumoulin, tapping the case papers with an agitated hand, had replied:

"I recognise that you are Jérôme Fandor, exercising the profession of a journalist — since it seems journalism is a profession! But that is not the question; the problem I have to elucidate! I have to ascertain when, and at what exact moment, one Jérôme Fandor took the personality of Corporal Vinson!"...

"I have already told you, Commandant!... Please read my deposition of the day before yesterday. I will recapitulate:

"Sunday, November 13th, at five o'clock in the evening, at my domicile, rue Richer, I received the visit of a soldier whom I did not know. He stated that he was called Corporal Vinson, and informed me that he had become part and parcel of the spy system; that he regretted it, and, not being able to extricate himself, he was going to commit suicide.... Desiring to give this unfortunate a chance of rehabilitating himself, desiring also to come to close quarters with this gang of spies, I decided to assume his personality, and take advantage of his entrance into a regiment where he was not known, and to go there in his place. It was in these conditions that I left eight days after, on Sunday, November 20th, for Verdun."

"You maintain that you did not assume the personality of Vinson before that date?"

"I do maintain that, Commandant."

"But that is the pivot of the whole business, and the important point yet to be proved!"

"That is not difficult," declared Fandor: "I have alibis who will support my statement."

The commandant raised his arms to heaven.

"Alibis! Alibis!... What do they prove, after all?"

"The truth, Commandant.... When I am in Paris it is evident I am not in Châlons or Verdun."

Dumoulin was evidently trying to find an argument to meet the accused's logic.

"Peuh!" declared he: "With fellows like you, who are perpetually disguising themselves, changing their faces as I change my collars, one never knows."... Suddenly Dumoulin's face lighted up.

"Tuesday, November 29th, you were in the shoes of Vinson — is that so?"

"Yes, Commandant."

"Very well. This same Tuesday, November 29th, you were at the Elysée ball as Jérôme Fandor! So you see!"

Dumoulin was triumphant.

"I had twenty-four hours' leave, Commandant — quite regular!" protested Fandor.

"Ah!" growled the commandant, glancing knowingly at Lieutenant Servin, who with impassive countenance was listening to this discussion: "Don't talk to me about leave!... Heaven alone knows how easily you spies succeed in obtaining leave!"

Fandor was about to protest vehemently against being numbered with the spies, when the commandant started another subject.

"Added to this, there is something very serious in your case."

"Good Heavens! What now?" ejaculated Fandor.

Dumoulin looked mysterious.

"We will speak of it later on.... The next step is to confront you with certain witnesses: Lieutenant Servin, see if the witnesses are there!"

Fandor himself had demanded this confrontation. He did not deny having assumed the personality of Corporal Vinson, dating from the day when the corporal entered officially on his duties as a unit of the 257th of the line, in garrison at Verdun. But the enquiry wished to establish that, anterior to this, Fandor had already taken the place of the real Vinson: the military authorities seemed to attach immense importance to this point. Fandor had then decided that the simplest way was to be brought face to face with soldiers who had known Vinson at Châlons: they would state that the Vinson presented to them in the person of Fandor was not the Vinson they had known.

Thereupon Dumoulin had sent for two men who, as orderlies at Châlons, had lived side by side with Vinson.

There was a momentous silence while Lieutenant Servin went to the end of the corridor and signed to the two waiting witnesses to come forward. The two men entered the commandant's office, facing Dumoulin in true military style.

Dumoulin, reading out the names of the two witnesses from a paper, started his interrogation with a haughty air.

"Hiloire?"

"Present, Commandant."

"What is your name?"

The soldier opened his eyes wide, and thinking he had to give his Christian name, stammered:

"Justinien!"

"What?" growled the commandant: "You are not called Hiloire?"

The bewildered man attempted some confused explanations, from which it could be gathered that Hiloire was his surname and Justinien his baptismal name!

"Good!" declared the commandant, who proceeded to question the second soldier as to his identity! When it was made clear that he was one Tarbottin, baptismal name Niccodème, the commandant questioned them together.

"You are soldiers of the second class in the 213th of the line, and fulfil the functions of staff orderlies?"

"Yes, Commandant."

"You know Corporal Vinson?"

"Yes, Commandant."

Dumoulin pointed to Fandor.

"Is he Corporal Vinson?"

"Yes, Commandant," repeated the two soldiers.

Lieutenant Servin intervened. He pointed out to his chief that the witnesses had replied in the affirmative without turning to look at the supposed corporal.

The commandant cried angrily:

"What kind of imbeciles are you? Before saying that you recognise a person you must begin by looking at that person! Look at the corporal!"

The two soldiers obeyed: they turned with precision and stared at Fandor.

"Is that man Corporal Vinson?"

"Yes, Commandant."

"You are sure of that?"

"No, Commandant."

Despite the miserable position he found himself in, Fandor could not help smiling at the bewilderment of the two soldiers: it was evident they could be made to say anything.

The commandant was growing more and more exasperated.

"What's that!" he shouted: "I will give you eight days in the cells if you continue to play the fool like this!...Try to understand what you are doing! Do you even know why you are here?"

After consulting each other with a look as to who should answer, Tarbottin explained:

"It is the sergeant who told us that we were being sent to Paris to recognise Corporal Vinson —well, then?"

"Well," continued Hiloire: "we recognised him!"

Then, speaking together, with an air of proud satisfaction:

"Yes, we got our orders. We have carried them out!"

The commandant was scarlet. With a violent blow of his fist he sent three sets of case papers flying to the ground. He turned to Lieutenant Servin.

"I fail to understand why the staff captain has expressly sent us the biggest fools he could lay hands on....What the deuce can you get out of such a pair?...Has the counter verification been carried out? Have they been shown the body of the real Corporal Vinson?"

Lieutenant Servin replied that this had been done.

"And what did they declare?"

"Nothing definite....I may say they were very much moved at the sight of the corpse — also, that it is decomposing rapidly."

Here Fandor broke in:

"Commandant, I am extremely surprised that you thought it necessary to summon only two soldiers! It is at least strange!...I have the right to expect that in the conduct of the enquiry connected with the action you wish to bring against me you should proceed more seriously than you are doing at present....A magistrate should be impartial!"...

The commandant had risen. He bent towards Fandor across his writing-table. Fandor also had risen — Dumoulin's air was threatening: he was furious.

"What do you mean by that?" he shouted.

"I mean to say," burst out Fandor, "that for the last forty-eight hours you have given proofs of a revolting partiality — against me!"

For a minute Dumoulin drew himself up, crimson, choking: he was an embodied protest. Suddenly he dropped the official and became the fellow-citizen. He cried:

"But I am an honest man!"

Dumoulin was a worthy official of the old school. Whatever his temperamental drawbacks, he undoubtedly aimed at a conscientious conduct of any case he had in charge. Fandor had made an exceedingly bad impression on him. He had been scandalised that a civilian, a mere journalist, had dared to treat the army with contempt, by so lightly taking the place of a real soldier. Unquestionably there were grave presumptions of Fandor's guilt: that was Dumoulin's opinion.

Considering the importance of the affair, the terrible consequences which might ensue for the accused were the case to go against him, it was imperative that the enquiry should be thorough down to the minutest detail....The commandant well knew the weak points in his procedure. There was this confrontation, with the absurd testimonies of the two soldiers: it had proved a ridiculous fiasco. Also, he would have great difficulty in showing conclusively that Fandor had been a certain time at Châlons under Vinson's uniform.

Dumoulin, mastering his emotion, resumed his official tone.

"Fandor!"...

He stopped short, glared indignantly at the two soldiers planted in the middle of the room.

"What are you two up to now?" he cried.

The ridiculous pair saluted, but did not reply.

"Lieutenant, remove those men! We do not want any more of them here! Take them out of my sight!" growled Dumoulin.

The commandant felt he must have a breath of fresh air, collect his thoughts, and calm down before resuming conduct of the case.

"We shall continue this interrogation in ten minutes' time," he announced and left the room.

The short interval had done its work. The commandant had calmed down, Fandor had regained his self-possession. No longer was it an irascible officer facing an inimical accused: two men, fellow-citizens, were prepared to argue and talk together.... The formal interrogation recommenced.

"Fandor," began the commandant in an amiable tone, "you have evidently been drawn on by unforeseen events to commit irregularities. Name your accomplices!"...

Fandor replied in a similar tone.

"No, Commandant, I have not been drawn into the spy circle really, nor have I practised spying.... I considered it right to assume the personality of Corporal Vinson solely to obtain information regarding the relations this unfortunate maintained, compulsorily and quite against his better judgment, with the agents of a foreign power. When I had obtained the facts I sought, my intention was to leave the law to deal with them."

"In other words," said Dumoulin: "you aimed at playing the counter-spy!"

"If you like to put it so!"

The commandant smiled ironically.

"They always say that!... In the course of my career, Monsieur Fandor, I have had to examine three or four spy cases: well, the defence of the guilty man is always the same — you have taken up an identical position: I sell secret documents in exchange for more important ones!... This system of defence will not hold water!"

"I cannot take up any other position!" declared Fandor.

"The Council will take that at its proper value," announced the commandant.

Fandor was asking himself how he was going to get out of a position that was growing worse, and that in a very curious way!

The commandant's next question struck a shrewd blow at the accused.

"Fandor — How about those accomplices you refuse to name?... Have they not remunerated you for your pains?"

"What do you mean to imply by that?" demanded Fandor.

"Have they not given you money?"

"No!"

"Think carefully, and be frank!"

Fandor ransacked his memory.... Ah!... What of that interview in the printing works of the Noret brothers? Would it be best in accordance with his aims to deny it? It went against the grain of his naturally frank nature to tell such a lie.... Nevertheless he had vowed to himself a well-considered vow that he would not reveal what he had learned: it would be a grave mistake at present.

He lowered his head as he persisted in his declaration:

"No, Commandant! I have not received money from the spies."

The commandant called to the reporter:

"Make a special note of that: underline it with red pencil. This is a most important statement!"

The commandant turned over some papers in his drawer, drew out a sealed envelope, opened it, extracted another envelope.

Fandor asked himself, with a thrill of foreboding, what this new move of the commandant's meant.

From a third envelope, Dumoulin took out several bank-notes, yellowed and crumpled. He held them up for Fandor to see.

"Here are three fifty franc bank-notes — new ones!... They bear the following numbers: A 4998; O 4350; U 5108. They were found, with others, concealed in your baggage at the Saint-Benoit barracks at Verdun. Do you recognise these notes as having been in your possession?"

"How do you think I can know that?" countered Fandor. "One bank-note is not distinguishable from another!"

"Yes they are: by the numbering," asserted the commandant…. "I willingly admit that it is not usual to write down for reference the number of every bank-note which passes through one's hands!... We have a better way of demonstrating that the notes I have in my hand were in your possession."

"What exactly is he going to spring upon me now?" Fandor asked himself.

There was an impressive pause.

"These notes," declared Dumoulin, "have been carefully examined by the anthropometric service. It has been demonstrated that they bear distinct traces of your finger-marks…. I hope, Monsieur Fandor, that you do not contest the exactitude of the Bertillion method?"

"No," replied Fandor simply. "I accept the evidence of the anthropometric method."

The commandant looked more and more satisfied.

"You acknowledge then, that these notes were in your possession?"

"Yes, I do."

The commandant again addressed the reporter:

"Note that important confession! Underline it with red pencil!"

Dumoulin fired a point-blank question at Fandor.

"Did you know Captain Brocq?"

"No."

"You did know him," insisted the commandant.

"No," repeated Fandor. He questioned in his turn:

"Why?"

"Because."… The commandant hesitated, then continued:

"You are not ignorant of the fact that an important document was stolen from the domicile of this mysteriously murdered man?"

"I know it," admitted Fandor.

"That is not all," continued Dumoulin: "A certain amount of money was also stolen from this unfortunate officer. Now, Brocq was in the habit of putting down in his pocket-book the exact sums he possessed and — mark this well — also entering the numbers of his bank-notes!... Now, bank-notes have disappeared from his cash drawer. The missing notes bear the numbers: A 4998; O 4350; U 5108; the very notes found in your pocket-book!"

There ensued a dreadful silence. Fandor was thunderstruck…. Everything seemed in league against him…. Oh, he was caught like a mouse in a trap!... These must be the notes that the red-bearded man — probably one of the Noret brothers — had slipped into his hand!... Evidently, from the time of his leaving Paris in Corporal Vinson's uniform, the traitorous gang he meant to expose had known him for what he was! Without suspecting it, he had been the hunted instead of the hunter: and this chaser of damaged goods and trumpery wares had been caught in his trap like a fool!... These unscrupulous wretches had hatched an abominable plot against him!... Fandor felt that each instant saw him deeper in the toils! His whole being was invaded by a terrible anxiety, an immense fear. Who could be so powerful, so subtle, so formidable as to have made a fool of him in such a fashion, to have led him into such traps that even Juve himself could do nothing to save him?

One being, and one only, was capable of such a diabolically clever performance; and Fandor, who would not believe it some weeks before, when discussing the question with Juve, had now to accept his hypothesis as a certainty: his acts caused his unseen personality to hit you in the eyes! Only one person could pull the strings with such a demon hand!... Yes, Fandor could no longer doubt that his desperate plight was due to the terrific, odious, elusive Fantômas!

Our journalist was now in the lowest depths. He attempted to keep calm and cool, but he had lost grip of himself…. He stammered, he mumbled confusedly, justifications, excuses, charging the Noret brothers with having given him those terrible bank-notes.

Dumoulin, on his side, was convinced that his examination had made an immense step in the right direction. He considered that the interrogation might well end with a last word, a last sentence. He turned to the wretched, over-strained Fandor, and in tones of the utmost solemnity administered his finishing stroke.

"Jérôme Fandor, not only are you accused of the crimes of treason and spying, but, taking into account the formal avowals you have just made, I, here and now, declare you guilty of the assassination of Captain Brocq, of the theft of his documents, and of his money!"

XXXI
A CARAVAN DRAMA

The night was dark and stormy. On the Sceaux road a gipsy was braving the tempest, making difficult headway in the teeth of a gale which flapped her long cloak with impeding force, soaked her to the skin, dashed masses of water in her face, plastered streaming locks to her forehead, taking her breath with its suffocating rush. Shielding her mouth with her hand, the gipsy pressed steadily forward.

A church struck eleven slow strokes, borne on the wind. Lashed by the tempest, the gipsy pressed on, muttering as she moved:

"Vagualame told me that he would be at the first milestone beyond the aviation sheds....I must get there! I will get there!"

It was Bobinette, struggling on in blind obedience to him whom she considered her master, towards the strange meeting-place fixed by the bandit five days ago.

Under her looks of Parisian delicacy, Bobinette had a valiant spirit, a high-strung temperament and a will of steel....Bobinette wished to reach the appointed trysting-place: she would reach it.

But gipsy Bobinette had her fears. She was painfully impressed by the obscurity of the night — sinister, menacing. From the marshy fields flanking her to right and left unaccustomed sounds, weird noises reached her straining ears through the gusty darkness.

Then what did her master want with her here, and at such an hour?

Never had Bobinette confessed to herself that Vagualame's real identity was unknown to her. What dark personality was hid behind that familiar figure? She asked herself that now, with shuddering apprehension. She had remarked certain coincidences, noted certain details: she divined that this enigmatic accordion player might well be none other than — Fantômas.

Fantômas! That name was it not a frightful symbol of all the crimes, all the atrocities, the monstrous synthesis of unpunished evil?

In her tormented brain those three syllables of sinister intent were sounding like a funeral knell....At thought of Fantômas and Vagualame co-mingled, Bobinette's terror-filled heart fainted within her. Yet, prey to haunting terrors as she was, Bobinette pressed unfalteringly forward towards what Fate held for her.

One reassuring thought came to hearten her. At every step she took the sequins of her gipsy circlet moved and shook and tinkled on her forehead. They reminded her of the words chanted by the old second-hand dealer when he sold her the string of sequins, words from the celebrated song of the Andalusian gipsies.:

"The coral shines on my skin so brown —
The pin of gold in my chignon:
I go in search of my fortune."...

Was she truly hastening towards good fortune through this night of wind and rain?...Why not? Bobinette felt comforted. She said to herself that since Vagualame had summoned her to meet him in gipsy costume, it must be because he intended to help her to escape: otherwise why had he foreseen the necessity for such a disguise?

To make sure of finding the rendezvous, she had taken a reconnoitering journey along the Sceaux road the night before....She knew now she was close to the famous milestone.

Bobinette jumped as though she would leap out of her skin!

On the left side of the road tall trees, stripped of their leaves, stood swaying like skeletons in the wind. Just there her eyes had seen something dark, a black patch, blacker than the surrounding night.

What was it?

A strange sound issued from the darkness, a low, dull, deep, complaining sound breathed from some infernal throat! Was it a cry, a growl, a snarl?...She halted, shivering with fright, her ears humming, her heart contracted in the grip of an indescribable terror, doubting her senses, doubting the reality of the sound she had heard.

Bobinette stood motionless.

The wind whistling through the branches conveyed another sound to her senses. She heard a mocking voice, harsh, imperious, a menacing voice, a voice whose orders she had obeyed many a time and oft, a voice she had never heard without secret terror, the voice of her master — Vagualame!

"Go forward, you fool! Why do you halt?"

As though galvanised, Bobinette with a supreme effort of will obeyed. A few seconds and she was by the side of Vagualame, who had come to meet her.

"Did you hear?" she gasped.

"I heard the bellowing of the wind," laughed Vagualame: "I heard the sound of sleety rain, I heard the noise of trees writhing and creaking in the wind — nothing more!"

"Someone or something cried out!"

"Who could?... We are alone here!... Bobinette you are alone here with me!"

There was a pause. Vagualame's voice was once more mocking.

"Am I to think you are afraid?"

"No, Vagualame, I am not afraid; but."...

"But you are trembling like a leaf!" cried Vagualame, with a burst of laughter which sounded strangely false. He seized Bobinette in an iron grip and forced her forward.

"Come! Come under shelter!" They moved towards the black blot Bobinette had not yet identified. Almost directly they were leaning against a gipsy van drawn up at the side of the road.

"Your future domicile," said Vagualame, showing the van to the bewildered Bobinette. "But this is not the time to install yourself — there are things to be said first — between you and me, Bobinette!"

The bandit was enveloped from head to foot in a dark cloak. All Bobinette could see of him was his profile: his features were concealed by a soft felt hat with turned-down brim, which showed at intervals against the sky when the lightning flashed and flickered.

The girl shivered: her master's last words were full of some dark menace.

"What do you want to say?" she murmured.

Vagualame took a few steps forward, then returned to where the girl was leaning against the van.

"Listen to me, Bobinette, listen, for, by Heaven, the words I am about to utter are the last you will ever hear."

Before Bobinette could interrupt, Vagualame continued:

"Tell me, do you know of anything more wicked, more contemptible, more vile, more shameful than treachery, than betrayal, than a trap set, a snare laid to catch one who has always been your friend, your defender?... Tell me, Bobinette, who is more hateful than the Judas who sells you with a kiss?... Tell me, Bobinette, who is less worthy of pity than the cowardly criminal who betrays his accomplice?... Than the bandit who delivers up his chief for money, perhaps for less than money — because of fear — who betrays his master to save his own skin?"...

Bobinette did not seem to understand one word of this apostrophe. She kept silence, terrified, crushed, in front of the awful abyss she divined.

Vagualame seized her by the shoulders and shook her brutally, thrusting her fiercely against the side of the van.

"Speak! Reply, Bobinette! I command you!"

"I do not understand you! I am afraid!"

A shout of ferocious laughter burst from Vagualame.

"You do not understand me! You are afraid?... Ah! If you are afraid it is because you understand well enough!... Bobinette! You know well enough what I have to reproach you with!... What I have to force you to expiate!"...

A hoarse cry escaped the girl's parched lips:

"You are mad, mad, Vagualame!... Pity!... Pity!"

In a voice so hard, so biting, that the words seemed arrows piercing her quivering flesh, the bandit addressed his victim:

"Bobinette, you deceive yourself strangely! I am not of those to whom one cries for pity!... I know not the word, nor such weakness. I have never had it, and never shall have it for any living soul."

The bandit paused. Then, in a tone of rising anger, he continued:

"And you think me mad? But what sort of woman are you, Bobinette, to try and deceive me? What madness is yours to think, to imagine you can dupe me?... To confess that with such words and speeches as your feminine mind can think of you are going to ensnare me, make me alter my decision, turn me from my vengeance — that you should decide how I shall act — I?... I?... Vagualame?"

The bandit pronounced "I?" with such an accent of authority, with such terrific pride, that Bobinette, with a sound as though the death rattle were in her throat, cried:

"Vagualame! Who are you? Tell me!... Tell me!"...

"You ask me who I am?... You wish to know?... It be according to your wish!... Who am I?... Look!"...

Slowly, with a movement firm and dignified, Vagualame unfolded the long cloak which enveloped him. He tore off his hat and flung it at his feet. With arms crossed he apostrophied Bobinette:

"Dare to utter my name! Dare to name me!"

Before Bobinette's distracted eyes a terrifying outline showed itself.... The beggar of a moment ago, his cloak removed, his hat thrown to the ground, appeared no more a bent old man: he stood there, upright, young, vigorous, superbly muscular. He was sheathed from head to foot in a tight-fitting garment, black as Erebus!

Bobinette could not see his face, a black hood covered it: two gleaming eyes alone were visible, eyes that to the distraught girl seemed lit by fires from hell!

This vision, the vision of this man without a face, resembling no other man, this apparition with nameless mask, its body like some statue cut from solid darkness, was yet so definite in its mystery that Bobinette, uttering the indescribable cry of some inhuman thing, articulated:

"Fantômas!... You are Fantômas!"

The bandit spoke:

"I am Fantômas!... I am he for whom the entire world is searching, whom none has ever seen, whom none can recognise!... I am Crime incarnated!... I am Night!... No human sees my face, because Crime and Night are featureless!... I am illimitable Power!... I am he who mocks at all the powers, at all the efforts, at all the forces!... I am master of all, of everything; of all times and seasons.... I am Death!... Bobinette, thou hast said it — I am Fantômas."

His wretched listener could not breathe. She felt death in her veins: she felt the earth dissolving into dust.... She sank on her knees.

"Pity, master! Pity!... Fantômas, have pity!"...

"You join those words together!... Fantômas and Pity!"... A furious anger seized the bandit. "Fantômas knows not what mercy is, I tell you!... Fantômas ordains that whoso resist him shall perish — shall disappear!"

"But, Master!... What have I done?... Master!... Fantômas, what have I done?"

Slowly the bandit enveloped himself once more in his cloak.... Bobinette was on her knees, as one nailed to the earth!... Fantômas had hypnotised her into immobility, as the bird is hypnotised by the cat watching its prey. He played with her. He could seize and master her at his pleasure.

In a voice cold and hard as the nether millstone, he denounced his victim:

"Bobinette, you aimed at my betrayal!... You pointed out the Nihilist's haunt to Juve, to Fandor, to my most personal enemies, to those who would hound me to the guillotine!"

"I never did!... I did not do it!... I swear it!" shrieked the maddened girl.

Fantômas, convinced that Bobinette, and she alone, was the traitor here....

"You are to die; but not by my hand!...The hand of Fantômas does not deal death to those who once served him, to the traitorous wretches once in his employ!...But you shall die, Bobinette! I deliver you to death!"...

Fantômas laughed. He laughed because the body of this woman, huddled in the mud, crushed to the earth, was a pleasing thing, because Fantômas was happy when he made human creatures suffer, when he tortured, when he wrought sweet vengeance....

Far away sounded the church bells....The carillon was ringing....Church bells were chiming through the night. To Bobinette, the abject creature grovelling in the mire of the roadway, the bells sounded vaguely serene, far, far away....

She seemed to be floating in some indefinable element, floating like thistledown on an irresistible breeze....Suddenly she had the sensation that she was sinking, falling, that she was rolling down, down, into the depths of a bottomless abyss....

When she opened her eyes, tried to move, sat up, she knew she was not dreaming....She knew she had lost consciousness and was coming back to life....She asked herself could she possibly be alive? Fantômas had threatened her with death, and yet she lived....Where was she?...Bobinette felt so weak and giddy that she remained in a sitting posture....What exactly had happened?...Ah! — yes! — when Fantômas had announced she was to die, she had fallen down on the road: her skirt was still wet and muddy, her testing fingers told her that! She was cold! What had happened since?...Bobinette heard the wind blowing rain as still falling, but she noticed none fell on her face.

"Where am I?" she asked aloud. Clear came the mental answer:

"Fantômas has shut me up in this van! I am imprisoned in this van!"...She felt about her with her fingers. She was certainly sitting on rough boards....She knelt, she stretched out her arms: she touched rough boards....Yes, this was the van she was in!...Was Fantômas quite near? He might appear again! She was not saved!...But in Bobinette who, terrified at being confronted with Fantômas self-confessed, had tasted the bitterness of death, a powerful reaction had set in: she was becoming mistress of herself once more.

Fantômas had said to her: "Thou shalt die!" She now decided that she would live, would save herself!...She must escape!

"If Fantômas were there I should hear him," she thought. "He must have gone....I must at all costs escape from this prison before he returns."

Bobinette got up....The van must have a door, a window. She would force her way out somehow. She was strong, and she was fighting for her life!...She would make a tour of the van!...She felt her way by fingering the wooden side of her prison....The van must be empty, she thought, for she had not encountered any furniture — when, suddenly, she felt her hand come into contact with something soft and warm, which moved. What was it?...

Bobinette jumped back....She must be mad to imagine!...She waited a few moments — she stepped forward — anew her fingers touched something....She could not say what!...But while she tried to define the strange object her fingers touched, she felt the unknown thing was drawing back — was avoiding her caress!...

The van was now filled with a formidable growling. She recognised it as a repetition of the sound she had heard when nearing her sinister rendezvous.

Bobinette understood!...She knew!...It was a bear!...It had been asleep. She had waked it!

Fantômas had shut her in with a bear: she was to be devoured alive!

Bobinette softly withdrew to the other side of the van. She waited. No growling sound reached her. The bear must have gone to sleep again. She could hear its heavy breathing. As the air became exhausted in the confined space the noisome odour of the beast caught her by the throat....What was she to do? Bobinette asked herself this again and again as the slow and dreadful hours of that night wore on.

"The bear sleeps," she said to herself; "but he will wake in the morning hungry: he will hurl himself on me and I shall be done for!"

After interminable hours of waiting, of aching immobility, of dull agony of mind, the interior of the van was becoming slowly visible....She had listened to the lessening fury of the wind: the rain had ceased. The wan light of early day came through the cracks in the planking. Bobinette could see the bear waking up: it turned, yawned: suddenly it fixed its eyes on her and crouched.

What should she do? What could she do?

Bobinette had once read that the human eye could frighten a wild beast into submission: she forced herself to stare at the animal with concentrated energy. Alas! she was too frightened herself to terrify a ferocious animal into harmless submission!

The bear licked itself. As though sure of its prey, which he would presently fall upon and rend, he took his time and proceeded to make his toilette.

It was grotesquely tragic, the leisurely tranquillity of this beast face to face with this girl who could count the seconds of life remaining to her.

Now and again Bobinette could hear the rapid passings of motor-cars on the high road outside, speeding to Paris or Versailles, passing the van abandoned, left derelict by the wayside. Far, indeed, were these passers from suspecting the terrible drama of which it was the theatre.

Call out?

That were madness! Her cries might pass unheeded. Why should she suppose the drivers of these cars racing on their appointed way would stop, locate the cry, and succour her? No, it would but excite the anger of the bear, rouse it to action, thus hasten her own dreadful end!...

A man was walking on the Sceaux road — walking fast. He wore the clothes of a working man. He was leading a sorry nag....The man halted and let the nag go free. A sound had caught his ear — a growling sound.

He listened intently.

"Did I imagine it?" he murmured.

Again that growling, punctuated by a woman's sharp scream. The man was off at racing speed towards the van, which was but a hundred yards away.

"Great Heaven! Shall I arrive too late?" ejaculated the man.

Reaching it, breathless, he glued his ear to the door. The van shook with the movement and growling of some beast of prey about to spring.

The man drew back, rushed forward, hurled himself against the door and drove it inwards.

A shot broke the silence of the morning.

The man rolled over the body of the bear, shot dead through the heart. The man freed himself; escaped the convulsive movement of its limbs, and crawled towards a crumpled heap huddled in a corner of this tragic stage. Bobinette's poor face, exposed to view, was slashed and torn: it bore the dreadful claw-marks of the bear.

The man placed his hand on her heart.

"She lives!" he said softly.

Supporting her with infinite gentleness, the man addressed her in a voice trembling with emotion:

"Do not be afraid, Bobinette! You are saved! It is Juve who is telling you so! It is Juve!"

XXXII
FREE AND PRISONER

Isolated in the cell which had served him as dwelling-place for the past fortnight, Jérôme Fandor had had his ups and downs, hours of deepest depression, hours of violent exasperation when he suffered an intolerable martyrdom between his four walls — suffered morally and physically.

Yet his imprisonment had been rendered as tolerable as possible. He could have his meals brought in from outside and obtain from the library such books as there were.

How he longed for a talk with Juve; but that detective was rigorously excluded from the prison. Juve was to be a witness at the trial.

As Fandor was to conduct his own case there were no consultations with his counsel to relieve the monotony of the days; nor were newspapers allowed him. He had no friends or relatives to visit and console him or divert him.

In his sleepless hours Fandor's thoughts would revert to his past, to the frightful drama of his boyhood, to the assassination of the Marquise de Langrune, when he, a youth of eighteen, had been suspected, had even been accused of committing this murder, the accuser being his own father![8]

He remembered that, commencing the very day after the discovery of the crime, his existence had been that of a pariah flying from the police, from those who knew him; remembered how he had assumed disguise after disguise, denied by his father, ignored by his mother, an unfortunate woman who had lost her reason and was shut up in a lunatic asylum.

The only gleam of happiness which had come to illumine the dreary darkness of his youth resolved itself into a memory picture of a pale dawn when the lad, Charles Rambert, leaving a wine-shop, had been caught by Juve, who, believing in his innocence, had taken him under his protection, had given him the name of Jérôme Fandor, and helped him to start a new life.[9]

From then onwards that timid lad, disheartened by his misfortunes, had regained courage and hope, and had boldly plunged into the struggle to live.

His heart and soul were in his journalistic work. Of an enquiring turn of mind, Fandor had not been content with the episodic work of a mere reporter: he eagerly pursued the guilty, took a lively interest in the victims, and became Juve's valuable collaborator, with whom the bonds of friendship strengthened day by day.

Thus Fandor, in Juve's company, was drawn into the hurly-burly, into the troubles and torments of criminal affairs so mysterious, so phenomenal, that, for several years in succession, they created a sensation, not only in Paris but throughout France.

He constituted himself one of the most implacable enemies of Fantômas. The more so, because he was satisfied that the "Genius of Crime," as this monster had been called, had had a considerable share in the vicissitudes and troubles of his own life. Fandor felt that this monster's sinister influence was still being exercised against him.

Too often, in those wakeful hours when he reviewed his life, following the course of it in a kind of mental cinematograph, did Fandor think of Elizabeth Dollon. It was with sad yet sweet emotion, with a piercing regret, but with an unfailing hope, that he saw before his inner vision the charming, the adored face, and figure of Elizabeth Dollon, for whom he had felt, and felt still, an affection profound and sincere. He loved her: he would always love her.[10]

He thought of her brother's death and the extraordinary disappearance of his body, of his own pursuit of the assassin, of the discovery, made with Juve, that the murderer of Jacques Dollon was none other than the elusive Fantômas.

Assuredly that ill-omened bandit was responsible for the sudden departure of Elizabeth, immediately after Fandor had obtained from her charming lips the sweet avowal of her love....He owed to Fantômas that he had been unable to join his life to that of this exquisite girl: to Fantômas he owed it that he could not trace her to her unknown retreat. Was she still in the land of the living? It was ultimately to Fantômas that he owed his present dreadful position — to this thrice accursed Genius of Crime — Fantômas.

That evening Fandor's absorbing reflections were broken into by the turning of a key in the lock of his cell at an unusual hour. Through the half-opened door he heard the close of a conversation between his jailor and an unknown person.

"I also give notice, my good fellow, that my secretary will come to join me presently," said the strange voice. The jailor replied:

"That is quite understood, Maître. I will warn my colleague, who will come on guard in my stead in ten minutes' time."

Fandor saw a barrister entering his cell. He supposed him to be the official advocate prescribed by the Council of War.... Not in the least disposed to unbosom himself to this defending counsel imposed on him by law, Fandor was about to give him a freezing reception, but at sight of the new arrival's face our journalist stood speechless. He recognised under the barrister's gown someone whose features were deeply graven on his memory, though he had not met him but once.

"Naarbo."... escaped his lips.

A brusque warning movement of the new-comer cut Fandor short. At the same time he closed the door with a lightning quick movement. The pseudo advocate then approached Fandor, saying in a low tone:

"Do not seem to recognise me. Yes, I am de Naarboveck.... It is thanks to a subterfuge that I have been able to get near you."...

Fandor was nonplussed. A hundred questions rose to his lips, but he did not speak. He had better await developments. As de Naarboveck had run such risks to enter his cell so disguised, he must have something extraordinary to say to the prisoner, Jérôme Fandor!

De Naarboveck seated himself on the one bench the cell contained. He invited Fandor to sit close to him, so that they might converse in low tones.

"Monsieur," began the baron, "I obtained a permit to visit you as the official advocate allotted to you by the president: that official's visit is due to-morrow.... Well, a favour is never lost when one is not dealing with the ungrateful!... Some weeks ago, when you came to interview me with regard to the deplorable assassination of Captain Brocq, I spoke freely to you, and at the same time asked you to give me your word not to put into print a number of those personal details with which journalists like to sprinkle their pages."...

"I remember," agreed Fandor.

"I confess I did not put much faith in your discretion, being a journalist," went on the baron. "I was then agreeably surprised to find that I had been interviewed by a man of tact. Since then I have followed with sympathy the tenebrous adventures in which you have been involved.... It was not without emotion that I learned of the grievous position you are now in. I will come straight to the point — I am here to extricate you from that position."

Fandor caught de Naarboveck's hands in his, and pressed them warmly.

"Can what you tell me be true?" he exclaimed.

The diplomat hastily withdrew his hands from Fandor's grasp, opened a heavy portfolio such as advocates carry, and drew from it a black gown like his own, an advocate's cap, and a pair of dark coloured trousers.

"Put these on as quickly as possible," said de Naarboveck, "and we will leave here together."

Fandor hesitated: de Naarboveck insisted.

"It is of the first importance that you leave here! I know where proofs of your innocence are to be found.... We have not a minute to lose: besides, as a member of the diplomatic service, it is of the utmost interest to me that the document stolen from Captain Brocq should be recovered.... I know where it is. I want you to return it to the Government. That will be the most striking proof possible of your innocence."

Fandor's critical faculties were momentarily suspended: he seemed moving in some dream. Mechanically he clothed himself in the get-up which the baron had thought good to bring him.

Fandor had seen so many extraordinary things in the course of his adventurous existence, that he did not stay to question the reason for this diplomat's interest in his poor affairs — an interest so strong that he had run serious risks to reach the prisoner and make himself the accomplice of that prisoner's flight.

Out of prison, free, Fandor could and would act!

The two apparent men of the law gently opened the cell door. De Naarboveck cast a rapid glance up and down the corridor, on to which half a dozen cells opened.... The corridor was empty and silent. De Naarboveck and Fandor stepped out, gently closing the cell door.

"The opening of the prison door is our next difficulty to be overcome," whispered de Naarboveck: "I warned the jailor that I expected my secretary. Let us hope he will take you as such and let us pass out unmolested."

The military prison of the Council of War of Paris is not like other prisons: that is why de Naarboveck's plan had a fair chance of success. It would certainly have failed had it been attempted at La Santé or at La Roquette.... This building had been a private hotel of the old style.

On the first floor, the former reception-rooms had been divided into small offices, and the principal drawing-room had been transformed into a court-room. On the ground floor, what were evidently the kitchens and domestic offices in the last century now constituted the prison proper, for in these quarters are arranged the cells where the accused await their appearance before their judges. No one unacquainted with these arrangements would suspect that the low door, scarcely noticeable in the vestibule facing the staircase leading to the first floor is the entrance to the prison.

Yet those who pass through this low door find themselves in the corridor lined with prison cells.

At the door of the prison a warder is posted, whose rôle is not so much to watch the prisoners and prevent any attempt at escape as to open to persons needing to enter that ill-omened place. At night-time supervision is relaxed. The warder has to keep the offices in good order, and when he has his key in his pocket, certain that the heavy bolts and locks cannot be forced, he comes and goes about the house.

De Naarboveck was not only well posted in these details, but was aware that up to the day of Fandor's trial, in view of the extra coming and going, it had been decided to give the guardian an assistant, and that this assistant would be at his post from six o'clock onwards.

It was past six o'clock.

The chances were, that when the false advocates knocked from the inside, the prison door would be opened to allow them egress by the supplementary guardian. De Naarboveck tapped on the peephole made in the massive door.

The noise of heavy bolts withdrawn was heard; the prison door was half opened: the warder's face appeared. Fandor stifled a sigh of satisfaction: it was a jailor who did not know him: it was the substitute counted upon.

"Ah!" cried he, saluting the gentlemen of the long robe: "Why, there are two of you!"

"Naturally," replied de Naarboveck: "Did not your colleague let you know that my secretary had joined me?"

"I knew he was coming, but I did not understand that he had already come," replied the man. De Naarboveck laughed.

"We leave together — what more natural?"

"It is your right," grumbled the man: "Have you finished your interrogation of the accused Fandor?"

As he asked this pertinent question, the jailor made a movement to enter the prison and make sure that the prisoner's cell was locked. De Naarboveck caught his arm.

"Look here, my man," said he, slipping a silver coin into the jailor's hand: "We are not suitably dressed for the street, and our ordinary clothes are at the Palais de Justice. Will you be kind enough to stop a cab for us? We can get into it at the courtyard entrance!"

The jailor decided that he could safely postpone his visit to Fandor's cell. He went out into the courtyard with the two apparent advocates. Standing on the step of the courtyard gate he looked out for a passing cab.

A taxi-driver scented customers. He drove alongside the pavement. In a moment de Naarboveck and Fandor were seated inside it, and, whilst waving his hand to the respectful and gratified warder, he instructed the driver in a clear voice:

"To the Palais de Justice!"

As soon as they reached the rue de Rennes, de Naarboveck changed his destination....

He turned to Fandor.

"Well, Monsieur Fandor, what have you to say to this?"

"Ah, Baron, how can I ever express my gratitude?"

De Naarboveck smiled....He gazed at the journalist. There was something in the situation he found amusing....

Following the baron's directions, the taxi went up the rue Lapic, and reached the heights of Montmartre. It stopped at last in a little street, dark and deserted, before a wretched-looking house, whose front was vaguely outlined in a small neglected garden.

De Naarboveck paid the driver, passed under a dark arch, crossed the garden, and reached a kind of lodge. He let himself in, followed by Fandor. They went up a cork-screw staircase to the floor above. De Naarboveck switched on a light, and Fandor saw that he and his rescuer were in a studio of vast proportions, well furnished.

Thick curtains hung before a large glass bay: it was a lofty room with very slightly sloping walls.

Two or three rooms must have been thrown into one, for several thick supporting columns of iron crossed the middle of the studio.

Fandor failed to find either piece of furniture or picture he could recognise: everything in the place was new to him.

De Naarboveck had slipped off his gown at once. He was in elegant evening dress.

Fandor also threw off the advocate's gown. He wore the black trousers de Naarboveck had brought him, but was in his shirt sleeves. The Vinson uniform had been left in the cell.

Having sufficiently enjoyed the surprise of his protégé, the baron asked:

"Do you know where we are, Monsieur Fandor?"

"I have not the remotest idea."

"Think a little!"

"I do not know in the least; that is a fact!"

"Monsieur," said de Naarboveck, coming close to Fandor, as though he was afraid of being overheard: "You know, at least, by name a certain enigmatic individual who plays an important part in the affairs of which we both are victims, in different ways....I will no longer hide from you that we are in this individual's house!"

"And," gasped Fandor, "this individual is called?"...

"He is called Vagualame!"

"Vagualame!"

Fandor was aghast! Had the devil himself appeared before him he could not have been more dumbfounded. Vagualame, the agent of the Second Bureau — Vagualame, whom Fandor, for some time past, had taken to be a spy with more than one string to his bow — it was he, then, who was the author of the crimes for whom search was being made, in whose stead Fandor himself was suffering humiliation and imprisonment, with further dreadful possibilities to come! Fandor recalled his conversation with Juve the day after Captain Brocq's assassination: in the course of their conversation Juve had asserted that Fantômas was the criminal.

Fandor himself had not followed the mysterious evolutions of this sinister accordion player as had Juve; but now he wondered whether there might not be a connection between Vagualame and Fantômas....All this was obscure: Fandor felt he was groping amid dark mysteries....

De Naarboveck was moving hither and thither in the studio: at the same time he was observing Fandor, listening to what he had to say: he seemed to be reading Fandor's thoughts.

"Your friend, Juve, has been hotly pursuing this Vagualame for some time," remarked De Naarboveck: "Famous detective as he is, he has suffered more than one check, has been routed, rebuffed, discomfited, on several occasions by this same Vagualame, who has proved that he is not such a fool as he looks! Possibly Juve will soon have a further opportunity of realising the truth of this — however."...

Fandor interrupted:

"I hope my friend, my dear friend, Juve, does not run any risk!... I beg of you, Monsieur, to tell me whether he is in danger!... You see, I am free now."...

"Attention, Monsieur Fandor!" de Naarboveck cut in. "Bear in mind that you are an escaped prisoner, that your flight must not be known! Be on your guard, then! As to your friend, Juve, be reassured on that point!"

Abruptly he changed the subject.

"Vagualame had a collaborator, a young person whom you know — Mademoiselle Berthe, called Bobinette.... Bobinette has done wrong, very wrong, but we will speak no more of her — peace to her memory — she has expiated her crime!"

"Is Bobinette dead, then?" asked Fandor.... Immediately a conviction seized him that the girl had fallen a victim to this mysterious assassin whom no one could lay hands on.

The studio clock struck ten.

The lights went out.

Fandor stood startled, in deepest darkness.

Before he could utter an exclamation, move a finger, he was swathed in a cloth, seized, bound, with the utmost brutality. Mysterious hands fixed a supple mask on his face, pressed something on his head. Dragged violently along, the cords cutting his flesh, Fandor realised his attackers were fastening him to something which held him stiffly upright. It must be one of the iron columns.

Fandor thought he heard a receding voice mutter: "As Bobinette died, so shalt thou die — through Fantômas!"

Had he heard aright? Was it some illusion of sense and brain?... Was it not he himself who had cried it? For Fandor, whose mind had been full of Vagualame, had, at the moment of attack, spontaneously thought of Fantômas.

Fandor strained at his bonds and thought of the baron.

"Naarboveck — To me! Help!" he shouted.

No answer came through the darkness.

Did he hear a distant, stifled groan?

Dazzling light flooded the studio.

Fandor, who could see through the eyeholes of the mask, supple as skin, stared about him with intense curiosity.

This extraordinary studio revealed a blood-freezing spectacle.

Facing him, immobile, rigid, was stationed a being whom Fandor had had a fleeting glimpse of two or three times in his life. He had seen this enigmatic and formidable being under circumstances so tragic, on occasions so phenomenal, that this being's outline was graven on his memory for ever!

There was the cloak of many folds, dense black; the hooded mask, the large soft hat shading the eyes; the strange inimitable outline!... Fandor was facing Fantômas!

Fantômas!

With bent shoulders and straining muscles, Fandor made desperate attempts to free himself, the while his eyes were fixed on the terrifying apparition confronting him!

It was a mocking Fantômas he saw; for the abominable bandit was mocking him — was imitating his every gesture to the life!...

Fandor's gaze was fixed in an observing stare....

Did he not see cords binding the limbs of Fantômas? cords binding him about the middle, constricting his whole body?

Was he in some hell nightmare?...Was he mad?...Who was this facing him?...Why, *himself*!...

Fandor, whose image was reflected in a mirror facing him a yard or two away! Fandor had been endowed with the outline of — Fantômas!...

From the throat of this Fandor-Fantômas issued a long-drawn howl of rage!

XXXIII

RECONCILIATION

"Which do you prefer, Mademoiselle? The multi-coloured cockades or the bows of ribbon in one shade? We have both in satin of the best quality."

Wilhelmine de Naarboveck hesitated. The representative from "The Ladies' Paradise" continued:

"The cockades of various colours do very well: they are gay, look bright; but the bows of ribbon also produce an excellent effect — so distinguished! Both articles are in great demand."

Wilhelmine answered at random:

"Oh, put in half of each!"

"And what quantity, Mademoiselle?"

"Oh, three hundred will be sufficient, I should think."

The shopwoman displayed her assortment of cotillion objects. She did her part ably. But Wilhelmine de Naarboveck gave but a perfunctory attention to this choosing of cotillion accessories.

The saleswoman was more and more astonished. She considered that were her customer's orders executed to the letter she would have the oddest assortment of cotillion accessories that could be imagined. She adroitly called Wilhelmine's attention to this.

Realising that she had been giving orders at random, the absent-minded girl came to a decision.

"We have every confidence in your house being able to supply us with a cotillion complete in every detail. You know better than I what is necessary. I will leave it to you, then, to see that everything is done as well as possible."

The saleswoman was full of delighted protestations. Though satisfied with a decision that simplified her task, she was surprised that a young girl as free to act and order as Mademoiselle de Naarboveck seemed to be, did not take interest in the details of a fête which, as rumour had it, was given in her honour.

"Ah!" said the young woman, as she collected the patterns scattered over a table in the hall, "if all our customers were like you, Mademoiselle, and allowed us to carry out our own ideas, we should do marvellous things!"

Wilhelmine smiled, but — would this saleswoman never have done!

"Of course, Mademoiselle, we make similar ribbons for you and your partner; but would you kindly tell me if the gentleman is tall or short? It is better to make the ribbons of a length proportionate to the height."

This question troubled Wilhelmine.... The leader of the cotillion should have been Henri de Loubersac. Was not their betrothal to have been announced at the ball?... But the painful interview at Saint-Sulpice seemed to have put an end to all relations between them!

Who, then, would lead with her?

Little she cared!

"Really, Madame," replied Wilhelmine to the woman, who was astonished at her indifference: "I do not know how tall or short my partner is, for the very good reason that I do not know who he is!... Provide, then, a set of ribbons which may suit anybody!"

When the representative of "The Ladies' Paradise" had taken her departure, Wilhelmine went up to the library. Except for the stiff and solemn household staff, Wilhelmine was alone in the house. Her father was still absent: Mademoiselle Berthe had vanished.

The house was turned upside down from top to bottom. Decorators and electricians were in possession. Hammering had been going on all the afternoon. Furniture had been displaced, pushed hither and thither. The hall had been denuded of all but the table; even the privacy of the library had been invaded — and all in preparation for the ball of the day after to-morrow, to which the baron de Naarboveck had invited the highest personages of the aristocratic and official worlds.

What a lively interest Wilhelmine had at first taken in this fête!

The baron was giving it to set a public seal on his diplomatic position, for hitherto he had not been definitely attached to his embassy; now he was to be the accredited ambassador of a certain foreign power. Also he intended to announce the betrothal of the young couple.

Alas! this latter project had suffered shipwreck!

As Wilhelmine sat in lonely state in the library, she saw a dismal future opening before her. Not only had her heart been torn by the brusque rupture with Henri de Loubersac, but everything which made up her home life, such as it was, seemed falling to pieces....No doubt the diplomat was obliged to be continually absent, but Wilhelmine suffered from this solitude, this abandonment....She had become attached to the gay and companionable Mademoiselle Berthe, who had been the life and soul of the house. She had disappeared: no tidings of her doings or whereabouts had reached Wilhelmine. There must be some very serious reason for this....

The mysterious occurrences of the past weeks had altered her world, shaken it to its insecure foundations, and inevitably affected her outlook. Life seemed a melancholy thing: how gloomy, how helpless her outlook!

More than ever before she felt in every fibre of her being that she was not the daughter of the baron de Naarboveck, that she was indeed Thérèse Auvernois. But what a fatal destiny must be hers! An existence open to the attacks of misfortune, at the mercy of a being, enigmatic, indefatigable, who, time and again, had thrown his horrible influence across her destiny, was throwing it now — the sinister Fantômas!

Wilhelmine was torn from her miserable reflections by the irruption of a domestic, who announced:

"Monsieur de Loubersac is asking if Mademoiselle can receive him!"

Wilhelmine rose from the divan on which she had been reclining. In an expressionless voice she said:

"Show him in."

When the young officer of cuirassiers appeared, his air was embarrassed, his head was bent.

"You here, Monsieur?" Wilhelmine's voice and manner expressed indignation.

But Henri de Loubersac was no longer the arrogant unbeliever of the Saint-Sulpice interview.

"Excuse me!" he murmured.

"What do you want?" demanded Wilhelmine, her head held high.

"Your forgiveness," he said in a voice barely audible.

De Loubersac had come to his senses.

His intense jealousy had distorted his judgment.

Desperate after the Saint-Sulpice interview, when, so it had seemed to him, Wilhelmine had avoided a categorical denial of his accusation regarding her liaison with Captain Brocq, the frantic lover had flown to Juve and had poured out his soul to the sympathetic detective.

Juve had shown himself no sceptic. He believed Wilhelmine's story and statements. They coincided with his own prognostications: they explained why Wilhelmine went regularly to pray at Lady Beltham's tomb: they corroborated his conjectures, they confirmed his forecasts.

If he did not confess it to de Loubersac, he knew in his own mind that these statements indicated that between this Baron de Naarboveck and the redoubtable bandit he was pursuing so determinedly there was some connection, possibly as yet unfathomed, but in his heart of hearts he believed he had lighted on the truth. His conviction that de Naarboveck and Fantômas had relations of some sort dated from the night of his own arrest as Vagualame in the house of de Naarboveck. He had gone further than that.

"Yes," he had said to himself: "de Naarboveck must be a manifestation of Fantômas!"

Corporal Vinson's revelations regarding the den in the rue Monge had but strengthened Juve's impression. He had said to himself after that, "De Naarboveck, Vagualame, Fantômas, are but one."

Juve had reassured de Loubersac: he declared that Wilhelmine had spoken the truth, that she certainly was Thérèse Auvernois and the most honest girl in the world.

Juve calmed and finally convinced de Loubersac.

It only remained for the repentant lover to reinstate himself in Wilhelmine's good graces — if that were possible. Now, more ardently than ever before, he desired to make Wilhelmine his wife. See her, be reconciled to her, he must!

He arrived at a favourable moment. The poor girl, lonely and alone, was a prey to the most gloomy forebodings. Life had lost all its savour. She was in the depths of despair.

De Loubersac, standing before her, as at a judgment bar, again implored her forgiveness.

"Oh, how I regret the brutal, wounding things I said to you, Wilhelmine!" he murmured humbly, sorrowfully.

The innocent girl, so bitterly wronged by his thoughts and words, crimsoned with indignation at the memory of them. Her tone was icy.

"I may be able to forgive you, Monsieur, but that is all you can hope for."

"Will you never be able to love me again?" begged Henri, with the humble simplicity of a boy.

"No, Monsieur." Wilhelmine's voice was hard.

It was all Henri could do not to burst into tears of humiliation and despair.

"Wilhelmine — you are cruel!... If you could only know how you are making me suffer! Oh, I know I deserve to suffer! I recognise that!... All I can say now is — Farewell!... Farewell for ever!"

Wilhelmine sat silent, her face hidden in her hands.

Henri went on:

"I leave Paris shortly. I have asked for an exchange. I am to be sent to Africa, to the outposts of Morocco. I shall carry with me the memory — how cherished — of your adorable self, dearest of the dear!... It shall live in my heart until the day when, if Heaven but hear my prayers, I shall die at the head of my troops."

With that de Loubersac moved slowly to the door, overwhelmed by the conviction that he had irreparably wounded the girl he adored, that he had destroyed for ever the love she had borne him!

A stifled cry caught his ear.

"Henri!"...

"Wilhelmine!"

They were in each others' arms and in tears.

How the lovers talked! What plans they made! How happy would be their coming life together! What bliss!

Wilhelmine broke off:

"Henri, do you know that it is past midnight?"

"I seem only to have come!" cried her lover.

"Ah, but you should not have stayed so late, my Henri!... The baron is not here. I am alone!... Indeed, indeed, you must go!"

"Oh," laughed the happy Henri: "Why, of course the baron is not here!"...

Wilhelmine, all smiles, shook a finger at Henri.

"Be off with you!... Do, do be off with you!"

"Wilhelmine!"...

"Henri!"...

The lovers kissed each other — a long, lingering kiss....

XXXIV
A FANTÔMAS TRICK

Fandor stared at himself with wild eyes....

He must be in an abominable dream, a mad nightmare!...He must be!...

What was behind all this? This outrage? This Vagualame, criminal proprietor of this pavilion, was the author of it! To him he owed it that he was thus bound, masked, disguised!

That sinister menace was still ringing in his ears: "Through Fantômas thou shalt die!"

Well, however it might come, Death came but once! He would await the event!

Fandor's spirit rose once more — indomitable.

He closed his eyes.

He lived again, as might a drowning man, his hours of joy, of struggle, of triumph, of defeat, of high endeavour: all the thick-packed hours of vivid life. Ah, how Fantômas had haunted him from childhood onwards!

"'Tis but life's logic," he reflected: "I have fought Fantômas, and not always has the victory been wholly his! More than once I have called check to him! It is his turn to take revenge with the irrevocable checkmate. Well, I have lost. I pay."

The heavy silence of the studio was loud with menace.

Surrounded by it, he awaited Death's coming, in whatever guise....

The studio door swung open noiselessly. Some twenty men appeared, all clothed in black and masked in velvet. Their approach over the thickly carpeted floor was soundless.

Fandor stared at these strange figures.

Solemnly, silently, they ranged themselves in a half circle facing Fandor. He who was plainly the chief of them remained apart, arms crossed, head high, considering Fandor. He spoke:

"Brothers! You have sworn to defend Russia, to defend Poland, by every means in your power! Do you swear it still?"

The voices of the masked men vibrated as one:

"We swear it!"

"Brothers, are you prepared to risk all for our Cause?"

"We are prepared."

The man who posed as chief came nearer his fellow-conspirators, who bent their heads as he apostrophised them:

"Brothers, there is a man in Paris who has worked more harm to us than have all the police in the world: a man who has stirred up against us the indignant horror of public opinion by an accumulation of hideous crimes, the responsibility for which he has cast on us!...This man I, Trokoff, have vowed to deliver up to you, that you may wreak your vengeance on him!...Look well, brothers! He is before you! I deliver him up to you!"

The conspirators, as one man, stared at Fandor.

A murmur issued from the mouths of these masked men; a murmur breathing hate and menaces:

"Fantômas!...Fantômas!"

Fandor did not lose one detail of this scene.

"Ah," thought he, "the bandit's last trick!"

Trokoff was Fantômas! Fandor was sure of it! He was abusing the ardent faith and trust of his disciples, this false apostle! Wishing to rid himself of Fandor, he delivered him to the vengeance of his companions. Making him pass for Fantômas, he drove them on to murder, thus thrusting on to them responsibility for the crime, leaving them to reap what consequences might follow from the journalist's assassination.

How Fandor longed to shout:

"I am not Fantômas! Your Trokoff is a traitor!"

But how pull the scales from off eyes blinded by fanaticism? How to prove to them he was not Fantômas? Who among them could recognise the unknown, elusive bandit, Fantômas?

These Nihilists had for Trokoff an admiration beyond the bounds of reason. How could he show up Trokoff as he really was?

It would be madness to attempt it!

For Fandor divined that behind the mask of Trokoff lurked the evil countenance of Fantômas — Fantômas who was gloating over his confusion and despair, rejoicing in his agony, counting on his collapse, hoping for some act of cowardice.

Never would Jérôme Fandor play the coward!

At this stake to which they had bound him he would die without a sound! Fandor drove back from his lips the cry of despair they were about to utter. He awaited the event.

A Nihilist broke from the circle, went up to Fandor.

"Fantômas! You have heard? You are about to die! What have you to say in your defence?"

Fandor was dumb.

"Fantômas! You would die unknown! But it is good that we, having gazed on your face, should be appeased when we see you dead!... Your hood and mask — I tear them off you!"

Trokoff rushed forward, crying:

"Do not lay hands on him!... This wretch belongs to me!"

Turning to his fellow-conspirators, Trokoff demanded:

"My hand should strike the fatal blow! I brought him here! The right is mine!"

Trokoff continued, in a quieter tone:

"The police may have been warned of our gathering here! We are spied on, tracked! You know it well!... Suppose we stay to watch the dying agony of this wretch! Suppose the police descend upon us! They will snatch from us our just revenge and will arrest us all!... Hand over this monster to me and leave the place. If the police are watching you they will see you go!... Leave Fantômas to me, that, at my leisure, I may see him die as he deserves to die!"

Fandor shuddered: so a lingering agony, a fearful death was to be faced!... Yes, Fantômas meant to torture him, extract from his victim some appeal for pity, for the mercy this monster in human form could never know nor exercise! Yes, Fantômas had changed his plans: rid of the Nihilists, he could have it all his own way with Fandor!

The disciples, as with one voice, cried:

"We are thy faithful followers. What thou ordainest that we do!"...

Trokoff turned to Fandor. He shook a threatening fist in Fandor's face.

"Collect yourself.... You are to pay the price of expiation soon!"

This menace hurled at his victim, Trokoff drew his fanatical partisans together, made them quit the studio, and vanished with them....

"He will return," thought Fandor: "And then it is all up with me! Courage to face the worst!"

The door of the studio had barely closed on Trokoff and his dupes when Fandor heard a breathless murmur at his ear.

"Quick! Quick! Fandor! Trokoff, you have guessed it, is Vagualame! Is Fantômas!... Cost what it may we must get the mastery of him!"

Fandor could not turn his head, but he felt his bonds were being loosened.... A minute or two and he was free! He took a staggering step or two: his limbs were stiff and numb.... Close to him, watching his first difficult movements with an expression of ardent sympathy, our journalist perceived — Naarboveck....

"You," said he.

"I!... Fandor, I will explain!... Hold! Here is a revolver!... Ah! the bandits!... They took me too! Me also they have condemned to death! But I managed to escape!... Look out! He returns! We will fall upon Trokoff!... We will avenge ourselves!"

A heavy step was heard on the stairs; someone was mounting hurriedly.... Trokoff was about to reappear....

Fandor grasped the revolver de Naarboveck had just handed to him. He bounded to the door, ready to leap on the entering man.

De Naarboveck was ambushed on the side opposite to Fandor.

Suddenly Fandor shouted:

"Do not kill him! If it is Fantômas, we must take him alive!"

Before de Naarboveck had time to reply, the door was flung back against him, thus putting him out of action for the moment.

Fandor shot forward, seized Trokoff by the throat, and, rolling on the floor with him, yelled:

"To me, Naarboveck! Fantômas, you are taken! Yield!"

Fandor's grip and spring had been so sudden that Trokoff had not been able to defend himself. He and Fandor struggled, twisted, writhed, in a terrible embrace; panting, livid, with eyes of hate and horror!

De Naarboveck had laid hold of Trokoff, shouting:

"You shall die! You must die!"

This frightful struggle lasted but a few moments. Trokoff managed to free himself from Fandor's grip. The stupefied journalist heard a familiar voice crying:

"Look out, Fandor! It is Naarboveck we must take! Go it! Go it!"

The studio was plunged in darkness: a door banged: Fandor staggered, driven violently back into the middle of the studio. He felt a man was rushing away.

"He escapes! He escapes!"

Fandor did not know who had remained with him, who, had fled, whether he was on his head or his heels!... It was a momentary bewilderment; for the voice he had heard when the struggle was at its height was still speaking, calm, mocking.... It was the voice of Juve, saying:

"How exasperating!... These matches are no good at all!... Ah!... this one has decided to catch!"

In the uncertain light of the match flame Fandor perceived someone leaning against the wall — it was Trokoff! — Trokoff, who calmly went up to a table, took a candlestick, and lighted a candle! Throwing himself into an arm-chair, this Trokoff asked:

"Well now? Why the devil are you got up as Fantômas, my lad?... For a military prisoner this is not at all correct!"

Could Fandor believe his ears? his eyes?

Trokoff was Juve!

Fandor looked so bewildered that Juve-Trokoff laughed a merry laugh.

"Come now, my Fandor, try to gather your wandering wits together a bit and answer me!"

"You, Juve!... You are Juve!" gasped Fandor, exhausted in mind, and body with the emotions he had experienced.

"So it happens," replied Juve: "Well, I see I must speak first as you do not seem to be in a condition to talk!... Listen, then!...

"I know these Nihilists, who imagine I am their chief, Trokoff — that is my latest transformation!... I learned this evening that these imbeciles, believing they had got hold of Fantômas, were summoned here to-night to pass judgment on the bandit.... I accompanied them as Trokoff, who had called them together. When we entered, I can assure you that, bound to your pillar, you made a striking figure of Fantômas!... You took in even me — for a while! Luckily I noticed your hands, the only portions of you visible, covered as you were in that confounded hooded thing they muffled you up in.... You must know that the pattern of the veins on the hands is absolutely characteristic and individual; so much so that the anthropometric service in Vienna is entirely based on this principle!... That is how I recognized you, my little Fandor. You can imagine that my one idea then was to get rid of the Nihilists as soon as possible, and liberate you! But, by Jove, when I returned, you and Naarboveck between you attacked me so brutally that you nearly did for me! It was a narrow shave! He was throttling me! Had you fired your revolver at me you would almost certainly have killed me, and then you would have fallen a victim yourself to."...

Juve stopped. He questioned Fandor with a look. "De Naarboveck!... De Naarboveck, who is Fantômas," replied Fandor, who now understood the situation.

Juve crossed his arms.

"It is as you say. Vagualame, Naarboveck, Fantômas, are one and the same: and, be sure of this, we have not set eyes on the real face of Fantômas yet, for de Naarboveck is as much made up for the part as he is when playing Vagualame!... Also."...

"Juve! Juve!" interrupted Fandor.... "We are mad to stay talking like this!... Naarboveck has just vanished. He is certain to go to his place even if, feeling he is unmasked, he has decided to disappear forever. Do not let him escape! Juve, for Heaven's sake, hurry!"

Juve did not stir.

"How very violent you are, and how simple, my little Fandor! Look now, it is quite three minutes since de Naarboveck disappeared from here, and you imagine there is still time to catch him?... It is childish!"...

"But Juve! I tell you de Naarboveck must return to his house! Let us put a watch on him and trap him!"

Juve's voice trembled as he made answer:

"We cannot arrest de Naarboveck!"...

"Why?... What do you mean?"...

"Because, though I have the right to place my hand on the collar of Fantômas, I have no power to arrest de Naarboveck!"...

Fandor's reply to this was an uncomprehending stare.

"It's Greek to you, I see! Trust me, Fandor! At present I have no right to reveal this secret, but, take my word for it, Naarboveck is inviolable!"

Fandor understood that this was an official secret which Juve was not at liberty to divulge.

"Ye Gods!" he exclaimed.

"Bah! The game is not lost yet, Fandor, my boy! I have still a card to play against his, and I play it this very night.... Enough of that for the moment! I am dying to know how you, whom I believed peacefully reposing at Cherche-Midi, happen to be playing the part of Fantômas in deserted studios!"

Juve's coolness was infectious. Fandor was himself again. He told Juve the story of his escape. At the close he asked abruptly:

"Now what are we going to do?"

Juve shook his head.

"Attention, my lad! Don't mix up the questions!... What am I going to do?... What are you going to do?... You, Fandor, ought to return to Cherche-Midi straight away, and ask them to put you back in your cell. That is the wise thing to do, believe me, dear lad!... To get away like that was a mistake — a very grave mistake — the falsest of false moves.... To escape is equivalent to pleading guilty.... You are innocent.... Return, then, to your prison ... I can promise you that you will not remain there long."

"And you, Juve?"

Juve rose, yawned.

"Oh!... It is a nuisance, but I must get into evening dress ... and that I do not like ... I must go by train, too — confound it all!"...

In a sumptuously decorated study an elegantly clad Juve was listening to a personage. This personage was addressing our detective in a tone at once friendly and haughty.

"No. It is not possible. It is asking too much of me! You do not take into consideration, Juve, the many complications which such an intervention on my part would give rise to if, by chance, you are mistaken.... I have the greatest confidence in you, Juve, I know your ability: I have had proof of your loyalty: I have experienced your devotion, but — you are not infallible!... The story you have told me is so strange, so — improbable, that I have to take into consideration the possibility of there having been some mistake, some blunder. I have to consider the terrible consequences to which I should expose myself in such a case!"...

Juve frowned slightly.

"With all respect, I should like to point out to Your Majesty that it is a mere question of a signature to be given."...

"A signature, Juve, which commits me, my kingdom! It might fan the flame! Worse: it might put a match to the powder magazine."

"Your Majesty might consider that by such a signature the thing would be settled."

"Juve! For the hundredth time I repeat I cannot give you this order! However far back in our annals you might go, I am convinced you could not find a precedent for this!"

"Your Majesty will not forget that with his name, a line of his writing, all difficulties would be cleared away."

"Oh, as to that!... Have you considered that if this decree be unmerited, this document will be a shameful one, and will reflect shame not only on me but on my country? Do you not know that a king has no right to put his signature, his seal to an injustice?"

"Sire, I know that a king should be Justice! Sire, I know I ask nothing Your Majesty may not grant! Sire, I have urged, entreated! But Your Majesty must excuse me when I say that I am no longer a suppliant.... Your Majesty understands me?... It is Juve who requests the signature of Your Majesty!"

The king was visibly hesitating. At last he replied:

"I understand you, Juve. You would remind me of that official visit to Paris when you saved my life and the life of my queen at the risk of your own. I told you then that I should never refuse you anything you asked of me! It is to that you allude, is it not?"

"Sire, I should never call upon your Majesty to pay a debt you did not acknowledge.... I did not then foresee that a decree from Your Majesty would prove the solution of the most formidable problem I have ever had to solve! I would far rather not recall the debt.... Your Majesty has forced me to remind you of your given word."...

The king had risen and was pacing the room.

"If I grant you this decree, Juve, will you take it to the Chancellor's Office as soon as you reach Paris?"

"Yes, Sire!"

"You will not wait, Juve, to have further proofs of what you assert?"

"No, Sire!"

"I must, then, rely solely on your word for it, your certainty, your conviction?"

"Yes, Sire!"

"Juve! Juve! If you exact this in the name of the promise I once made you, I will sign this decree for you — but — you will forfeit my friendship! You will have taken my good faith by storm! Decide then, Juve! Exact this — I grant it you!"

There was a silence.... Juve broke it.

"Surely Your Majesty does not wish to put me on the horns of such a dilemma? Lose Your Majesty's friendship, confidence, or let pass a unique opportunity?"

"Yes, Juve.... That is what I wish."

"In that case, Sire, I do not exact payment! But Your majesty is breaking to pieces all that my life means! Sire, my own honour wills it that I bring this business to a conclusion, cost what it may! With Your Majesty's support it was possible.... With only my own resources to depend on all is lost!"

It evidently cost the king something not to give Juve the satisfaction he implored.

"Juve, this is cruel! I would rather you had exacted the decree.... But all is not ended.... I will order an investigation in a fortnight's time."...

"In a fortnight's time? Your Majesty knows it will be too late."

The king continued his pacing up and down. He was considering the question.

"Juve, can you bring me face to face with this man? Can you convict him of his imposture in my presence?"

"What exactly does Your Majesty mean?"

"I mean, Juve, that whatever might be the scandal, the humiliation it might result in for me, I would grant you here and now the decree you claim if I were assured that you had not made a mistake.... You bring me suppositions, Juve, but no proofs! Arrange so that this man throws off his mask, if but for an instant, and I will allow your justice to take its course!...Juve, forget that you are speaking to a king: think of me as your friend!...Whatever the risks to be run, can you bring us face to face under such conditions that the truth will be apparent to me?"

Juve reflected. He raised his head and looked at the king.

"Your Majesty," said he slowly: "I am going to ask you to take an extraordinary step....I am going to ask Your Majesty to perhaps risk your life. I am going to ask Your Majesty."...

Juve's emotion was such that he could scarcely speak. Mastering it, he said in a low voice:

"I am going to ask Your Majesty to accompany me in three days' time ...when."...

XXXV
AT THE COUNCIL OF WAR

"The Council, gentlemen!... Stand up!"

"Shoulder — arms!"

"Rest — arms!"

The seven military judges of the Council of War advanced solemnly, in single file. They were in full dress uniform — sabres, epaulettes, regulation plumes on helmets and caps. With all due ceremony they took their respective places at a long green-covered table.

This opened at one o'clock, on the afternoon of the twenty-eighth of December. The president was a colonel of dragoons, a smart, distinguished-looking man, whose fair hair was slightly tinged with grey at the temples.

On the right of the tribunal, before a bureau piled with voluminous case papers, was seated Commandant Dumoulin, redder in the face than ever. The place next him was filled by Lieutenant Servin, who showed himself the very pink of correctness and meticulous elegance. Seated near the lieutenant was a white-haired officer acting as clerk of court.

The government commissioners had their backs to the court windows which looked on to a very large garden; facing them was the dock, guarded by two soldiers with fixed bayonets; behind the dock was the table which stood for the bar where the counsel for the defence would plead.

The centre of the room was occupied by an enormous cast-iron stove, shedding cinders on every side, whose ancient pipes were scaly with age.

Behind the line of soldiers cutting the room in two were narrow seats and still narrower desks, where the representatives of the legal press were seated as best they could.

Behind the journalists pressed a tightly packed crowd, restless, overflowing with curiosity, leaning on the press-men's shoulders, peering between their heads, for whom the authorities had shown but scant consideration, and for whom the poorest accommodation was provided.

All Paris had done their possible to be present, begging cards of admittance, a favour which could be granted to a very limited number.

As soon as the interest aroused by the appearance of the members of the Council of War had died down the crowd's attention was concentrated on the hero of this sensational adventure: his doings had been the one prevailing topic of conversation during the past few days.

Jérôme Fandor, modest, reserved, appeared indifferent to the mute questioning of the hundreds of eyes focussed on him. Our journalist wore Corporal Vinson's uniform. He had begged the authorities to let him appear in civilian clothes: demands and entreaties had been so much breath wasted.

The counsel assigned him was a shining light of the junior bar, Maître Durul-Berton.

The audience on the whole was favourably disposed towards this well-known contributor to *La Capitale*. They knew that on many occasions this well-informed journalist had rendered immense services to honest folk and to society in general by placing his intelligence and energy at the service of every good cause.

Then there was one strong indisputable point in his favour. Though he had escaped from prison with the help of an unknown person, he had returned, had given himself up, declaring he would not leave the Council of War except by the big door with head held high, his innocence established.

The president announced:

"We shall now call the names of the witnesses."

There was silence in the court-room while a sergeant who filled the office of crier to the court, read out the names from a list in his hands. The call-over lasted ten minutes. Most of the witnesses were officers and men belonging to the garrisons of Verdun and Châlons.

Among these witnesses as they defiled before the tribunal Fandor recognised some whose faces were graven on his memory during his brief sojourn in the Saint Benoit barracks.

The first call resounded through the court-room:

"Inspector Juve!"

Juve approached the tribunal, proved he was present, then, in conformity with the law, left the court-room, as did the other witnesses called.

The presence of Juve reassured and comforted Fandor. Had not Juve said to him:

"You must face your judges, little son; but I am greatly deceived if a certain incident which will occur in the course of the hearing will not alter the speech for the government from the first to the last!"

More than this Juve could not be got to say: he had put on his most enigmatic manner and closed his lips.

The president of the Council addressed Fandor:

"Accused! Stand up!"

The president stared hard at the prisoner with his pale clear eyes like porcelain expressing neither thoughts nor feelings.

Fandor stood erect, waiting.

An hour had gone by.

Juve, the first witness called, was finishing his evidence. Of all the witnesses, he alone could give precise details which would confirm or nullify Fandor's statements.

Juve had given a rapid sketch of Fandor's adventurous career, but had carefully omitted to mention that Fandor's real name was Charles Rambert.[11]

His defence of his friend was a eulogy.

Nevertheless, the revelations of Juve did not simplify the problem as regards the grave charges of murder and spying brought against the prisoner.

When Juve had finished his panegyric, the president spoke to the point:

"All this is very well, gentlemen, very well — but the affair grows more and more complicated, and who will come forward to elucidate it?"

From the back of the court came a sound, sharp-cut, clear:

"I!"

The sensation was immense. Members of the Council looked at one another. There was a disturbance at the back of the room: the crowd swayed, and peered, and whispered.

The colonel-president frowned. He scrutinised the close-packed swaying mass. He shot a question at it.

"Who spoke?"

Sharp, distinct, a monosyllable was shot back.

"I!"

Someone, pushing a way through the audience, was approaching the military tribunal.

A murmur rose from the crowd.

"Silence!" shouted the colonel. He swept the crowd with an angry eye: he threatened.

"I warn you! At the least manifestation, favourable or otherwise, I shall have the room cleared: we are not here to amuse ourselves. I do not authorise anyone, either by gesture or by speech, to comment on what is taking place within these walls."

Having obtained comparative quiet, the colonel looked squarely at the person who had approached the witness-stand and was facing the military tribunal.

This would-be witness was a young woman, elegantly clad. She wore black furs, and a dark veil partially concealing her features, but revealing the strange pallor of her face. The audience, who had a view of the newcomer's back, noted her masses of tawny red hair, set off by a fur toque.

The colonel put her to the question at once.

"You are the person who said 'I'?"

The young woman was greatly moved, but she answered firmly:

"Yes, Monsieur. That is so."

"Who are you, Madame?"

The witness collected her forces, pressed her hand to her heart as though to still its frantic beating: paused. In a clear strong voice she made her declaration:

"I am Mademoiselle Berthe: I am better known as Bobinette."

Exclamations from the crowd, craning necks, peering eyes, murmurs.

When the excitement was suppressed, the colonel interrogated Bobinette.

"Why have you taken upon yourself to interrupt the proceedings of the court?"

"You asked, Monsieur, who could clear up this unfortunate affair. I am ready to tell you everything. Not only is it a duty imposed on me by my conscience, it is also my most ardent wish."

The judges were in earnest consultation. Commandant Dumoulin was shaking his head. He was angrily opposed to this witness being heard, a witness who had appeared so inopportunely to trouble the majesty of the sitting.

The counsel for the defence intervened.

"Monsieur the president, I have the honour to request an immediate hearing for this witness.... It is your absolute right, Monsieur the president: you have full discretionary powers."

"And if I oppose it?" growled the commandant behind his desk, with a vicious glance at the defender of his adversary.

Maître Durul-Burton replied with calm dignity:

"If you oppose it, Monsieur the commissaire, I shall have the honour of immediately deposing on the bureau of this tribunal conclusive evidence which will bring this sitting to a close forthwith."

An animated discussion ensued between the members of the council. It resulted in the colonel's announcement:

"We will hear this witness."

He addressed Bobinette:

"You are allowed to speak, mademoiselle. Swear then to speak the truth, the whole truth, and nothing but the truth. Raise your right hand and say: 'I swear it!'"

With a certain dignity Bobinette obeyed.

"I swear it!"

Then, in a low trembling voice, trembling from excess of emotion but not from timidity, Bobinette began her story.

A child of the people, honestly brought up, she had not always followed the straight path of virtue: there had been lapses. Intelligent, longing to learn, she had been well educated, and had intended to take a medical degree.... Again, at the hospital, she had succumbed to temptations, had led a life of idleness, and had renounced all idea of working for her doctor's diploma. Instead, she had become a hospital nurse.[12]

Here the colonel interrupted:

"What can these details matter to us, Mademoiselle? What we want to know is not your own history, but that of the guilty person — information pertinent to the case in hand."

In a strangely solemn voice, Bobinette replied:

"You would know the history of the guilty person?... Listen!"

The tribunal was impressed: the members, silent, attentive, let the witness have her way.

Bobinette touched on the various stages of her life up to the day when she came in contact with the Baron de Naarboveck. The care she had lavished on the youthful Wilhelmine gained the gratitude of the rich diplomat and his daughter. From that time they treated her as one of themselves: she became Mademoiselle de Naarboveck's companion.

"Ah, cursed be that day!" cried Bobinette.... "Misfortunes, tragedies, date from then. The worst is — I must confess it — I was the cause of them!"

"What do you mean by that?" interrupted Commandant Dumoulin.

"I mean to say that if Captain Brocq died by an assassin's hand, the blame is mine!... I mean to say that if a confidential document disappeared from his rooms, it is because I took it!... I was his mistress!... I am responsible for his death!"

There was a gasping silence: the sensation was intense. Juve, half hidden behind the cast-iron stove, alone remained unmoved.

Bobinette continued:

"My evil genius, gentlemen, was a bandit of the worst kind: you know him under the name of Vagualame. Vagualame, agent of the Second Bureau, and officially a counter-spy. Quite so. But, gentlemen, Vagualame was equally spying on France, a traitor in the pay of a foreign power: worse still, he it was who assassinated Captain Brocq: you know he was the murderer of the singer, Nichoune!...

"This Vagualame made of me his thing, his slave! Alas! I cannot pretend that it was under the perpetual menace from this monster I became a traitor! I have so many betrayals that must count against me: betrayal of my country, betrayal of Captain Brocq's love for me! I robbed him in every kind of way: I stole the document referring to the mobilisation scheme: I stole his money — bank-notes — with the excuse that it was to put the police on the wrong scent and make them believe it was an ordinary burglary.

"These notes, gentlemen, were found in the possession of the unfortunate Jérôme Fandor. It seems they constitute an overwhelming charge against him. Know then, that after having been stolen by my hands they were given to Jérôme Fandor by one of our agents, for the purpose of compromising the false Corporal Vinson....But if I have acted thus, it was not so much through a desire for the money they gave me for my treachery, not so much for the fallacious promises of eventual riches which Vagualame was always trying to dazzle me with — it was through rancour, spite, hate, it was through love!"

Maître Durul-Burton rose and, bending towards the half-fainting Bobinette, cried:

"Speak, speak, Mademoiselle!"

Bobinette went on slowly:

"Through love — yes. And it is an avowal which touches me nearly, wounds me in the depths of my soul, in my most intimate thoughts....

"Yes, I have given away to the vile suggestions of Vagualame, if I have let myself be drawn by him into horrible by-paths of spying and treason, it is owing to the spite and rage of an unrequited love, of an intense passion, intense beyond expression, which I have felt for a man — a man whose heart was given to another — for the betrothed of Mademoiselle de Naarboveck — for Lieutenant Henri de Lou — —"

The colonel-president, with a brusque gesture, interrupted this confession.

"Enough, Mademoiselle ...enough!...You are not to mention names here!...Be good enough to continue your deposition only as it relates to facts connected with spying."

Bobinette then recounted how she had consented to hide the famous gun piece brought to her one day by Vagualame; how she had helped the bandit to concoct the daring plan by which this piece was to be handed to a foreign power; how she had disguised herself as a priest in order to take Corporal Vinson to Dieppe. She did not know, at first, that she was dealing with Jérôme Fandor. Enlightenment came through Vagualame's telegram. She only then realised that the traitor Vinson and the soldier in her company were two distinct persons.

"And," cried she, "who killed the real Corporal Vinson but a few days ago in the rue du Cherche-Midi? I know. It was the murderer of Captain Brocq, the murderer of the singer, Nichoune — it was Vagualame ... Vagualame!" Bobinette was working herself up to a paroxysm of exasperation, shouting out her revelations like an apostle who means to convince, shouting his convictions as a martyr might at the worst moment of her anguish.

"Vagualame? You ask who he is, and you search among the thieves, the receivers of stolen goods and light-fingered gentry, you search among the secret agents, among that low unclean crowd which gravitates to your Staff Offices and circulates about them, forever on the watch, on the prowl to surprise some secret, to buy over some conscience, to sell and bargain over some purloined document!...Look higher than that, gentlemen — much higher! Look higher than the Staff Offices, than the leaders in the political world, than members of the Government, even — fix your attention on the accredited representatives of foreign powers."...

Bobinette was unable to continue....Commandant Dumoulin had been too excited to remain in his seat. He rushed towards the witness, who was making what he considered to be wild and outrageous statements: he put his big hand over her mouth, effectually silencing her....

The commandant turned to the colonel, shouting:

"Colonel! Monsieur the president!...I demand that this case be now heard in camera! Such accusations must not be heard in public!...I beg you to order that the rest of this case be heard behind closed doors!"

The counsel for the defence rose in his turn, and in a calm tone, which contrasted with the violence of Commandant Dumoulin, declared:

"I am in agreement with this demand, Monsieur the President....Will you order that the further hearing of this case be in camera?"

Here Commandant Dumoulin, to whom Lieutenant Servin had made a suggestion, intervened anew:

"Monsieur the President, gentlemen, having regard to the grave declarations made by this witness, I require her immediate arrest!"

Hardly had this demand been voiced when a loud cry rang out, electrifying the whole court. Bobinette had swallowed the contents of a small phial hidden in her muff!

Juve, guessing Bobinette's intention, had rushed to her, but, in spite of his rapid action, he reached her only in time to receive the fainting girl in his arms.

"She has poisoned herself!" shouted Juve.

The public broke bounds, knocked over chairs and benches, rolled in a surge of excited curiosity to the very feet of the Council of War, crowding round this fresh centre of interest — Bobinette!

Fandor was too stunned by the avalanche of incidents to move.

"The hearing is suspended!" shouted the colonel in an angry voice. There was nothing else to be done: the court was in an uproar!

It was nine in the evening, and a crowd as large and densely packed as before awaited the verdict.

Since Bobinette attempted suicide — she had been removed to the infirmary with the faint hope that life was not extinct and she might yet be saved — the hearing had been conducted in camera. But the revelations of the guilty girl had not only upset Dumoulin's course of procedure, but had also convinced the judges of Fandor's innocence. He had once more explained why he had concealed his identity beneath the uniform of Corporal Vinson.

The Council of War had come to the conclusion that they could not consider Fandor accountable to their tribunal.

At nine o'clock then, after a short deliberation, the Council of War delivered judgment through the mouth of its president, delivered judgment according to the solemn formula, commencing thus:

"In the name of the French People!"

Jérôme Fandor was acquitted.

The news of his acquittal was received with hearty cheers.

Fandor was free.

Congratulations, hand-shakings, questions followed.

Mechanically he responded, though he had a smile for Lieutenant Servin when he murmured, with a touch of irony:

"The judgment made no mention, Monsieur Fandor, of the clothes — the borrowed clothes — you are wearing: but it seems to be established that they do not belong to you. Be kind enough, then, to return them to the authorities as soon as possible! Otherwise we shall be obliged to summon you afresh for appropriation of military garments!"

The lieutenant had had his little joke, and departed laughing.

The crowd melted away. Only a few of Fandor's colleagues remained. To them he talked more freely of his troubles and trials. Then Juve arrived on the scene again. He was no longer the impassive listener of the trial: he was friend Juve, beaming and joyous.

He embraced his dear Fandor effusively, murmuring:

"Now, old Fandor, this is not the moment to linger! We must be off instanter. I shall see you to your flat, where you can change into clothes of your own; for this evening we have our work cut out for us!"

"This evening?" Fandor's curiosity was aroused.

Juve, as they went off together, became mysterious.

"Ah! you will understand presently!"

XXXVI

AMBASSADOR!...?...

"Hurry up, Fandor! We must be off!... We shall be late!"

Jérôme Fandor slipped on his overcoat and took the stairs at a rush in the wake of Juve.

"Well, I like that, old Juve! Here have I been waiting for you a good quarter of an hour!... You will have to give the coachman an address, anyhow, and that will tell me where you are taking me, why you have made me get into evening clothes, and why you are in that unusual get-up yourself — it's unheard of!"

"It is true, lad! I amuse myself making mysteries!... It is stupid.... Well, Fandor, we are going to a ball.".....

"A ball!"

"Yes — and I think we shall lead someone there a fine dance, or I am much mistaken."

"Who, then?"

"The master of the house!"

"You speak in riddles, Juve!"

"Not at all! Do you know where we are going, Fandor, lad?"

"I ask you that, Juve."

"Well, then — we are going to the house of — Fantômas — to arrest him!"

"Ye gods and little fishes!" cried Fandor.

Juve crossed the pavement and jumped into a carriage, making room for his dear lad beside him.

"But, Juve," remonstrated Fandor: "You declared to me the other day that it was impossible to arrest de Naarboveck — that he was inviolable — but you did not tell me why.... Isn't that true?"

"It is true."

"And it is so no longer."

"It still is so."

After all he had been through, Fandor was in a state of high tension. He caught Juve's hand and beat it with angry impatience.

"Don't quibble, Juve!... It is too deadly serious!... What do you really mean?... We know that de Naarboveck is Fantômas, but you swore to me that it is impossible to arrest Naarboveck. You still assert this: nevertheless, you now declare that we are going to arrest Fantômas! What the deuce do you mean?... I've had more than enough of your ironical mockery, old man!"

Juve took out his watch and, with finger on the dial, said:

"Look! It is half past ten. We shall reach de Naarboveck's about a quarter past eleven. It would be impossible for me to arrest him just then; but at a quarter to twelve, midnight at latest, it will be quite easy for me to put my hand on the collar of de Naarboveck — Fantômas! I shall not bungle it!"

"Juve! You and your mysteries are maddening!"

"My dear Fandor, do pardon me for not being more explicit. I told you Naarboveck was out of reach as far as arresting him goes. I also told you that we were going to arrest Fantômas. It is exact; because all that is subordinate to a will — a will I happen to have at my command for the moment, but also a will which may raise some preventing obstacle at the last moment, and so stop me from capturing the bandit straight away, enabling the monster to brazen it out in perfect safety."

"Whose will, Juve?"

"My lad, do not question me further! I cannot say more."

Fandor desisted: Juve's sincerity was obvious.

"All serene, Juve! I leave it to you. Whatever happens. I shall try not to lose sight of you. I shall stick to you like a leech — if you have need of me."

Juve held out his hands.

"Thanks, dear lad!"

With fast-beating hearts, thrilling with excitement, expectation, anxiety, the friends embraced.

"You know, dear lad," said Juve in quiet tones: "We are going to risk our skins?...I am sure of the final victory unless a stupid ball from a revolver.".…

Fandor was his old teasing self once more.

"Oh, that's all right! You are not going to frighten me with that old black bogey of yours!".…

At this moment the carriage turned the corner at the end of the Alexander bridge.…

The Baron de Naarboveck's mansion was brilliantly illuminated. The much-talked-of fête was at its height.

Below, the spacious hall had been turned into a magnificent supper-room — a veritable transformation scene — while dancers thronged the rooms above.… The end room only was deserted: it was the library. It had been made the receptacle of an overflow of furniture when the reception suite was cleared for dancing.

An orchestra, concealed by foliage plants, discoursed seductive waltzes in the principal ballroom, whilst crowds of lovely women and distinguished men listened, chatted, and looked on.

Madame Paradel, wife of the Minister for Foreign Affairs, was talking to her host. Observing Wilhelmine, all grace and smiles, she murmured:

"What a charming girl she is!"

Turning again to de Naarboveck, she remarked:

"But you must be in the depths of desolation, dear Baron! Have I not heard that the young couple are leaving for the centre of Africa?"

"Oh, that is an exaggeration," laughed the Baron. "As a matter of fact, my future son-in-law, de Loubersac, is leaving the Staff Office, and with the rank of captain. His chiefs are sending him, not, as you think, to the wilds of Central Africa, but only to Algiers! An excellent garrison!"

"Well, Baron, I like to think you will soon be paying a visit to your newly married pair."

The Baron bowed, and, as Madame Paradel moved away, he went towards the entrance of the gallery commanding a view of the hall and stairs.

The figures of two advancing guests had caught his eye.

In a tone at once enigmatic and perfectly correct, de Naarboveck accosted them:

"You are among my guests, gentlemen."

"That is obvious, is it not?" replied one of the new-comers.…"You may be assured, Baron, that neither my friend Fandor nor I would have allowed ourselves the liberty otherwise.".…

"I know! I know, Monsieur Juve!...Besides — I was expecting you!" An ironic smile curved the lips of de Naarboveck.

"We should have reproached ourselves, Baron, had we not come this evening to offer you the felicitations to which you have a right."

"Really?...No doubt you refer to the marriage of Wilhelmine?"

"No, Baron. I reserve such congratulations for Monsieur de Loubersac and Mademoiselle Thérèse — pardon, for Mademoiselle Wilhelmine."

When making this deliberate mistake in the name, Juve looked squarely at the diplomat — but de Naarboveck made no sign.

"What, then, do you refer to, Monsieur Juve?" he asked.

"I mean, my dear Baron, that I have recently heard of your new office, heard that your credentials have just been presented, heard that they will be ratified to-morrow.… From this evening, Baron, are you not then the representative of the kingdom of Hesse-Weimar?...I fancy, Monsieur the Ambassador, that you are satisfied with this nomination?"

De Naarboveck, smiling that ironical smile, bowed.

"It carries with it some advantages, certainly."

"Among them, Baron, the privilege of inviolability — ah, that famous inviolability!"

Juve laid stress on the word *inviolability*.

De Naarboveck did not seem to understand the insinuation conveyed.

"It is quite true, Monsieur," he said in a matter-of-fact manner: "I do enjoy the right of inviolability; it is one of the privileges attached to my office." On a bantering note he added:

"An appreciable advantage, is it not?"

"Appreciable indeed!" was Juve's reply.

A wave of fresh arrivals surged up the grand staircase and separated the speakers. The master of the house stepped forward to greet them, whilst Fandor drew Juve by the sleeve into the corner of a window recess. Speaking low, he asked:

"Juve! what is the meaning of this comedy?"

"Alas, Fandor! it is no comedy!"

"De Naarboveck is an ambassador?"

"For the kingdom of Hesse-Weimar, yes. He has been that for over a week — since that evening we failed to arrest him in the rue Lepic."

"And he is inviolable?"

"Naturally. In conformity with international conventions, every representative accredited to a foreign power as ambassador is an untouchable, inviolable person — wherever he may be.... Therefore, Fandor, when in this mansion, situated in the heart of Paris, we are no longer legally in France, but in Hesse-Weimar. You can understand the kind of consequences which must follow from such a state of things.... But all is not over.... Ah! excuse me ... there is something I must see to immediately!"...

Leaving Fandor, Juve made his way through innumerable dress-coats and magnificent toilettes, moving with difficulty in the press.

He approached a guest stationed apart, watching all that was going on about him. This guest, who stood unobtrusively aloof, was a distinguished-looking man of about thirty-five; he wore a blonde moustache turned up German fashion.

Juve bowed low before this personage, and murmured with profound deference:

"Ah, thank you, thank you for coming, Majesty!"

"Here, Monsieur, I am incognito — the Prince Louis de Kalbach: respect my incognito and do whatever you have to do quickly. My presence in Paris is not suspected. As you are aware, I am fortunately not known personally to my — to this individual."

Juve was about to assure the king that his wishes would be respected, but someone touched him on the arm. Juve, with a respectful inclination, turned away.

"Ah, Monsieur Juve, how delighted I am to see you!... But I was forgetting.... Monsieur Lépine was looking for you just now!"...

Juve was facing beaming Lieutenant de Loubersac.

"I will go to him at once ... but let me take this opportunity of congratulating you, my dear Lieutenant."...

Juve slipped away to join the popular chief commissioner of police, who was standing apart in the gallery overlooking the hall. Despite the amiable smile he cultivated, Monsieur Lépine looked anxious.

"Juve, are you on duty here?" he asked.

"Yes and no, Monsieur."

Monsieur Lépine looked his surprise.

"I will explain this to you later, Monsieur," said Juve.... "Things are still very complicated."

Wilhelmine de Naarboveck came into view. She was one beam of happiness and radiant beauty.

"Ah, Monsieur, I perceive you are not dancing," she said, playing the good hostess to Juve. "Will you not allow me to introduce you to some charming girls?"

"This is not the time," thought Juve: "and there is my age to be considered."

Making an evasive reply, Juve beat a retreat in good order, and followed Colonel Hofferman, who was talking to de Naarboveck.

"The work of the Second Bureau," declared that officer.

Juve heard no more — Monsieur Lépine confronted him. The chief commissioner of police was plucking at his pointed beard with nervous fingers.

Drawing Juve aside, he asked:

"Juve, what is Headquarters thinking about?"

"I do not know, Monsieur."

"What! There is a visitor here, unnoticed.... Are you also ignorant of the fact that the Baron de Naarboveck receives a king here to-night?"

"Oh, as to that, I know it — Frederick Christian II."

Monsieur Lépine was incensed at the detective's calm.

"You know it! You know it!" he grumbled, "and the administration knows nothing about!... Well, since you know so much, what is he doing here your king?"

"He comes to see me."

"Juve, you are mad!"

"No, Monsieur, But."...

Juve cut short the conversation, approached the king, and said a few words to him in a low voice.

The chief commissioner of police was surprised beyond words when he saw the king listening attentively to what Juve had to say, then nod acquiescence, leave the ballroom and enter the gallery on to which several rooms opened, including the library at the far end.

Juve glanced discreetly at his watch. He was startled. His expression altered. It grew severe, determined. He glanced about him, discovered de Naarboveck not far off, and went up to him.

"Monsieur de Naarboveck," he said: "shall we have a few minutes' talk? Not here — somewhere else.... Should we say?"...

"In my library?" proposed de Naarboveck, who looked the detective up and down — a measuring glance, cold, contemptuous. Their glances crossed, hard, menacing.

"You are set on it, Monsieur?" De Naarboveck's tone was irony incarnate.... "And what may I ask is your aim in forcing this conversation, Monsieur?"

Juve's reply came, distinct, determined:

"Unmask Fantômas!"

"That shall be as you like," was the diplomat's reply.

In the library, unusually full of furniture, Juve and de Naarboveck met for their duel of words and wits.

They were by themselves. Juve had made the Baron pass into the room before him. He knew there was but one exit — the door. If in order to get clear away, de Naarboveck meant to employ force or trickery, he would first have to remove Juve from the door, before which he had stationed himself.

Juve did not budge.

Certainly there was the window at the other end of the room looking on to the Esplanade des Invalides. Curtains were drawn across the window, but Juve did not fear to see his adversary escape in that direction: he knew — and he alone knew it — that between this window and the curtains there was an obstacle — someone."...

"Do you remember, Monsieur de Naarboveck, that evening when the police came here to arrest Vagualame?"

"Yes," replied de Naarboveck with his ironic smile: "and it was you, Monsieur Juve, who got yourself arrested in that disguise!"

"That is a fact." Juve's admission was matter-of-fact. "Do you recall a certain conversation, Monsieur de Naarboveck, between detective Juve and the real Vagualame at Jérôme Fandor's flat?"

"No," declared the Baron: "and for the very good reason that the conversation — you have just said so — was a dialogue between two persons: Juve and Vagualame."

"Nevertheless, this Vagualame was none other than Fantômas!"

"What then?" De Naarboveck was smiling.

Juve, after a short silence, burnt his ships.

"Naarboveck!" he cried: "It is useless to double like that! Vagualame is Fantômas: Vagualame is you, yourself: Fantômas is you, yourself.... We know it. We have identified you; and to-morrow the anthropometric test will prove in the eyes of the world what to-day is the conviction of a certain few only.

"This long time past you have known yourself pursued, tracked: you have noted that the ring has been drawn closer, tighter each day: so, playing your last trump card, attempting even the impossible, you have planned this abominable comedy, which consists in duping a noble king and getting yourself nominated as his ambassador, that you might take advantage of diplomatic inviolability — an advantage, let me tell you, you are in desperate need of!... Quite a good idea! Was it not?"

During Juve's virulent apostrophe de Naarboveck had maintained an ironic self-possession.

"You confess, then?"

"And suppose it were so?... No doubt, Monsieur Juve, you intended to denounce me, to prove that the Baron de Naarboveck is none other than Fantômas.... Well, it pleases me to admit your cleverness. I will even go as far as allow that you may quite well obtain authorisation to arrest me — in a few days' time."

"Not in a few days' time," interrupted Juve: "but now at once!"

"Pardon," objected de Naarboveck, cool, collected, while Juve had difficulty in containing himself: "Pardon, but the credentials I possess are authentic, and no one in this world can deprive me of my function, of my official position, and what pertains to it."

"Yes!" Juve flung the word at de Naarboveck as though it were a stone from a sling.

De Naarboveck's gesture might mean anything:

"Who?"...

Juve hurled another two stones in the shape of words.

"The king!"

De Naarboveck's nod was malicious.

"Frederick Christian alone can take from me my style and title of ambassador.... Let him come and do it!"

Juve lifted a finger slowly towards the far end of the library, in the direction of the window.

De Naarboveck, who had followed this movement mechanically, could not restrain a cry of stupefaction, a cry of anguish.

The window curtain had just been gradually drawn apart: slowly before the miscreant's eyes appeared the majestic form of King Frederick Christian II, King of Hesse-Weimar.

The king was livid with suppressed rage.

Juve approached him, his eyes on de Naarboveck. The king took a large envelope from an inner pocket and handed it to Juve.

"I am the victim of this monster's imposture, but I know how to recognise my mistakes and rectify them.... Monsieur Juve, here is the decree you asked me for, annulling the nomination of — Baron de Naarboveck."

During this brief scene, Naarboveck-Fantômas had gradually backed towards a corner of the room, his face was pallid and drawn: he had the look of a trapped beast of prey. But at the king's last words Naarboveck-Fantômas drew himself up to a semblance of stateliness. He also took from an inner pocket a document. He held it out to the king: his lips were curved in a smile of bitter irony.

"Sire," he said: "I, in my turn, hand you this! It is the plan stolen from Captain Brocq — the mobilisation plan for the whole French army — a plan your emperor."...

"Enough, Monsieur!" shouted the king.

The paper fell to the ground.

Juve bent quickly and picked up the document.

The king, as though to anticipate the suspicion which might be put into words, said:

"Juve, this plan belongs to your country. Never have we wished."...

The eyes of Juve met those of the king in a deep, questioning glance. A question was asked and answered then. But five seconds in time had passed. Juve's glance went back to Naarboveck-Fantômas.... The bandit had disappeared!

Juve kept his head.

"Michel!" he called: "Michel!"

Michel entered the library on the instant. He had been posted in the gallery close by. Behind him appeared several gentlemen in evening dress: they were detectives despatched on special duty from Headquarters.

"Fantômas is there, Michel," Juve cried: "concealed, but not escaped.... There may be some hiding-place in these walls — we must sound them — but no passage, no exit: I am sure of that. Let us carry out these pieces of furniture, which form a veritable barricade."

Some moments passed, tense with expectancy. At Juve's earnest request the king had left the room. He had fulfilled his promise and had best begone. Juve and Michel were guarding the door. The situation was dangerous, and well the policemen knew it! They had come to grips with a formidable criminal, to whom nothing was sacred, who would stick at nothing! Protected by some piece of furniture, he could take aim at his leisure, shoot his opponents through the heart, and could go on shooting till he had emptied his revolver.

"Start in!" cried Juve.

With six men to aid him, Juve began a systematic turn-out of the library, moving the furniture piece by piece, leaving no hole, no corner unsearched.

No Fantômas!

Yet Juve felt confident, felt sure he held the miscreant in the hollow of his policeman's hand: the library contained no trap-door, no secret door, no sliding panel covering his retreat: the floor had no opening in it: the ceiling was not movable.

"Take these pieces of furniture into the gallery," commanded Juve: "every one of them! Fantômas is not a being without weight and substance, though, for the moment, he is invisible. He cannot have left the room; therefore he must be in it!"

It was no easy task to move quickly, noiselessly, these heavy pieces of furniture into the gallery by way of the narrow library door. Soon they had carried out a comfortable leather arm-chair of unusual proportions, four other chairs, a stand, and various smaller pieces of substantial make.

And all the while, dancers whirled on in the ball-rooms, seductive strains of music were wafted on the air, mingled with the hum of joyous talk and gay laughter; yet in the background were these dark happenings with tragedy ahead!

Wilhelmine de Naarboveck appeared in the doorway, staring at the disorder organised by Juve.... Juve paused: speech failed him at sight of her.

"Monsieur Juve," said she, in quite ordinary tones: "I am so glad I have found you! The Baron de Naarboveck has sent me to you.";...

"Who sent you, did you say, Mademoiselle?"

Juve started forward.

"The Baron de Naarboveck asks for me?... Where? Since when?"

"Why Monsieur Juve, I have just this moment left him at the entrance to the ball-rooms. He had just come out of here!... But why are you putting all this furniture in the gallery?"

"What of the Baron, Mademoiselle?" cried Juve, on tenterhooks.

"Ah, yes! The Baron said to me: 'Wilhelmine, I feel a little tired, and am going up to my room for a few minutes; but go to Monsieur Juve, and tell him...'"

Not waiting to hear more, Juve rushed out to the gallery, but only to stop dead.... He had run up against a large, an unusually large, arm-chair standing apart. Thus isolated, it was remarkable. Juve paused to examine it. This arm-chair was astonishing, extraordinary! Yes — it opened in the middle — a kind of a double chair! Why — the interior could hold a man who knew how to pack himself in! It had a false bottom with a spring! One in hiding could escape that way!... Once closed on the person concealed within, the chair looked empty. A most ingenious hide-hole! Juve now knew the answer to the riddle of the bandit's disappearance. Within an ace of arrest, he had seized the chance offered by Juve's interchange of glances with the king, and with an acrobat's agility had slipped inside this chair! No sooner was the chair abandoned in the gallery than de Naarboveck-Fantômas had slipped out and away. When leaving his magnificent house forever, and all the securities and privileges of his position, he had sent Wilhelmine to announce his escape to Juve! Could cynicism — could mordant irony go further?

Juve felt crushed. It was too, too much.

"What ails you, Juve?" asked a gentle voice beside him. It was Fandor, who, knowing nothing of what had passed, but suspecting there was mischief afoot, had come in search of Juve. Had he not seen the diplomat whom he knew to be Fantômas, and Fantômas on the point of being arrested, cross the ballroom rapidly and disappear in the crowd of dancers?

Juve could not find words for speech.

Great tears rolled down his cheeks, hollowed and lined with an immense fatigue.

At last he gave low utterance to his feelings.

"Fantômas! I had got him!... And it was I who had that cursed chair taken out of the library — I did it ... I!... It is thanks to me!"

Juve could not continue. He burst into tears in the arms of his devoted friend....

Once again Juve had suffered shipwreck when coming into harbour! Once again the bandit had escaped! Ah, decidedly Vagualame, Naarboveck, Fantômas, were one!

Fantômas the evasive, the elusive, the shadowy Fantômas, genius of evil, had flitted by them, had disappeared! Whither?...

Would Juve ever have his revenge?

The future alone would decide....

THE END

Footnotes

1.   Hall of the Wandering Footsteps.

2.   See *The Exploits of Juve*, vol. ii, *Fantômas Series*.

3.   See *The Exploits of Juve,* vol. ii of the Fantômas Series.

4.   La Sûreté-Scotland Yard detective service.

5.   See *Fantômas*: vol. i, Fantômas Series.

6.   See *The Exploits of Juve*: vol. ii, Fantômas Series.

7.   See *Fantômas*: vol. i, Fantômas Series

8.   See *Fantômas*: vol. i, Fantômas Series.

9.   See *The Exploits of Juve,* vol. ii, Fantômas Series.

10. See *Messengers of Evil*: vol. iii, Fantômas Series.

11. See Fantômas Series: vols. i, ii, iii.

12. See *Fantômas*: vol. i, Fantômas Series.

www.ingramcontent.com/pod-product-compliance
Lightning Source LLC
Chambersburg PA
CBHW072136170626

46813CB00004BA/1585